The Bomb
That Never Was

A novel about World War II

J. R. Shaw

The Bomb That Never Was
A novel about World War II

iUniverse books may be ordered through booksellers or by contacting:

iUniverse
1663 Liberty Drive
Bloomington, IN 47403
www.iuniverse.com
1-800-Authors (1-800-288-4677)

ISBN: 978-1-4759-7061-6 (sc)
ISBN: 978-1-4759-7063-0 (hc)
ISBN: 978-1-4759-7062-3 (e)

Library of Congress Control Number: 2013900462

Print information available on the last page.

iUniverse rev. date: 10/20/2015

In Memory Of

J. L. Oehlsen, S. Oehlsen, H. Walker, N. Walker, L. C. Love, and H. D. Love

Appreciation

To all of you who helped me and counseled me while I wrote this book, thank you.

J. Kendrick, H. Love, Joseph P. DeSario, Robert L. Aaron, Ken Krom, James Yagelski, Larry Simon, William Cooper, Allen Klein, Dan Heagy, Sarajoy Pickholtz, Arden Orr, Theodore W. Grippo, the folks at Ruben & Goldberg, LLC, The Silich Group at Morgan Stanley Wealth Management, Krebs Custom Guns, members of the Barrington Writers Workshop, Joel Platt, Dr. Colman Seskind, Dr. George Burica, Osvaldo Leandri, and the staff at iUniverse, Sarah Disdrow, Amy McHargue, Nolan Estes, Holly Hess, Tracy Anderson, and all the others.

To the Glenview, Skokie, Wilmette, Morton Grove, and Lake Forest Public Libraries for pulling articles and recommending books to read so I wouldn't embarrass myself by making too many mistakes.

To the authors and publishers of books I bought and read for research purposes, and to Al Gore for inventing the Internet.

Maps and Drawings

Maps

Drawings

Photograph

Toward the end of the 1930s and into the 1940s, the Nazis tried mightily to develop nuclear weapons. Everything that's been made available to the public by the Allies since the war indicates the Nazis were never successful in building those types of weapons.

But governments don't always tell the truth, do they? This was demonstrated once again in 2003 with claims made about Iraq's possession of "weapons of mass destruction." So can it be said with certainty that the Nazis were not the first to enter the atomic age?

And if the Nazis did build such weapons, what happened to them?

Prologue

Clutching her much-loved doll in one hand while holding onto the bedcovers with the other, the little girl swung her legs over the edge of her "big person's" bed and used the tips of her little toes to find the floor. Tiptoeing as quietly as she could down the second-floor hallway to where the balustrade overlooked the first-floor parlor, she hid behind the posts, watching her big sister, Karin, tidy up the parlor.

"Hey, you!" Karin called out, catching a glimpse of the child peeking through the posts. "I thought by now you'd be in dreamland."

"We're not tired," little Elsa told Karin, holding up her doll as she ran back to her bedroom.

Karin went up to Elsa's room, hoping to find a way to bring sleep to the little girl. She lit a kerosene lamp, making the room cozy. While they read about dancing rabbits and prancing horses, the child watched in fascination as the shadows cast from the kerosene lamp danced on the walls. Seeing the child's eyelids grow heavy, Karin picked up the little girl, careful not to wake her. She softly kissed the child good night and, for the second time that evening, carefully placed her in her "big person's" bed.

Karin heard loud knocking on the front door downstairs. She was concerned the racket might wake the child. The young woman raced out of the bedroom. She ran downstairs and, without looking to see who was making all the noise, opened the door. A man in a faded fedora bulled his way past Karin into the foyer. He threw her against a wall.

"Who are you?" she demanded. "What do you want?"

"Gestapo!" the man barked as two other men entered the house.

"Get out of here!" she yelled, panic mounting as she backed away.

"Quiet, Jewess!" the first man said, smirking.

"I'm not a Jew," she told him, confused by his remark. She had barely spoken when a second man backhanded her, knocking out a tooth. The force of his blow caused Karin to lose her balance and fall to the floor. Immediately the first man, the one in charge, reached down, grabbed a handful of her beautiful blonde hair, and yanked her back to her feet.

"Don't lie to me, Jewess," he ordered. "This morning your daughter was seen parading around a park with a Star of David hanging from her neck."

"She's not my daughter. She's my little sister," Karin sobbed, the pain in her mouth causing her eyes to tear. "She was given the Star by a little girl she met in—"

But before she could finish explaining what had happened, the leader slapped her again. Suddenly all three men stopped and looked upward. A shrill scream was coming from Elsa, who was perched at the top of the stairs. "Get up there, Bruno," the leader said to one of the men, pointing to Elsa. "Lock that screaming little bitch in her room. Hugo will stay here with me, and we'll have some 'fun' with the mother. We'll let you have her later." Turning his attention back to Karin, the man in the faded fedora started dragging her around by her hair, yelling, "Where is your husband, Jew?"

I'm not married," Karin said, barely managing to stay conscious. "I told you before," she moaned. "The child upstairs is my *sister*." Karin found it difficult to speak because of the pain in her mouth. Slurring her words, she managed to say, "We're here in Munich, visiting friends of my parents. The family that lives here went to the theater this evening. Why are you doing this to me?" she cried before slipping into semiconsciousness.

"Left you both here by yourselves, did they? Such poor hosts," the man said, sarcasm dripping from every word. "You know Jews aren't permitted to attend Reich productions. Now, where's your husband?" he demanded. Getting no response, he released her hair, grabbed the front of her blouse, and pulled Karin's now-unconscious form upward and toward him. Forming a fist with his other hand, he struck her in the face, breaking her nose. As she fell backward, the weight of her body ripped open the buttons on her blouse.

"Well, what do we have here, Hugo?" the man holding Karin asked his henchmen. "Let's find out." And with that he lecherously yanked off one of Karin's bra straps. Without the strap, her breast became exposed. Before he touched it he spat out orders: "Hugo, go upstairs and find out what Bruno's doing. Before we entered the house, I thought I saw a lamp burning upstairs. Bring it down."

"What about her?" Hugo asked, pointing at Karin.

The man in the fedora smiled. "I'm sure she'll be here when you get back."

The flames from the shattered kerosene lamp quickly engulfed the house's first floor. Outside, the three Gestapo hoodlums watched as the fire burned its way to the second floor. When the ruffians heard the sound of fire engines in the distance, they briskly walked away into the night.

When Elsa heard the front door slam shut, she crawled out from under the bed. "The bad men are gone, Dolly. It's safe to come out. Karin will give us cookies and milk." Tears were streaming down Elsa's cheeks. She gripped her precious doll to her tiny heaving chest and ran from her bedroom toward the stairs, crying out for her sister. The flames were licking their way upward, blocking the stairway. Elsa first smelled the smoke. Then she saw the fire. Becoming confused, she ran back to her room, slamming the door shut behind her. She climbed onto the bed and pulled the covers up over her head. "Don't worry, Dolly, we'll be all right," she murmured, cradling her doll in one hand while clenching the Star of David pendant in the other. Elsa was given the Star by her new friend Sarah that afternoon in the Marienplatz while they fed the pigeons.

Part I

1.

On the last day in January 1943, Hitler along with members of his inner circle were cloistered behind closed doors. The mood was grim. The subject under discussion was how to keep Stalin's Slavic hoards from taking back what the armies of the Reich had won in the East and what to do about the Americans and British about to do the same in the West. No one proposed a solution the others would support. The debate dragged on for hours. As usual none of the Reich's top military leaders, her Field Marshals, Generals, and Admirals—the ones that were actually fighting the war— were present to make suggestions. The exception was "Leave it to my Luftwaffe Göring," head of the Reich's Air Force. At this stage in the war Göring was nothing more than a placeholder due of his dependency on drugs.

Every one was tired. Most were bored, having had the same discussion a hundred times before.

No one took the time to look out the room's giant picture window to view the beauty and tranquilty beyond the slightly frosted panes of glass. The mountains in the distance cast blue-gray shadows on the newly fallen snow. The shadows were starting to lengthen, signaling the day was coming to an end. Smoke was curling up from the chimneys and lights were twinkling in the windows in the homes in the valley below. It was a perfect picture of a winter wonderland.

One thousand miles to the east the winter picture was not so wonderful. There the snow was red with the blood of two opposing armies. There the sun never broke through the smoky haze of war to cast shadows. The place was Stalingrad and the German Sixth Army under General Friedrich was losing, badly.

The conference room, where this no-resolution discussion was taking place was at the Berghof, Hitler's alpine retreat high in the mountains of southern Barvaria, a cozy place, far away from the dirty business of war. In the hallway, outside the conference room two men waited for the giant doors in front of them to open. The younger man, the soldier in uniform, was waiting to tell his Führer that the Reich had a new "wonder weapon," a weapon so powerful that its use practically guaranteed the Reich's victory in the war. Naturally there was a caveat and that was if everything worked out as planned. The young man making the presentation was Karl Strassburg.

◄━━▊▶

Before being wounded in 1941, during Operation Merkur, the German airborne invasion of Crete, Strassburg had been a Major in the *Fallschirmjagers*, the German paratroopers. Due to wounds he received on Crete, Strassburg was no longer on active duty. He only wore his uniform for interviews, photography sessions, occasions like today. Strassburg could have passed for a movie star. He stood just over six feet tall, was broad shouldered, and had a full head of dark hair, with hints of gray sprouting around the temples despite being only twenty-five years old. Worry lines were etched at the corners of his mouth and crow's feet were taking shape at the end of his eyes; they were telltale signs of the price he paid for his Knight's Cross with Oak Leaves and Swords, the award that hung around his neck on a red,

5

white, and black ribbon, an award equivalent to the US Medal of Honor. Strassburg was a Hero of the Reich.

He also was a physicist. His university studies began in the fall of 1936 under the famed chemist Otto Hahn and his two assistants, Fritz Strassmann and Lise Meitner. They were the first scientists to discover when an atom of uranium is bombarded with neutrons it splits, releasing energy. At the end of his third year, Strassburg decided to experience life outside of Germany, so he transferred to England's prestigious Cambridge University for half a year. Then he returned to Germany, resuming his studies at the Kaiser Wilhelm Institute for chemistry, where he earned high honors in applied physics before joining the *Fallschirmjagers*.

◄━━█◗►

The man standing next to Strassburg was his mother's cousin, Dr. Wilhelm Ohnesorge, Minister of Post for the Third Reich, a long-time friend and confident of Hitler. Their friendship went back to the 1920s, when the two were inmates at Landsberg Prison in southwest Bavaria. Those were dark days but nowhere as dark as the days ahead if the Reich failed to get one of the three major Allies, aligned against them, out of the war—soon. The two friends were sentenced to five years at Landsberg, punishment for the unsuccessful 1924 "Beer Hall Putsch," the plot to overthrow the elected German government. In Landsberg, Ohnesorge worked with Hitler on his political manifesto, *Mein Kampf*. This act endeared Ohnesorge to Hitler and when Hitler became the Führer, Ohnesorge became Minister of Post.

It was Ohnesorge who got Strassburg his job at Baron Manfred von Ardenne's laboratories at Lichterfelde-Ost after recovering from the wounds he received on Crete. Ohnesorge and the Baron were good friends. Their friendship started when Ohnesorge, with Hitler's approval, diverted huge amounts of Reich postal funds to finance the "new wonder" project at von Ardenne's laboratories under the supervision of General der Waffen SS Dr-Ing Hans Kammler, Strassburg's boss.

It was Kammler who suggested using the Baron's facilities as the place to build the "wonder weapons," knowing that Allied Intelligence never bothered monitoring von Ardenne's facility because Admiral Wilhelm Canaris, head of the Abwehr, Nazi Military Intelligence, had skillfully spread the word that the Lichterfelde-Ost laboratory was focused solely on medical research.

◄━━█◗►

Hitler liked presentations made by Heroes of the Reich, especially when they delivered "good news," which lately rarely happened. However, today's news was extremely good. Kammler should have made the presentation, but for reasons unknown to Strassburg he was given the job.

"Although you're still slumping a bit, your back seems a lot better, Karl," Ohnesorge commented, hoping to strike up a lighthearted conversation that would help take Strassburg's mind off his upcoming presentation.

Strassburg's mood darkened. "You do realize those boneheaded nitwits at the Air Ministry's Technical Equipment Division—the ones who came up with the design for our chutes—are partially responsible for what happened to me on Crete, don't you? Who in their right mind would design a chute where the jumper has no

6

choice but to land on his knees and fall forward? Before they ever put those shrouds of death into production, they should have talked to the *Fallschirmjagers* who'd be using them. Whoever designed those things, should be shot!"

This obviously was not the lightedhearted banter Ohnesorge sought. Realizing now was not the time to make small talk he stopped talking and instead looked up, pretending to admire the coffered details of the ceiling.

Free from unwanted conversation Strassburg focused on more important issues. Namely the complex personalities of the men he'd be presenting to: Hitler and the top Nazi leaders he nicknamed "The Committee."

Adolf Hitler was the only one who could approve or disapprove Strassburg's proposal. The Führer had met Strassburg at a Hitler Youth rally years ago. According to Ohnesorge, Hitler had followed Strassburg's *Fallschirmjäger* exploits with great pride and interest.

Then there was The Committee.

Dr. Joseph Goebbels was the Reich's Minister for Propaganda and Enlightenment. He had met Strassburg during a photography shoot for *Signal* magazine, the propaganda publication of the Wehrmacht, the German army.

Albert Speer, the Reich's Minister of Armament, was the only member of The Committee Strassburg collaborated with on development of the Reich's top-secret "wonder weapon." He enjoyed working with Speer and their solutions to problems typically were successful. The thing Strassburg and Speer found annoying was Kammler's almost constant flow of sarcastic comments.

Reichsmarschall Hermann Göring—second only to Hitler in the government, head of the Luftwaffe, the German Air Force, and the *Fallschirmjägers*—had presented Strassburg with his Knight's Cross with Oak Leaves and Swords. Göring was an acclaimed fighter pilot during the Great War, now referred to as World War I. He was awarded the *Pour le Mérite*, commonly referred to as Blue Max, the German World War I version of the US Medal of Honor.

Martin Bormann was Hitler's obsequious personal secretary. He administered an enormous fund, "The Adolf Hitler Gifts," a kitty to which German industrialists contributed money in order to receive state and military contracts. Bormann used the contributions to build Hitler's Berghof, the Eagle's Nest, the mile-high teahouse atop the Kehlstein, and the huge Obersalzberg complex up the road from the Berghof.

Heinrich Himmler—ex-chicken farmer, Aryan racial purity zealot, and head of the feared SS—was Kammler's boss. One of Himmler's assignments was the overseeing of construction, staffing, and operations of the Reich's internment camps. Strassburg figured, from what Ohnesorge told him, that if Hitler had a favorite on The Committee, it most likely was Himmler.

Feeling the need to resume their conversation, Ohnesorge told Strassburg not to worry because everyone behind the doors had met him, knew about the weapons, and with the exception of Hitler, knew about *his* target proposals. Nothing would go wrong. They all liked *his* proposals, pending Hitler's blessing, of course. "Don't worry, Karl, everything will go smoothly. You'll see."

Pointing to the film canister under Strassburg's arm, Ohnesorge smiled and said, "I can't tell you how pleased Hitler will be when he sees *that* film. Today will be remembered as the turning point in the war. Once Hitler approves the targets you're recommending, the real work will begin."

Hearing Ohnesorge say, "you're recommending," Strassburg knew his neck was on the chopping block if Hitler didn't like what he saw or heard. Strassburg, like his father, never liked Ohnesorge. "Willie's a snake," his father repeatedly told him when the two were alone. Strassburg rubbed the back of his neck. *Life had been so much simpler before my mother received that damn letter.*

"You feeling all right, Karl?" Ohnesorge asked.

"Never better. You know, Willie, I had nothing to do with the weapon itself," Strassburg reminded Ohnesorge. "Kammler and Houtermans were the geniuses behind it, especially Houtermans. He was the one who came up with the moderator to enrich U-238, natural uranium, to weapons-grade material, U-235."

"Moderator smoderator. Who cares who did what at this point! The only thing that matters now is that with this new weapon we'll win the war," Ohnesorge gleefully told Strassburg, throwing his hands up, exuding ecstasy. "Stop worrying, Karl. You're beginning to sound like your mother."

Before Strassburg could address Ohnesorge's tasteless remark, the conference room doors swung open, courtesy of the pudgy hands of *Reichsmarschall* Göring.

Crossing the threshold, Strassburg was taken aback. He didn't know whether to cry or laugh. The conference room had all the trappings of some huge theatrical set.

Directly behind Göring was an oversized oak conference table with Hitler at its head. The men sitting around the table seemed dwarfed by its size.

On one side sat Bormann and Goebbels. Next to Goebbels was an empty chair. On the table, in front of the empty chair, was a huge plate of food. Behind the food were two plates piled high with cleanly picked chicken and beef bones, obviously Göring's place at the table.

On the other side was Himmler, standing and finishing his presentation. Bormann sat next to Himmler, and next to Bormann was a place for Ohnesorge.

The long sideboard, hugging one of the walls, contained the latest gramophone, along with hundreds of classical music recordings by the Berliner Philharmoniker on *Deutsche Grammophon*. To Strassburg's surprise, tucked amongst the classical music collection were many British and American jazz and show-tune recordings.

The conference room walls were oak paneled from the marble flooring up to the chair rail. A giant clock with a massive bronze eagle crouching on top sat against the far wall. Huge paintings—contemporary and classic nudes, along with Gobelin tapestries—hung above the chair rail. The heavy velvet curtain dividing the room into two areas—the conference area and the living area—were tied back. Hitler's beautiful Alsatian dog, Blondi, Bormann's birthday gift to his Führer, was sprawled out in front of the great stone fireplace, enjoying the fire's warmth.

Behind the men was, what Strassburg thought had to be, the world's largest picture window. Outside the window was a scenic background of epic proportions and spectacular beauty. A mile or two in the distance, nestled in the valley, was the beautiful, tranquil alpine town of Berchtesgaden surrounded by majestic snow-covered mountains as far as the eye could see.

Our Führer lives well, Strassburg thought.

Everyone in the room looked fatigued. From the look on Hitler's face, it was obvious to Strassburg the previous discussions had not gone well.

Himmler, finishing his report, continued looking at his notes as he nervously polished his glasses, ignoring the entrance of Strassburg and Ohnesorge. "As you can tell from the report," Himmler started to summarize, "the January 20, 1942, Wannsee Conference was a total success. Now we have agreement from all parties involved on the best way to exterminate all the Jews in countries occupied by the Reich."

Pausing to gauge the reaction of those around the table, Himmler continued, "Now we can execute the Final Solution to our Jewish problem, and do it without causing undue trauma to those running the program and be sure the children of these undesirables will not be around to avenge their parents."

Strassburg was stunned by what he heard—so shocked—he forgot to salute his old boss. *Reichsmarschall* Göring attributed Strassburg's error to pre-presentation jitters, having never before given a presentation to Hitler and The Committee.

"Relax, Major. We're all friends here. We've just been fed, so we're not hungry for young red meat," Göring whispered in a jovial voice.

Strassburg saluted.

"Thank you, *Reichsmarschall*. That's good to know."

Watching Strassburg's eyes as they gazed around the room, Göring said, "Impressive, is it not, Major?"

"Yes, *Reichsmarschall*, impressive doesn't begin to describe it."

Actually it scares the hell out me, Reichsmarschall, Strassburg thought. *Hitler lives in a fantasy world advised by people Freud would have given his eyeteeth to put on a couch.*

Strassburg kept staring at the conference room's coffered ceiling, with its massive dark wooden beams and carved panel inserts. In the center of the ceiling was a massive wheel-shaped chandelier, its outer ring sprouting twenty to thirty electric candles projecting a sense of drama and foreboding.

"Beautiful, yes?" Göring asked, noticing the Major's fascination with the ceiling. "It's modeled after a ceiling at Neuschwanstein, the fairy-tale castle built by Ludwig II, the mad king of Bavaria."

Hearing Göring mention Ludwig II, and then looking at Hitler and The Committee, Strassburg couldn't help but think that acorns really don't fall far from the tree.

Seeing Strassburg and Ohnesorge enter the conference room, Hitler smiled and stood, motioning the others to follow suit.

"Please, please, Major, come in, a pleasure to see you. I think the last time we met you were a young boy in lederhosen. I've followed your heroics for the Reich with great interest. I'm told by everyone here you have good news."

"My Führer," Strassburg replied somewhat stiffly, "you now have the most powerful weapon on the planet, a nuclear bomb. In fact, you have *two* of them!"

Hitler beamed. "At last!" he cried, shaking his fists triumphantly over his head as his eyes became moist. "Can this be so? Those weapons I've heard so much about—are finally mine? Now, I can finally bring my enemies to their knees? Tell me, Major, how do you know these new wonder weapons of yours will work? Whenever I talk with Heisenberg and the others in charge of our *official* program, they tell me we won't have such weapons before the end of 1945."

Before Strassburg had a chance to answer, Göring barged into the conversation. "As you know, my Führer, these bombs were developed outside of Heisenberg's organization. Let me assure you Germany has two of these weapons, and they work! The Major here will tell you what targets to use these weapons against in order to bring this dismal war to an end—a plan we know you'll agree with."

No sooner had the words "we know you'll agree with" passed Göring's lips than anger clouded Hitler's face. No one said a word. Everyone was waiting for the hammer to fall. Göring immediately realized in his excitement he had overstepped—badly. Lowering his head, as a dog does in submission, the *Reichsmarschall* said, "My apologies, my Führer, a plan we *hope* you'll consider."

Hitler said nothing.

You're such a damn fool, Hermann. If you keep using those painkillers, we'll surely end up losing the war, Speer thought, his elegant hands toying with his platinum cigarette case left unopened in deference to Hitler's adamant no-smoking policy.

Göring's addiction to painkillers was due to wounds he received during World War I. Hitler knew about the problem and refused to do anything about it, because their friendship went back to the founding days of the Nazi movement.

Speer raised his hand to be recognized. He feared if someone didn't step in immediately—and take Hitler's mind off Göring's faux pas—Hitler might scuttle the presentation, explaining why the bombs would work.

At one of the many conferences held in the years before the war, Speer had met Jun Noguchi, the driving force behind Japan's industrial empire in Korea. After the two got to know and trust each other, they discussed areas where they might be able to help one another. One of those areas was nuclear-weapons development and testing. Under their agreement, if Germany developed a bomb, Noguchi agreed to let her test it near Konan in northern Korea, where the Soviet Union (USSR) and the United States couldn't monitor the test. In return, Speer agreed to keep Noguchi informed about the work being done by Heisenberg and others in Germany's quest to build a bomb.

What Speer didn't know until later was that Kammler had hired Dr-Ing Fritz Houtermans to create a bomb in a project parallel to Heisenberg's and that Heisenberg and his team knew nothing about this.

"Don't forget mentioning how Kammler got the ore to build the bombs, Minister," Himmler piped up, in effect, ensuring Hitler wouldn't forget the SS's key role in the bomb's development.

"Thank you, Heinrich, for reminding me," Speer courteously said but obviously annoyed at Himmler's self-serving interruption.

When Houtermans told Kammler how much uranium ore would be needed to build the bombs, Kammler searched for an appropriate source. He couldn't take the ore from Germany's existing reserves without Heisenberg and the Allies knowing about it. If that happened, the trail would lead to Lichterfelde-Ost. In a matter of days, the Baron's laboratories likely would be bombed into dust.

Realizing this, Kammler went digging. He found that in 1940, prior to the fall of France, Canaris's Abwehr had stupidly let the French underground smuggle a huge cache of uranium ore out of France, owned by the Curie organization in Paris. The ore ended up in the hands of the British somewhere in North Africa. After more digging, Kammler found where the British had taken the ore, launched an operation to retrieve it, and transported it to Germany without the British or anyone else knowing the ore was spirited out of North Africa. With the Curie ore, Houtermans built three bombs—the two still at the laboratories in Lichterfelde-Ost and the third successfully tested in Korea under the agreement Speer made with Noguchi. Before developing plans for their use, Speer, Strassburg, and Kammler had to make sure the bombs worked.

Hitler waved his hand, signaling he heard enough. "Thank you, Speer. I've read this in Kammler's report. I've also read reports by Heisenberg and his cronies. All anyone ever shows me are reports and more reports! I'm sick of seeing reports!" Banging his fist on the table in rage, spittle flying off his mustache, Hitler turned to Strassburg. "Major, the film canister under your arm I know what's in it. Show me what happened in Korea!"

With that, Ohnesorge walked over to the opposite wall and pulled back one of the Gobelin tapestries, revealing a movie screen and projector. Strassburg placed the film reel he'd been carrying on the projector. "My Führer, while you're watching this film, we'd like you to consider this: of the three major Allies aligned against the Reich only one is really important. Because without that one, the armies and navies of the other two can—and will—be defeated by our next generation of armor, aircraft, and U-boats coming on line during the middle of 1944. Only the United States—due to her location, almost limitless raw materials, manpower, manufacturing, and industrial might—can defeat Germany. If we fail to force the United States out of the war *this* year, Germany will lose the war during the first half of 1945."

Hitler and the others said nothing. Strassburg signaled Ohnesorge to shut the curtains on each side of the giant picture window. Strassburg turned on the projector. What they saw was the bomb's detonation, just before dawn. It was filmed behind nine inches of ballistic glass from inside a four-foot-thick concrete bunker. Because the light was dim, nothing much appeared until fifty-two frames into the film. Then everything went white, followed by a growing burn spot in the center of each frame. The spot became so large the rest of it was edited out. A brilliant light, thousands of times brighter than the sun, caused the spot. What followed was a mushroom-shaped cloud, which rose steadily into the atmosphere. Over these frames someone had scratched 47,811 feet, indicating the height of the cloud, and three million degrees Celsius, denoting the temperature at the explosion's core. Directly under the blast the heat turned the sand into glass. Next came a series of aerial and slightly elevated ground views within a one-mile radius of ground zero. Nothing was there: no trees, no vegetation, no buildings, and no vehicles. The film's final frames showed a series of panoramic vistas of the surrounding seven-square-mile area from ground zero, an area of total devastation.

As the end of the film started slapping against the side of the projector, the reel stopped. There was no clapping, no cheering—just silence. Hitler, visibly shaken, sat staring at the empty screen. The others—even though they previously had viewed the film—were so cowed, they sat motionless and dazed. Strassburg asked Hitler if he wanted to see the film a second time. The Nazi leader was silent, so Strassburg repeated the question.

"No, Major, seeing *that* film once was quite enough. When this presentation is finished, see to it this copy, the negatives, and any other copies you have are destroyed."

Then, after making eye contact with each one in the room, Hitler said, "No one here has ever viewed this film, understood?" Turning his lifeless gray eyes to Strassburg, Hitler said, "You have split the earth open and shown us hell. Please continue with your presentation, Major."

"As you saw, the uranium bomb works. As for the two targets in America," Strassburg said, while placing the film reel in its canister, "they must be so important that once they are destroyed the American public will demand that Roosevelt abandon the war, leaving Churchill and Stalin to their fates."

Ohnesorge threw open the curtains, letting what daylight remained to flood the room.

"Assuming you approve the targets," Speer said, addressing Hitler, "General Kammler, Major Strassburg, and I will come up with specific plans and timetables for delivering *your* bombs to their targets."

"New York!" Bormann shouted, not waiting for Hitler's approval to speak—a mistake, as he was about to find out. "It's America's biggest city, their financial center, a deepwater port, a naval shipyard, a major railway hub."

Not to be upstaged, Himmler jumped up. "Then that Jew Roosevelt, and his mongrelized country, will know the power of the Reich!"

"Sit down! Both of you! No more outbursts," Hitler barked. "Thank you for your enthusiasm, but no more comments until the Major has finished briefing *me*. Naturally, New York will be the primary target. We've planned for that all along."

Göring sheepishly looked elsewhere once he realized Hitler's caustic comment about bombing New York was directed at him because the Luftwaffe lacked a bomber that could carryout the mission. But the fact was that no nation in 1943 had an aircraft capable of crossing the Atlantic without some type of refueling. America got its bombers to bases in England and Scotland using ground refueling sites in Newfoundland, Canada, Greenland, and Iceland. Germany didn't have similar bases. In 1939, before the war started, flying boats made sixteen Atlantic crossings using Flight Refueling Ltd.'s aerial refueling system.

Days before the presentation, Speer mentioned to Strassburg that Göring and members of Germany's aviation industry had at the beginning of the war discussed the possibility of building a transatlantic bomber capable of reaching America's East Coast and returning to Germany without refueling. Several manufacturers had submitted prototype plans. But recently Hitler and Göring deemed development of such a revolutionary aircraft "inopportune" due to the scarcity of resources. Soon the RLM, the Ministry of Aviation, would notify the manufacturers of that decision.

"Please, continue, Major," Hitler urged.

"While the bomb has massive destructive power, it could never destroy all of New York City. That's why we're proposing Wall Street, their Financial District, as the center of the attack."

The room became quiet, everyone waiting for Hitler to ask Strassburg how he intended to get the bomb to Wall Street when the Reich didn't have a bomber that could cross the Atlantic. Being a politician, Hitler was also an actor. He knew how to read his audience and throw them off balance. Knowing everyone was expecting him to ask Strassburg how he intended to get the bomb to the US, without an aircraft, Hitler didn't ask. He wanted to see everyone's reaction, especially Strassburg's.

"So what are *you* recommending as the second target, Major?"

Everyone in the room, except Hitler, knew Speer and Strassburg's recommendation and why they were recommending it. They also knew there was a good chance that once Hitler heard it, Strassburg would be cut loose, and Strassburg— well, others had been shot for less.

Strassburg knew the risk he was about to take He also knew "you only live once."

A memorable moment, Strassburg thought. *Hitler isn't asking The Committee members for their opinion. He's asking me for mine.*

"The second target should be Boulder Dam in their Southwest, my Führer."

"That's absurd, Major, if the *Reichsmarschall* can't get a bomb to New York how do you propose he bombs a dam in their Southwest? Get one of Dönitz's U-boats to fly it there, and why this dam? Where exactly is it?"

Seeing the others smirk—as if to say, "We told you so"—Speer immediately interjected, "Let me answer your last question first, my Führer. But before I do, I need you to come with me over to the globe in the corner."

Speer spun the globe, stopping it at the US landmass. "Boulder Dam is here, on the border between the states of Arizona and Nevada. This is Lake Mead behind it. The dam is one of the most ambitious engineering projects of this century. What's important here is what it provides for the American war effort and the effect it will have on American morale once the dam is destroyed. This dam holds back trillions of gallons of water in Lake Mead—nearly two year's flow from the Colorado River."

Spinning the globe again, Speer stopped it at Lake Konstanz, bordering Germany, Austria, and Switzerland. "As you can see by comparison, Lake Konstanz, Germany's biggest lake, is smaller than Lake Mead, and Mead is still filling up with water. That water irrigates one-third of all the farmland in their Southwest. It provides hydroelectric power for approximately one-third of all their West Coast cities and industries. Those industries produce arms and munitions used against Germany and Japan. It provides all the power for the world's largest copper and aluminum mines. The dam's destruction will cause widespread hysteria and ruin."

When Speer said "widespread hysteria and ruin," Hitler's gray eyes seemed to glow.

"Just as Wall Street, in lower Manhattan, represents the epitome of their corporate and financial power," Speer added, "Boulder Dam represents the pride and accomplishments of their labor and industry. It's the power that keeps their West Coast industries alive and growing by leaps and bounds. The dam is inland and remote. Destroying it will convey a message to all Americans: there is nowhere in the States you can hide and escape the fury of the Reich."

"As for how we plan to get the bomb to Wall Street and the dam," Strassburg said, "we're asking you to trust us to work that out. Just as we worked out a way to build the bombs—in secret."

Hearing Strassburg ask Hitler for his trust, every member of The Committee, except for Speer, backed away. None of them wanted to be associated with Strassburg's request for trust, fearing Hitler would not react favorably.

Hitler remained silent for a minute before speaking.

"Minister Speer, please join the others at the conference table. I want a moment alone with the Major."

Then, as a father would regard a son, Hitler placed one hand on Strassburg's shoulder and with the other hand examined the Knight's Cross with Oak Leaves and Swords on the ribbon around Strassburg's neck. Then in a tone only Strassburg could hear, Hitler said, "I now realize why you're wearing this Knight's Cross with Oak Leaves and Swords. No one in this room, except maybe Speer, would have had the balls to say to me what you said moments ago, asking for my trust. You're a 'smart boy,' Major, but remember, always leave your audience wanting more. Make sure you deliver what you just promised. I hope for your sake you can pull this off. Good luck. Now go!"

Releasing Strassburg, Hitler turned and faced his Committee of ashen faces. "I'm approving both missions," he said. "Minister Speer and the Major have convinced me both targets have merit. The Americans will never suspect we're capable of destroying their dam or Wall Street. When we do, there will be hysteria across America. They'll beg for mercy, and when they do we'll be merciful. Naturally, it will be on *our* terms. Just like it was with the French in that railroad car in the forest of Compiègne in 1940—the same railroad car and the same forest where Germany was forced to sign that humiliating armistice on November 11, 1918, the end of the Great War. 'America the beautiful' will soon not be so—beautiful."

Hearing what Hitler said, everyone stood up, clapped, and congratulated each other.

Strassburg left the meeting, his thoughts spinning like the arms in a centrifuge—the calm way Himmler delivered his report on the plan to annihilate thousands, perhaps millions, of people; The Committee's acceptance; and Hitler's violent mood swings. *This is not my Germany. This can't be happening.*

2.

The night's January mountain air felt like millions of tiny pinpricks attacking his lungs. After saluting the SS guard on duty, outside the Berghof's front door, Strassburg turned up the collar on his greatcoat for protection against the howling wind and whirling snow. He walked several steps to the curb, where a 170V Mercedes was waiting to take him to the nearby Hotel Platterhof. The short uphill walk to the luxurious hotel would have been enjoyable had the weather not been so brutally raw. Even with the car's heater turned up high, it was cold inside the car's plush interior.

The hotel was in the Obersalzberg compound above the Berghof. The compound began as two simple home sites: one for Bormann and one for Göring. That way the two could be near Hitler when he was in residence at the Berghof.

The compound expanded, under Bormann's direction, due to The Committee members, their staffs, Generals and Admirals, along with their wives and girlfriends needing to spend more and more time at the Berghof as the war became increasingly difficult to manage. Prior to the expansion the closest accommodations were in Berchtesgaden, the town in the valley. Not a pleasant drive, uphill or downhill in winter.

The compound was surrounded by two rows of chain-linked fencing, each row topped with barbwire. The space between the two fences was patrolled twenty-four hours a day by SS Guards with dogs. There were guard towers, sporting machine guns, every hundred or so feet along the perimeter. The compound's exterior appeared to have been designed by the same people who designed the exteriors of Himmler's "resort" camps. Inside the wire, it was a completely different matter. Here every building appeared part of a resort. The quarters occupied by bodyguards and sentries looked nothing like the ones found on military bases. There were shooting ranges for pistol, rifle, trap, and skeet; a post office; a grand garage housing luxury transportation for VIPs; a military motor pool; a kindergarten; staff housing; kitchens; Göring's home; Bormann's home, and the luxury Hotel Platterhof, where Strassburg was staying.

Bormann told Strassburg the hotel cost millions—millions of new 1933 German marks—to construct. Bormann spared no expense, making it the world's finest hotel.

Hitler insisted the hotel be limited to two floors, insuring it would fit in with the region's distinctive alpine architecture. The interior was a combination of twentieth-century German simplicity and the Nazi preference for the neoclassical. The common rooms, hallways, and lavish lobby had exotic wooden floors adorned with thick-piled Persian carpets. Guest rooms, more appropriately called suites, featured bathrooms with marble walls and floors. The suites boasted ceilings adorned with lavish gold-plated fixtures; sitting rooms equipped with telephones; and bedrooms with antique French beds and armoires—courtesy of the Wehrmacht after the 1940 defeat of France.

The first floor housed the lobby; a huge reception hall that doubled as a ballroom, adorned with "liberated" paintings, museum-quality furnishings, and a floor-to-ceiling mirror; a reading room/library; a beer hall, and a breakfast room. The breakfast room ceiling reportedly cost twenty-five thousand new Reichmarks. The only things the rooms didn't have were listening devices. The Committee members—with the exception of Himmler—insisted on it.

The Platterhof was off-limits to the public, but had that not been the case, it would have rated four stars in the finest travel guides. The barbershop, beauty parlor, cleaners, haberdasher, and women's dress salon were staffed with the best and brightest from countries occupied by the Nazis.

Standing in the hotel's posh lobby, looking at all the opulence, Strassburg kept thinking, *The National People's Hotel indeed! Where "common people" stay while meeting their Führer. I imagine precious few "common people" will ever see the inside of this palace, a tribute to extravagance and indulgence.*

Three civilians—two men and a woman—stopped Strassburg as he made his way through the lobby to the front desk to retrieve his room key. They recognized him as a Hero of the Reich from photos splashed on Goebbels's propaganda posters. The woman asked Strassburg for his autograph, a souvenir for one of her children.

After writing a brief message and signing it, Strassburg walked up the ornately embellished double staircase leading to his suite on the second floor.

"I thought one of the articles I read about him said he was twenty-six. He's really handsome, but he looks to be at least thirty-six," the woman said to one of the men.

As he walked down the corridor toward his suite, Strassburg unbuttoned his uniform blouse, his mind was on a hot bath, and his eyelids were heavy.

3.

Hauptmann (Captain) Lothar Bergen had a problem. He was the pilot of Göring's Ju 290A-7, the Luftwaffe commander's personal aircraft. His copilot was hospitalized with appendicitis and the next day they were scheduled to fly the *Reichmarschall* back to Berlin from the Berghof. With the Luftwaffe's deteriorating pilot pool—the result of tremendous casualties as the war droned on—finding a last-minute replacement was a big problem. Bergen started calling in favors. A friend at Blohm & Voss, one of Germany's leading aircraft manufacturers, dispatched B&V's senior test pilot from the company's flying-boat division to copilot the transport on the flight back to Berlin. Bergen watched with envy—from inside the Ju 290A-7 hangar—as the replacement copilot started his final approach. The pilot was flying a Bf109G-2 Trop fighter, which only a few of the Reich's top pilots could handle.

"Shit, that bastard can really fly," Bergen murmured with jealousy.

The pilot taxied to a stop in front of the hangar. Switching off the fighter's powerful 1200-hp liquid-cooled engine the three-bladed prop stopped spinning. Wheels were chocked. The pilot pushed opened the canopy.

Bergen could hardly believe his eyes. *Son of a bitch! He's a goddamn she. That bastard sent me a woman.*

Not only was the pilot a woman, she was stunningly attractive—blond, tall, gorgeous. She had the longest legs Bergen had ever seen. Her highly tailored, powder blue flight suit was skin-tight, appearing painted on her inviting body.

Oh, to be that flight suit.

"Phew," she said, unzipping the top of her flight suit, revealing a modest amount of cleavage. Smiling, she held out her hand, "I'm Anna Prien from Blohm & Voss. You're Hauptmann Bergen, right?"

Bergen was silent. His mouth was open but no words came out.

Prien continued, "Someone from B&V will pick up the Trop tomorrow. Right now, I'd like to freshen up so if there's nothing you want me to do, I'd like to go to the hotel. Dr-Ing Vogt, my boss, told me it's fantastic."

Bergen just stood there—staring.

"Hello in there, you are Lothar Bergen, right?"

"You're a *woman!*"

"Yes, the last time I looked in the mirror, everything seemed to indicate I was a woman. So, Hauptmann Bergen, do you want me to stay and help you, or can we find someone to drive me to the hotel?"

Regaining his composure, Bergen thought there was a lot Prien could help him with. Unfortunately, that had nothing to do with airplanes.

"Hook up that tow bar to your Trop and I'll get someone to drive you to the hotel."

Upon entering the hotel's well-appointed lobby Prien received a chorus of catcalls. Ignoring the stares, she walked up to clerk behind the reception desk, pulled out her B&V identity, and Luftwaffe assignment paper. Before she said a word the clerk asked, "Where is your luggage, Fräulein?"

"I flew here in a Trop. There's barely enough room in the cockpit for me, let alone luggage. I didn't bring any clothes. My boss at B&V told me the hotel could launder the clothes I'm wearing in time for my trip to Berlin in the morning."

"It will be our pleasure to do so, Fräulein Prien," the clerk said. "But you'll need clothes for the evening's festivities in the ballroom. Someone on *Reichsmarschall* Göring's staff requested your attendance. Here's the request."

Anna was irate. "Didn't you hear what I said? I have no other clothes than the ones on my back. Even if your laundry gets them back to me in time for these festivities—whatever they are—I'm not going anywhere other than an airplane hangar in my flight suit. Please convey my regrets to whoever gave you the request. Now give me my key and tell me where my room is."

Overhearing the exchange between Prien and the desk clerk, the man standing next to the clerk, with the cross keys on both lapels, interceded. "Permit me, Fräulein Prien, I'm SS Hauptmann Max Hubbell, the hotel's concierge. I couldn't help but hear your conversation. I fully appreciate your situation. Permit me—the hotel's dress shop, beauty salon, and cleaners are all at your disposal. SS Schuetze Marks here will show you to your suite. Take a hot bath, pamper yourself, and relax. I'll have a matron deliver you suitable clothing so you can go to the dress shop. Leave everything you're wearing in your suite and you'll have it back nice and clean by eleven tonight."

"What is this? A command performance?" she asked.

"Well—something like that," he told her, smiling.

Prien spent nearly twenty minutes relaxing in a tub large enough to accommodate three Göring-sized people. After toweling herself off, she dusted her body with talc and felt like a woman. Neatly arrayed on the ornately carved antique French bed—likely "liberated" from some French château—was lounge wear fit for a queen, and much to her surprise, everything fit.

How in hell did they know my size?

Prien turned and looked at herself in the mirrored doors of the armoire. Stairing back at her was a young woman she hadn't seen in months.

All the parts seem to be holding up pretty well, she mused, *even after years of stress—stress from flying experimental aircraft.*

Turning side to side, she absently twirled a strand of blonde hair, still moist and curled from the bath. She looked at her breasts, her mind drifting back to the time when Stefan, her first boyfriend, asked her if he could touch them. She had just turned sixteen.

How young and innocent we were, she thought. *How bashful Stefan was when I told him he could touch me.*

Memories of that moment cascaded from the recesses of her mind. Anna laughed as she remembered how she grabbed Stefan's quivering hand, licking the tips of his fingers, following the advice of a girlfriend. How she moaned with delight, as he timidly rubbed his fingers on the tips of her nipples. Remembering how she pulled his hand away quickly, when her panties moistened.

19

Stepping into the panties, left on her bed by the hotel matron, she giggled, savoring the feel of silk caressing her thighs. The panties barely covered the dark blonde triangle of hair between her legs.

How nice it would be if Stefan's fingers were inside these panties, making me moist. Anna smelled the pungent odor of her musk. For the first time in months she felt sexy.

Her father, an independent aircraft-engine designer of some repute had been the one who introduced Anna and her brother, Dirk, to the wonders of flight. Both siblings loved to fly, but it was Anna who had the instinct for soaring among the clouds. She remembered how her mother always scolded her father about his desire to make a pilot out of their daughter. Under his tutorage Anna honed her flying skills. In her teens she was recognized as one of Switzerland's up-and-coming young pilots.

Soon after Germany's 1938 annexation of the Sudetenland, a region of Czechoslovakia, an assistant director at Blohm & Voss was attending an air show on Switzerland's Lake Zurich and saw Prien perform aerial stunts with a floatplane. After the show, impressed with her performance, he offered her a test-pilot job at B&V's Flying Boat Division, testing the company's new BV 222 flying boat. Prien remembered holding out her hand, accepting the offer on the spot.

While she loved her job, her love life was a disaster. Prien dated many single men. However, when they found out she was a test pilot none of these eligible bachelors asked her out a second time. She clearly was a threat to their masculinity.

"How can we be of assistance, Fräulein?" the manager of the hotel's dress salon asked Prien.

Prien explained how she came to be at the hotel and that she'd been invited to attend the evening's festivities in the hotel's ballroom and like Cinderella she had nothing to wear. Being tall she was skeptical the salon could outfit her on such short notice.

The manager showed Anna three dresses. All of them, with minor alterations, would fit her perfectly. After trying on the dresses, she was unable to make a decision. The manager chose a creation by the famed Italian fashion designer Elsa Schiaparelli. It featured a haltered neck, a floor-length sheath with a slit on one side to mid-thigh, and a slight train in back. The halter started just below the navel, looped around her neck, and barely covered both breasts. The flawless beauty of her ivory white skin was enhanced by the dress's black polished silk. The problem was the back. There wasn't one. It was open from the halter around her neck to the cleft in her buttock, revealing the top of her panties—not good.

The manager observed it really would be a shame if she wore her panties. The gown was designed to be revealing and there just wasn't a suitable undergarment that accommodated the dress's daring design.

"But I'd feel so naughty not wearing something," Anna replied, twisting and turning as she viewed herself in the salon's full-length mirror. "What would my mother say if she knew I wasn't wearing panties?"

"So don't tell her, dear," the manager said, somewhat bewildered by Anna's innocence.

Anna completed the outfit with black evening gloves and Ferragamo patent leather three-inch pumps.

If only this could have happened with someone special.

While seamstresses made final adjustments to the stunning gown Prien was wearing, the hostess summoned a hair stylist, who carefully studied Prien to determine the appropriate hairdo.

"What a waste!" the stylist said, referring to Prien's natural beauty. "This young woman has no idea how gorgeous she is."

"I know," the manager replied. "How refreshing and how rare."

4.

Prien energetically hugged and profusely thanked the salon's staff for transforming her from a test pilot to something akin to a fashion model in record time. She literally ran out of the salon, realizing she was close to being late for the evening's glittering party.

Prien headed for her suite, clutching her undies and lounging wear in her left hand and the gown's elegant train in her right hand. She murmured to herself as she hobbled around the corridor's second bend, "Damn it, I'm late. I took too long in the bath and the salon."

The salon manager had volunteered to have her things returned to her suite so Prien could go directly to the hotel's lavish ballroom. But, she stubbornly refused.

Strassburg was exhausted. Head down, his mind adrift, he never considered what might be heading in his direction around the bend in the corridor. Prien was fixated on getting to her suite, as fast as possible, dropping off her clothes, and somehow getting to the ballroom without tripping on her train. She never thought someone might be coming toward her from the opposite direction, a train wreck in the making. The two collided. Prien landed on her back, legs spread apart as far as the Schiaparelli would allow. Strassburg landed facing her, chin up, unconscious.

The corridor was dimly lit. Prien didn't realize Strassburg was out cold and his eyes were closed. All she noticed was his head was up and appeared to be looking at her private parts.

"Like what you see? she asked, her voice filled with indignation, her face turning scarlet. "I'm sure you've seen it all before." Scrambling around on the floor, with all the grace of a Mack Sennett comedy starlet, she finally managed to lessen her embarrassment without ripping her gown. "Show's over," she howled. "So get up. I'm talking to you."

No response, no movement, nothing. Crawling towards him she raised her arm to slap him. Then she realized he was unconscious or worse, maybe dead.

Oh my god! Prien panicked. She forgot everything she knew about treating an unconscious person. Instead of rolling him over slowly she flipped him over as she would a pancake. She put her face near his nose and mouth. *Thank god you're still alive. Hopefully you're not someone important.*

Then she saw it—the Knight's Cross with Oak Leaves and Swords dangling from the ribbon around his neck. *Shit! You are important! You're the one on that damn Nazi propaganda poster in the hotel lobby.*

Prien stood up, kicked off her pumps, gathered the Schiaparelli up around her waist, kicked open the door to her suite, and dragged Strassburg inside. Before the door slammed shut behind her she went back into the hallway, picked up what the two of them dropped, and managed to make it back in before the door slammed shut. Lucky the collision occurred where it did, if front of her suite. Strassburg was still unconscious. She grabbed one of the pillows off her bed and bent down to put it under his head. The ripping sound that followed reminded her of a window shade going up accidentally. Anna started to cry. *What's next? Now the damn dress is ripped.*

Wiggling out of the dress as if she were a snake shedding its skin, Prein grabbed the silk robe off the bed, wrapped it around herself, and went back to address her number one problem. The man on the floor, who still wasn't moving. She went into the bathroom, returned with a moist towel, and placed it on his forehead. He still was lifeless. Now she was crying. *Please, please, wake up!*

She got down on the floor, lifted his head onto her lap, and unbuttoned his tunic. What she saw made her gasp. His well-muscled body was a mass of scars. Tears clouded her eyes. *Oh my god! So that's the price you paid for that stupid medal around your neck. Please, please, please, wake up!*

For some impulsive reason, she held his head to her breast. Tears kept streaming down her cheeks as she cradled his head in her arms like a mother comforting her baby. She kissed him on his forehead. Slowly his eyes began to open.

Then, without warning, he shot up out of her arms, his head barely missing her chin.

"What the hell?" he moaned in a state of half-consciousness. "Where am I? Who are you?" he asked, slurring his words.

She looked at him for a second and said, "We bumped into each outside my suite. You fell, hit your head on the floor, and didn't get up."

"Why are you in a robe and my uniform blouse is unbuttoned?"

"I'm sorry, I panicked. When you didn't get up I thought you might be dead and your Nazi friends—well."

Strassburg said nothing. He stood up, held out both of his hands for Anna to grab and pulled her up. For a few awkward moments they stood facing each other.

"What makes you think I'm a Nazi?" he asked.

"You're on one of those propaganda posters in the lobby."

"I'm not a Nazi. I'm just a guy fighting for his country and—" Strassburg didn't finish. "Don't look so scared. You're not in any trouble. But you still haven't answered my question. Why are you in a robe and why is my blouse unbuttoned?"

Prien briefly explained everything. Who she was, what she did, why she was at the hotel, and why she was in a robe?

"You still want to go to that dinner dance, or whatever it is?" Strassburg asked. My head still feels like it was hit with a hammer and we haven't eaten, so if you're game let's go."

"When I pulled you in here I ripped the dress."

"Sorry, I forgot about the dress. How bad is the rip?

"Why?"

"If it isn't too bad maybe no one will notice?"

"But we'll be late," she reminded him.

"Believe me, with that crowd no one's going to notice."

"You really don't like these people, do you?"

"I told you. I'm not a Nazi and the sooner this damn war we started is over the better for everyone—except Germany. No one is going to forgive us for what

23

we're doing."

Prien wondered what he meant with the strange reference to "what we're doing." But she let the comment pass.

"By the way, what's your name? Please forgive me for not asking."

"Anna Prien. What's yours?"

"Karl Strassburg," he said, as she walked into the bathroom and closed the door behind her.

He had just finished buttoning his tunic when she exited the bathroom and did a little twirl. "What do you think?" she asked.

For a moment Strassburg just stood there dumbstruck. "You're the most beautiful woman I've ever seen."

She didn't know what to say. She just looked at him, thinking *he* was the most handsome man *she* had ever scene.

"Well?" she asked. Are you just going to stand there or are you going to come over here and kiss me?"

They never made it to "whatever."

5.

Next morning, the clerk at the hotel desk handed Strassburg an envelope. Inside was a note from Prien, saying how much she was looking forward to spending the following weekend with him. She also piqued his curiosity with a cryptic comment about having a "surprise" for him.

After last night, how many more surprises can she have?

On the flight back to Berlin, Strassburg sat in the rear of the aircraft, away from the others, deep in thought. The last eighteen hours had brought many more complications into his life. Going into the briefing, Strassburg realized he had to accomplish two things: remain calm, no matter what happened, and gain Hitler's trust if he had any chance to stop the madness he was involved in. He accomplished both.

Consequently, Strassburg was ensured a continuing prominent role in the planning of the two bombing missions against the United States, placing him in a unique position to sabotage those missions. The question was: How?

Strassburg loved his country but hated the Nazis. He feared if the Allies won the war, Germany would be divided into pieces and never reassembled. However, if Wall Street and the dam were destroyed that might not happen. But that also meant the Nazi's would still be in power. So the question was: How to get rid of the Nazis and preserve Germany? But his mind kept churning over Himmler's presentation—'The Final Solution," the annihilation of the Jews. Because of that, he realized the two "wonder weapons" he talked about in the meeting must never be used regardless of what happened to his beloved Germany.

Strassburg realized that he badly misread Hitler. Going into the presentation he thought Hitler would scuttle the US attacks and demand the bombs be used against the Soviets or the British. If Hitler had made that decision he'd have needed a new plan, triggering a series of long-winded, drawn-out discussions between various members of The Committee over which of the two were the biggest threat. Strassburg speculated that those talks might take one or two years and while The Committee jabbered, he'd find a way to destroy the weapons or get the Allies to obliterate them.

Now, with the two targets in America approved, Strassburg didn't have even six months to destroy the bombs. He had to move quickly. He had to find ways of keeping both missions from happening.

This triggered troubling moral questions. By working to destroy Germany's new superweapons, Strassburg knew he was committing treason. He'd be crossing the line, violating the oath he took as a German officer—that was until he reminded himself of what Himmler told The Committee and the letter given to him by his father. The letter that woman in Munich sent his mother.

If all these complicated and deadly thoughts swirling around his mind weren't enough, now he had to add another: Prien. Now that there was a woman in his life and the possibility of a relationship, perhaps even marriage, Strassburg was beside himself. Before last night he hadn't given much thought to the fact that his opposition to the Nazi bomb project might cost him his life. Now life was a much more precious commodity. Tension was building in his mind over his commitment to sabotaging the bomb versus the prospect of a long life with Prien.

Maybe the best thing would be if he canceled their upcoming weekend plans. Break off all further contact. If they continued seeing each other, it might endanger her. Should he—or shouldn't he—tell her why seeing each other wasn't a good idea? Strassburg wasn't sure what to do. In the past, his father had always been there for counsel, when he needed advice. Now his parents were in Switzerland, and he was alone. *Problems and more problems!* he thought as he stared out the plane's window.

Arnold Strassburg, Karl's father, was a prominent Berlin international corporate lawyer before he retired. He never thought much of Ohnesorge, his wife's cousin, or Ohnesorge's Nazi friends.

"Crooks, scoundrels, thugs," he often muttered while he and his son listened to Hitler's radio broadcasts or read newspapers together.

After the tragic death of his two daughters, Arnold grudgingly asked Ohnesorge to use his Nazi connections to arrange for him and his wife, who was Swiss by birth, to leave Germany and move to St. Gallen, Switzerland. Her doctors had proposed the move, thinking she might recover quicker from the loss of their daughters if she was among family and friends in Switzerland. The day after the March 1938 German *Anschluss*, the annexation of Austria, Arnold and his wife moved to St. Gallen.

The Strassburg's originally had three children: Karin, Karl, and Elsa. Karl was two years younger than Karin, and Elsa was twenty-three years younger than Karl. He remembered his baby sister trying to act grown-up at her last birthday party by putting on some of Karin's makeup. Their mother smiled at the mess, sending Elsa to the bathroom to scrub off the makeup. All three children had their mother's thick dark hair, fine features, and beautiful skin.

Arnold often joked that Karl pursued the sciences because one lawyer in the family was enough. The last time father and son spent a good deal of time together was in the spring of 1936, when Karl accompanied his father on a business trip to the United States.

Luftschiffbau Zeppelin, or DZR, the builder of rigid airships, was one of Arnold's clients. In the spring of 1936, DZR's manager, Dr. Hugo Eckener, asked Arnold to travel to the States to persuade the powers-that-be in Washington to lift America's ban on helium sales to Germany. At the time, the United States was the only country in the world with supplies of helium, a nonflammable gas, unlike hydrogen, which was used in Zeppelins to keep them aloft.

Arnold, lacking US government connections, hired Manning Dorff, an attorney with the Washington law firm of Schmidt, Guthrie & Dorff, to assist him in getting the helium ban lifted. Dorff's firm was well connected to many members of the US Congress and Cabinet secretaries in President Roosevelt's administration.

While Dorff's connections failed to get DZR their helium, Arnold and his son got to vacation in the States before returning to Germany. Among the places they visited was Boulder Dam on the Colorado River in Arizona.

Karl hadn't seen his father since August 1939, when Arnold returned to Germany on business, a few days before Hitler's troops invaded Poland, launching World War II.

The military transport Strassburg was aboard landed at one of the recently constructed airdromes outside Berlin. A few yards from the transport, a *Kübelwagen*, a Jeep-type vehicle, waited to take him to the office of Albert Speer, Minister of Armament. The day had just begun. The craters in the streets from the previous night's bombing had yet to be filled. Getting there would not be easy. His one-armed driver continually had to swerve the *Kübelwagen* in order to avoid the unfilled creaters. Every street, road, and boulevard they traveled down took on the appearance of a lunar landscape. Smoke still rose from ruins, another sign of the nocturnal attack. Noise from fire-engine sirens invaded the normal sounds associated with the start of a new day.

"Bad night?" Strassburg commented to his one-armed driver.

"Nah, more like a walk down the Wilhelmstrasse at night before the war."

"Where did you serve?" Strassburg asked, thinking the driver's reply was rather cavalier.

"Russian steppes in winter."

Strassburg, as always, was amazed at the enormity of the building that housed Speer's empire, the Ministry of Armament. All the buildings the Nazis constructed were huge but somehow the Ministry of Armament semed bigger. The only thing missing over the entrance was the ubiquitous gigantic granite eagle, the Nazi symbol of everlasting power, the thousand-year Reich. Thinking about the missing eagle caused Strassburg to laugh as he walked up the steps toward the entrance. *Maybe the eagle's absence is another war shortage. Could be the Nazis are running out of eagles.*

Having worked with Speer on the presentation given to Hitler, Strassburg found him extremely intelligent, a problem solver, and a gracious host—traits not shared by Bormann, Himmler, Göring, or Goebbels. Speer also lacked the others' arrogance, most likely due to his upper-class background. Unlike the others on The Committee, Speer was a latecomer to the Nazi inner circle. He gained his position after the Nazis' chief architect, Paul Troost, died in 1934.

Speer was known as the "Architect of the Reich" due to the many buildings he designed and built for the Nazis during the 1930s, all in close collaboration with Hitler. As the Reich's Minister of Armament, Speer was in charge of all war production and distribution of resources. This made him unquestionably one of the most powerful men in Nazi Germany.

Speer was highly organized. His giant desk, the centerpiece of the Ministry of Armament portion of his office, displayed that trait. Reports and documents, prioritized by date, were piled high in neat stacks on his desk, ensuring that his secretary or some assistant could easily find any paperwork needing the Minister's attention or approval. That was Albert Speer: bureaucrat—manager—administrator.

But Speer remained an architect in his heart. On the architect side of his office, the centerpiece was a well-worn but much-loved drafting table. Blueprints unrolled on top were held in place by four pieces of beautifully carved B.C. Roman marble, given to him by Mussolini, the Italian fascist leader, Hitler's junior partner in the Axis alliance.

Several baskets surrounded the table, containing rolls of blueprints, sketches, and architectural renderings in various stages of completion. It was obvious to anyone from a casual glance that no one could find anything in that mess except Speer. This was Speer's personal territory, his art, and his hobby. This was the "escape" that allowed him to review and complete all the work contained in those neat stacks of paper on his gigantic desk—work necessary to keep the Reich humming along as best it could.

"Good morning, Major," Speer said in a welcoming tone.

Strassburg smiled and nodded a warm hello as he sipped a cup of the Minister's special-blend coffee, something he enjoyed immensely.

"So sorry I wasn't here to greet you when you arrived." Speer was warm and gracious; his smile was broad, his handshake exuberant. "And congratulations," he added, "on what was probably the most brilliant presentation Hitler ever received. After the meeting, we all stood around congratulating ourselves about how astute we were for choosing you to make the presentation.

"If Houtermans, who created the bomb, had made it, it would have been a disaster. His endearing and condescending manner might have gotten him a one-way ticket to one of Himmler's "vacation" camps. Well done, Karl, well done."

"Thank you, Minister, for all your support. It wouldn't have gone as it did without you bringing Hitler over to the globe and showing him the geography we're dealing with."

While Strassburg talked, he noticed the workaholic lines deeply etched in Speer's face, the thinning hair, and the drooping shoulders. Speer was in his late thirties. He looked much older. However, as usual, Speer was impeccably dressed in what others called the "Minister's uniform"—a dark-colored, double-breasted, civilian-cut suit, perfectly tailored to fit Speer's tall, lean frame, with only the slightest bit of Nazi symbolism—the small round swastika pin on his lapel, given to him by Hitler for something Speer did that pleased the Führer immensely.

Speer glanced at the window. "Unfortunately Karl, your boss—the always friendly and amenable SS General Kammler—should be here any minute. While we're waiting for his lordship, I'd like to go over a few things with you without the benefit of his caustic comments."

6.

SS GruppenFührer Dr-Ing Hans Kammler was born in Stettin, Germany, around the turn of the century. Schooled as a civil engineer, Kammler was one of Germany's best. The "Dr-Ing" before his name, a mark of academic success, signified he'd earned a doctorate in engineering.

Kammler was happily married. His wife was beautiful. The couple had five children. The family lived in Lichterfelde-Ost, a suburb of Berlin, where the SS had one of its main administration centers, Baron von Ardenne had his laboratories, and where Houtermans built the bombs.

Early in his career, Kammler joined the SS's *Wirtschafts und Verwaltungshauptamt*, or WVHA, the Office of Economic and Administrative Development. Other SS units were *Sicherheitsdienst*, the SD or Security Service; *Kriminalpolizei*, the Kripo or criminal police; *Reichssicherheitshaupptamt*, the RHSA, or the Reich Main Security Office; and the *Schutzpolizei*, or Schupo, a branch of the state-level police of the various German states.

Kammler was ambitious. He knew advancement would be slow if he joined a private engineering firm after graduation from the university. By joining the WVHA, he knew his career would progress much faster.

His early assignments included assisting the Luftwaffe in constructing airfields and research facilities. Some months after the war started, Kammler met Baron von Ardenne at a social event, sponsored by the Baron at his Lichterfelde-Ost laboratories. Kammler was impressed.

Realizing Werner Heisenberg—head of the Uranverein, Germany's officially recognized nuclear energy program—and the others in the program hadn't a clue as to how to build a uranium bomb, Kammler suggested to the Baron they collaborate on building a uranium bomb. The Baron agreed.

Kammler told his boss, Reichsführer SS Heinrich Himmler, about the agreement, and Himmler convinced The Committee it was in Germany's best interest to have two nuclear programs—a public one headed by Heisenberg and a secret one run by Kammler.

Besides the bomb program Kammler was also charged with constructing the Reich's two new underground cities, one in the Jonastal region of Thuringia and the one at Nordhausen. The one in the Jonastal region would house what was now the government in Berlin in the event the German capital became uninhabitable due of the ravages of war; a "Vengeance" weapon plant, where V-1, unguided cruise missiles, and V-2, ballistic rockets, would be assembled; a Junkers's airplane-engine assembly plant; a U-boat and aircraft component plant; and housing for all the bureaucrats, engineers, workers and their families. The tunnels connecting all the parts would stretch more than twenty miles. The second underground city, similar in scale, was Nordhausen where V-1, V-2, U-boat, and aircraft components would be manufactured.

En route to the meeting with Speer and Strassburg, Kammler's driver was continually zigzaging, trying to avoid the many craters in the road caused by the previous night's bombing raids. The car continually swerved making it difficult—nearly impossible—for Kammler to sift through his paperwork. Documents kept tumbling from his highly organized file folders. Frustrated, the SS General finally jammed everything back into his briefcase, sat back, sunk into the salon's posh seating, and tried to relax. He had to admit he liked the sensation of sitting on velvet, one of the many "perks" bestowed on an SS General.

While not working, Kammler found the car's rocking motion relaxing. It allowed his mind to drift back to one of his many coups, specifically a meeting with the cantankerous physicist Dr-Ing Fritz Houtermans in the summer of 1941, when he told Houtermans he wanted him to build a uranium bomb.

Houtermans was a genius. He was also a loner, an introvert, and one big pain in the ass. He found it near impossible to work under anyone's supervision. He was tactless and impatient with those he deemed less gifted than himself. He was overbearing and condescending. He found it impossible to maintain collaborative relationships with colleagues—unless, of course, they did everything his way. These traits caused him to be an outcast among his peers, especially with Heisenberg, the self-appointed head of Germany's "official" nuclear-bomb development group, the *Uranverein*.

Prior to the formation of the *Uranverein* the major players at various universities and laboratories throughout the Reich working on the uranium bomb were independent. When the *Uranverein* was formed that changed. All those previously independent projects were consolidated under the leadership of one man, Heisenberg, who in 1932 won the Nobel Prize in Physics for the creation of quantum mechanics. The consolidation was done to gain efficiencies. What ended up happening was nothing but a number of endless theoretical arguments and academic talkathons taking place—none of which got the Reich closer to having a bomb. The biggest stumbling block was a lack of agreement about how best to enrich uranium ore found in nature, U-238, into weapons-grade uranium, U-235.

Realizing what was going on at the *Uranverein*, Kammler knew something had to be done, and done fast, if the Reich wanted to have an uranium bomb before the Allies developed their own. That meant someone besides Heisenberg and his *Uranverein* would have to do it.

Kammler found that someone in Houtermans. When Kammler told everyone on The Committee the Reich had three uranium bombs, they all thought he was a genius. When he told them who built the bombs—Houtermans, someone Heisenberg and his group considered a nobody—they all laughed.

Due to Houtermans's "easy-going" personality, Kammler decided the best way to deal with him was using "the carrot" and "the stick." Kammler's "carrot" was giving Houtermans everything he needed to build a bomb.

But before the "carrot," Kammler thought a small amount of "stick" was in order. The "stick" was having Houtermans wait for almost an hour before Kammler consented to see him. And when he did see him Kammler ignored him; said nothing, never looked up, just kept doing paperwork. Then with a sweep of his hand, he motioned Houtermans to sit down. By this time Houtermans was beet red. Now it was time for the "carrot."

The "carrot" was allowing Houtermans to ask one and only one question. Houtermans being Houtermans asked Kammler a number of questions. Did Kammler know anything about building a bomb? Did he have any idea of the amount of ore needed to build a bomb? Where was Kammler getting the ore because Heisenberg controlled the ore?

Before Houtermans could ask more questions Kammler held up his hand, signaling Houtermans to stop. Then he told the physicist what he asked was none of his business. So much for the "carrot."

Then Kammler asked Houtermans a question. What did he intend to use as a moderator to enrich the ore into weapons-grade material.

Satisfied with the answer, Kammler smiled—back to the "carrot." This time the "carrot" was telling Houtermans he had the job. Houtermans's color returned to normal. He even managed a weak smile.

Kammler balked at answering Houtermans's query about the source of the critically needed uranium ore for a very simple reason: The fewer who knew, the better.

From the beginning of the war, the Allies knew the exact amount of uranium ore held in the Reich's reserves. Every month reports were received from carefully placed spies about how much, if any, ore had been withdrawn. Small amounts were of no concern. Large withdrawals meant Heisenberg and his *Uranverein* had succeeded in finding a way to enrich U-238 to weapons-grade U-235. The next step was building a bomb. The Allies couldn't allow that to happen. No matter the cost, the Allies would bomb every building, every factory, and every outhouse if they thought it was part of a Nazi nuclear-bomb project. By the time they'd finish pummeling the Reich with bombs, it would look like a moonscape.

For that reason the Reich's "known" uranium reserves had to remain untouched and known to the Allies. What the Allies must never know was the Reich had another uranium source, which Houtermans, an unknown, was tapping to build the bombs—weapons constructed at von Ardenne's laboratories at Lichterfelde-Ost.

Back to the "stick." Kammler loved delivering "sticks." After telling Houtermans he had the job, Kammler told the scientist he needed three bombs—not just one—and all of them had to be the same size, weight, and yield, and he needed them the following year.

Kammler recalled with glee how Houtermans's complexion turned a very pale white when he heard the price of failure. If Houtermans botched the bomb-building project, Kammler assured him he would spend the rest of his life cleaning ovens at one of Himmler's "resorts," better known as concentration camps.

Kammler began to laugh as the memory of Houtermans chocking down bile became more vivid in his mind.

Oh, what a great day that was.

Now Kammler was enjoying the ride.

31

7.

Frédéric Joliot-Curie and his wife, Irene, received the Nobel Prize in Chemistry in 1935. The couple continued to research radioactive elements until France fell in the summer of 1940.

When Hitler's armies occupied northern France, including Paris and all the cities along the English Channel, the French moved their capital from Paris to Vichy. Vichy, all the area south of Paris down to the Mediterranean, and France's colonies in North Africa, were known as the "unoccupied zone." While the Nazis didn't occupy those areas they greatly influenced their policies and the people living there.

When it became obvious the French Third Republic would be crushed by the Nazi blitzkrieg, or lighting war, two of the Curies' research assistants, Fritz von Halban and Lew Kowarski, along with the French underground, smuggled tons of Curie uranium ore out of Paris. The Curies had amassed the ore for research. The ore was taken by truck to the port of Marseilles on France's Mediterranean coast. The Nazis's never questioned what was in the trucks because the ore appeared to be nothing more than construction debris. At Marseilles, the ore was loaded on ships and taken to Morocco, in North Africa. The British, fearing the Nazis might steal the ore, moved it from Morocco to a secret location down the coast toward Egypt.

Before the fall of France, the Abwehr, Nazi military intelligence, established a shell company, Cellastic, in a building sharing a common wall with the Curies' research facility on Paris's famed Champs-Élysées. The Nazi's knew about the ore by way of listening devices they installed in the common wall. Eventually the information about the ore reached the SS and made its way to Kammler. But by then the ore was in North Africa.

After following a number of dead-end leads concerning the ore's location, one of Kammler's sources discovered it's whereabouts, the small British air base at Sidi Rezegh near Tobruk in Libya.

In February 1941, German Field Marshal Erwin Rommel and his Afrika Korps landed on the sands of North Africa. Prior to Rommel's arrival the British and their Commonwealth armies were trouncing the Italians, the Reich's Axis ally. The Reich couldn't let that continue. If the British drove the Italians out of North Africa, they'ed be poised to cross the Mediterranean and invade the southern part of France, the "unoccupied zone." If that happened the Reich would have to fight a two-front war in Europe.

By July of 1941, Rommel had the British in disarray, tightening the noose around Tobruk. The territory between El Agheila, the coastal city at the bottom of the Gulf of Sidra in Libya, and Salum had changed hands so many times, neither side knew what was buried under the sand. So many senior British commanders had been replaced, captured, or killed that none of the present commanders knew anything about the importance of the pile of rocks at the end of the runway at Sidi Rezegh.

Rolf Muller, a young German attending school in England, returned to Germany in 1938, when he realized war was on the horizon. Muller volunteered for service, received a commission, and began *Fallschirmjager* training. After which Muller was assigned to the newly formed 7 Flieger-Division, achieving the rank of *Hauptmann* (captain) by 1940. His unit, the III/FJR, was tasked with taking the Waalhaven airfield on the island of IJsselmonde near Rotterdam in Holland.

Muller and his men immediately came under heavy machine-gun fire from the Dutch defenders when they landed at the airfield. If Generalleutant Hans von Sponeck's division couldn't land at Waalhaven in their Ju 52 "Iron Annie" transports, the Nazis' timetable for occupying Holland would need to be revised—drastically.

After a short, one-sided fight, the *Fallschirmjägers* gained control of most of the airfield. Only one stubborn Dutch anti-aircraft battery remained operable. But that one battery kept shooting down von Sponeck's transports. After several attempts failed to silence the battery, Muller decided the only way to get the job done would be to take it out using hand grenades.

But the battery was four hundred yards away. That meant Muller had to run and weave his way toward the battery while his men provided covering fire. Muller made his run, took out the battery, and in the process was severely wounded. Muller was awarded the Knight's Cross for valor, for his heroics.

Because of his wounds, Muller's doctors recommended he be placed in a pool of officers no longer fit for combat. This unit provided staff replacements for soldiers killed in combat or others who were transferred.

When Kammler read about Muller's military exploits, science background, and his knowledge of English, he had him assigned to Lichterfelde-Ost.

"Young Muller," as Kammler referred to him, soon became one of his favorites. Muller was exceptionally bright, a hard worker, and personable. Muller often was invited to dinner with Kammler, his wife, and his children. Kammler's children loved being around Muller, and he enjoyed playing with the youngsters.

But Muller was a warrior. He missed being with his fellow *Fallschirmjägers*. Kammler suspected this would be the case and had just the assignment to make Muller one very happy *Fallschirmjäger*.

On the night of November 14, 1941, Muller was lying in a patch of wet sea grass near Beda Littoria on the Libyan coast. Beda Littoria was the site of Rommel's headquarters. Three nights later, a British raiding party landed at Beda Littoria, hoping to find Rommel and kill him.

Scanning the water to his front, using powerful *Kriegsmarine* (navy) binoculars, Muller was looking for a freighter. The ship was loaded with three platoons of Generalmajor Hermann-Bernhard Ramcke's *Fallschirmjägers*, along with British lorries, trucks the British abandoned on the beaches of Dunkirk, where in 1940 more than three hundred thousand Allied troops escaped the European continent, leaving behind great amounts of supplies and equipment.

What first appeared to be nothing more than a speck on the horizon slowly transformed into a ship's silhouette. Lying there in the serenity of the moonlight, hypnotized by the grass weaving slowly back-and-forth, Muller failed to realize the transformation. That was until he heard the splash of the anchor followed by the sounds of men's boots splashing in the surf. Three hundred yards from the water's edge, four rafts, heavily laden with supplies, were being pulled ashore by men he recognized: *Fallschirmjägers*.

The man in charge of the landing party, Oberleutnant Fritz O'Gorsky, broke ranks after securing the beachhead. O'Gorsky was looking for Muller and when he failed to find him he feared something was wrong.

"Where the hell are you Muller?" O'Gorsky muttered under his breath. Then, just as he was about to turn and go back to the beachhead to warn the others, a hand flashed across his face, grabbed the top of his helmet, jerking his head back, exposing his neck to the flat side of the blade of an open-gravity knife, the knife of a *Fallschirmjäger*.

"Damn it, Muller! What took you so long?" O'Gorsky ranted. "That Knight's Cross of yours, slowing you down?

"Good to see you to too, Fritz. Word's out the Russians think you've got a cute ass," Muller joked, referring to O'Gorsky's recent stint on the Eastern Front. The two men hugged, remembering when they served together in Holland.

"Let's get back to the others before they start spreading rumors we 'like' each other," Muller quipped, patting O'Gorsky on his back.

Once all the men and equipment were off the freighter Muller gathered the men and explained the mission—as much as he could.

"The deal is when we're dressed up as Tommies, we all speak English. We only speak German when we're wearing German uniforms and our English lorries have Iron Crosses on them."

"Jolly good, old boy!" O'Gorsky replied, mocking the British. "Pip, pip, and all that rot! Before anyone got on the freighter, I personally checked out everyone's English. They all speak it like a Brit. Everyone here was scheduled to be part of the vanguard for Sea Lion." O'Gorsky rolled his eyes. "What made us ever think we'd invade England? Hitler's no William the Conqueror."

"True, but before Hitler and Göring got a wild hair up their ass and switched from bombing British industry to bombing London, it might have happened, Fritz."

"Don't get me started, Rolf."

"Okay! Okay! I thought by now you'd put that one behind you. Sorry."

"So who are we going after, Auchinleck, the British commander?"

"I wish," Muller told him. "No such luck. We're going to snatch a couple of tons of rocks."

"We're what? You can't be serious? Who had the brain fart this time?"

"Sorry, I can't tell you more, so don't ask."

"Boy, hearing you say *that* really gives me confidence."

"Don't worry, Fritz. If this comes off as planned Germany will come out of this mess, smelling like a rose."

Hearing that, O'Gorsky got serious, bowed his head, shaking it side to side.

"You know that isn't going to happen. And this Russian thing is not going to end well. Germany doesn't have anywhere near the manpower or the resources needed beat the Ruskies. And when the Allies cross the Channel—and they will—it'll all be over."

"I hope you're wrong, Fritz," Muller said with a lilt of doubt in his voice.

"You see these guys, here," O'Gorsky began, "who you're going to have pick up rocks in the desert, they're the toughest fighters in the world. But when we got the news we were going to North Africa, we all should have jumped for joy. You know what we did? We balled like babies. You know why? Because we knew we'd never see those guys, who weren't coming with us, ever again. Russia is a fucking meat grinder. Hitler should have learned that lesson from Napoleon."

While the men loaded the vehicles, Muller told O'Gorsky where the rocks were located and where O'Gorsky should take them if Muller was killed. After that the two split up. O'Gorsky checked all the vehicles's Afrika Korps markings for correct size and placement and Muller made sure all the men were in Luftwaffe tropical uniforms and everyone had their British and German identity papers, tags, pay book, and field orders.

Deception was a key element of Muller's mission. The Afrika Korps had salvaged numerous British lorries, other vehicles, and equipment the Tommies had abandoned following several North African battlefield defeats. After rebuilding them, they applied Africa Korps's markings on their bumpers and sides and used them to fight the British. But Muller's British vehicles were a little "different." Hidden in his vehicles were British markings, British uniforms, British weapons, and other British military gear. These bogus British markings would be put to good use once Muller and his convoy crossed into territory controlled by the British. This flexibility—the ability to swap at will German and British markings, uniforms, and equipment—allowed the *Fallschirmjagers* to freely cross friendly and enemy lines unmolested.

Their British papers and vehicle markings showed they belonged to a small, very hush-hush Eighth Army quartermaster unit stationed in Alexandria, Egypt. Since the unit was top secret, no local British commander would challenge the authenticity of Muller's orders. Things were tough enough at the front. Why stir up a hornet's nest inquiring about a platoon-size unit in lorries whose orders were to pick up a pile of rocks at the Sidi Rezegh airfield?

Seeing the fake orders, O'Gorsky laughed. "When you told me back there in the grass we were here to collect rocks I thought you were bullshitting me. I'm sure when those guys we left back in Russia run out of ammunition, they'll appreciate getting those rocks."

The following night, the column headed south, driving deep into the Sahara, careful to avoid areas where the sand wasn't packed hard enough to support the vehicles.

Muller stopped the convoy at sunup. The men put camouflage netting with strips of sand-colored burlap woven into the netting over the lorries to shade themselves and aid their sleep. The idea was to travel at night and sleep during the day, minimizing the withering effect of the blazing North African sun.

After eavesdropping on German and British radio traffic during daylight hours on November 15, 1941, Muller determined his convoy was well beyond either combatant's southern flank. When night fell and the air cooled, Muller started up the convoy and turned east. He continued in that direction until the night of November 16, when he turned the convoy north. When they hit the coast road, he veered west toward Tobruk.

Around 3 a.m. on November 17, during a break, the night's serenity was abruptly broken. The next chapter in the battle of North Africa was about to be written.

"Sorry to disturb you, sir," a young radiotelephone operator (RTO) whispered in Muller's ear. "But I thought you should hear what's coming over the wireless at Rommel's headquarters at Beda Littoria."

"Go on."

"Around 2:35 a.m., a British Commando unit, size unknown, landed and attacked Beda Littoria. When I left to get you, there seemed to be bedlam on both sides."

Upon entering the radio tent, illuminated by the eerie red glow from a single overhead bulb, all they could hear coming out of the speaker was static and confusion. Minutes that seemed like hours passed. Finally the familiar roar of Rommel's Tiger I tanks's 88-mm guns came blaring over the speaker. No more guessing which side was winning. Seconds later the British ceased all radio transmissions.

"So, their prelude to battle didn't seem to go well for our British cousins," Muller sarcastically remarked to O'Gorsky, who entered the tent moments before the sound of the 88s came roaring over the speaker.

"Seems that way," O'Gorsky replied. "The British never would have staged such a raid if they weren't planning a major battle."

The chessboard was set for a clash of Titans. Additional crackling radio traffic during daylight confirmed O'Gorsky's conclusion. The main Commonwealth force was moving westward. As yet, none of Rommel's forward reconnaissance units had spotted the Commonwealth vanguard. Heavy rains and the Brits' brilliant use of camouflage hampered the German effort.

Since neither side knew the other's location, Muller figured the British would screen their front, spreading their armor brigades between Bir el Gubi and Sidi Omar. Rommel would deploy the bulk of the Afrika Korps between Gambut and Sidi Azeiz, screening his flanks and rear with his 88s. This meant the area around Tobruk would be ground zero for the upcoming battle. Muller's best chance to get to Sidi Rezegh before that happened was riding the coattails of the British

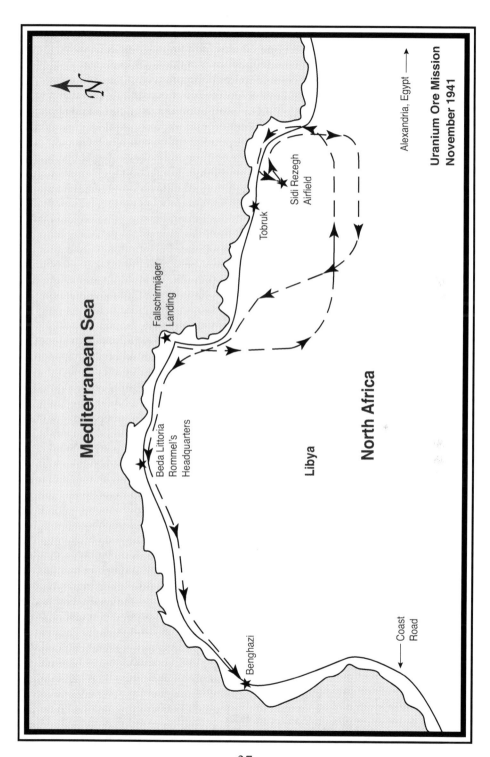

Mediterranean Sea

Fallschirmjäger
Landing

Beda Littoria
Rommel's
Headquarters

Tobruk

Sidi Rezegh
Airfield

North Africa

Libya

Benghazi

Coast
Road

Alexandria, Egypt ⟶

Uranium Ore Mission
November 1941

7th Armoured Brigade (AB) as it moved west along the coast road towards Tobruk.

When the 7th AB stopped for a break, Muller, as commander of the 8th Army quartermaster unit stationed in Alexandria (the unit that never existed), rode up to the front of the column and asked the 7th AB commander if his quartermaster unit could pass. After reading Muller's orders, the 7th AB commander was beside himself with laughter. When he regained his composure, the commander told Muller he could pass and good luck getting the rocks.

An Afrika Korps's forward reconnaissance unit encountered the British advancing toward Gabr Saleh late in the afternoon of November 17. Being told of the advance, Rommel called off his assault on Tobruk and turned the Afrika Korps and the Italians to deal with the British advance.

Muller and company reached Sidi Rezegh on November 19. He told the base adjutant he was there to "pick up a bunch of rocks." The adjutant thought it was a joke and, like the commander of the 7th AB, started laughing until he read Muller's orders. Scratching his head, he walked away in disgust, muttering, "Take whatever those fools in Alexandria told you to take, but do it fast. Jerry will be here any minute. There's food in the mess hall, if you want it."

Muller thanked the adjutant, adding, "If the battle goes like the others, we'll be lucky to get out of here with anything other than the clothes on our backs. So, if you don't mind, we'll eat once we're back on the coast road heading towards Alexandria."

The adjutant complimented Muller on making a wise decision.

They worked in shifts through the night, so by 4 a.m., November 20, all the ore was loaded onto the lorries. The men were dead tired and Muller knew tired men make mistakes. So, instead of leaving the base when the ore was loaded, Muller told O'Gorsky to have the men eat, post two guards, and have the rest get as much sleep as possible before moving out at 7:30 a.m.

Initially, the convoy traveled east, toward Alexandria, away from the upcoming battle. An unexpected rain came down in buckets. Spotting a medium-size wadi, Muller had O'Gorsky pull the column off the coast road and wait for the day's scorching heat to pass. Sleep was what the dog-tired men craved, but while sleep proved elusive, the men rested. With the coming of night, refreshing breezes began blowing inland off the Mediterranean, cooling and drying off the surface layer of sand. Off-roading appeared possible, so Muller had the column head south into the endless desert. But then the lorries started bogging down. Realizing the subsurface sand hadn't sufficiently dried out to support the vehicles's weight, he turned the column west. Gas gauges were tilting toward empty. If Muller didn't angle the column north and a smidgen west soon the ore would never reach Germany.

Radio traffic indicated the battle was raging in earnest. Weighing his options, Muller decided it best to wait where they were.

On the morning of November 21, the waiting was over. Muller headed the convoy northeast toward the coast road leading to Benghazi, careful to stay far away from the battle thundering on their right flank. At Benghazi the ore would be loaded on U-tankers (large U-boats used to resupply German *Wolfsrudels*, or "wolf packs,") and taken to Germany.

Vehicles were starting to break down. The desert was taking its toll. The chances of complete breakdowns increased with each passing mile. Fuel would soon be a problem. The men were reduced to walking zombies, making mistakes due to punishing heat and sleeplessness. Both Muller and O'Gorsky wondered if they'ed even reach Benghazi. The ore might remain in Africa.

The next day, November 22, the battle reached its zenith. While Muller and O'Gorsky listened to the static-laden radio traffic, the pace and sounds of war kept getting more confusing, a jumbled mass of death and destruction on both sides. It might take a day or two for the results—winners and losers—to unfold; Muller knew he couldn't wait that long.

Steam was coming out from under the hoods of two of their lorries. Soon the engines would seize up, the result of little or no water in their radiators. It was then that Muller and O'Gorsky held a strategy session and decided to take a riskier but shorter route to Benghazi. They couldn't continue as they had, skirting the edges of the battle area, a safer but longer route. The men and machinery could no longer take the punishment the desert was handing them.

Having made their decision, they knew they were greatly increasing the risk of coming face-to-face with some battle-weary unit, lingering in the area, still capable of fighting, and having more firepower than Muller and his men. Having faced the fog of war, Muller and O'Gorsky knew edgy men do foolish things—that smoldering embers from a battle could easily erupt into fire.

On the positive side, both men thought it likely that Rommel had won the battle. If that were true, then the Afrika Korps would have scrounging rights in the area they were planning to pass through. They'd be safe in their *Fallschirmjäger* uniforms and German vehicle markings, a platoon of Herman Bernhard Ramcke's *Fallschirmjägers*. Under their own colors they cautiously began weaving their way across the field of death.

Muller and O'Gorsky rode in the lead lorry. The first things they saw that clearly defined the conflict were long, thin plumes of grayish-black smoke on the horizon carried aloft by high winds.

O'Gorsky was the first to speak. "If it wasn't for the heat I'd swear this was the Russian steppes. In this light, sand looks like snow. It gives me the willies."

Eventually, their nostrils picked up the smell from hell. The smell that no one who's ever experienced mechanized warfare forgets. The sweet pungent smell of burned flesh mixed with diesel fuel and cordite.

"Damn it," Muller commented.

"Ya, the same smell," said O'Gorsky, nodding agreement.

"Same as at Waalhaven, when those poor bastards were burning in those Iron

Annie transports, shot down by the Dutch."

"I'll never forget it. One moment they were men."

"Seconds later they were black smoldering ash. I wonder why God lets us do these things to each other?" Muller asked. But at the same time not really asking.

"God has nothing to do with it, Rolf," O'Gorsky said in a cold, emotionless voice. "He gave us free will. We do this to one another because we like to."

As they passed through the battlefield, littered with burned-out vehicles and twisted wreckage, O'Gorsky's mood changed. He smilled, "You gotta hand it to Rommel. By my count, the Tommies lost this one—big."

Their gamble paid off. The only units they encountered as they drove through the battle area were German Panzers salvaging anything of value they could get their hands on for the next battle. A *hauptmann* (captain) in one of the Panzer recovery units recommended to Muller he put Afrika Korps's panels on the canvas tops of his lorries, so low-flying German Bf109 fighters wouldn't mistake Muller's lorries since they were British. Muller thanked him, deciding against the Hauptmann's advice. While the British didn't own the desert, they did own the sky above it.

Eventually, after a long, hard slog, Muller's lorries reached Benghazi intact. During the night of November 25, two U-tankers—U-116 and U-549—sailed from the city's docks, their holds filled with "rocks" bound for Germany.

Kammler was not a sentimental man, a man given to fits of nostalgia. But, riding in the backseat of his black Mercedes, en route to his meeting with Speer and Strassburg, he became somewhat wistful about Rolf Muller.

I'll never forget the day you reported back to me at Lichterfelde-Ost, he recalled, thinking of Muller. *It was one of those rare days in December when tunics replace greatcoats. Having just returned from the desert, you found the air— as mild as it was—a bit chilly.*

When I invited you to come home with me for dinner, you beamed your endearing smile, saying how nice it would be to have a home-cooked meal and see the children. And when I told you what a magnificent job you had done, you became modest, self-effacing. You said all the credit should go to O'Gorsky and his platoon of Ramcke's Fallschirmjägers.

Such a dear boy you were.

You played with the children after our wonderful dinner. We sipped cognac; we smoked cigars in the garden. It was like you were part of the family.

Too bad I had to have you killed. But at least it was painless.

Oh, Rolf, I do miss you dearly. But you knew too much.

8.

"Sorry to disturb you, sir, but we're here," his SS driver announced to Kammler, who was still reminiscing in his mind about Muller and the ore.

What an ugly building! Kammler thought, stepping out of the car and looking up at Speer's dominion. *And he's supposed to be this great architect!*

"He's here, Minister," Speer's executive assistant said, poking his head through the half-opened door. The pronoun "he" was used because the assistant knew how much Speer despised Kammler and was irked whenever he heard his name.

Strassburg joined Speer at the window. They watched as Kammler—his gaunt figure wrapped in a flamboyant black leather greatcoat, his hat with its death head insignia rakishly cocked to one side—stepped out of his black hearse-looking prewar Mercedes. Two SS double lightning rune flags on each fender fluttered menacingly in the breeze. Kammler waved to Speer and Strassburg, his crooked smile adding nothing to his persona.

"Damn it," Speer said to no one as he walked away from the window. "They're all just so damn arrogant."

With a swagger typical of the SS, Kammler strode authoritatively into the room. Strassburg saluted, prompting Kammler to say, "At ease, Major, at ease. As long as there's just the three of us here, let's dispense with formalities. We all know each other, and we'll be here many hours—probably days before we figure out a way to get those two bombs to their respective targets in the States. In the meantime, I don't want to keep bringing my arm up, returning your salute, every time I come back from the crapper, understood?"

Strassburg forced a thank-you smile. Kammler sat down.

"I suppose, Albert, you've already been here for hours in this monstrosity of a building," Kammler chided as he opened his briefcase and pulled out a number of files, papers, and documents, arranging everything in neat stacks.

Turning to Strassburg, he commented, "Albert, here, is like a rooster. He thinks the sun can't rise until he does." The three chuckled, two of them trying to make it sound natural. With Kammler's attempt at humor out of the way and everyone seated, Speer began the discussion about how to get the Reich's Manhattan Financial District bomb to its destination.

Speer opened his platinum cigarette case, offering one of his special blends to Kammler. Speer knew Kammler didn't smoke. Toying with his lighter, Speer lit up a cigarette and pointed to the obvious. "Hans, as you know, neither the Reich nor the Allies have bombers capable of crossing the Atlantic, even one way, without some sort of in-flight refueling. You're also aware that while there have been instances of successful in-flight refueling, no country has developed a system capable of doing it under wartime conditions."

"Not to mention," Kammler pointed out, "no one has a bomber that can carry a nine thousand-pound bomb. So tell me something I don't know."

Always have to butt in and have the last word, don't you? Speer thought.

"Anyway, Hans, we took a good look into Göring's toy box of prototypes—"

"And you found none," Kammler butted in, drumming the tips of his fingers on the table. "Can we get on with this?"

Speer turned to Kammler, smiling. "What about one of those new wonder weapons you and von Braun are always touting?"

"You're referring to a V-2 rocket, correct?" Kammler asked, not expecting a reply. "You both know the bomb's way too heavy to be carried inside a standard V-2 rocket. Besides, even with what's on the drawing board range still would be a problem.

"But if weight wasn't a problem, Hans?" Speer asked tauntingly. "What about using one of those new-generation V-2s and launching it from a merchant ship outside US air and sea defenses?"

"Forget it. Even the next-generation will need completely stable platforms for a successful launch. The biggest surface ship in the world on a glassy calm sea still rolls. A surface ship could never provide the kind of stability needed for a launch. Any platform we launch from has to be anchored solidly to the ground for stability."

Speer pressed on. "Just for a moment, forget about the stable platform thing. What we're asking you is can the next-generation V-2 carry a nine thousand-pound payload?"

"Probably—yes I suppose it could if we repositioned some of the rocket's parts so the damn thing wasn't top-heavy. Yes—that might work."

Kammler's mind was a calculator, capable of processing information and coming up with answers that took most people days to figure out. "But no more than one hundred and fifty miles. But there's still the problem of stability," Kammler told the two, not wanting to hear more of what *didn't* work, only what *did* work.

"How about this, General?" Strassburg piped up. "We put the bomb into one of those new-generation V-2 rockets. Put the rocket in a watertight container, tow the container to the waters just off their coast, and fire the rocket?"

Hearing this, Kammler perked up. "Brilliant, Major, brilliant! That's the fucking Steinhoff plan. It's nice to see you've both done your homework."

Speer smiled.

Dr. Ernst Steinhoff worked at Peenemünde, the Reich's "Vengeance" weapons development center in the Baltic. In 1941, Steinhoff and his brother Fritz, Kommandant of the U-511 came up with the concept of putting a V-2 with a warhead inside a watertight container and using a coastal U-boat to tow the container to a firing position off the British coast. Once the container or U-barge, as the brothers called the container, was in position, the firing crew inside the barge would detach the barge from the U-boat, have it float to the surface and re-ballast the barge from horizontal to vertical with the nose of the barge slightly above the waves, and stabilize it by firing anchors attached to cables into the seabed. Once that was done, they'd open the above-water bow doors on the barge and fire the rocket. Once the rocket was on its way to the target, the crew would cut the stabilizing cables, re-ballast the barge back to the horizontal, radio the U-boat to hook up the barge to the U-boat, and tow it back to France, where the cycle would begin again.

The Steinhoff brothers' plan was approved by Grossadmiral Karl Dönitz, head of the *Ubootwaffe*, Germany's U-boat command, but went no further. The reason was that Göring, head of the Luftwaffe, insisted he be in charge since the "Vengeance" weapon program was his turf. Hitler scuttled the program after becoming frustrated and angry over the bickering by Göring and Dönitz over who should control the program.

"The Americans do have reconnaissance aircraft, you know," Kammler sneered. "What makes you two think the Americans wouldn't see the barge from the air even though it's underwater?"

Looking at Speer, who gave an imperceptible shrug, Strassburg reached under the table and came up with a nautical chart of the waters off the coast of New Jersey.

Strassburg unrolled the chart, and Speer stood up and pointed to a red X.

"I believe if you'd care to look at where I'm pointing, Hans," Speer said coldly, "it might answer your concerns. It marks the spot where the US Coast Guard sank a small Canadian coastal freighter in 1926. The ship was caught running illegal liquor from Canada to the States during America's Prohibition era. From the air, if we were to anchor a barge with a rocket inside right next to the wreck it would appear to be part of the wreck.

"Okay," Kammler begrudgingly acknowledged, "that takes care of spotting the barge from the air, but what about the stability problem?"

"I'll let the Major answer that one."

But Strassburg didn't answer immediately.

Something's wrong, Strassburg thought, looking at the chart, *but what? I've looked at this chart maybe fifty times, and now I think something's wrong?*

Strassburg tried to wrap his mind around what was amiss. What was bothering him?

"I'm waiting, Major" Kammler snapped. "How do you intend to solve the stability problem?"

Jarred back to reality by Kammler's curt question Strassburg answer. "Sorry, General, I was going over some numbers in my mind, making sure my answer to your question would be correct."

"Like Hitler told me," Kammler sneered, "you're a bright boy, Major." Please, continue to amaze me."

Strassburg's concept was a variation of Steinhoff's plan. It involved creating a U-barge made up of two hulls and placing a new-generation V-2 rocket, forty-six feet in length, along with everything needed to launch the rocket, in the inner hull, the one that was watertight. The two hulls mated together, Strassburg estimated, would be one hundred and twenty feet in length. A series of giant "O" rings would separate the inner hull from the outer hull, allowing the inner hull to move up and down while the outer hull was anchored to the sea floor. Pumping seawater in or out of the area between the bottoms of two hulls would either raise or lower the inner hull with the V-2 rocket inside.

Strassburg needed the bow of the barge's inner hull in its most downward position to be eighty-three feet below the waves in order to keep it from being spotted by US reconnaissance aircraft. That meant finding a shipwreck fifty to one hundred and fifty miles out from the coast where the water was two hundred and twenty-three feet deep. The approximate depth of the seabed and distance from Wall Street where the 1926 wrecked Canadian coastal freighter laid burried in the Atlantic.

The barge would be stabilized and leveled by extending eight massive hydraulic legs with feet and cables, evenly placed along the exterior wall of the outer hull, and anchoring them to the seabed. Crew access to the barge would be through an air lock.

Before dawn, on a day when the surface of the water was a smooth as glass, the inner hull's clamshell bow doors would be pushed up above the water's surface. The crew would open the doors and fire the rocket, and with luck America's Financial District in lower Manhattan would cease to exist. The crew would then close the doors, lower the inner hull, flood the interior, and leave by rubber boat for the Jersey Shore.

"Bravo, Major, bravo!" Kammler told Strassburg, standing up and clapping after hearing how everything worked. "What you and Speer have come up with is absolutely brilliant. When I tell Hitler what *we* came up with, he'll do his little jig until he drops. Congratulations!"

Speer abruptly cut off Kammler's "celebration," dryly telling him there was more to the plan, which included using a revolutionary new U-boat to push or pull the barge into position adjacent to the wreck.

When Kammler heard the word "revolutionary," a smile crossed his pockmarked face. He instantly asked if this "revolutionary" U-boat had anything to do with a U-boat designed by Professor Hellmuth Walter, reminding Speer and Strassburg that the SS's eyes and ears were ubiquitous.

"As I'm sure you both know," Kammler pontificated, "Walter is one of our most talented and innovative underwater boat designers. He's probably the best in the world. But what you may not know is he's also one big pain in the ass—just like Houtermans."

Before going out on his own, Walter was employed by Germania, a company that supplied Dönitz with most of his U-boats. Walter's V-80 U-boat was his first radical design. He used a wind tunnel, usually associated with aircraft design, to test the V-80s hull. Walter was convinced the hull should be shaped like a fish to reduce drag. He also equipped the V-80 with a single propeller rather than the standard

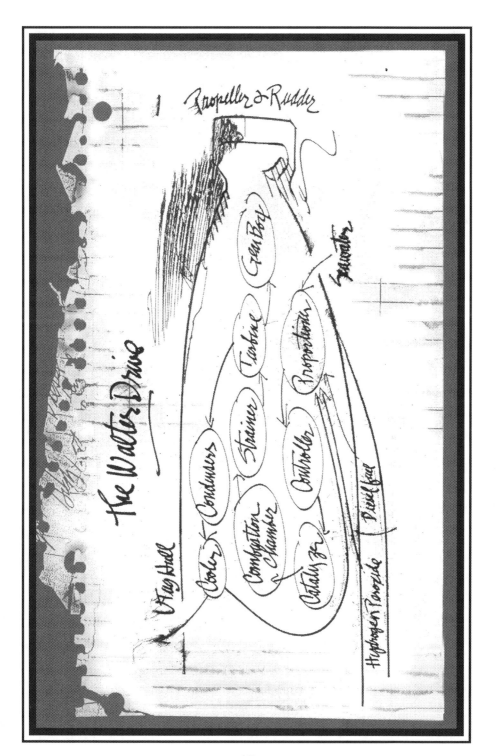

The Walters Drive

Propeller & Rudder

Gear Box

Turbine

Generator

Proportion

Strainer

Controller

Condensers

Cooler

Combustion Chamber

Catalyzer

V Flag Hull

Hydrogen Peroxide   Diesel Fuel

two on other boats. His design also scrapped the forward hydroplanes. Realizing Germania would never send such a radical design to Dönitz, he set up his own company, Walterwerk. The V-80 had one significant problem: it lacked stability caused by using only one control stick to steer both lateral and vertical movement. While the V-80 was extremely maneuverable underwater, it was an absolute nightmare to handle at periscope depth.

The problem of stability was supposedly solved with Walter's V-300 design. But the V-300 never got beyond laying the keel due to squabbling between Walter and Germania, his former employer, which Dönitz selected to manufacture the V-300.

"The quarrel was started by Germania. Attempting to squeeze Walter out of the U-boat business. They were out to protect their near monopoly designing and building U-boats," Speer reminded Kammler.

"You've done your homework, Speer," Kammler acknowledged. "And the V-300 was sacrificed. But the incident convinced Dönitz and the *Ubootwaffe* high command that Germany was best served if there was competition to build future U-boat prototypes. Whoever builds the best prototype receives the contract to build all U-boats in the series. As a result, Blohm & Voss and Germania were put under contract to build future prototypes."

"Before you arrived, Hans, I was telling the Major about my impressions of Walter's latest prototype U-boat. The ones I saw in their dry docks being built by Blohm & Voss and Germania. The B&V boat, the Wa-201, has a much better internal layout. But what really sets the B&V U-boat apart is its workmanship."

"Too bad neither boat will ever reach production," Kammler announced, the ever-present smirk at the corner of his mouth widening.

"What!"

"Sorry, Speer," Kammler chided, "I thought you of all people, being the Minister of Armament, would have known that someone at Germania talked to Dönitz and convinced him that additional wind-tunnel testing was needed on the model before more work on either prototype should proceed. Those tests confirmed the Wa-201 still has maneuverability problems near the water's surface at low speeds, just like Walter's V-80."

"So what happens now?"

"It's back to the drawing board for the 'good' professor," Kammler told him. "And you know how things work, Speer. Those two prototypes, sitting in their dry docks, will never to be completed. There's no way Walter would ever be able to correct those near-surface maneuverability problems enough to satisfy Germania even though each boat would have maneuvered underwater like a dream. Such a pity really—with that new propulsion system they'd be fast, thirty knots underwater, and could have stayed submerged for days, not just for hours like our current U-boats."

"The Major and I both know about Walter's new propulsion system. So what's your point, Hans?"

"Simply that you killed Walter's new propulsion system because of the amount of hydrogen peroxide it uses. You're an architect, Speer, not an engineer. I'm convinced that with further research it's possible to reduce the system's gulping

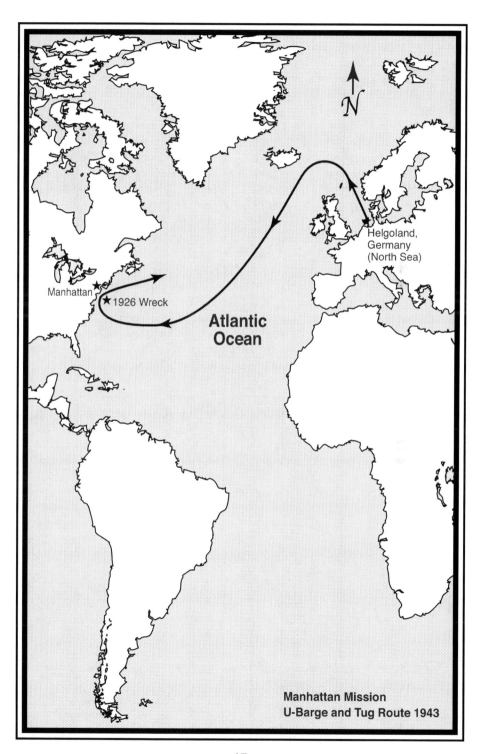

Manhattan

★ 1926 Wreck

Helgoland,
Germany
(North Sea)

**Atlantic
Ocean**

**Manhattan Mission
U-Barge and Tug Route 1943**

47

of hydrogen peroxide—a propulsion system that would have given us control of the seas."

"Hold on, General!" Speer shouted. "It's impossible at this stage in the war for Germany to generate enough hydrogen peroxide for a fleet of Walter U-boats, as well as existing programs in aircraft manufacturing, maintenance, V-2 rockets, and torpedo fuel."

"I know, I know!" Kammler replied in his usual sarcastic tone of voice. "But we're not talking about fueling a fleet of Wa-201 boats, are we? We're talking about building one—and it's waiting for you at B&V's shipyard on the island of Kuhwerder, near Hamburg. So, as the Reich's Minister of Armament, write a note to Dönitz, tell him that since both hulls will never be finished—and you need all the fucking steel you can get—the Ministry of Armament is taking possession of both prototypes and cutting them up for scrap. In fact, here's my pen. Write it now!"

Kammler often bullied people and Strassburg had seen him do it repeatedly. But Speer was a member of The Committee, equal in rank to Heinrich Himmler, Kammler's boss. Apparently that didn't make any difference. Speer might be the Reich's Minister of Armament, but Kammler clearly was the one in charge.

"When we break for lunch," Kammler said to Speer, "I'll call the good professor and impress upon him how important it is that he cooperates with you and does what you tell him to do. I'll also tell Walter that he needs to keep his mouth clamped shut. No talking to Dönitz or his staff about this. He'll also need to know about the barge. After all, when the U-boat and barge are submerged, they need to work as a unit."

Strassburg had been sketching while Kammler lectured Speer. Once Kammler completed his "request" of Speer, he turned his attention to Strassburg. Seeing the sketch prompted Kammler to sarcastically comment, "I hope we're not boring you with our discussion, Major."

"Not at all, General," Strassburg replied, ripping the sketch from his notebook. "It shows the various parts of the Walter Drive and how everything flows. I thought this might be of some help later on."

Kammler looked at the sketch and handed it to Speer. "Very nice, Major, very nice. But, if I were you, I wouldn't look for a job as a sketch artist until after the mission."

"Thank you, General," Strassburg replied, dismissing Kammler's snide remark. "But what about the ballast problem?"

"What ballast problem?" Kammler asked, showing concern that Strassburg knew something that he didn't.

"There could be a ballast problem for the U-tug on her return trip to Germany."

"Explain."

"If the tug ends up pushing the barge instead of pulling it, the barge's stern will be attached to the U-tug's bow."

"So?"

"So, General, on the return trip the barge won't be attached to the tug. Without the barge, the tug's crew will find it hard to maintain trim. Her bow will constantly want to rise up, making her a bear to control."

"That's the tug captain's problem, Major. Let him deal with it," Kammler flippantly snapped. "We have bigger problems to solve."

Speer and Strassburg looked at one another. Neither could believe Kammler's solution to a serious problem was so ridiculously cavalier. Both thought there was something Kammler wasn't telling them.

"Problems like?" Speer asked.

"Like determining, through testing, if there's a problem detaching the barge from the tug two hundred and twenty-five feet below the surface of the Atlantic or anchoring the barge to the seabed or the inner cylinder, failing to go up with eighty-three feet of water pushing down on its bow. Or, god forbid, the clamshell doors in the nose of the inner cylinder not opening. These are things we need to be concerned about—not if the tug gets back to Germany."

Strassberg caught the "if."

It should been "how" the tug gets back to Germany, General, not "if" the tug gets back.

Speer caught the "if" too. But like Strassburg said nothing.

"Professor Walter will design and oversee the conversion of Blohm & Voss's Wa-201 U-boat into our tug. He'll also construct the inner and outer cylinders of the U-barge at their shipyard on the island of Kuhwerder near Hamburg. He'll leave the outfitting of the barge's inner cylinder, the part housing the rocket, the crew, etc., to be done at Peenemünde."

"When will Houtermans install the bomb in the rocket, Hans?"

"At Peenemünde, where the decision also will be made about whether the barge will be pushed or pulled. Of course, Walter's opinion will be sought on these and other issues."

Now that the plan of "how everything works" was more or less worked out it was obvious to Strassburg and Speer the mission had become Kammler's, they where there only as "things" Kammler could point to as "causes" if problems arose.

"Where will the barge and tug go from Peenemünde, General?"

"Through the Kaiser Wilhelm Canal at Kiel in the Baltic to our U-boat pens at Helgoland in the North Sea. Any last-minute, fine-tuning can be done under the safety of Helgoland's million-ton concrete roof. Are we all clear on this?" Kammler asked, sternly looking at Speer and Strassburg to make sure they clearly understood who is in command.

"Good, then this meeting is over. Hitler and the others will be pleased. A very productive morning, gentlemen, we're off to a good start. I'm looking forward to this afternoon, when we discuss a plan to deliver our second bomb to our American friends at Boulder Dam in the middle of nowhere."

Maybe it's been a good morning for you, Hans, but not for me! Speer thought, realizing he was now working for Kammler. *And if I'm working for you, does this mean I'll soon be working for Himmler?*

Speer remained calm throughout the rest of the morning. He realized the importance of not displaying even an inkling of fear in the presence of a predator like Kammler.

Looking at his watch, Speer said, "As you pointed out, Hans, a very productive morning. I've arranged for lunch to be sent in. Why don't we gather up our notes, charts, everything concerning the two missions, and lock them in the safe while the staff sets up lunch. In the meantime, I'll show the two of you Hitler's 'broken dream.' It really is remarkable. The man's a visionary."

Visionary my ass, the man's a psychopath. Strassburg thought.

Speer opened the door.

"You have to be joking," Kammler said before breaking into laughter. "There's nothing here but a bunch of furniture covered with sheets."

Speer's smile indicated otherwise. Following Speer's lead, Strassburg grabbed a sheet, carefully removing it from part of a large architectural model, depicting what would have been the Reich's architectural centerpiece, the Nazi capital for all Nordic people, Germania, Hitler's "broken dream."

With a broad sweep of his hand, Speer told Kammler and Strassburg what they were looking at was a "labor of love," a place Hitler used to regularly visit, a place where Hitler sat for hours, planning and sketching his vision of the future. But, with the war going so badly, Speer confided, Hitler had abandoned the room. He found it too depressing. In fact, Speer was skeptical that Hitler even remembered his grand and glorious dreams for Germany and the world.

Not used to surprises, Kammler gasped. "Oh my god! If that had been finished, it would have been the world's largest dome."

In an instant, Kammler shifted mental gears. He swiftly altered himself from "Kammler the Schemer" to "Kammler the Engineer." He carefully studied the model with his trained engineer's eye and silently read a plaque at the model's base: *"Volkshalle, the People's Hall."*

"It makes the Brandenburg Gate look like a toy, doesn't it?" Speer asked. "The hall beneath the dome's apex would have been more than seven hundred and twenty feet in height, and the floor space under it would be able to accommodate one hundred and eighty thousand people."

Seeing the look of amazement on the faces of his colleagues, Speer asked Kammler and Strassburg to help him remove all the sheets, revealing the entire model of Hitler's vision, the New Berlin. The model hadn't been touched since it was completed in 1937. Speer then went on and told the two that Hitler thought Berlin looked dirty, provincial, and old-fashioned. He motioned his two colleagues to a framed sketch hanging on a wall.

"Hitler drew that in 1925," Speer said with pride. "Even then, before he became Führer, the vision was there."

Strassburg shook his head in disgust. *So that's why our Führer's not terribly concerned that Göring's Luftwaffe can't stop the bombing of our once beautiful capital. He wants it destroyed, so if we win, which we won't, Speer can build him his "vision" of a city surpassing the magnificence of ancient Rome on the ashes of the Berlin I love.*

Now everything makes sense. This is the real reason for those underground cities Kammler's building in the south, so we all can live underground while Berlin

50

is reduced to rubble.

Strassburg was livid, yet he knew the worse thing he could do was to show it.

The three sat down for lunch and the conversation around the table drifted back to Germania. Kammler was greatly impressed by the model of the *Volkshalle.* He asked Speer for a copy of its structural specifications, telling the Armament Minister he wanted to check the calculations himself.

"Still the engineer, Hans?"

"As much as you're still the architect!" Kammler snapped back. "So let's cut the crap. Are you going to give me those specifications or not? I might be able to use your *Volkshalle* in one of my projects. The way things are going, I doubt you'll be building your People's Hall anytime soon."

Satisfied he put Speer in his place, Kammler returned to the business at hand: bombing the dam. His timetable was explicit. He told Speer and Strassburg the dam must be blown up no more than three days after Wall Street was a pile of rubble.

"Why's that?" Speer asked, puzzled.

"Because once we prove to the Americans we can reach their East Coast, they'll immediately redeploy their military resources along that coast, hoping to stop other attacks on major cities like Philadelphia, Boston, and Washington, DC. So, with the Americans looking east, we'll attack them in the west."

Then Kammler reminded the two of Hitler's explicit directive. If the bomb directed to take out Wall Street failed to do the job, then the bomb destined to take out the dam would somehow be redirected to Wall Street.

We'll be lucky if we get the bomb to the dam, let alone redirect it to Wall Street, Speer and Strassburg thought.

After a most pleasing lunch, Speer started the discussion about the dam.

"I'm sure as an engineer," he began, "you'll appreciate what the Americans accomplished."

With the luncheon dishes removed, the table was clear, allowing Strassburg to place several rolls of dam plans and drawings on the table in front of Kammler. Speer knew how Kammler loved to be the center of attention during planning sessions. Speer seemed more relaxed than he was before lunch.

Strassburg explained that Boulder Dam was built to hold back the waters of the mighty Colorado River and other rivers that flow into it. Its principal purpose was to prevent flooding and drought. He explained that the dam had transformed arid Southwest lands into acreage for farming and ranching.

"Once Lake Mead, the lake behind the dam, fills up," Strassburg reminded Kammler, "it will generate enough electrical power for most of the major cities and industries in Southern California, Nevada, and Arizona."

Kammler, ignoring Strassburg's "lecture," having heard it before, thumbed through several US geological reports Strassburg had placed on the table along with the dam's plans and drawings.

"Hmmm, say's here the canyon walls, where they anchored the dam, are igneous andesite, some of the hardest and most durable rock on the planet. Just think, Albert, if things had worked out differently, you might have gotten enough American andesite while they were building the dam to build your thousand-year *Volkshalle*. Then again, if these bombs fail to get the Americans out of the war before the end of September, the Reich won't be around for more than two years. Right, Major?"

Strassburg ignored Kammler's remark.

"The Americans may be a bunch of mongrels," Kammler pontificated, "but they really are superb engineers. The dam's location and design are brilliant. Couldn't have designed it better myself."

"The dam's also beautiful," Strassburg told his boss, "especially viewing it from the front. When the sun's west of it, reflecting off all that white concrete at the end of the day, it's absolutely breathtaking."

Strassburg reminded the two that he saw the dam in 1936 when he accompanied his father on a business trip to the States. Once the business was concluded, Strassburg and his father traveled around the country. One of the sites they visited was Boulder Dam.

Strassburg described the dam's turbine room, calling it amazing. "But even more amazing, was when we rafted a quarter of a mile downstream and looked back at the dam. It took on the appearance of a glacier coming out between a narrow crack in the earth's crust. The temperature at the bottom of the canyon was cool even though the air on top was over a hundred degrees Fahrenheit. Seeing the dam towering over us made me think about how many millions of tons of water that wall of concrete was holding back. Our guide told us there was enough reinforced concrete in the dam to pave a two-lane highway from San Francisco to New York."

The three continued talking about the dam and the endless problems associated with destroying it for the rest of the afternoon.

"A very productive day, gentlemen," Kammler said. "I'm leaving. I'll see you here around eleven o'clock tomorrow morning."

Once Kammler left, Speer said to Strassburg, "Suppose it was something I said?" He smiled when he referred to the abruptness of Kammler's departure. "Let's hope it was and I remember to say the same thing tomorrow, only earlier."

Strassburg returned to his hotel. While picking up his key at the front desk, the manager gave him a message to call a friend, Oberleutnant Fritz O'Gorsky. The message said O'Gorsky was in Berlin, attending a conference, and Strassburg should call him to see if they could get together for some "serious" drinking. Strassburg knew O'Gorsky was part of the *Fallschirmjäger* contingent Kammler had dispatched to North Africa to recover the uranium ore Houtermans used to build the bombs. Strassburg wanted to hear more about O'Gorsky's North African exploits, as well as talk about things in general.

Strassburg telephoned O'Gorsky's hotel. He told the hotel's operator that he wanted to talk to O'Gorsky. The operator directed his call to the hotel's manager.

"You're a friend of Oberleutnant O'Gorsky, correct?" the manager asked.

"Yes, my name is Major Karl Strassburg. Why?"

"I'm terribly sorry, Major, I have bad news. Oberleutnant O'Gorsky was struck and killed by an automobile this morning in front of the hotel. The car didn't stop."

"Have his parents been notified?" Strassburg asked, trying to cope with the shock of the somber news.

"I don't know," the manager said. "When I reported what happened to the police, the SS showed up and took over."

"Thank you."

You'll be missed, Fritz. You were so much fun, especially that tale you always told of bedding those loved-starved nuns at the convent outside of Aube in the Champagne-Ardennes region in northeastern France. Each time you told the tale, there were always more nuns requesting your services!

After thinking about O'Gorsky, Strassburg decided to call Rolf Muller, another *Fallschirmjäger* Strassburg served with, and O'Gorsky's boss during the North African ore mission. He didn't have Muller's number so he called Muller's mother.

"Hello, Mrs. Muller, this is Karl Strassburg. Do you have Rolf's number I need to talk to your son."

"Oh, Karl!" she said. From the sound of her voice, Strassburg knew she'd been crying. "We haven't heard from Rolf since he returned to Berlin from some secret mission. The family was planning to see him after he got back. He never could tell us the name of his boss, someone in the SS, or we would have called him to ask about Rolf. It's not like Rolf to do something like this. We're all afraid something terrible has happened. But they would have told us, wouldn't they, Karl?"

"I'll let you know if I find out anything," Strassburg said.

"Oh, thank you, Karl. Thank you so much."

Oh my god! Karl thought. *Fritz killed in a hit-and-run and now Rolf has disappeared. A coincidence? Unlikely. Aside from Kammler and myself, no one knows Rolf, Fritz, and his platoon of Fallschirmjägers were the ones who pulled off the uranium-ore heist in North Africa. Kammler's fingerprints must be all over this.*

9.

The sun had barely edged up over the horizon when Strassburg met Speer at his office. The two wanted to review several ideas for destroying the dam between themselves without the benefit of Kammler's comments before he arrived at 11 a.m.

As they floated ideas back and forth, Speer noticed Strassburg seemed preoccupied.

"Is everything all right, Karl?" Speer asked, his voice laced with concern.

"I learned last night that an old friend from my university days—someone I also served with in the *Fallschirmjägers*—was killed yesterday in an accident."

"How terrible," Speer said, showing genuine concern.

Kammler arrived precisely at 11 a.m.

"Good morning, everybody," a somewhat bubbly Kammler effused.

"Sit down, Major. Please sit down. Remember, no formalities when it's just the three of us. I suppose the two of you already have figured out how we're going to get the bomb to the dam, right?" Kammler's voice was dripping with his trademark sarcasm.

"I think we might be onto something, Hans," Speer replied cautiously, "but we have some questions that need answers."

Kammler, posturing like an oracle, dismissed Speer's concerns with a wave of a hand.

Noticing, as Speer had done earlier, that Strassburg appeared distracted, he asked, "Something bothering you, Major? We need everything your brilliant mind can give us if this project is going to succeed."

Strassburg told Kammler what he had told Speer—that he just learned that a friend had died.

"How awful. Berlin traffic is still dangerous even with fewer cars on the road," Kammler said dismissively.

Funny, no one said anything about Fritz being killed in a traffic accident. Did someone tell you that? And, if that's the case, why didn't you tell me? You know Fritz and I were friends? Or were you behind Fritz's death—and if that's the case it wasn't an accident, it was—murder.

Kammler was oblivious to his mistake—a big mistake. He had misspoken. The SS General, unconcerned about what he had said, kept removing papers from his overstuffed briefcase, head bowed and gazing intently at the satchel's contents.

"Let me begin," Speer said, "by reminding all of us the area around the dam is sparsely populated. The dam itself is not well protected from aerial attacks. In fact, most of the precautions taken by the Americans are aimed at preventing sabotage."

Kammler already knew this and was irritated at Speer for wasting his time. "I know this, Speer," he barked. "We talked about this yesterday. There's no need to go over something we already know. We looked at a map of the area yesterday, deciding the dam was way too far inland to deliver a bomb using another rocket."

Speer painfully agreed, adding, "Besides, if we used a rocket, we could never redirect it to take out Wall Street if our first attempt—using the V-2 rocket —failed."

"Again, thank you for telling me something I already know. So, tell me what we can use to get the bomb to the dam and, if needed, switch gears and get the bomb to Wall Street," he bleated. "Something I don't know."

Speer, also showing indignation, said he could do that but, with his own blast of sarcasm, griped that it would take all the "fun" out of the presentation he and Strassburg planned.

"Well, let me make a wild guess at what you two have come up with," Kammler said, his eyes narrowing. "You're planning to use a flying boat to deliver the bomb to the dam. You'll establish refueling and maintenance stops along the route—a route you and Strassburg plotted before I arrived."

Now how the hell did he know that? Strassburg thought.

Speer smiled, showing no signs of surprise. "My grandma, what big ears you have," Speer said, referring to what Little Red Riding Hood said to the Big Bad Wolf.

"One of the perks of being SS, dear Speer, is hearing and learning a lot of things. One of my associates informed me this morning that both of you have been calling every manufacturer of flying boats in the Reich, asking if they had an aircraft capable of carrying a nine thousand-pound payload. And if they did, how high and how far would it fly?"

"You amaze me, Hans," Speer said in a flat tone, pretending no shock at what Kammler had said. "So, tell me, why is it with all your eavesdropping, Germany doesn't seem to be winning the war?"

Kammler ignored Speer's barb and continued his monologue. He told the pair things they already knew. The Reich Air Ministry had issued a decree, effective in a few weeks, halting all flying-boat designs and prototype testing. This decision likely would sabotage plans framed by Speer and Strassburg. But Kammler, warming to their idea, cryptically said he might have "something" that would work. However, he needed time to make some phone calls before lunch in the—rubble.

Strassburg was puzzled. "Lunch in the rubble?"

"You heard him correctly, Karl," Speer said, smiling. "Hans said he'll meet us in the—rubble."

"I don't understand. Some bombed-out building?"

"You don't have to understand, Major, just go with Speer. Good-bye! I have to make some telephone calls. Hopefully they'll prove productive—and save your plan. I'll meet you both as soon as I can."

Speer's driver drove the two a short distance down the Wilhelmstrasse, Berlin's major thoroughfare. Before the war, the Wilhelmstrasse—the north–south roadway lined with palaces and government buildings, architectural treasures from Germany's imperial period—was one of the world's most picturesque drives. Now, only gaunt ghosts of once grand buildings lined the pockmarked pavement.

Speer ordered his driver to stop in front of a heap of rubble. The chauffeur ran around the front of the car and opened the door on the passenger side of Speer's customized maroon-and-black 1932 Maybach Zeppelin DS8. Speer stepped out. Strassburg remained seated, gazing at the rubble.

"This used to be one of Berlin's most exclusive men's clubs. I remember my father bringing me here." The more Strassburg looked around, the more he thought this was some kind of sick joke. Finally, he said to Speer, "Okay, Minister, fun's fun, but where do we eat?"

Speer motioned for Strassburg to step out of the car. "I'll show you," Speer said mysteriously and mischievously.

Taking in the three hundred and sixty-degree view, a scene of vast destruction and debris, Strassburg closed his eyes, visualizing the neighborhood as it was before the bombs fell. *Beautiful old linden trees lining both sides of the street, charming stone exteriors of buildings considered the most exquisite examples of Germany's imperial era. Gone, nothing left of the past.*

"We can't bring back the past, Karl." Speer said, guessing what Strassburg was thinking. "But we can recreate some of it."

Speer placed a gentle hand on Strassburg's shoulder, motioning him to follow the two SS *Feldwebels* (Sergeants) who seemingly appeared from nowhere.

"Watch your step, gentlemen. The elevator is over here," one of the *Feldwebels* cautioned.

From the outside, the elevator appeared as just another piece of rubble. But inside it was an almost exact reproduction of the prewar men's club's elevator, which Strassburg remembered. The only difference from those long lost days was that now the elevator descended rather than ascended.

What will I see when the elevator door opens? Strassburg wondered.

It was as if the war hadn't happened. Time wound itself backward as Speer and Strassburg entered an exclusive world, a world only a privileged few in prewar Berlin experienced. The club's imperial grandeur, its opulence, was flawlessly reproduced—from the aged dark-wood paneling and burgundy-colored drapes to the paintings of sweeping nineteenth-century battles and portraits of Germany's great heroes, soldiers, and statesmen, like Moltke and Bismarck.

The light was bright, a stark contrast from Berlin's drab winter skies. Waiters served water from crystal carafes. Stewards offered an extensive wine list to well-dressed patrons. The tone and texture of the place were clearly designed to help club members forget the war going on above them while they dined safely beneath thousands of tons of rubble and debris.

Speer and Strassburg followed an immaculately attired maître d' to their table. Other luncheon patrons were eyeing the famous duo—the powerful Minister of Armaments and the bemedaled Hero of the Reich, who was on the covers of so many German magazines and was the subject of so many propaganda posters. Their heads turned and their tongues wagged as they speculated about why the two were together. Occasionally, as Speer weaved his way through the dining room he nodded an acknowledgment to an influential acquaintance.

This still was a place where deals were brokered. Gossip was on the menu. Patrons trolled for snippets of information about how the war was going on various fronts. When Kammler arrived fifteen minutes later, more gossip and speculation were added to the brew.

Kammler, snapping his fingers for service, immediately got the waiter's and wine steward's attention, the two trying to outdo one another with the elegance of their service. After ordering, Speer removed a cigarette from its case, tapped it on the table, lit it, and inhaled deeply.

"Without getting into particulars here," he said to Kammler, "did your phone inquiries prove helpful, or are we back to square one?"

"I can't say for sure," Kammler truthfully replied. "More details need to be worked out. But it appears *we* have come up with the solution. I'll fill you in when we're back at your office. For now, no shoptalk."

10.

The lunch was brief. Kammler was bored—disinterested—in Speer and Strassburg's banter about the influence of Pablo Picasso on twentieth-century art.

The trio returned to Speer's office following lunch and continued their deliberations about razing the dam using a long-range flying boat to deliver the nine thousand-pound bomb. Speer started the discussion by reminding Kammler about phone calls he and Strassburg made to all the Reich manufacturers of flying boats, and how they were stonewalled.

"Naturally," Kammler told them, as if they should have expected it, "you asked them to tell you about flying-boat prototypes in the wake of the *Reichsluftfahrtministerium* telling them to halt all flying-boat production, a decision that came from Göring and Hitler. They must have thought the two of you were nuts. None of those companies can afford to alienate the RLM, which means alienating Hitler and Göring."

Kammler noticed Strassburg's expression. "You're a 'smart boy,' Major. I'm surprised to see you so bewildered. The companies you and Speer contacted were fearful if they released information to either of you on a 'killed' project they'd face retribution. Meaning they might lose their existing contracts and for sure the chance to bid on future contracts."

Strassburg argued logically that since Hitler had already approved the dam's destruction, it made sense to contact Dornier and the other manufacturers and ask them if they had a flyable prototype that met certain criteria. Then Strassburg went on to remind Kammler they were going to have Walter redesign his Wa-201 prototype U-boat for the Wall Street mission, a project Dönitz killed. So what was the difference between getting a scrapped U-boat prototype or a scrapped flying-boat prototype?

Kammler, showing mounting impatience, chided Strassburg as a "brilliant physicist and idea person" but scorned him for lacking political savvy.

"Because, Major," Kammler lectured, "the two situations *are* different, entirely different. Dönitz killed Walter's prototype because it failed to meet the needs of the *Ubootwaffe*, and that will allow Speer to confiscate the B&V prototype boat for scrap without raising any questions. As for the second-generation V-2 rocket, it was already under development, so my siphoning off a 'prototype' won't raise any questions."

Speer saw where this was going but decided to say nothing for the time being. Instead, he opened his cigarette case, placed a cigarette between his lips, and savored the ceremony of bringing flame to tobacco.

Kammler was now Strassburg's teacher, a position he relished. Any time Kammler could lecture anyone and point out how things worked in governments—the Reich, in particular—he was happy. "This morning when Dornier and the other aircraft manufacturers started getting phone calls from the Minister of Armament and some *Fallschirmjäger* Major about flying-boat prototypes, and knowing neither one of you had anything to do with the RLM or its policies, naturally they clammed up.

Why was Speer, a member of our exalted Committee, an equal of Göring, making calls that could be considered meddling in Göring's business? Speer, you should have asked Göring to place those calls. Even more interesting was why the two of you were interested in developing one of those monsters to fly by the end of this August."

Hearing this, Strassburg also knew where Kammler was going but decided, like Speer, to say nothing and let him finish.

"You both have to remember that if any one of those manufacturers answered your questions, the other manufacturers would know about it, and faster than shit flows through a goose, they'd tell Göring, hoping he'd show his gratitude when the RLM bids out their next project."

"But if you, General, being SS," Strassburg began, "had asked instead of Minister Speer and myself, you would have gotten answers and those manufacturers would naturally have kept their mouths shut."

"And if word ever leaked out about what I asked, they and their families simply and quietly would disappear. Forever. See, Major, you really are a 'bright boy.'" Once again that crooked smile appeared.

You really are one evil piece of shit, Strassburg thought, finally grasping the unlimited reach of Kammler's very sinister power.

"My sources told me," Kammler said to Speer, "that one of the companies you called this morning was Blohm & Voss and they told you to talk to Göring about getting one of his BV 222 flying boats, which isn't a prototype. You had Strassburg, here, do some digging, and he found out there were only ten to thirteen of these aircraft in service, and while you knew, as built, they could never deliver the bomb to the dam, you were both hoping to modify one of them to carry our five-ton 'friend' and find a way for it to fly high enough and fast enough to escape the shock wave when the bomb exploded. And how were you planning to install a bomb bay in the flying boat's underbelly and not compromise the flotation hull?"

Speer, peeved, asked Kammler, "So, why are you telling us something you know we already know?"

"A lesson needed teaching," he replied. "We're a team, one big happy family. And since I'm the father, I get to know everything. One of you should have told me what you were planning, and this little lesson wouldn't have been needed. Understood?"

Silence.

When Kammler calmed down, he conceded that *your* concept—not *our* concept—was absolutely brilliant, noting that he should have thought of it himself.

"The only problem," Kammler pointed out, "is that you picked the wrong aircraft."

"It's the only one we could find, Hans," Speer countered.

"Ah, and that's why you need *me*," Kammler crowed.

Kammler, satisfied he'd taught both men a valuable lesson (why they needed to get his advice on everything they did), changed the subject and asked which one of them came up with the flying-boat concept. When Speer credited Strassburg with the clever idea, Kammler smiled.

Then Kammler played his trump card. Moments ago, he faulted Speer and Strassburg for "picking the wrong aircraft," but now he circumspectly revealed the "right" aircraft, the one *he* discovered. Kammler was always cagey. He always wanted to be in control, so he doled out information slowly and cautiously. He told them the aircraft "we need," the only one ever built, was under a massive camouflage net on Lake Schaal near Hamburg. He described it as not finished but in "flyable condition." Kammler said the flying boat was the brainchild of Dr-Ing Richard Vogt, the chief designer at Blohm & Voss—the same person who designed the BV 222.

Then turning to Strassburg, Kammler said, trying to make it sound as an afterthought, "Oh, I almost forgot, Major, your girlfriend, who by the way is very beautiful, Anna Prien, works for Vogt. She's the aircraft's test pilot."

This malicious nugget of information clearly was served up by Kammler to let Strassburg know he was on a short leash. However, Strassburg showed no emotion when he learned Kammler knew about his relationship with Prien. Kammler didn't anticipate this reaction.

After a few moments of awkward silence, Kammler briefed Speer and Strassburg about the "mystery" aircraft's history. In the autumn of 1941, the RLM awarded a contract to B&V to replace the BV 222 flying boat with a much larger aircraft, the BV 238. The larger airplane had to be capable of carrying more than forty-four thousand pounds. The first of four prototypes was supposed to be completed in the spring of 1944. Vogt, the aircraft's designer, decided he wouldn't need that much time to design and build the new aircraft. Only five people knew the first prototype had flown in the autumn of 1942. Fearing if the RLM found out what he had done—not adhering to the agreed-upon schedule—B&V might lose pending contracts, Vogt took great pains to hide the flying boat after its maiden flight, hoping to avoid problems with the RLM.

Speer listened intently to Kammler's soliloquy, growing increasingly baffled and wondering why he, the Minister of Armament, hadn't heard even a whisper about the BV 238. Kammler, intently watching the expression on Speer's face, instinctively detected the Minister's thought.

"You never asked the right people or looked in the right places," Kammler said, rebuking Speer. "But even if you had, I doubt if anyone at B&V would have mentioned the BV 238 for fear of pissing off the RLM and Göring. But for now let's put that aside. You never asked about prototypes that had already flown—only prototypes that could be made to fly—by June of this year. Then today when I heard whom you two were calling, I asked your questions of the same manufacturers and got answers the old-fashioned way. Any questions, gentlemen?"

I think, General, we all know your old-fashioned way, Strassburg thought.

Kammler returned to his "lecture" about flying boats. He began by telling Speer and Strassburg that Göring's Luftwaffe had a fleet of fourteen BV 222 flying boats. He then recounted how he convinced his boss, Himmler, to coax Hitler into having Göring transfer one of his BV 222s to the SS.

Yes, Hans, hearing about your cleverness is giving me a headache, Speer thought, blowing smoke rings with his cigarette.

"When the transfer's complete," Kammler went on to explain, "I'll have someone fly the BV 222 to Lake Schaal, when the lake is covered with fog. They'll land, taxi as close as they can to the BV 238, and switch the camouflage netting from the BV 238 to the BV 222. Then they'll fly the BV 238 to a base where I'll have it refitted for the Major's bombing mission. When the fog lifts from the surface of Lake Schaal, observers, either on the shoreline or in the air, will see a camouflage net over the silhouette of a flying boat. I believe the Americans call this 'bait and switch.'"

Speer objected. His incisive mind spotted a flaw: one aircraft was much larger than the other.

"I thought the same thing," Kammler said, "until I saw these two photos. The one under the netting on the left is the BV 238, the larger aircraft. The one under the netting on the right is a BV 222 in Norway. Both photos were taken from different shores, but the distances from both shorelines to the aircraft were approximately the same. Now, I'll turn both photos over, shuffle them as I would cards, and turn them back faceup. Can you tell the difference?"

Speer and Strassburg studied the photographs. Their facial expressions told the story. The silhouettes under the netting looked identical. Viewed from a distance, Kammler's slight-of-hand trick worked, and unless both flying boats were moored next to each other, the size difference would never be noticed. Furthermore, when just one aircraft was viewed with nothing near it to indicate scale—no one would suspect the switch. There were smiles all around.

"It works," Speer said. "Damned, if it doesn't work."

Kammler abruptly changed the subject. He said he was surprised that neither Speer nor Strassburg reacted to his comment about Strassburg heading the dam mission and Prien being the BV 238's lead test pilot.

"When you said *my* bombing mission, General," Strassburg said, "I assumed you meant my recommendation of Boulder Dam as the second target. I can't lead the mission because I'm no longer in the Wehrmacht. The only reason I'm wearing my old uniform is that I work for you, and because everybody on The Committee wanted me to wear it when I presented to Hitler. I'm really a civilian in uniform. As for Fräulein Prien, what can I say? She's great under the sheets but, boy, does she have a temper."

Kammler, always energized by mind games, dropped the Strassburg–Prien angle—at least for now—and decided to try to drive a wedge between Speer and Strassburg.

"Speer, I thought you of all people would have told the Major about his leading the dam mission," Kammler said, his voice laced with sarcasm.

"You know damn well, Hans, I knew nothing about this," Speer angrily replied, his hands shaking slightly as he lit another cigarette.

Kammler conceded Speer's point, admitting only that morning in a conversation with his boss, Heinrich Himmler, that he learned Hitler had ordered Strassburg to command the dam mission. Kammler, with irritation in his voice, dismissed his "announcement" of Strassburg's role as "a little fun." The SS General opined that Strassburg likely won the plum assignment following his well-received presentation to Hitler and The Committee.

"After hearing you make your presentation," Kammler said, "and seeing you decked out in your nicely pressed *Fallschirmjäger* uniform, the Knight's Cross with Oak Leaves and Swords hanging from your neck, you fulfilled Hitler's fantasy of some Wagnerian hero. We all know how our Führer loves his heroes. Except for your hair color, Major, you are Hitler's perfect hero. You're also a very 'smart boy,' aren't you, Major? So, welcome back into the fold. After that marvelous presentation to Hitler, you're back as a Major in the *Fallschirmjägers*."

You're a 'smart boy,' Major, Kammler thought, his lifeless blue eyes showing no emotion. *And that's exactly what Hitler said to me after everyone left the conference room the night you gave him that presentation at the Berghof.*

11.

Now, two of the dam mission's greatest unknowns were resolved. Strassburg was the attack's leader and Blohm & Voss's BV 238 flying boat would haul the powerful, weighty bomb, the thousands of miles across oceans to Boulder Dam.

With those issues out of the way, planning now focused on the mission's routing and logistics. What were the best routes, the safest and most covert routes, to get the bomb to the United States? Where should the resupply points be located? How would resupply points be stocked and who would man the resupply points? And most important, what was needed to convert the monstrous flying boat into a bomber? That would be a difficult engineering challenge because the aircraft's floatation hull had to be maintained.

Their spontaneous back-and-forth exchange of "what if we do this or that" stopped the moment Kammler revealed the aircraft's altitude ceiling. Hearing this, Strassburg told the others the dam mission had just become a suicide mission. Flying boats weren't designed to climb beyond twenty thousand feet. At that altitude, Strassburg and his crew simply could not survive the blast.

Kammler listened to Strassburg's concerns about crew survivability while he filled his water glass from a carafe. After taking what amounted to a theatrical sip, he blandly told Strassburg not to worry.

"The answer, gentlemen," Kammler began in his most matter-of-fact tone, "is Blohm & Voss's BV 8-246 *Hagelkorn* glide-bomb." He showed the two a somewhat vague drawing of the *Hagelkorn*, as well as some scribbled performance specifications compiled by one of his minions. Speer and Strassburg were dumbfounded. They never had heard of the contraption. Kammler might be a despicable person, but he also was an extraordinary resource: Houtermans, the uranium ore in North Africa, the BV 238 flying boat, and now the BV 8-246 *Hagelkorn*. Kammler had eyes and ears everywhere.

According to the scribbles, the BV 8-246 glide bomb, equipped with a preset gyro guidance system, could be loaded with one of Houtermans's nine thousand-pound bombs—released at twenty-thousand feet, the BV 238's ceiling, and glide one hundred and thirteen miles to the dam—ample distance for the crew to escape the bomb's deadly shock wave.

Having covered the major points about the *Hagelkorn*, Kammler said sarcastically, "From our prior 'what if we do this and that' conversation, I'm assuming you two have already plotted refueling and maintenance points to the dam. We'll go with what you came up with later. For now let's just stick to the bombing portion of the mission. So, after the Major arms the bomb and launches the glide bomb, he and the crew fly south and land in the Sea of Cortez. The crew opens the plane's seacocks, the aircraft sinks, everyone paddles to shore, and lives in Mexico while the Americans sue us for peace."

"Hold on Hans," Speer objected, "there's still the problem of the flying boat's flotation hull. How do we convert it into a bomber?"

"We don't have to, Speer. Didn't I tell you? The nose of the BV 238 opens up for loading cargo. So there's no need to figure out a way to put bomb-bay doors in the bottom the aircraft. We just open the bow loading door, extend the glide-bomb's wings, the glide-bomb floats out, and that's, that."

"Sounds like you've got everything under your usual anal control, Hans," Speer said while lighting another cigarette.

"Thank you, Speer, for noticing."

"Major Strassburg," Kammler began, "remember me mentioning Fräulein Prien being the BV 238's test pilot? Well, you'll be pleased to know she'll be the crew's instructor. Himmler," he gloated, "thought this might please the two of you."

What a shit you are, Hans! Speer thought, stubbing out his freshly lit cigarette in a gesture of disgust.

Strassburg did everything he could to appear nonplussed by Kammler's news about Anna.

"Yes, well, please thank *Reichsführer* Himmler for getting us the best test pilot Blohm & Voss has. She shouldn't be a problem, but like I indicated to you earlier, she does have a mind of her own. Oh, and by the way, did your 'ears' tell you I'm going out with her this weekend? If it ends up being like last time, we'll—well—I guess you can fill in the blanks. She's gorgeous and one hell of an athlete in bed."

Kammler smirked.

Nicely handled, Major, no emotion, no stumbling around for words. Maybe Himmler was wrong and Fräulein Prien is nothing more than a wartime fling. Either way, you both will bear very close watching.

Several problems were solved. They had an aircraft capable of carrying a nine-thousand pound bomb in its belly to the dam. The crew had a way to survive the blast, all of this courtesy of Kammler.

"Okay, now I think we're ready to hear your brilliant fuel and parts positioning plan for the Major's journey to the dam," Kammler told them, smugness filling his face.

Speer forced a smile and stood up, a lit cigarette dangling from his lips. He pulled a world map from under the conference table and unrolled it, placing bricks on the edges so it wouldn't roll up.

His voice was edgy. "I'm surprised, Hans, that you haven't read our minds about where we planned to position maintenance and refueling points."

Strassburg was silent. He peered at the map, scribbling some numbers on a scrap of paper.

"Major, I'm waiting!" Kammler barked.

"Sorry, General," Strassburg replied as he continued fiddling with his calculations.

"Now that I know what aircraft we're using and the weight it's capable of carrying," Strassburg explained, "I'm adding together what the bomb weighs, the Hagelkorn's weight, a guesstimate of what the spare parts weigh, and the weight

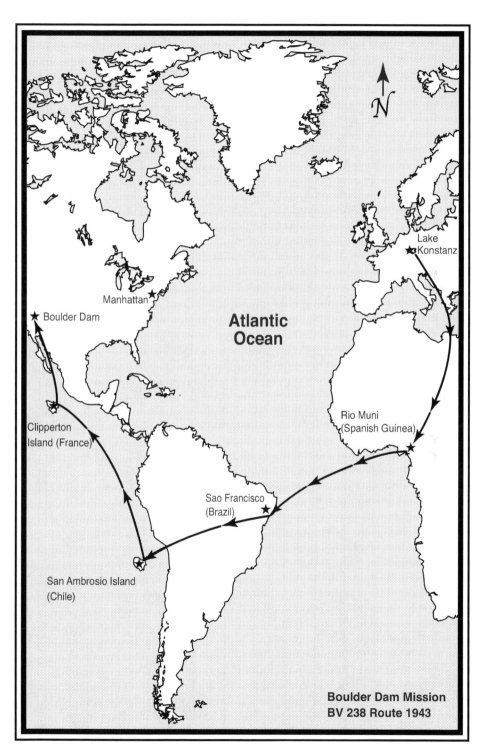

Boulder Dam
Manhattan
Atlantic
Ocean
Lake
Konstanz
Clipperton
Island (France)
Rio Muni
(Spanish Guinea)
Sao Francisco
(Brazil)
San Ambrosio Island
(Chile)

**Boulder Dam Mission
BV 238 Route 1943**

of the fuel in its topped-off wing tanks. I've subtracted that number from the total amount of weight the aircraft is capable of carrying, and that number tells us how much extra fuel we can carry in fuel bladders, fuel we'll need to extend the range of the aircraft. Based on the extended range of the flying boat, I've chosen several refueling points."

"How many points, Major?" Kammler demanded.

"Four should do it, General, depending on where we start."

Kammler was fretting about whether there'd be sufficient fuel during the final leg of the flight to divert the BV 238 from the dam to Wall Street if the V-2 failed.

Silence.

Strassburg again started fiddling with the known variables in an attempt to put Kammler's fears to rest. Kammler was envious of Strassburg's dexterity with numbers.

"Yes," Strassburg finally said, looking up from his calculations, "it appears that we will have enough fuel to fly to New York if for some reason that second-generation V-2 rocket fails to perform. But how do you propose we avoid being shot down while we fly across the States, General?"

Kammler cryptically said he had the perfect solution and would brief them about it later.

Speer pushed Kammler to reveal the mission's all-important jumping-off point. Kammler hesitated—making a mental judgment about whether now was the right time and place to reveal such critical information. Then he realized that, without it, Strassburg could never determine the exact location of any of the four refueling sites. These locations needed to be checked out before setting up the refueling and maintenance stations.

"Lake Konstanz," Kammler laconically replied. "For now, neither of you need to know the exact location on the lake."

While both men were irked by Kammler's evasiveness and secrecy, they accepted the fact that he always would be nothing more than a rude "son of a bitch." Strassburg, putting his feelings aside, began discussing the four refueling sites, while Speer pointed them out on a map. These sites were Strassburg and Speer's "best guesses" before Kammler told them about the BV 238 and its performance capabilities.

The first site was the Rio Muni's delta in Spanish Guinea on the coast of West Africa in the South Atlantic, more than four thousand two hundred and fifty miles from Lake Konstanz. The second refueing and supply site was across the South Atlantic at the estuary of the Sao Francisco River, near the small coastal town of Penedo, Brazil, a distance of three thousand four hundred miles from Rio Muni. The third— San Ambrosio Island, six hundred miles off the coast of Chile in the South Pacific, a perilous three thousand six hundred-mile odyssey going west from Sao Francisco on South America's East Coast then over the majestic Andes Mountains, which in some places stretch to a height exceeding the flying boat's twenty

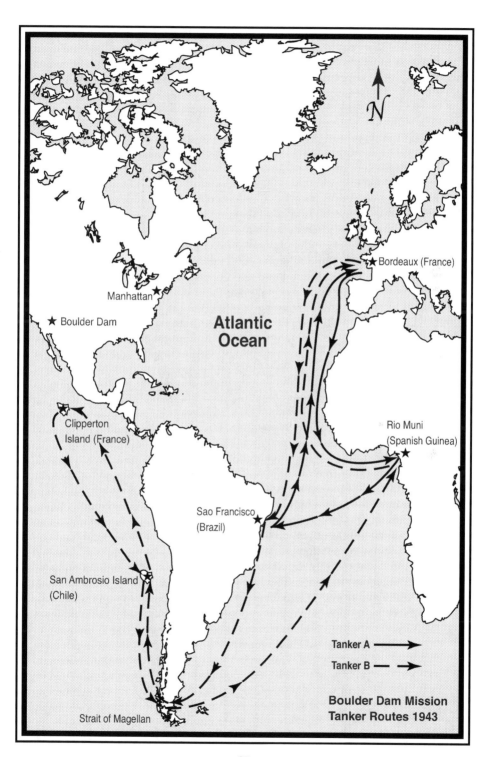

N

Bordeaux (France)

Atlantic
Ocean

Manhattan

Boulder Dam

Clipperton
Island (France)

Rio Muni
(Spanish Guinea)

Sao Francisco
(Brazil)

San Ambrosio Island
(Chile)

Tanker A ⟶
Tanker B ⟶

Boulder Dam Mission
Tanker Routes 1943

Strait of Magellan

67

thousand-foot ceiling. The fourth site—Clipperton Island—was four thousand miles north of San Ambrosio, off the coast of Central America.

Kammler did a slow burn as he watched Speer point out the route and listened to Speer describe the locations of the four refueling sites. He was rash and failed to think through their rationales for the route. He argued their routes were unnecessarily long and arduous—that Hitler would never approve such a globetrotting journey.

"There have to be shorter routes," Kammler blurted out.

"Yes, there are shorter routes," Strassburg conceded in a sharp tone bordering on disrespect. "But we're losing the war, General. And that means we're also losing friends. The route we chose and the places we picked as refueling and maintenance depots are located in colonies and countries that remain friendly to us. They're also out-of-the-way places, where a giant flying boat with a German crew is not likely to be seen."

Kammler mutely pondered the logic of Strassburg's argument before grudgingly accepting it.

⋘▬▬◗▬▬▷

Strassburg resumed his detailed explanation of the mission's route, starting with a brief history of Clipperton Island, a small atoll once ruled by a rapist who declared himself king. The island atoll, after its discovery, changed owners—British, French, and US—many times. Despite being abandoned by the Americans, the US Navy still randomly patrolled the waters surrounding the atoll.

Kammler immediately pounced on the fact the Americans sometimes roamed the waters surrounding the island. That fact, according to Kammler, made Clipperton a poor choice as a refueling and maintenance way station.

Speer shot right back. He pointed out that the US patrols were haphazard, perhaps once every six months, and when they happened, US forces never set foot on the island. They checked it from afar, using binoculars. He also noted that US ships were too large to sail over the coral reef surrounding the island, and the reef's openings were in very shallow water, which also barred big ships getting close to the island.

Kammler still balked at Speer's explanation. He remained worried the US Navy would show up precisely at the moment the flying boat was being refueled. Stubbornly, he kept pressing the point, sensing a major flaw in Speer and Strassburg's plan to use the atoll as the fourth refueling point.

Speer was fed up. "Tell you what, Hans," he barked. "You're Mr. Know-It-All. Here's the damn map. Pick another spot you think is less risky. Sell it to Hitler. I'm finished."

Kammler was stunned—speechless.

Strassburg stepped in, pointing to the map and told Kammler the distance from Clipperton to the dam was only one thousand eight hundred miles. If the V-2 failed to take out Wall Street, they'd still have enough fuel to get to Wall Street. Hearing this, Kammler ended his objection to Clipperton as the fourth refueling point. Regaining his equilibrium, once again the man-in-charge, assertive and commanding, Kammler reminded Strassburg to monitor all American civilian radio networks along the route to the dam to find out if Wall Street was destroyed and if not to proceed to New York.

"If that's the case, then we have placed Major Strassburg in command of a suicide mission," Speer said, chastising Kammler.

Kammler, again being secretive and evasive, simply said, "For now, just be assured that if the V-2 fails, the Americans will gladly escort the Major and his flying boat to their East Coast. Once the Major's within thirty miles of Wall Street, he'll release the Hagelkorn, and *poof*, no more Wall Street. During the ensuing chaos and confusion he'll broadcast a Mayday, informing whoever is listening his aircraft is coming apart. Everyone bails out, the plane crashes, and everyone goes to Mexico and lives happily ever after. When we win the war they'll come home to Germany. It's simple, really."

Strassburg wondered. *What's the bastard holding back? Doesn't he trust us? What could it be? Why would the Americans "gladly escort" us to their East Coast?*

Kammler looked at his watch, letting his "colleagues" know his time was valuable. Picking up on Kammler's coy hint to keep things rolling, Strassburg continued.

The afternoon light was fading. Shadows grew longer. Kammler, Speer, and Strassburg drew up their individual lists of supplies and parts to meet every contingency the BV 238 flying boat might encounter on its way to Boulder Dam.

Their lists were tallied, paying particular attention to the weight of aviation fuel and equipment deposited at the four maintenance and refueling sites. When they saw the results, it became clear what they'd need to support the mission: two IXD U-tankers from Dönitz's rapidly diminishing tanker fleet.

Hitler recently had ordered Dönitz to convert all but three of his IXD U-tankers into minelayers, laying mines in The English Channel. Hitler thought if enough mines were laid, the looming Allied cross-Channel invasion of France would be disrupted. Dönitz pleaded with Hitler not to do the conversions. He reasoned that the number of mines the converted tankers could lay in the time allowed would not affect the cross-Channel invasion. However, if the tankers were used as intended, his wolf packs could sail farther, sinking more Allied shipping. But, Hitler insisted on the conversions, leaving Dönitz with only three IXD U-tankers.

"Don't worry about getting the IXD tankers. I'll get them," Kammler assured Speer and Strassburg.

"How? By killing Dönitz?" a passionate Speer asked.

"Let's just hope it doesn't come to that?" Kammler joked.

Neither Speer nor Strassburg laughed. Kammler then asked Strassburg to brief him on how the tankers would reach the four resupply points.

Strassburg explained that each tanker had a range of thirty thousand five hundred miles. Opening a map, he pointed out their routes. Both tankers would start from Germany's U-boat pens at Bordeaux on the French coast in the English Channel, giving them fuel-saving access to the North Atlantic.

Tanker A, sailing the shortest route, would head south into the Atlantic to the delta of the Rio Muni in Spanish Guinea on Africa's west coast. After dropping off aviation fuel, spare parts, and half her maintenance crew, she'd head west across the South Atlantic, to the estuary of Brazil's Sao Francisco River. Here she'd deposit the balance of her aviation fuel, spare parts, and the other half of her maintenance crew along with her unneeded diesel fuel, which would now be available for tanker B.

After doing that she'd return to the sea and wait for the BV 238 to arrive for refueling. Once the flying boat was airborne, tanker A would resurface, the maintainance crew would sanitize the area, reboard the tanker, and head back to Bordeaux.

Kammler halted the briefing. He was puzzled by Strassburg's reference to submarine tanker A's unneeded fuel. The Major explained—without getting into numbers—that both tankers would be topped off with marine diesel at Bordeaux. Tanker A wouldn't need all the fuel in her tanks for her journey to Rio Muni and the Sao Francisco River and back to Bordeaux. But tanker B needed more fuel than she could carry in order to make it to her two drop-off points and back to Bordeaux.

The solution was simple: transfer tanker A's unneeded fuel into specially made fuel bladders at the Sao Francisco refueling and maintenance site and have tanker B stop at Sao Francisco and pick up the fuel.

Kammler smiled, complimenting Strassburg on his solution to the fuel problem.

Once tanker B's tanks were topped off with marine diesel left by tanker A, it would sail south through the Strait of Magellan at the tip of South America, turn north into the Pacific, and head for San Ambrosio Island. At San Ambrosio, she'd drop off half her load of aviation fuel, spare parts, and maintenance personnel. Tanker B would then set a northerly course for Clipperton Island. At Clipperton she'd off-load the balance of her aviation fuel, spare parts, and the maintenance crew. Then tanker B would go back out to sea beyond the reef, submerge, and wait for the BV 238's arrival.

Once the BV 238 was fueled and on her way to the dam tanker B would pick up unneeded spare parts, and the maintenance crew at Clipperton, sail south to San Ambrosio, pick up the other half of the maintenance crew, clean up the island, go back through the Straits of Magellan, and head northeast to the mouth of the Rio Muni. At Rio Muni she'd pick up the maintenance crew, left by tanker A, then head back to Bordeaux.

Soon after, a knock on the door interrupted the planning session.

"Tell whomever it is we're in a conference and can't be disturbed!" Kammler barked.

"Sorry, Hans," Speer retorted, annoyed. "Until I'm told otherwise, this is still my office. I give the orders here. Not you."

Kammler fumed at Speer's moxie.

Speer opened the door, and one of his assistants handed him a document for his signature.

"Minister, I think you'll want to see this."

"Thank you," Speer courteously told the man.

Speer looked carefully at the document. He grinned and laconically said, "Hans, Major, we no longer have a problem."

Kammler and Strassburg showed surprise. Speer remembered being handed the document before lunch and not reading it. He had placed it on top of a stack of papers he planned to read once the day's meeting with Kammler and Strassburg ended.

"I should have looked at this before we left for lunch, Major," he contritely commented. Waving the document in the air, he added, "If I had, I wouldn't have muddled over how to go about getting those two tankers from Dönitz."

The document was a work order, requesting Speer as Minister of Armament to convert U-180 and U-195, the types of tankers needed to support the dam mission, into minelayers. The request was signed by Dönitz but lacked a completion date. Speer could not sign it without a completion date.

Kammler, recognizing this fortuitous circumstance, immediately tossed cold water on the situation.

"How are you going to avoid telling Dönitz his work request is undated?" he asked.

Speer, smirking, bluntly replied, "I'll use a play taken directly from your SS 'dirty tricks' playbook, Hans. When Dönitz asks why the refitting work hasn't' started, I'll tell him that since the work order wasn't dated, I assumed there was no rush."

"But what happens when he asks you the whereabouts of his two U-tankers?" Kammler countered.

Speer, greatly enjoying this exchange of wits, said, "I'll simply throw up my hands and tell him since I never signed for his tankers, the Ministry of Armament can hardly be held responsible for their location. I'll also encourage him to pay more attention to his paperwork in the future. But I'll save the best part for last—"

"Which is?" Kammler asked.

12.

"Since misplacing two tankers is a serious matter," Speer glibly said, "I intend to tell Dönitz it's appropriate we bring the matter to Hitler's attention. Something I doubt he will want to do."

Kammler was skeptical of Speer's ploy, pointing out Dönitz was more likely to launch his own probe into the "missing" tanker's whereabouts.

"Maybe," Speer partially agreed, "but if he does look for the two 'misplaced' tankers' the trail will lead directly to your front door, Hans. You're the cunning son of a bitch in this tight little trio. You deal with the problem."

Strassburg was surprised by how boldly Speer confronted, even challenged, Kammler.

Kammler's face flushed.

"Nice move, Speer. You played your hand well. You've learned a lot from me. But learning and doing are two different things."

Kammler remembered Dönitz becoming livid after being told by one of Hitler's naval attachés to refashion all of his IXD tankers, except for three, into minelayers. Dönitz went directly to Hitler and pleaded his case, failing miserably.

"Dönitz doesn't waste time on lost causes," Kammler lectured Speer. "He's already written off those tankers. He also knows that dumping more mines into the English Channel will do nothing to stop the coming Allied invasion of France."

Silence followed. Kammler restarted the conversation after an uncomfortable interval.

"Tell me, Speer, when the two tankers are back in their pens at Bordeaux and Dönitz says, 'Looks like you found my missing tankers, Minister,' what do you intend to tell him?"

"How about this, Hans? 'Talk to Hitler, Admiral.'"

"That wouldn't sit well with anyone, Speer. Use the time before those two fish come back and think up something more appropriate for all our sakes."

The hulls of the two IXD tankers wouldn't require reinforcing since the cargo—aviation fuel, spare parts, maintenance equipment, and crew—weighed less than the normal load of marine diesel and parts each tanker carried on routine missions to support the *Ubootwaffe's* wolf packs. The conversion involved refitting areas in the tankers with rubber fuel bladders with galvanized seams. If aviation fuel were placed in tanks once filled with marine diesel, it would be contaminated.

"You'll need a hell of a lot of bladders," Kammler commented.

"And that's precisely why you're around, Hans," Speer replied. "If I were to requisition them through the Ministry of Armament, it would take years. But you, using your SS connections, can get it done in—let me guess—days, weeks at the most."

Speer's bold assertion triggered another awkward moment of silence, while the two stared at each other. Once again it was Kammler who broke the quiet, warning Speer, "Don't tweak the tail of the tiger and expect it not to bite. Once I receive a bladder prototype from you and the Major, I'll deliver the goods in a month."

The uneasy tension between the two seemed to find no end. Speer was emboldened. Kammler felt threatened, a rare circumstance for the ego-driven, malevolent General.

Strassburg recognized the strong animosity between Kammler and Speer. He tried to break the mounting antipathy by explaining to them the only difficult part of the journey for tanker B would be its passages through the Strait of Magellan at the bottom of South America. But because of what Germany learned about those turbulent waters from *Reichsmarschall* Göring's Antarctic escapade, the passage shouldn't be a problem. That was all it took. Both Kammler and Speer broke into laughter.

"That little 'adventure,'" Kammler quipped, "was such a 'bargain.'"

"Oh, yes," Speer replied in a mocking voice. "Who else but Göring could get away with spending millions of Reichsmarks for a few penguins and get a medal for doing it?"

What the trio was talking about was a secret 1938–1939 Nazi expedition to the Antarctic, at the behest of Göring, with the goal of annexing some territory to benefit Germany's growing whaling fleet.

Strassburg returned to voicing his concern about tanker B's hazardous undertaking—submerged or on the surface—going through the Strait of Magellan, twice. He explained the Strait was noted for its high winds, fog, heavy waves, and occasional icebergs. Consequently, Strassburg argued such dangers called for a very experienced tanker B commander.

"So, where do we get such a commander—and crew—without Dönitz finding out what we're up to?"

"I'll take care of it, Major," Kammler asserted. "Leave that to me."

Thinking more about it, Kammler said, "Actually, we'll need three U-boat commanders and crews—one for the Walter Drive boat, the one towing or pushing the barge with the rocket inside, and one for each of the tankers."

Kammler paused, appearing lost in thought, thinking about what Strassburg said about the Strait of Magellan. Eventually, he said that both tankers *must* depart Bordeaux before winter comes to the Strait, a much more turbulent season in the southern Atlantic than winter in the North Atlantic.

"Do you know the tankers' speed?" Kammler asked.

"On the surface, twenty knots max," Strassburg replied. "Submerged, 7.9 to 9.2 knots. Once the tankers clear the Allied convoy lanes, they'll run on the surface whenever conditions allow."

◄━◖▌▐◗►

A knock at the door intruded on the conversation.

"Sorry to disturb you like this, Minister," a guard said, "but it's getting dark. I have to close the blackout curtains. Orders."

This signaled the meeting's end. Kammler, Speer, and Strassburg gathered their papers.

Speer addressed Strassburg, "Since its Friday, Karl, and we're not meeting this weekend, let me put your notes and materials in my safe. I'll give them to you on Monday before our flight to Peenemünde. What about yours, Hans?"

"Thank you, but I'll need them this weekend. Monday, at Peenemünde, we'll meet briefly with Professor Walter about the tug and the barge. Remember, no mention of the rocket. After that, Albert, we'll see an old retired friend of yours, Dr-Ing Gerhard Cranz. I've already made travel arrangements for the three of us. Plan for an overnight stay. If the weather holds, there'll be a V-2 launch on Tuesday. It's been a long but very productive two days. See you Monday at the aerodrome. Any questions?"

"Just one, Hans," Speer said. "Do you want me to verify the data on the *Hagelkorn*?"

"Certainly not!" Kammler thundered. "The SS always gets things correct! I thought you of all people would know that. Oh, and Strassburg, be sure to give my regards to Fräulein Prien and, please, give her these. One of my SS associates picked them up in Paris. I'm sure they'll fit her nicely. "

13.

Hauptmann Lothar Bergen would not be flying left seat, piloting Göring's massive Junkers Ju 290A-7 transport, his usual spot, on the way back to Berlin. Today Anna Prien was flying the *Reichsmarschall* in his luxurious transport from the airstrip outside the Obersalzberg compound to Berlin. After seeing Prien and hearing about her exploits, the rotund and politically powerful Göring ordered the change in pilots. Göring, the World War I flying ace of Manfred von Richthofen's Flying Circus, was infatuated with Prien's classic blonde beauty. Once the plane landed he insisted on accompanying Prien off the transport as she walked to the terminal. During the walk, he whispered in her ear, telling her she was to remain "on loan to 'his' Luftwaffe" and would soon be given a very special assignment. In the meantime, she'd spend her days overseeing maintenance and inspections on a diverse number of aircraft in the Reich's inventory. Göring kept rubbing his pudgy hand just below the small of her back as they walked. Occasionally his hand would drop lower, and Prien found the incident annoying and embarrassing.

While overseeing the maintenance of various aircraft, a job requiring extreme attention to detail, Prien had to remind herself to focus on what she was doing. But, her thoughts constantly drifted back to the night she had spent with Strassburg at the Platterhof. His warm reassuring smile, those mischievous dark eyes, and the memory of his intimate touchings kept interrupting her concentration. Prien couldn't understand how fast she'd fallen for a stranger.

She wasn't even sure anything really happened—besides his fingers inside her, causing her to want more. *Those damn fingers. Every time I moaned, he kept probing deeper. I can't ever remember feeling that naughty. The way we fell asleep next to each other, it felt so—very natural*, she thought. *What must he think of me? Anyway, he probably has women stashed all over the damn Reich.*

Occasionally her thoughts would drift to her parents in Switzerland, giving silent thanks they were out of danger. They thought she was relatively safe as a civilian test pilot. They were unaware B&V had "loaned" her to fly Göring's transport.

In a very real sense, Prien was a prisoner of the Reich. She was unable to visit her parents at their ski lodge outside Interlaken in the canton of Bern due to the war and her test-piloting responsibilities. Her letters said little more than "I love you, all is well, and I hope everything back home is fine." She wrote nothing of her work, which was top secret.

Finally it was Friday, the workweek was over. Her pulse quickened now she was free to think about their upcoming date. But Strassburg hadn't called. The last time they talked was the night they bumped into each other at the Platterhof. *What if he doesn't show up tonight?*

Strassburg had packed for the weekend and checked out of the hotel that morning, before beginning his and Speer's lengthy—and sometimes contentious—

meeting with Kammler. He did that so he could pick up Anna and head off to her "weekend surprise" for a quiet weekend. Where that "suprise" was, he wasn't sure since she was the one making the arrangements. The idea was to get out of Berlin before the British and their Lancasters began another night of bombing. Strassburg was driving a gray-and-black BMW 327 Cabriolet, courtesy of Kammler, who assigned it to him from the SS barrack's motor pool at Lichterfelde-Ost.

En route to Anna's billet, he wondered if it was a good idea to even see her now that he was leading the dam mission and she'd be training the crew. His future prospects—with or without Anna—seemed dim.

Should I just knock on her door and tell her I had second thoughts, let her slap my face and leave? That's probably the sensible thing to do.

But Strassburg wasn't sure he wanted to be "sensible." He also toyed with the idea of throwing caution to the wind and telling Anna *everything*.

But what if she panicked? Something unlikely since she was a test pilot. What if she tells Kammler I'm a traitor?

Strassburg, usually the epitome of logic, was having a hard time thinking logically as so many contradictory ideas and emotions spun around in his head. He knew that whatever his decision, its basis wouldn't be logic. He was in love—logic and common sense were unimportant.

So the only thing to do is tell her everything, he concluded. *The trick will be finding the right time and place—a place where the walls don't have ears.*

Anna's quarters were at one of the many small prewar civilian landing strips on Berlin's outskirts. When the war came, the government commandeered these airstrips, upgrading and converting them to military bases.

A single guard stood watch at the main gate. Nowhere were barracks or housing in sight. Strassburg could see only a few derelict aircraft scattered about the taxiways along with two dilapidated vintage 1920s aircraft hangars.

He was confused. Had he somehow missed the main gate?

The lone guard approached his car, saluted, and asked for identification. He checked Strassburg's name against others he had on a sheet of paper attached to a clipboard. The guard again saluted, raised the gate, and told Strassburg to drive to the first hangar.

He stopped the car in front of the shabby-looking hangar's closed doors, which immediately slid back, revealing an interior filled with old unusable parts and equipment. Two guards instantly appeared from the shadows, the only light from a dim overhead bulb.

One of the guards motioned Strassburg to drive onto a rectangular metal platform in the middle of the oil-stained concrete floor. The other guard chock blocked all four wheels of his car and told him to set the emergency brake before stepping out of the Cabriolet.

The guards saluted. One of them with a hint of sarcasm said, "Hold onto the door handle, Major. Welcome to the new Germany. Soon everyone will be living underground. Only the cockroaches will live aboveground."

The smooth hum of well-maintained machinery came to life and the BMW along with Strassburg and both the guards started descending into the earth.

As more and more of the shaft's exposed rock wall wizzed by one of the guards looked over at Strassburg to see how he was "enjoying" the ride.

"Amazing isn't it, Major, and the best part is yet to come. This facility is actually a small city, it's the second one built. It's designed and built to provide housing and dining facilities for VIPs traveling by air around the Reich. Eventually installations like this will ring all our major cities."

"So the airfield—" Strassburg started to say.

"Completely operational," the second guard said. "You can't tell from the air, unless you get up close to them on the ground, but those bomb craters on the runways are really three-dimensional paintings of bomb craters. From the air the runways appear to be completely inoperable. Makes the British and American bomber crews think they've done their job."

Amazing, Strassburg thought.

The platform stopped with a shudder more than three hundred feet below the surface.

"When you want to return topside, Major," the first guard said, "call the front desk, and by the time you get back here your car will be waiting."

"Heil Hitler!" both guards snapped to attention and said in unison."

"Heil Hitler!"

Strassburg checked in at the desk. A clerk telephoned Anna, announcing his arrival. Moments later a young Luftwaffe *flieger* (Air Force private) with a pale complexion drove up in an electric cart. He saluted Strassburg and took him on the next leg of his subterranean journey. They chatted as they drove through a network of crisscrossing tunnels to the living quarters area. Strassburg learned the *flieger* had just turned fourteen, had been a member of the Hitler Youth, and wanted to become a *Fallschirmjäger* so he could do his part for the Fatherland.

He's only a child, Strassburg thought. *He's getting no sunlight down here. I had no idea things were this bad.*

Soon they came to a hub marked "VIP Living Quarters." Up to this point, everything was bland—concrete, steel, and industrial lighting. Here the decor changed. Walls were covered in exotic wood paneling adorned with artwork. Floors were terrazzo overlaid with Oriental runners. Ceilings were coffered, set off with soft recessed lighting.

Another credential check, a different cart, another young driver. This time a perky young girl, a member of the *Nachrichtenhelferin*, Woman's Auxiliary Services, chauffeured Strassburg on the next leg of his journey.

Judging from her looks and manner, Strassburg thought she was about the same age as the young *flieger*. After a short drive and a delightful conversation, she stopped the cart in front of Anna's suite.

Strassburg stepped off the cart and thanked her for the ride. The cart took off.

The door flew open before his knuckles could rap a knock.

"Damn you, why didn't you call?"

Anna was in a fit of passion. She pulled Karl into the room, turned, and kicked the door shut behind them. She had expectantly waited for their "rendez-vous" all week even as she fretted that Strassburg might stand her up.

Karl placed a hand over her mouth. The index finger of his other hand placed against his lips—a clear sign she shouldn't say another word. Anna was wide-eyed but nodded her head, indicating she understood. Karl gently pushed her away. He snatched some paper off the nearby desk and pulled out his pen. He wrote a brief but chilling message: "The walls have ears. I've missed you more than you'll ever know. Just follow my lead."

Anna gasped. She mouthed, "We're being spied on!"

Karl grabbed her again and held her tight, all the while kissing her, as if consoling a child. He realized they had to quickly resume their conversation. Their silence would arouse suspicion from those who surely were listening. He casually said, "Sorry I didn't call, but work's been a bear."

Anna pushed him away. Clapped her hands, hoping it sounded like she slapped his face.

"That's for not calling me," she said in a loud voice. "You think you're the only one with problems at work?" she shouted, faking anger.

"Okay! Okay!" Karl said, playing along. "I apologize for not calling. But come on! We're not married."

"And I doubt you ever will be," she said, continuing the charade. "No woman in her right mind would put up with not hearing from her husband even if a war is going on."

"Fine!" Karl shot back, smiling as their fictitious lover's spat unfolded. "If that's the way you feel, do you want to go out or don't you?"

Strassburg reached in his pocket and pulled out a pair of women's silk stockings. They were the stockings Kammler had given him for Anna.

"Look!" he roared. "Maybe these will put you in a better mood. My boss had an associate bring these back for you from Paris."

"Oh, my!" Anna said, trying not to laugh at the peace offering. She pulled up her skirt and held the stockings to her legs. They laughed.

"They're a little short," she said, mock disappointment in her tone. The stockings weren't short, but exactly the right length.

"It's wartime, Anna," Karl said with fake rebuke. "And while I wouldn't know myself, I'm told women's silk stockings are hard to come by."

Anna changed the tone of her voice to honey. "Then they'll just have to do, won't they? I'll write a thank-you note to your boss while you go change to your civvies in the bathroom. In the meantime, I'll put on a garter belt—maybe I can stretch these stockings out so when I sit down—"

"Can I stay here and watch?" he asked, a sheepish grin filling his face.

"Go change in the bathroom and close the door. No peeking."

Karl exited the bathroom some ten minutes later wearing a double-breasted suit, white shirt with spiffed collar, school tie, and wingtips. "How do I look? Karl asked, doing something of a parody of a model's pirouette.

Anna pursed her lip.

"It's a good thirties look but—well—sure, why not."

"Dated?"

"Kinda. What about these stockings?"

"They're Argyles—Okay?"

"Not yours, dummy. These!" she said, slowly raising her skirt just above the tops of her stockings.

"Sure, why not."

14.

It was close to 8:30 p.m. when they arrived at Anna's "weekend surprise," an inn just outside of Werder on the banks of the Havel River. Here they were safe, far away from the prying eyes of the Abwehr, German military intelligence, and Kammler's SS.

The inn, originally a petty nobleman's hunting lodge during the late nineteenth century, was sold to its present owners in the early 1920s. The new owners, recognizing the inn's potential, remodeled and updated it without destroying its original charm.

The exterior still showed the rich architectural blend of brick and timber. Only the wattle had been replaced with twentieth-century waterproof stucco and the bricks had been tuckpointed in 1936. The roof remained thatch, preserving the soft warmth and coziness its builders intended. Inside was the usual mixture of taxidermy lining the lobby's walls. Exposed beams dominated the walls and ceilings of the entrance, sitting area, dining hall, stairways, and guest suites. Dark-stained, wide-planked flooring set off oriental runners and rugs of nomadic design, which decorated every floor.

The innkeeper and his wife—short people—were friendly, warm, and courteous, traits that were disappearing in cities and towns across Germany in the Nazi era.

Karl and Anna signed the guest register. The innkeeper was nonplussed when they didn't register as husband and wife.

"Look, Mama," he said to his wife, "he's that Major on the cover of *Signal*, the *Fallschirmjäger* who was awarded the Knight's Cross."

The innkeeper's wife, duly impressed, sheepishly asked Karl to autograph a magazine article about him, gushing that her thirteen-year-old daughter has a "terrible crush on you."

Karl smiled. Anna rolled her eyes.

"I'd be happy to sign this," Karl solemnly said, "as long as you both promise to tell no one I'm here."

"Here's your key. Do you want me to bring up your—one piece of luggage?"

"We'll be fine," Karl told the innkeeper, as he grabbed the baggage and followed Anna up the stairs.

"You're famous," Anna said once they were alone, somewhat dreamy-eyed, as she cocked her head to one side. She rested her head on his shoulder and grabbed his free hand. They walked slowly down the hallway toward their suite. If anyone was watching they might have thought the two were happily-married honeymooners with not a care in the world in spite of the war.

"Whether you're in or out of uniform, people recognize you. You seem troubled by this. Why?"

"Like I told you when we met at the Platterhof, I'm not a Nazi, I'm a German. Unfortunately, when people see me in my uniform—or out of it—they see me as a Nazi. I'll tell you more when we're in our suite and I've checked it for listening devices."

"You can't be serious," she exclaimed, showing great surprise. "Here, in this inn, in the middle of nowhere, you think there might be listening devices?"

"I don't know, Anna. I just don't know. For now, let's freshen up, have dinner, and once we're back in our suite, then we'll talk." But Karl was impatient. He couldn't wait. "Are you on Göring's staff?"

"No!" she emphatically replied, showing indignation. "I work for B&V. I told you that. I'm only copiloting Göring's plane—"

"I thought you said you were the stand-in copilot?"

"Please let me finish. I'm flying Göring around until his regular copilot gets out of the hospital. But yes, for now I'm the pilot. When that fat pig saw me he made me the pilot. Don't worry, it's only until B&V gives me my new assignment. Then it's bye-bye Göring—Okay."

Shit, Kammler wasn't kidding. You'll be the instructor.

Karl decided to wait to tell her about her "new assignment."

"My brother, Dirk was killed in the Battle of Britain." She became teary-eyed, having mentioned her brother's name. "Against my parents' wishes he enlisted in the Royal Air Force. Many of our boys did after Hitler marched into Poland. I hate being in Germany, but they won't let me go back to Switzerland because of what I do at B&V."

"Do you still have anything to do with a huge flying-boat prototype, the BV 238?"

Anna was stunned. "No! But how do you know about the BV 238? My boss kept it so hush hush. Only a handful of people even know it exists. The first prototype wasn't supposed to be ready until sometime in the spring of 1944. I was the test pilot for the maiden flight. Then everything came to a halt." Anna's eyes grew big. "I don't know where it is now. So no, I don't have anything to do with the program. You're scaring me Karl! Should I be scared?"

"Shit!" he exclaimed. "Sorry, but this really complicates things. You're the only one at B&V who knows how to fly the thing?"

"No," she said. "I'm the only one B&V trusted to fly it. It's a monster. It's huge. It's either the hardest or close to the hardest airplane I've ever flown. Why?"

"Damn! I was afraid you'd say that," Karl said. "Look, it's complicated, so for now let's just wash up and have a great dinner. Just don't drink too much. I want you to be clearheaded because afterwards I need to tell you some things. When you hear them, you might not want to have anything else to do with me."

Anna bit her lip. "You're really scaring me, Karl!"

"I'm scaring myself."

Their dinner was a tense affair. Efforts to amuse each other with small talk failed miserably.

Once the two returned to their suite, Karl locked the door, took off his jacket, and loosened his tie. Anna approached him from behind, threw her arms around him, and placed her head against his back.

"What's this all about, Karl? Please tell me everything is going to be Okay." Her voice was soft and shallow. "I was afraid throughout dinner and I don't even know what's frightening me."

Karl reached inside his jacket pocket. He pulled out a battered envelope containing a letter.

"Anna, read this," he said, handing her the tattered letter. "This is how Germany collapsed around myself and my family."

12 July 1941

Dear Frau Strassburg,

I am a neighbor and a friend of Liesl and Konrad Brandt. They gave me your address in the event something should ever happen to them. As you may or may not know, the Gestapo took the Brandts away when they returned to their home, the evening it burnt down with your two daughters inside of it. While no one dares mention this, moments before the fire started the same three men, who were seen taking the Brandts away, were the same men who came out of their house before the fire started.

The afternoon before the fire, I talked to both your daughters when they came back to the Brandts' after your little daughter, Elsa, played with some of her friends in the park. I noticed Elsa was wearing some sort of Jewish necklace around her neck, and when I asked your older daughter, Karin, about it she said one of the little girls Elsa was playing with gave it to her. I think that might have been the reason the Gestapo went to the Brandts' home. Someone must have reported seeing a little Jewish girl at the Brandts' that wasn't registered. The Brandts have never been seen since they were taken away. Please don't contact me about any of this, as I fear for my safety. If my husband found out I wrote this letter to you, he would be furious. As a mother myself, I could not do otherwise. I'm so sorry for your loss.

Alfreda Huber

Anna looked up, her eyes streaming with tears. "Oh, Karl, now I understand why you avoided talking about your sisters when we spoke about our families."

Karl told Anna when 'it' happened, his sister, Karin, was twenty-eight years old and engaged to be married to a man named Alex, a lieutenant in the *Kriegsmarine.*

"I used to tease Karin about her being a spinster before her engagement."

Karl, having a tough time holding back tears, explained that his four-year-old sister, Elsa, was a late-in-life surprise for his parents. Elsa, Karl fondly remembered, always tried to act grown-up when he was on leave from the *Fallschirmjägers*.

"I wish now I had paid more attention to her," he confided to Anna. "I often thought of her as a pest. She always would hang around me, chattering, wanting to play games with her dolls." Memories washed over him of Elsa climbing up on his lap, tickling her, and making her laugh, as only a little girl can.

Karl's voice cracked. Anna held his hand. Using the back of it, she wiped away some of her tears. After taking in a deep breath, Karl continued, "The summer before Karin's wedding, my mother thought it would be good for Karin to get away—to broaden her horizons, so to speak, before settling down to married life with Alex. Our cousins, Liesl and Konrad Brandt, the ones mentioned in the letter, were delighted to have Karin and Elsa visit them. They didn't have children of their own to fawn over."

Karl paused again to collect his thoughts and control his emotions.

"I was home when 'it' happened. We hadn't heard from Karin in more than a week, so my father called the Brandts. When he couldn't reach them, he and I went to Munich. We saw what happened to the house—the fire. We asked neighbors if they knew anything. No one told us a thing. Everyone said, 'Talk to the authorities.' We did, and nothing happened. Absolutely nothing."

Karl's remorse was turning to tears of anger.

"At that point my father contacted Willie, my mother's cousin. Willie is the Reich's Postmaster General, a good friend of Hitler, a member of the Führer's inner circle. He looked into the matter. After a few days, Willie told my father to talk to the Nazi civilian district commander in Munich. That moron," Karl said, his voice trembling with anger, "couldn't even tell us where my sisters were buried. Do you know what that damn son of a bitch told us? 'These things happen in wartime.' That's what he said. 'These things happen in wartime.'"

"My father couldn't—he wouldn't—accept that. He found the coroner who performed the autopsies on my sisters. At first he was reluctant to say anything. But he finally told my father that Karin had several broken bones in her face and that those injuries didn't have anything to do with the fire."

"What about—" Anna started to ask.

"Rape?" Karl asked. "The coroner said he couldn't tell. Thank god little Elsa was untouched." Karl, clearing his throat, explained that they were unable to discover anything about the Brandts—what happened to them or their whereabouts. "Those pigs," he fumed, "whoever did this thought they were Jewish, and since Dachau is only a few kilometers away—"

"What's Dachau?" she asked.

"Dachau is something Himmler and his SS swine dreamed up when they were having a bad day. I'll tell you all about Dachau and Himmler's 'The Final Solution' later."

Eventually, Karl talked to Anna about his mother. How she blamed herself for suggesting that Karin go on holiday. That she never recovered from the shock of losing Karin and Elsa. How his father talked to her doctors and decided it was best for them to move to St. Gallen in Switzerland since his mother is Swiss and her family and girlhood friends live in St. Gallen.

"Has your mother gotten any better?"

"The last letter I received from my father, which was a while back, seemed to indicate she is improving. But the doctors were very, very cautious."

Anna, trying to boost Karl's crestfallen spirits, optimistically said he might see the Brandts after the war. Karl walked over to the fireplace. He placed another log on the grate and stirred up the ashes.

"Anna—the Brandts are dead—or they soon will be."

The rejuvenated fire did little to stem the chill running through Anna's body.

"Remember what I said a few moments ago about Himmler and his Final Solution. Here's what's happening throughout Germany and the occupied territories to Jews, political dissidents, gypsies, anyone the SS deems to be 'impure'—young, old, rich, poor, it doesn't matter. Millions are being shipped in railroad cars, as if they were cattle, to internment camps all over Germany and the occupied countries. The night we bumped into each other at the hotel, I had just come from giving a presentation. But before I spoke, Himmler was wrapping up his presentation. That's when I heard what these bastards were doing, the Final Solution."

Anna was horrified.

"Karl, there must be some mistake. This is the twentieth century. Things like that don't happen. The Nazis can't be doing this. Germany is a civilized country."

Karl faced Anna.

"The people they're killing—the Jews and all the others—well, the Nazis are confiscating their homes, investments, art, jewelry—everything they own. If any of these people are unable to work at these camps, they're gassed. Once they're dead, their dental work is removed before their bodies are cremated en masse, then the remaining corpses are bulldozed into mass graves.

"Kammler, my boss, redesigned the ovens to accommodate twelve thousand cremations a day. Himmler was voicing concerns—complaints from the people who live near the camps—about the smell."

"The smell?" Anna seemed puzzled. Then it hit her. "Oh my god, Karl, you mean!"

"Exactly!"

Karl walked over to the edge of the bed. He sat down beside Anna.

"Perhaps I should start at the beginning," he somberly said.

"Like most young Germans who grew up after the Great War, I felt my country was humiliated and oppressed under the terms of the armistice, the Treaty of Versailles. My family was fortunate. It had investments outside Germany when the Reichsmark plummeted. Most Germans weren't that lucky. People were pushing wheelbarrows of valueless banknotes to stores for just a few groceries. When the Nazis came to power, all that changed—almost. I thought it was a miracle. My father, on the other hand, thought it was a disaster. I accepted the Nazis. I chose not to be concerned with the obvious. Like so many others, I thought it would pass. I saw the average German, proud once again to be German. I dismissed what I found distasteful about the Nazis. I thought everything I disliked about them would go away as soon as Germany was back on her feet."

"What about the singling out of the Jews and Communists?" Anna asked.

"At first they seemed to be unfounded rumors. Jews were loyal Germans; they fought against the Allies in the Great War. Sure, a few Communist agitators were placed in 'protective custody.' But visits by the Gestapo to people's homes in the middle of the night, none of that could be true. And if any of it were true, it would only be for a few months until order was restored. After all, Germany was *the* leader in the sciences and the humanities. As you said, 'this is the twentieth century.' Germany is a 'civilized' country."

"What about the annexation of Austria in 1938?" Anna asked.

"My father saw it for what it was—a power grab," Karl replied. "I viewed it as a German-speaking country becoming part of a German-speaking union. Even when we began marching through Europe, I truly believed we were liberators. It was our divine destiny to build an empire under German enlightenment to protect Europe from the horrors of Communism and the Soviet Union. When other countries didn't stop us from annexing Austria and the Sudetenland, I thought—or wanted to think—we had their support."

"Silence amounts to consent," Anna said in a hushed voice.

"Exactly! So I joined the *Fallschirmjägers* to serve my country, to help guide Europe into another age of enlightenment—a German Renaissance destroying European colonialism. Even if that meant fighting a humane, short war, a fast war, like it was turning out to be. First Poland, then France, a new way of fighting, the blitzkrieg, no more prolonged wars like the Great War. No more having men slugging it out in trenches for a few hundred yards of land a week. At the time, it seemed the right thing to do. God forgive me. I killed many in the service of my country only to find out how evil she'd become."

Karl laughed bitterly.

"In the process I became a Hero of Hitler's Reich, which really isn't Germany. And now the Reich—or Germany, whichever you prefer—has a new weapon, two of them, in fact, and that's the other thing I need to talk to you about."

But, before Karl confided details of Germany's biggest wartime secret to Anna, he had to learn more about her—much more about her. The questions he posed were painful to ask. They were brutally personal and bluntly political. They probed Anna's character and loyalties. For example, how do you ask the woman you love if she's a spy, working for Kammler?

Anna was shocked—and more than a trifle insulted—by Karl's interrogation. Yes, she admitted, her employer Blohm & Voss was contributing to Germany's war effort. But, she passionately argued she had no choice. She either worked for B&V or she'd earn a one-way ticket to a camp for aliens.

Tears wetted her eyes and face. She unleashed a tirade about how she hated the war—all the fighting, all the death, all of the destruction. Anna hated the Nazis. She said Hitler and Company turned her stomach. Anna despised Göring and all of his groping, gluttony, and unabashed hunger for power. Anna said she hated serving as Göring's copilot. Anna's body started to shake when Karl asked her if she was spying on him under orders from Kammler. Her face flushed. She started to move her arm and open hand, but stopped. No matter how much she was angered by this conversation with Karl, she simply couldn't slap him.

"Spy for Kammler? Are you crazy? I'm ashamed that I even know who he is."

Anna was emotionally spent. Karl rushed to her side; holding her in his arms, he caressed her. Their eyes were blurry with tears. They crouched together sobbing on the floor.

"I'm sorry, I'm so, so sorry," he whispered. "I didn't mean to hurt you. I'd never intentionally hurt you. But, I had to know. I had to know if I could trust you."

"So what's the verdict? Do you trust me?"Anna asked in a soft, emotionless voice.

Karl gently kissed her on the lips. "Yes."

Emotionally drained, Anna had cried her eyes dry, but Karl wasn't finished. He had more to tell her. The growing bond he felt for Anna compelled him to share with her his biggest secret. Karl's growing hatred of the Nazis had reached a crescendo.

"Because of all this—and much more—I've decided to stop them from doing more harm."

"What are you talking about?"

He hesitated. "I have to stop these 'wonder weapons' from being used. But now that I've met you, I also want to live."

"Karl, I can't lose you."

He hesitated again, this time the pause was longer. "The one thing I can't do is endanger—you." Karl explained what the Reich's "wonder weapons" were. He spoke in great detail about the bombs, Hitler, The Committee, Kammler, Houtermans, Baron von Ardenne, and the laboratories at Lichterfelde-Ost. His monologue reached its climax when he described the two targets in the States: Wall Street and Boulder Dam.

Anna was mute, unable to utter a word; her mind was churning after listening to Karl's shocking account of Nazi affairs. Finally, she mustered her thoughts.

"What I don't understand is why you were the one they chose to pick the targets? No offense, but you're just a Major."

"They chose me because of my science background, I know what these bombs can do. Where they'd do the most harm. And most important—I'm expendable."

"So, Hitler or Kammler would have fired you if they didn't like your recommendations, so what? You'd have been out of all this madness."

"Just one little problem, Anna, no one gets fired knowing what I know. If Hitler hadn't liked what I told him, Kammler would have seen to it I disappeared like my friend, Rolf. Besides, at the time, I couldn't think of a better way to sabotage the project than to stay involved with it."

"And because Hitler liked what he heard when you made your presentation, you're stuck?"

"Exactly."

Suddenly terrible thoughts flashed through Anna's mind. Her eyes opened wide. A knot formed in the pit of her stomach. "What if the Americans, with all their science and technology, are developing similar weapons? What if they plan to use them against us—against Germany? Do you think the Americans know about Germany's 'wonder weapons?' Maybe you could just warn them. Let them take it from there."

Karl squelched Anna's desperate idea pointing out he didn't have the contacts needed to warn the Americans. And even if he did, who'd believe him? He wasn't someone known to be involved with Heisenberg and the *Uranverein*. It was a matter of credibility. He acknowledged the Americans might be working on similar weapons, but he doubted they'd use them against Germany unless the Reich struck first. He also didn't think the Americans needed the bomb to defeat Germany. But Japan was a totally different matter, especially if Tokyo refused to surrender and the Americans had to invade the home islands.

"An invasion of the Japanese home islands could cost the Americans a million lives. Under those circumstances, they'd use nuclear weapons, if they had them. Remember, Anna, just one of those super bombs can destroy a medium-size city."

Anna was curious about how the Reich was able to develop the bomb in such secrecy. Karl explained the Reich had two programs: the one under Heisenberg and the *Uranverein*, which the Allies knew about, and Kammler's program, the one they knew nothing about. Kammler had compartmentalized his program so that only The Committee and fewer than twenty others knew it existed.

"Two of my closest friends, Rolf Muller and Fritz O'Gorsky, risked their lives to get the ore Houtermans used to build his bombs. One is dead. The other has been missing for months. We served together in the *Fallschirmjägers*. Both were good soldiers, good Germans."

"Are you sure that Kammler's the one behind yours friend's death?"

"Yes," Karl said, rage building in his voice. "Back in Speer's office, when we were planning how to get the bomb to the dam, I mentioned that Fritz had been killed in an accident. I didn't say what *kind* of an accident. Kammler piped up and said, 'Traffic in Berlin is so bad.' Who knows how he did away with Rolf?"

Anna shuddered. "First, your friend O'Gorsky is killed, and Muller is missing. You're next in line, aren't you?"

Karl didn't answer. She understood. He didn't want to worry her.

"What haven't you told me, and don't tell me there isn't something else? Something occurred during the week besides what happened to your two friends that's causing you to act the way you are."

Karl said nothing. He looked away.

"What about the drive to the inn?" she asked. "All we talked about was our families. I kept dropping hint after hint for you to pull over. I let my skirt creep up to the tops of my stockings. All you did was keep on driving. And that wonderful romantic dinner we just had?" Anna sarcastically asked. "Twice I stuck my toe between your legs under the table hoping to take your mind off what happened and both times you pulled away. I just wanted to lighten up your mood. But there's something else. Please tell me everything—please.

"Remember when I asked you all those questions about Göring? I asked what you did at B&V, if you had any connections with that prototype giant flying boat, the BV 238."

"Oh, no!" she cried. "You mean—"

"Yes, Anna, that's the plane I'll be using for the dam mission."

"*You'll* be using?"

"Yes Anna, I'm the mission commander and you'll be instructing me along with the crew to fly the damn thing. That's why no one—absolutely no one—can know how we feel about each other. If anyone suspected we're lovers and told Kammler, that evil son of a bitch would hold you hostage, knowing I would do anything—and I mean anything—to keep you safe.

"So starting now," Karl said passionately, "let's hold each other and cry until we have no more tears. Then, if you're up to it, let's make love because it'll be the last time we do it—for a long time—maybe—"

Karl didn't finish.

"Maybe—never—you were about to say, weren't you?" Anna said, finishing the sentence.

"Yes, Anna, maybe never. Starting tomorrow we've got to convince everyone the night at the Platterhof and tonight were nothing more than two people having some wartime fun. No deep feelings for one other, just two people having some fun."

15.

Three weeks prior to Kammler, Speer, and Strassburg's scheduled visit to Peenemünde, the Baltic island where the Reich's "Vengeance" weapons were developed and tested, half a squadron of US Army Air Force P-38, twin tail-boom Lightning fighters, previously assigned to North Africa, was secretly transferred to a base in Northern Scotland.

Two of the squadron's top pilots—Jack "Jockstrap" Mahoney and Wilhelm "Rottweiler" Schultz (both Captains)—sat bitching and moaning in one of the base's recently built and unheated Quonset huts in the land where "real men wear skirts" (better known as kilts), while waiting to be briefed by the unit's XO (Executive Officer).

"So, Rot," Mahoney began in jest, "I take it you're looking forward to visiting death and destruction on some unsuspecting pickle-helmet member of your goose-stepping clan?"

Mahoney's "clan" remark referred to Schultz's German ancestry, the "pickle-helmet" to the headgear worn by German soldiers in World War I. The "goose-stepping" alluded to the marching style of the Third Reich's army during parades and reviews.

"Unlike your Mick ancestors," Schultz replied, "who came to America because they couldn't get rid of some potato bug, mine came to the US in style, tossing their cookies over the side of some stinking square-rigger. But once their feet touched the New World, they got the lead out and helped Washington cross the Delaware."

"Now that we've gotten that bullshit out of the way, what's your take on why only half the squadron's here in this freezing tropical paradise?"

"To begin with, Jock, I doubt if we're here—"

Before Schultz could finish the squadron's XO abruptly walked in, ending the Schultz-Mahoney banter.

"Please, don't bother getting up on my account," the XO deadpanned with a mock sarcastic tone in his voice, "even though I outrank you two clowns. Who knows, the way you two are adding swastikas to the port side of your Lightnings— shooting down Göring's finest—I might soon be working for you guys."

After some lighthearted ribbing, the XO told the two "double aces" why they were in Scotland.

"Boys, the Mighty Eighth is having trouble continuing its unescorted daylight raids over Germany. The new P-51s you've heard so much about won't be here until March. With belly tanks, they'll be able to fly with the B-17s anywhere in the skies over Germany and back to England. But, in the meantime, we need to keep Göring's Krauts looking over their shoulders. That's where you two—and those other guys come in."

"Gee, boss, it's not every day you're told you're doing a good job, but soon you'll be replaced," Mahoney wisecracked.

The XO ignored the wisecrack.

"In order for you and those other bums to stick it to Fatso Göring's Luftwaffe we're equipping your Lightnings with droppable fuel tanks, similar to the ones that will be on the Mustangs. We're also upgrading your Allison engines, so they won't crap out on you in this shitty weather."

The XO abruptly changed the direction of the conversation, a ploy to allow what he had just told the two hotshot pilots to sink in.

"By the way, Schultz, I know why they call you Rottweiler because you're such a tenacious bastard in the air. But Mahoney, what's with the Jockstrap thing?"

Schultz laughed. "Next time Jack's in the shower, pop in—you'll have your answer."

16.

The sky over Berlin in the hours just after sunrise on February 1, 1943, was gray and bleak. The mood of Hitler, his Generals, and members of The Committee matched the sky. The previous day, Generalfeldmarschall Frederic von Paulus surrendered what was left of his Sixth Army to the Soviets at Stalingrad. The battle cost Germany more than two hundred thousand men. Allied air raids on the German capital added to the deep gloom.

Kammler, Speer, and Strassburg were departing for Peenemünde. Their early morning flight minimized chances of encountering British bombers returning to England after nighttime raids and a few American bombers going out on daylight missions. More and more fighters, bombers, and aircrews were rolling off US assembly lines. At the same time, the Reich was running out of trained pilots. Göring knew it was only a matter of time before his Luftwaffe could no longer defend the skies he once boasted as being impenetrable by the Reich's enemies. Under these stark conditions, Hitler ordered Göring to assign first-line fighters to escort all unarmed transports.

Kammler and Strassburg—waiting to board the flight to Peenemünde—didn't clap when they heard the announcement that two Messerschmitt Bf109E fighters would be flying escort duty.

"What a great way," Strassburg whispered to Kammler, "to attract the cat to the mouse."

"Yes, Major," Kammler, replied shaking his head in agreement. "They might just as well have painted 'Here We Are' in big letters on our aircraft. The two fighters flying escort are sure to attract trouble—not keep it away. The way the numbers are stacking up against us, every VIP flight will soon need not just two but an armada of fighters for genuine protection. Translation, we could be fucked!"

One by one they boarded the strange-looking aircraft. The head steward, who welcomed them, said the airplane was the prototype for the Luftwaffe's first heavy bomber, the Ju 89 V3, but the German Air Ministry canceled the project. Subsequently, the bomber was converted to a transport, the Ju 90.

The trio settled into their posch leather seats, buckled their seat belts, and hoped for a smooth and uneventful flight to Peenemünde. Kammler attacked his ever-present pile of paperwork. Speer and Strassburg chatted about Peenemünde. Strassburg knew little about Germany's rocketry research. Speer, always willing to play the role of teacher, gave Strassburg an impromptu history lesson.

Peenemünde, at least for the time being, was the site of *all* Nazi rocket research, development, and production, a tempting target for Allied bombers. The plan was once the underground cities at Nordhausen and Bleicherode were completed, Kammler would move everything out of Peenemünde and into those two cities. Manufacturing and assembly would move to Nordhausen and Bleicherode, theoretical work to Garmish-Partenkirchen, and wind tunnel testing to Kochel.

Logistics aside, Speer briefed Strassburg about the history of German rocket research, which began after World War I. Triggered by restrictions in the Treaty of Versailles—restrictions barring Germany from having a government-sponsored aircraft and rocket industry—Hitler, in 1935, decided to secretly support all such work. When the program became public, it became part of the *Heereswaffenamt*, or the weapons office, which established various subdivisions for work on different types of rockets.

Kummersdorf was the first rocket testing area. Generalmajor Walter Dornberger was put in charge and hired two hundred fifty of Germany's best and brightest young scientists, charged with developing rockets capable of delivering payloads of explosives, impossible for conventional artillery and manned aircraft. When they outgrew Kummersdorf in 1937, everything moved to Heeresversuchsstelle, the army testing ground at Peenemünde on the Baltic island of Usedom at the mouth of the Oder River on the Polish border.

"How much did all that cost?" Strassburg asked Speer.

Kammler piped in, "Well over one hundred twenty million new marks, Major."

Kammler, always interested in ways to showcase his knowledge, joined the conversation. He pointed out that Peenemünde is immense, housing more than two thousand scientists. The site was chosen because it looked like any other sleepy German coastal village from the air and because of its distance from Germany's southern industrial areas. On the north side of the island was a small landing strip, the main testing area, and launch pads. The rocket production plants lay along the coast, and the south end housed staff and military personnel.

The ground fog was beginning to lift as Kammler rambled on about Peenemünde. The assistant steward was busy taking breakfast orders from the passengers. The Ju 90's four 830-horsepower engines turned over, belching blue smoke until all motors were purring nicely. Alongside the transport, the two Messerschmitt Bf109E escorts revved their engines.

The three-plane formation took off and climbed above the clouds. The head steward and his assistant—both SS—began serving breakfast to the seventeen passengers. They ate off fine china and used highly polished sterling silver flatware.

The seats, like those on a train, were designed to face in any direction. Strassburg faced forward, sitting by himself, facing Kammler and Speer. In between bites of breakfast, he occasionally looked out of the planes port window.

We must be at about nine thousand five hundred feet above the cloud cover, Strassburg thought, *heading north. The Messerschmitts were holding steady at thirteen thousand feet.*

"Relax, Karl, everything's fine," Speer remarked. "Look, you're on the cover of *Signal*, looking like a movie star. Your parents will be proud." *Signal* was the German army's propaganda magazine.

Strassburg ignored Speer's flattering comment.

"Listen to the Minister, Major," Kammler said, looking up from his paperwork. "Now that we're above the cloud cover, our escorts can see for miles. Relax, there's nothing to worry about."

"Jockstrap, this is Rottweiler. Over."

"Rott, this is Jock. Over."

"See that smidgen a little over three and a half miles off your eleven o'clock, approximately fifty-two hundred feet below us? Looks to me like two of a kind escorting one butt-ugly looking bitch. All three holding tight, about six five zero above the cloud cover. Over."

"I'm seeing something, Rott, but my peepers aren't as good as yours. Hold on! Got 'em! What's the plan? Over."

"We go up two more thousand and come out of the rays with guns ablazing. You take out the starboard douche bag. I'll plant the port guy. Then we'll take turns hammering that ugly bitch they're escorting. Over."

"The old four 'F'? Over."

"You got it, Jock! Find 'em. Fix 'em. Fuck 'em. Forget 'em. Over."

"Sounds like a plan. Jock out."

"Sorry, Minister," Strassburg said, apologizing to Speer for removing his food tray so fast he almost spilled it. "Something just caught my eye."

"Sit back, Major, and relax," Kammler ordered.

"I thought I saw a—" was all Strassburg managed to utter before their port Bf109E escort peeled off, trailing smoke, before exploding.

Flipping open his seat-belt clasp, Strassburg quickly stood up and screamed, "Get out of your seats! Now! Lay flat in the aisle we're under attack!"

The Ju 90 transport banked hard to starboard and then reversed direction, banking violently to port. The next few seconds gave the passengers a false sense of hope, as the aircraft resumed level flight. But then the transport rolled back to the starboard followed by a steep dive toward the clouds, four thousand five hundred feet below.

The passengers bounced around the cabin like rag dolls.

Strassburg crawled on all fours to the cockpit. Once again the plane leveled off. Seconds passed. Strassburg was about to reach up, grab the handle, and open the door to the cockpit. Something inside him said to stay down and hug the floor. Then it happened. The first, second, and third propeller blades came off the number two starboard engine's spinner. Pieces of blades tore through the transport's thin aluminum skin, shredding the airframe and sending hundreds of large and small shards of metal through the exotic hardwood paneling lining the cabin's starboard interior wall.

Some of the passengers began standing upright, thinking the worst was over. Legs and arms were instantly amputated. One passenger's head was split down the middle like when a sharp knife splits open a watermelon. Those who weren't standing—the fortunate ones—received milder injuries. The truly lucky passengers were just bruised.

Death infected the cockpit.

The pilot, slumped over the controls, was missing his head—almost. It was barely attached to his body by a tendon. It kept bouncing up and down as if it were a ball attached to a paddle by a rubber band, someone's sick version of paddleball. His heart still was pumping blood out the top of his neck. His brain hadn't told it to stop.

The copilot was barely alive. Buckled into his seat he seemed to be looking down, his eyes wide open. Blood continued to flow out of stumps, where moments before there were legs. The man was in shock.

The navigator, also dead, was lying on the cockpit floor, blocking the entrance to the flight deck. Small pieces of metal had assaulted his body, shredding virtually every major organ.

The pilotless aircraft was back in a dive. If the descent continued, the already shattered airframe would break apart before it crashed into the ground.

The Ju 90's abrupt downward momentum flung Strassburg forward; he hit the cockpit door so forcefully the door popped off its hinges, propelling him into the flight deck.

What Strassburg saw would have made those unfamiliar with the horrors of combat and bloodshed lose the contents of their stomach, bowel, and bladder. Strassburg, a combat veteran, had become hardened to such scenes. He'd witnessed too much death and destruction to slow him down from doing what had to be done. He sprang into action like an automaton. He popped the quick release on the beheaded pilot's chair harness and pushed his lifeless body onto the cockpit's bloody floor. Stepping over the body, Strassburg slid into the dead pilot's blood-soaked seat. With all his might, he pulled back on the yoke, hoping the controls were sufficiently functional to get the aircraft's nose up, ending its death dive. Strassburg was surrounded by an array of broken dials, loose wires, and wayward electrical sparks. The controls were sluggish, but they responded to his pulling back on the yoke.

His immediate problem was getting rid of the now-dead copilot in the starboard seat. A piece of flying metal damaged the mechanism that kept that chair upright. Without that gadget, the copilot's body was slumped forward on the controls, making it virtually impossible for Strassburg to continue his Herculean effort to right the aircraft.

"General!" Strassburg yelled over his shoulder. "Get in here! I need your help, *now!*"

Strassburg knew Kammler was a pilot.

The dive was sufficiently steep that it created a partial vacuum that sucked oxygen out of the fires ravaging the Ju 90's two starboard engines. With two of the aircraft's four engines running, even poorly, chances for survival leaped from impossible to a "definite maybe."

Kammler entered the cockpit as the aircraft plunged to three thousand feet. He immediately recognized the problem. He released the copilot's harness and pulled the dead, legless man out of his seat. Kammler climbed into the copilot's position and started pulling back on the yoke, assisting Strassburg in bringing the Ju 90 out of its dive.

"Nice going, Major, I'll take it from here. I didn't know you could fly."

"I can't."

Strassburg checked the navigator's pulse as he left the cockpit. There was none. The man's skin already was turning the grayish color of death.

When Strassburg entered the main cabin, those passengers who could began clapping.

"Damn it, man," Speer said with sincerity, "if it hadn't been for you, we'd all be dead. You're a hero, Karl, a fucking hero. Where did you learn to fly like that?"

"The General asked me the same thing. The answer is: I can't. But during Operation Merkur, I was forced to take over the controls of a Ju 52 Iron Annie transport. The difference between that situation and this one is that both the pilot and copilot were conscious and told me what to do."

"Oh my god!" Speer gasped. "You're bleeding. You're covered with blood."

"I'm fine, the blood's from the pilot and the copilot.

"Will they live?"

"They're dead."

"Who's flying the aircraft?" Speer asked with a tinge of panic in his voice.

"Kammler, and let's pray it holds together until he lands—and those fighters don't make more passes."

Strassburg ordered the passengers to get back into their seats, help the wounded do the same, and buckle up.

Kammler started his landing approach, hoping the farm field ahead was devoid of tree stumps and other obstacles hidden by the snow. He killed both port engines thirty seconds before landing. He knew if he botched the landing the nose of the aircraft would go down into the earth and with the propeller blades on two of the engines still spinning they would shear off their spinners. If that happened, the landing would be a repeat of what happened minutes before at nineteen thousand feet. The blades would come crashing into the aircraft's fuselage.

Strassburg's eyes were glued to the window, looking for signs of the two Allied fighters that had caused the mess they were facing.

Kammler did a superb job of landing the aircraft; especially since the starboard landing gear, damaged during the aerial confrontation, buckled the moment the wheel touched the snow-covered frozen ground. Another wave of anxiety careened through the passengers as the starboard wing dropped, digging into the snowy earth when the landing gear crumpled. Finally the aircraft slid to a stop.

Danger was still with them. Strassburg gave a flurry of orders for the passengers to scurry out of the crippled aircraft and tend to those in need of assistance. With everyone off the listing Ju 90, except Kammler and the steward, Strassburg yelled to the steward, "Give me the key to the arms locker!"

Kammler, departing the cockpit, saw Strassburg insert the key into the locker.

"What the hell are you doing, Major?" Kammler screamed, straining the veins in his neck. "Get off this aircraft before those fighters return. That's an order!"

Strassburg ignored Kammler's order. He shoved a 7.92-mm MG34 machine gun along with a saddle-drum magazine into the arms of the screaming General.

"Take this with you!" Strassburg ordered. "I'll meet you at the tree line. Your life depends on doing exactly what I'm telling you to do. Now go! Give me your dagger."

Kammler was slow to respond. Strassburg, impatient, pulled the dagger from its sheath and jumped off the aircraft. He used the blade to puncture holes in the Ju 90's fuel tank before following Kammler to the tree line. Out-of-breath Strassburg threw the dagger, sticking it between Kammler's feet.

"Thanks for the dagger," he bluntly said. "Now get down. I hope this works."

Dropping down behind the MG34, he inserted the saddle-drum, cocked the weapon, and fired short bursts into where the aviation fuel was leaking from the Ju 90's ruptured fuel tank. Nothing happened.

Strassburg shouted at the steward, "The damn magazine was marked white phosphorous. How come the rounds aren't cooking off the aviation fuel?"

"Keep firing, sir, they will," the steward assured him. "Only this time put the WP rounds in the wing ahead of where the fuel's leaking out."

That did it.

The aircraft exploded like it was an ammunition dump hit by an artillery round. Everyone was hugging the ground under the cover of the pines when the explosion occurred. Even though the shock wave passed harmlessly over their heads, everyone felt the heat from the blast on their faces and gloveless hands.

Thirty seconds later, as a lion is drawn to the sound of its prey, Strassburg and the others heard the unmistakable guttural hum of two aircraft engines coming from somewhere above them in the clouds.

"Look, there it is," the steward whispered, as if the pilot of the incoming Lightning might hear him.

The clouds started to part. Out of the sun, a speck appeared. As the fighter came closer, it flew parallel to the wood line, no more than twenty feet off the ground, speed well over three hundred and fifty miles per hour. The pilot was cocooned in the command pod set between two engines, and the trademark twin tail of the Lightning brought gasps from the mouths of the people on the ground.

"What in god's name is that?" the steward asked. "It's way too big to be a fighter."

"Oh, it's a fighter," Speer said. "It's an American P-38 Lightning. Our pilots in North Africa nicknamed it *Der Gabelschwanzer Teufel*, 'the Fork-Tailed Devil.'"

Moments after the Lightning's flyover people who could started to stand up.

"Stay down and don't move," Kammler screamed. "It's not over."

Kammler, like Strassburg, realized from the way their two fighter escorts and transport were manhandled there must have been two enemy aircraft in on the kills. Since one just made a recon of the crash site, the other wouldn't be far behind.

"Crafty bastards," Kammler mumbled to Strassburg, scanning the sky for the second Lightning.

"Yes," Strassburg murmured, looking right and left to make sure everyone remained on the ground motionless.

"The first one flies by, doesn't shoot unless he's shot at," he explained. "You think it's all over. Feeling confident you've outfoxed him because he's left the area, you come out of your hiding place. As soon as you start to stan—"

Strassburg stopped talking. He pointed. "Look, in the distance, there's the second one. He's coming in low like the first one."

"Everyone, be still!" Kammler shouted. "Keep your heads down."

Speer and Strassburg stood up after the second Lightning passed overhead. Strassburg had just started checking the condition of the wounded when Kammler grabbed his shoulder, spun him around, and screamed, "What the hell did you think you were doing, pushing that machine gun in my arms, taking my dagger, and then throwing it between my feet? I could have you court-martialed."

Things had been simmering between the two ever since Strassburg started working for Kammler. Now, their mutual resentments boiled over. Strassburg stood his ground; he didn't back down.

"How about I was saving your ass," he barked. "Will that do, General?"

Kammler was livid, speechless.

One of the Ju 90 passengers who was ambulatory approached Kammler and bluntly said, "General, what the Major did was absolutely brilliant. He didn't have time to explain anything. By causing the fuel to explode, that ugly beast that shot us down thought we all died. That's why he flew by never strafing the area. The American didn't think there were any survivors."

Hearing the outburst everyone started looking at Kammler.

Shit! Kammler thought. *Damn his ass, he's right, of course. Now I look stupid in front of all these people.*

In the meantime, the steward dispatched his assistant to a farmhouse across the field, seeking medical help and transportation. While that was happening, the steward accompanied Kammler on a search, hoping to find at least one of the BF109 pilots—alive.

An hour passed before the steward's assistant returned with the farmer driving a tractor that was pulling a wagon filled with straw. Everyone huddled under the straw for warmth. Soon after Kammler and the steward returned, finding no trace of the pilots or their Bf109 fighters, Kammler told the farmer to take them to the nearest town with a telephone, so he could call for assistance.

The drive took hours. Everyone aboard the wagon kept replaying in their minds what happened and how lucky they were to be alive. Hardly anyone talked. Strassburg knew that for the first few hours after experiencing the violence of warfare that sparse conversation was a natural part of the healing process. Kammler also knew that with Speer being an eyewitness to the hair-raising events they just gone through that Hitler and The Committee would be well aware of Strassburg's heroics. They also would be informed of Kammler's blunders. Hitler, a soldier in the Great

War, and Göring, a highly decorated pilot in that war, would understand the significance of Strassburg's actions. Kammler, on the other hand, was in the unenviable position of having to save face.

Kammler lay down in the straw next to Strassburg. At first he remained silent. Finally he spoke, hoping to twist his "blow-up" into something positive.

"Remember back there, when we were the last two on the transport and I ordered you to get out. Instead you disobeyed me and shoved that machine gun, along with the saddle drum, into my hands. Then you grabbed my jeweled SS General's dagger out of its sheath. For a moment I thought you were going to kill me. Never do something like that again. Because if you do," he joked, "I might have to have you shot."

Strassburg appeared not to be listening.

"I had no idea what you had in mind," Kammler continued. "Next time, if something like that happens, before you do anything, tell me what you have in mind."

Then the peace offering, "By the way, what you did was brilliant."

Kammler, thinking he'd reestablished his dominant position, waited for Strassburg to apologize.

Strassburg lay there, saying nothing, hands folded across his chest, the brim of his hat shielding the bright February sun from his eyes. Finally he turned his head. His gray-blue colored eyes, the eyes of a predator, the eyes of a wolf stared at the SS General he so vehemently despised.

This got Kammler thinking that Strassburg needed some serious attitude adjustment. Kammler was a playground bully and like most bullies when they obtain power they treat others badly, especially when people don't stand up to them. Speer was a good example of this. He ran the Ministry of Armament and had way more power than Kammler, yet Speer let Kammler belittle him and push him around, something the SS was good at.

Before Kammler continued, Strassburg spoke.

"General, if I had taken the time to explain things to you, we'd all be dead. And since I've been in similar combat situations and you haven't, situations where there's no time to talk, you either act or embrace death. You either lead—because you know how to lead—or get out of the way and let someone who can lead, lead. Have I made myself clear? That was the case with what just happened."

Kammler didn't like the way the conversation was going, but said nothing.

"So while I respect your rank, what you've achieved, and you are my boss, I'm not in the SS and I'm barely in the Luftwaffe. But I'm still a German. And as a German, I intend to do whatever is in the best interest of my country. If that means telling you, without any explanation, to take that bloody machine gun off that fucking plane and run like hell with it into the tree line, as if the devil was about to crawl up your ass, I'll tell you to do it every time."

Strassburg smiled. "By the way, General, you did a hell of a job landing that airplane. I hope Hitler gives you a medal."

Kammler was inwardly fuming, stunned, and horrified. Never before had a subordinate had the gall to lecture him.

Fuck you, Major, you know I can't replace you because our beloved Führer would never approve. Besides, I don't have the time. Even if I did have the time, who would I replace you with that Hitler would approve? You know the plan. You know how everything works. You've seen combat. You're a war hero, the ideal leader, and one of Hitler's favorites. If only Hitler hadn't personally appointed you to lead the dam mission, I would have picked someone in the SS to lead it like I've done for the Wall Street mission. You figured out which of the three countries the Reich absolutely had to get out of the war if there was any hope of victory. Your choice of targets was absolutely brilliant. Everyone knows this. Removing you, as I did Muller and O'Gorsky, never would work. So for now I'll just have to eat shit—won't I?

17.

Kammler, Speer, and Strassburg arrived at Peenemünde an hour before their late-morning meeting with Professor Hellmuth Walter, the brilliant U-boat designer. Walter was nothing like Strassburg imagined. He was taller than average, around age forty, fit, a bushy head of hair, and a walking gait of a man in his early thirties.

Walter shook Speer's hand vigorously, as if they were old friends, thinking Speer was in charge of the group since he was Minister of Armament.

"Ah, Minister Speer," he gushed, "I'm so glad to meet you. Admirals Dönitz and Raeder keep singing your praises. Of course, I have many questions. Who is this obnoxious fellow, Kammler, who had one of his assistants call and say, 'No excuses, you have to make this meeting'? Who does he think he is? He's not even an Admiral."

Strassburg stood back and smiled, barely able to keep from laughing. Kammler was about to explode.

Kammler pushed Speer out of the way. His face was inches from Walter's, when he introduced himself. "I'm the SS General whose associate called your office for this meeting. What you'll be doing is for me, not Minister Speer. And as for you asking me questions—how can I put it? — The SS doesn't answer questions. We ask them."

Walter's initial buoyant mood abruptly changed. His eyes froze on the hollowed-out eyes in the skull of the SS death's head insignia on Kammler's hat. Those horrible no-eyes stared back at him. Beads of sweat started to appear on Walter's upper lip.

The Professor was cowed. For someone who continuously talked, Walter found it impossible to say anything, let alone ask questions.

Kammler, instantly recognizing his total dominance, declared, "Good, I'm so glad we had such a quick meeting of the minds."

Walter kept sweating. Kammler kept talking.

"I'll be the one taking over your defunct Wa-201 undersea boat project," Kammler asserted, "the one in Blohm & Voss's shipyard on the island of Kuhwerder. If anyone asks about it, tell him the Ministry of Armament has commandeered it for scrap. The Ministry needs the metal and parts for other projects.

"Good, still no questions," Kammler sarcastically remarked. "Then we are off to a good start, aren't we?"

"Relax, Herr Professor," Speer interjected. "He's not going to bite you."

Walter wasn't sure about that.

Kammler told Walter what his needs—the SS's needs—were. They wanted a tug to push or pull a barge underwater from a Baltic port to the southernmost tip of South America. The barge needed to be roughly one hundred twenty-five feet long.

"And back?" Walter asked in a barely audible voice.

"Now, we weren't going to ask questions, were we, Professor?" Kammler snidely responded, dropping the "Herr." "But just this once, I'll answer you. No, it's

100

a one-way trip."

Kammler told him this because the round-trip from the U-boat pens in Helgoland, where the mission would begin, to the 1926 wreck site—one hundred-plus miles from Wall Street—was a shorter distance than sailing from Helgoland to the tip of South America.

You crafty bastard! Strassburg thought. *You intend to keep Walter in the dark about the purpose of the barge, don't you?*

Speer was confused. Unlike Strassburg he had yet to figure out Kammler's gambit.

The SS General continued "briefing" Walter, telling the Professor the barge would need to be repositioned from the horizontal to the vertical. The bow of the barge facing upward, absolutely stable no bobbing around like some—

Walter interrupted Kammler, as a precocious child would do hoping to impress his classmates and teacher. "Yes, General, I know all about Dr. Steinhoff and his brother's plan to put V-2s inside containers, tow them to a position off the English coast, and fire them at British targets. Reusable, mobile, underwater launchers are much harder for the enemy to find and destroy."

"Thank you for interrupting," Kammler whimsically replied. "You've just told me something I have no use for. Unless, of course, Himmler has put *you* in charge of this project—has he? Well, has he?"

Kammler's tone was intentionally on the verge of being confrontational. Walter was on edge. He started mopping his damp forehead with a handkerchief.

"I was just trying to—" was all Walter managed to say before Kammler cut him off.

"Just shut up! Do you ever stop talking?" Kammler snapped. "Let me finish! As I was saying, keeping it from bobbing around like some cork while we unload extremely valuable pieces of *art*. Now, do we push the damn thing, or do we pull it? That's the question, Professor, and thank you for letting me finally finish my question," Kammler growled.

"Pushing it would be best, General," Walter meekly replied. "I hope you'll consider using my revolutionary hydrogen-peroxide drive to propel the U-boat you're going to use to push the barge. The underwater and surface speeds are—" it was fast becoming a contest of interruptions, pitting Kammler against a wordy Walter—"superior to existing U-boats."

"I know all that! Stop interrupting me!" Kammler was exasperated. He was turning red and far passed the point of being amused by the quirky Professor's antics. Walter gauged Kammler's testy temperament and remained mute.

"Since you're familiar with Steinhoff's concept," Kammler curtly continued, "and you know the general length of the barge and the circumference of the barge's hull has to match that of your rusting Wa-201's hull—B&V's unfinished prototype—and will be pushed, powered by your 'fabulous engine,' so I'll leave it to you and Dr. Cranz to work out the details.

"Just remember, Walter, Dr. Cranz—not you—is the boss. If he calls me, complaining you're argumentative and a big pain in the ass, which you usually are, I will personally make sure you are part of the U-tug's ballast. Understood!"

Fear, already rising in Walter, turned to terror when Kammler leveled his next blast at the overly inquisitive scientist.

"When you leave this room an SS Major named Hoff will be your constant asshole companion. If I find out you blabbed any of this to anyone—especially Dönitz and Raeder, now or after the war—you and your entire family will regret the day all of you came out of your mothers's wombs."

The damp and growing stains of profuse perspiration in the armpits of the Walter's jacket were clear signs he understood the situation.

"And remember, Professor," Kammler barked, "the U-tug will carry a crew of forty.

"*Now*, do you have any questions?" Kammler snidely asked, smirking.

Walter ran his hand through his thick and unruly hair before answering. "No questions, General," he haltingly answered. "But just be aware there is one problem."

"Go on," Kammler replied, rolling his eyes.

Walter hesitated. "With the two mated together—the Wa-201 in back, the barge in front—it will be like a locomotive pushing a train. Once they get going, their combined mass will be hard to stop. Turns needed to evade enemy depth charges will be impossible."

Kammler said nothing. Walter expected another series of rebukes. Kammler just smiled.

"That won't be a problem, Professor" he replied. "The barge and tug won't be attacking Allied convoys. Oh and remember, the artwork inside the barge is no concern of yours. Cranz will take care of that. Just make sure your part of the project works."

"Of course, General. Of course!"

As the three left the meeting, leaving Walter to bemoan his fate, Speer wondered whether the Professor had bought the part about transporting the "artwork." Speer whispered his concern to Kammler.

"Of course, he didn't buy it," Kammler replied. Sounding miffed that Speer had even brought it up. "The man's difficult to work with, but he's not an imbecile. I just want to scare the shit out of him so he keeps his mouth shut tighter than a tick's ass."

That afternoon the three met with Dr-Ing Gerhard Cranz, doctor of engineering, in a secure conference room. Cranz, recently retired, still maintained a small office at Peenemünde. He divided his time between theoretical rocketry, his life's work, and cataloging his vast postage-stamp collection. Strassburg immediately noticed the respect Speer and Kammler showed the jovial elf-like man. Kammler never showed respect to anyone but Hitler and Himmler.

After greetings and handshakes, Cranz singled out Speer, and asked Kammler if he might have a moment or two alone with the Armament Minister. Off to one side Cranz spoke to Speer, as an aging father would talk to his son.

"You know, Albert," the retired rocket scientist began, "I haven't seen you, Margarete, or the children for over two months. I know you're busy, but I'm not go-

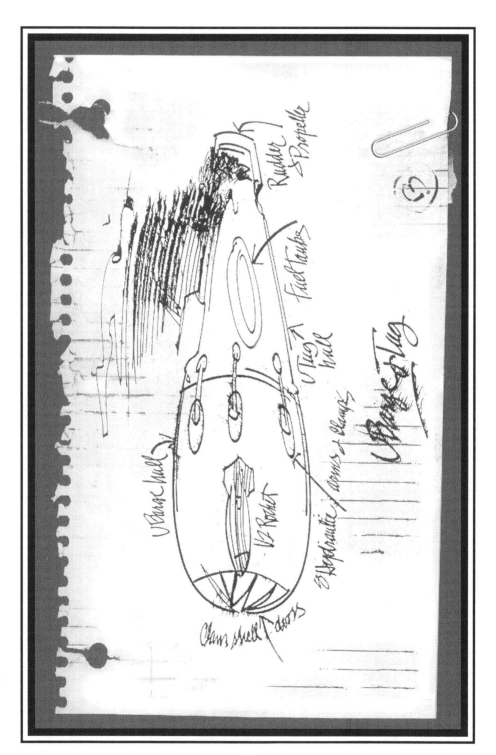

103

ing to be here forever. Make some time for an old man. See me more often, please?"

Speer hugged the old man, nodding yes.

Inside the conference room Cranz motioned the three to take seats.

"Gentlemen, we've a lot to talk about. General Kammler has done a fantastic job of explaining what you need and when you need it. As you can see by the charts, plans, sketches, and photographs on the walls, as well as my scribblings on the blackboard and the papers in front of you, we may not get out of here before nightfall."

"This is overwhelming, Dr. Cranz," Strassburg said. "Am I free to take notes? Make sketches?"

"Ask General Kammler, Major," Cranz replied. "He's the one who can say if it's okay."

Kammler nodded, giving Strassburg the green light for his notes and sketches. Cranz went on to explain the conference room they were in was designed as a vault. There were no listening devices or cameras. If they wanted they could leave their notes and papers in the room overnight. SS guards would see to it that no one entered the room during the night. Cranz got down to business. He briefly reminded the trio they weren't the first to promote the idea of placing V-2 rockets in submersible containers.

"I doubt very much," Cranz, said, smiling, while polishing his eyeglasses, "Dr. Steinhoff ever envisioned his concept being used for such an ambitious undertaking, crossing the Atlantic and using one of our V-2 rockets to deliver a nine thousand-pound nuclear bomb to Wall Street. Brilliant. Absolutely brilliant."

But something was bothering Cranz. Kammler, ever perceptive, saw a hint of reservation in the scientist's facial expression. Cranz was concerned the mission was pushing Nazi technology to its limits. Cranz noted that unless every gyro, gimbal, and a million other parts inside the rocket work absolutely perfectly together, the nine thousand-pound bomb would never reach Wall Street. Kammler liked Cranz's straightforward approach. He wasn't sugarcoating the odds.

"What I can guarantee," Cranz told the three, "is that Walter will never know the barge he's building will house a rocket. How's that?"

The three smiled.

"What you may not know, General," Cranz continued, a twinkle in his eye, "is that the Reich Air Ministry recently gave Steinhoff the go-ahead to develop his floating container concept to launch a V-2 rocket off England's south coast. There's even a code name for it, Prufstand XII. We're supposed to have a prototype by late 1944."

Kammler told Cranz what the RLM wanted had absolutely nothing to do with the Wall Street mission–to keep the two projects separate. Kammler cautioned *their* project was to remain "absolutely secret" and completely divorced from Prufstand XII.

"If anyone asks you about what you're doing for me," Kammler told Cranz, "have them talk to me."

Kammler reminded Cranz about the meeting he, Speer, and Strassburg had

with Walter earlier that morning, a meeting to ensure that Walter "understood the length of his tether and who was at the other end holding it." That "understanding," Kammler told Cranz, guaranteed the rocket scientist would have absolutely no trouble getting Walter to cooperate.

Kammler then faced Strassburg. "Now might be a good a time to give Dr. Cranz the sketch you did, based on what I told Walter I wanted him to do."

While Cranz studied the sketch, Kammler told him what he told Walter, about the barge carrying artwork to the tip of South America. Cranz laughed, realizing what Kammler said to Walter about the tether also applied to him. Cranz was a veteran of numerous turf battles. His scientific and diplomatic aptitudes had allowed him to hone his bureaucratic and political survival skills.

"What Walter comes up with is always amazing," he said, as if he were again in the classroom, addressing a group of graduate students. "And how the three of you saw the potential of using one of his most radical designs is absolutely brilliant. Better yet, it was a design that Dönitz had no use for. Then combining it with Steinhoff's concept, in order to get around the problem of not having a bomber capable of delivering your bomb to Wall Street, was a stroke of genius."

Cranz paused, as if getting his second wind.

"But, my friends," he said, "we'll need to have Walter make a couple of design adjustments to his Wa-201 and Steinhoff's barge concept. I'm sure General Kammler, in his own sweet way, told Walter he might have to make some modifications. Yes?"

This triggered a big laugh.

Cranz reminded the three that even on dry land, where there is no wave motion or currents, it's difficult to achieve successful rocket launches and accurate targeting. He asked them to imagine the problems associated with pushing the barge up from the seabed, opening the watertight clamshell doors in the bow, firing the rocket, and hitting Wall Street one hundred and fifty miles away.

Speer asked if Cranz thought the mission was a pipe dream.

"The mission," Cranz said, "is possible but difficult. The barge cannot move when the rocket is readied for launch, during launch, or moments after the launch."

Cranz asked the group to look at a chart tacked to a corkboard. It was a copy of the chart Speer sent him showing the position of the 1926 shipwreck, where the rocket-bearing barge would be located. Cranz described the location as perfect.

"The currents, shown on the map where the wreck is, are weak, and the ocean bottom seems relatively free from silt. That means there should be solid ground for the barge's legs to rest on and fasten the cables."

While Kammler, Cranz, and Speer demurred, Strassburg viewed the chart through a magnifying glass supplied by Cranz.

How could I have missed this? The mission will never happen. Strassburg was smiling.

"Like Dr. Cranz said," Strassburg told Kammler, looking up from the map, "we couldn't have picked a better spot."

The V-2 rocket's performance had improved over the life of the project.

Among major advancements were its ability to carry heavier and more complex payloads, fly farther and faster, and improved fuels. The same could not be said for the rocket's reliability. V-2s continued to fail during liftoff. The problem was traced back to the milling machines. While the machines themselves were the best in the Reich they consistently failed to hold the finite tolerances needed for parts to perform under the stress of liftoff. The solution was securing the latest Swiss-made milling machines that could hold these higher tolerances—consistently. After hearing Cranz describe the problem along with the solution, Kammler told him he was sure the SS could find a way to persuade their Swiss neighbors to look the other way a time or two and sell the Reich some of their latest milling machines.

The rocket used for the Wall Street mission would be a second-generation V-2, bigger and more powerful than its predecessor. Normally, the nose cone section at the top of the rocket would house the payload, the bomb. But due to the size and weight of the bomb, it would be placed above the rocket motor; otherwise the rocket would be nose-heavy. Houtermans would install the bomb in the rocket, as it was assembled at Peenemünde and before it was placed in the barge. The detonator would be installed and armed prior to launch. Kammler worried about the bomb being placed so close to the engine.

"Not to worry," Cranz told him, "we'll install plenty of insulation to keep the bomb from being cooked like a bratwurst."

Cranz's flip response triggered a spate of laughter.

Cranz continued his description of the rocket. Kammler hung on his every word.

Normally the section under the warhead would be the control and instrument section—four feet eight inches in height, accommodating instruments, gauges, widgets, and gadgets weighing nine hundred seventy pounds. However, in this "custom" V-2, the control and instrument section needed to be housed in the nose cone. Next were the two fuel compartments, taking up most of the space. The top tank contained a seventy-five percent /twenty-five percent blend of alcohol and water, respectively, and the bottom tank held liquid oxygen, or LOX. Directly below the LOX tank was the nine thousand-pound bomb. The last section was the rocket motor, including supporting structure, HTP turbine, fuel pumps, catalyst, control gear, directional-control vanes, and other equipment weighing four thousand pounds and measuring fourteen feet eight inches in height.

Speer had known Cranz since childhood. Listening to Cranz's monologue, he feared a shoe was about to drop and told this to his old friend.

"You're correct," Cranz replied. "This is all leading up to my concerns. You must hear me out before you three decide if you want to go ahead with what is basically a Steinhoff delivery system. For the time being, let's just stay with the rocket. We'll deal with the barge later."

Kammler agreed, speaking for the others. Lines of concern began wrinkling his brow.

"We'll test the rocket sections before assembling them," Cranz began, clearing his throat, "and then have Houtermans install his bomb and place the rocket with the bomb in the barge. From this point forward, I have concerns because once the rocket is in the barge—with everything hooked up and working—that doesn't mean everything will keep working."

Speer looked confused, but Kammler and Strassburg knew exactly what was coming next.

"The distance from our U-boat pens at Helgoland, where Walter's U-tug and Steinhoff's barge will start their journey, to a spot one hundred and fifty miles off the coast of Manhattan may prove to be too great a distance to transport such a delicate one of a kind device. If the journey itself doesn't cause a problem, rotating the barge ninety degrees to its launch position, extending its eight legs to the seabed, then anchoring it with cables and testing the barge to make sure it goes up and down may be the straws that break the camel's back. I say this because under normal conditions—with all our prior checks and tests—we still have a huge number of failures."

Cranz then stopped talking about the rocket and began discussing the barge, his usual upbeat tone returning to his voice. He described it much as Strassburg had to Kammler in Speer's office in Berlin.

Walter would build the barge and rebuild his Wa-201 at Blohm & Voss's shipyard on the island of Kuhwerder near Hamburg to accommodate the barge.

The tugs outer hull diameter would be the same as the barge's, twenty-nine feet one inch. The barge's stern being concave and the tug's bow convex, when mated together would appear to be one extremely long U-boat. The feet on the barge's eight legs would also serve as the female parts of a revolutionary hydraulic-clamping system. The male parts of the clamps attached to the tug's hull. Both parts designed to work like latches on a steamer trunk.

The barge's inner hull housing the rocket would be shorter than the outer hull and have an outside diameter of twenty-six feet two inches. Walter would have nothing to do with outfitting the inner hull. That would be done at Peenemünde.

Because the inner hull needed to slide up and down in the outer hull, the inner wall of the outer hull would be polished to a mirror-like surface then coated with a corrosion-resistant material protecting the surfaces from the seawater corrosion. Two giant "O" rings, made up of a material resistant to the destructive properties of salt water, would be installed between the two hulls. The "O" rings allowing the inner hull to go up and down in the outer hull, much as the rings on a piston allow it to move up and down in an engine cylinder.

Once the tug and the barge were completed testing would begin. A non-functional V-2 rocket the size and weight of the actual rocket with the bomb inside would be installed in the barge. The barge-tug would under go a number of attachments and detachments to see if the clamping system worked as designed. After that the barge would under go a series of reballasting tests, going from horizontal to the vertical and extending its eight legs down and away from the hull, allowing more seawater to enter the ballast chamber and sink the barge to a depth of two hundred and twenty-three feet—the depth of the shipwreck—where anchor cables from the barge would attach it to the seabed for greater stability. Once those maneuvers worked flawlessly more seawater would be pumped into the outer hull's ballast chamber raising the inner hull up towards the surface. When the nose of the inner hull broke the surface the clam door would be opened and closed to see if the mechanism worked as designed. If it did water would be pumped out of the outer hull's ballast chamber allowing the inner hull to retract into the outer hull.

When Cranz was through explaining the testing Kammler signaled he had a question. "When do you plan to do a live test? Firing a rocket with a dummy nine thousand-pound warhead out the barge's inner hull.

"I was just getting to that, General," Cranz replied.

"And?"

"When we think everything will work."

This time no one laughed at Cranz's joke.

"But you do think there'll be problems, don't you, Gerhard?" Speer asked while lighting up a cigarette with none of the usual pleasures he derived from smoking.

"Does a baby teethe?" Cranz said.

"What?" Speer asked.

"Because this one surely will, Albert," Cranz replied. "I'm hoping we'll be able to take care of all his teething problems while he's here. But just remember, he may still upchuck a little when he goes on his first boat ride. He could get seasick, so it's important that General Kammler gets him some good nannies. "

At this point, the meeting adjourned for dinner.

As the four men walked toward the cafeteria, an aide approached Kammler and gave him a small sealed envelope. The SS General excused himself, saying he might have to reply to the envelope's contents.

"It's probably a note from his tailor," Cranz wisecracked. "You know how the SS love their uniforms."

Their dinner was pleasant, more so since Kammler wasn't there and the table talk avoided any mention of Wall Street. Afterward, the three returned to the conference room where Kammler joined them and work continued.

Cranz made it clear the technicians in charge of the launch faced a narrow launch window once the barge was in position off the coast of Manhattan. The surface had to be extremely calm, the early morning hours moonless, no rain, and a cloudless sky.

"I know you have some tolerance issues due to the milling machines you're presently using, so I take it we're not at the stage where we can push a few buttons, throw a few switches, and twenty minutes later the Kremlin's dust?" Kammler asked sarcastically.

"Wouldn't that be nice," Cranz replied. "No, I'm afraid you'll have to wait

110

twenty-fve years for that. Because of all the hundreds of different relays, transducers, switches, cables, pipes, and gauges—all having to work in harmony—some careful tinkering is always needed for a successful launch."

Cranz continued to discuss his anxieties.

"Getting a competent mission crew may prove impossible. I don't know where you're going to find a crew skilled enough for the mission," he said, "but they better know their stuff, and they better be small. They'll be working in extremely close quarters."

Cranz fretted over a host of issues, including the high vibration levels the rocket motors created during liftoff. He cautioned that valves and relays often freeze up because of those vibrations. He told Kammler that men had to be stationed at points of concern and make split-second decisions.

"This is not a job for amateurs or dummies," he warned.

Kammler had enough of Cranz's caveats and cautions.

"Dr. Cranz, is this going to work?" he bluntly asked.

"Ahhh, finally one of you asks the ultimate question," Cranz said. "In fact, I thought one of you would have asked it long ago."

"And?' Kammler asked, nearly losing his patience.

"The answer is yes, General, with a but. The important thing to remember is that with any new technology there are always the 'buts.' You and others like you," Cranz said philosophically, "hold Germany's future in your hands. That future can only be assured if you're willing to take risks to learn things. Before this century is over, we'll travel to the moon—someday the stars. But it won't be rockets that get us there. It'll be the minds of men dreaming about doing things, things that seem impossible. We have to be willing to fail because that's how we learn and bring our dreams to reality. Failure is always the first step in going forward.

"Tomorrow, when you view the V-2 launch, you must see beyond that sleek, shiny piece of metal on the launch pad. It's that mess of spaghetti beneath the surface that counts.

"The presentation I just gave wasn't meant to scare you. It was meant to impress you with all the fantastic accomplishments of German science and engineering, to make you aware that as great as the V-2 is, it's only the beginning.

"When one of you finally asked me if I thought the V-2 would work for your mission, I said yes 'but.' None of you stood up and walked out of the room. That was wonderful. It meant you are all dreamers and not ordinary men overwhelmed by your project. Congratulations!"

Strassburg was the first to stand up and clap, followed by Kammler and Speer.

18.

Strassburg went directly to his room after the meeting/presentation was over. While placing his key in the lock to his room, a beautiful young woman walked toward him. Something didn't seem right.

The woman with some ceremony stopped at the door next to Strassburg's, but before putting the key in the lock she overdramatized recognizing him.

"Weren't you on the cover of *Signal* some months back? Aren't you that *Fallschirmjäger* who received the Knight's Cross?"

Strassburg nodded a somewhat shy acknowledgment.

"I'm Olga Berger," she announced, as if they knew each other when they were children but didn't kept in touch. "I just got here. I'm doing a Reich Air Ministry audit here tomorrow. Can you believe it? They lost my luggage.

"These are the only clothes I have," she complained, pointing to her outfit, "and I'm seeing one of the deputy directors first thing in the morning. I hope there's an iron in my room. Look at me, my clothes are a mess."

"You look fine," Strassburg told her, nonplussed by the conversation, as he unlocked the door to his room. "Whoever you're meeting tomorrow won't mind a few wrinkles."

Minutes after Strassburg turned off his bedside reading light, there was a knock on the Jack and Jill bathroom door, the bathroom he shared with Berger. Not quite asleep, not quite awake, he threw back the bedcovers, walked to the door, unlocked and opened it. There was Olga in her slip; standing on her tiptoes, hanging her freshly washed panties, bra, hose, and garter belt on the shower rod. In his stupor, Strassburg forgot he was wearing nothing but his boxers.

"Sorry to bother you, Karl," she said, her back toward him, her slip having creeped up past her thighs, revealing the lower part of her derriere. "Could I trouble you for some toothpaste?"

As Olga turned to face him, one of the straps on her slip fell off her shoulder, revealing a firm breast and a dark chocolate–colored, very taunt nipple.

"Sorry," she said, pushing everything back under the lace.

"How did you know my name?" he asked, thinking her immodest even if it was wartime and standards were relaxed.

"I—I remembered it from when we exchanged introductions in the hallway. How could you forget?" she said, sticking out her lower lip in a mock pout, as if she were a little girl.

"And would you happen to have an extra blanket?" she asked, changing the subject. "It's really cold in my room."

"Wait here while I get the toothpaste and blanket."

"Here they are. Look, maybe I'm getting this all-wrong and if I am, please accept my apology, but I just broke up with a girl, and right now all I want to do is get some sleep, so good night. I hope your meeting tomorrow goes well, with or without clothes."

Strassburg locked the door behind him and went back to bed.

Sorry Olga, but that small SS rune tattoo on your inner left thigh was a dead giveaway. I hope Kammler doesn't spank you too hard for failing to pry information out of me—information he could use against me. It would be a shame if he damaged those beautiful cheeks.

Part II

19.

During the first week of February 1943, while no one admitted it openly, Hitler and the members of The Committee realized if something wasn't done soon Germany would lose another global war during the first half of the twentieth century. The blitzkrieg war, the mobile warfare that worked so well in 1939 and 1940 (the only type of war the Reich could win) was now a myth. With each passing day, the Allies gained ground on all fronts.

This time there would be no armistice as there was in 1918. This time the Allies wouldn't stop until Germany was a pile of rubble, the rubble divided into smaller piles of rubble, and those piles divvied up among the conquering Allies. Germany would no longer be Germany. Instead of a "thousand-year" Reich, as Hitler promised, it would take the next thousand years to put Germany back together if the two bombs failed to get America out of the war. Germany would become the Humpty Dumpty of Europe because "all the king's horses and all the king's men" couldn't put Germany back together again.

Signs of this started to appear in 1942. In March and April, the Allies bombed Lubeck and Rostock. May began with raids on Kiel and Dortmund. On May 30, a thousand-plane raid attacked Cologne, Berlin, and Hamburg. Even with Göring's Luftwaffe inflicting unbelievable damage on the Allied bomber force, the Luftwaffe was incapable of doing to the Allies in 1942 what the RAF did to Luftwaffe bombers in 1940 during the Battle of Britain: stop them.

On November 2 Rommel, once referred to as the "Desert Fox," started a two thousand-mile retreat from El Alamein to Tunis. With the Allies holding all the major North African ports, it was just a matter of time until the Axis surrendered.

Things weren't going any better in Russia. Field Marshal Frederic von Paulus surrendered to the Soviets what was left of his surrounded and decimated Sixth Army at Stalingrad on January 30, 1943.

The *Reichsmarine* wasn't doing any better. With the sinking of the battleship *Bismarck* on May 27, 1941, Grand Admiral Erich Raeder's High Seas Surface Fleet made its last offensive war cruise in the Atlantic. By November 1941, the Royal Navy had cleaned the high seas of Germany's surface fleet.

The only bright spot was Dönitz's U-boats. But even there, the Allies' anti–U-boat technology was gaining the upper hand. Dönitz knew time was growing short until his U-boats felt the full force of his opponents's new technology and tactics.

The destruction of Wall Street and Boulder Dam was the only hope the Reich had of winning the war.

It was a day like most others in February 1943 on the island of Peenemünde, located off Germany's Baltic coast—cold, sunless, and the sea mist so thick you could push it aside as if it were cobwebs in an attic.

Speer and Strassburg had just entered Peenemünde's VIP dining hall for breakfast. Away from the other tables, Kammler was deep in conversation with an SS Major, who departed as soon as he spotted Speer and Strassburg entering the room.

"Hans doesn't look too happy, Karl," Speer remarked, smiling.

"Maybe he failed to get someone to sleep with him." Strassburg replied, smirking, remembering Olga Berger.

"What are you talking about, Karl?" Speer asked, looking confused.

"Nothing, Minister, just a little joke between the General and myself."

As they neared Kammler's table, Strassburg noticed Speer's cultured mannerisms and bearing returning, his elegant hands ceremoniously opening his gold cigarette case and lighting a Dunhill.

"Bad night, Hans? Our pillow a little too lumpy?"

Kammler ignored the jibe.

"Due to the weather there won't be a V-2 launch today. Once we've eaten breakfast, the Major and I will be on our way to Lake Konstanz. As usual, Speer, it's been grand."

Speer disregarded the part about their collaboration "being grand."

"If you don't mind me asking, Hans, how do you intend to get there in this ugly weather? The runways and taxiways are covered with ice. No pilot is going to chance flying in these conditions."

"We have ways, Minister," Kammler replied, mimicking Nazi movie characters in Allied films.

"But before the Major and I order breakfast, I need to go over his flight crew with him. Naturally you can stay and listen, if you like, Speer."

Speer saw this as maybe his last opportunity to tweak his nemesis before he flew back to Berlin.

"That's a splendid idea, Hans. In case something should happen to you or Himmler, I could take over your duties. Yes, I'd be happy to listen to how the truly great ones pick a crew."

"Have it your way," Kammler said, tired of sparring with someone he felt offered no challenge.

⟨━▮⬤⟩

Kammler started pulling four thick folders from his briefcase. At the same time he told Strassburg and Speer that while he and Himmler would have preferred an all-SS crew, that wasn't possible. Hitler and the others on The Committee wouldn't hear of it. So they abandoned that idea and narrowed their search for the best personnel—a pilot, copilot, crew chief, and mechanic from the ranks of Göring's minions and the Reich's flying-boat manufacturers.

"Oh, that must have hurt *our* ego a little." Speer said, taking a long drag on his Dunhill.

Kammler didn't reply.

⟨━▮⬤⟩

The pilot, Max Horst, was recognized as one of the best flying-boat test

118

pilots Dornier had at their Friedrichshafen test site on Lake Konstanz. When the war started in 1939, Horst volunteered for the Luftwaffe to fly fighters. Horst was thirty-four years old at the time and considered too old and valuable at Dornier to be a fighter pilot. His family had been in Holland visiting relatives when the war broke out. During the fighting a Dutch mortar round killed his wife and three children. If he didn't make it back to Germany after the dam mission, there wouldn't be family there to miss him.

The copilot, Wilhelm Ritter was young and unmarried. Ritter flew BV 222 Staffels on reconnaissance missions supporting Dönitz's U-boats in Norway's Trondheim Fjord. During a routine patrol searching for Allied convoys, he received a radio distress call from a U-boat. It surfaced because its bow planes were stuck and the U-boat couldn't dive. While the crew was trying to fix the problem, a British Beaufighter attacked. With the odds against him, Ritter dove his BV 222 directly at the fighter. The fighter pulled up and got on Ritter's tail. Somehow he missed shooting down Ritter. Leading the Beau away from the U-boat while skimming wave tops, Ritter got lucky—the Beau's port prop caught a wave, causing it to flip over and sink. When Ritter returned to base and reported the incident, he was grounded for recklessness. When Dönitz heard about Ritter being grounded he was furious. He awarded Ritter the *U-Boots–Kriegsabzeichen*, the Knight's Cross of the Iron Cross over Göring's objections.

"Hearing about Ritter's Knight's Cross, Speer blurted out, "Good for him," his voice charged with emotion.

"Now, here's where the turf war begins," Kammler continued. "With his nose out of joint over Dönitz's actions, Göring promoted Ritter to an administrative position, guaranteeing he would never fly again."

Speer shook his head in disgust

"Exactly, what an ass," Kammler acknowledged, in response to Speer's show of emotion.

Kammler found out about Ritter from one of his aides. After viewing Ritter's file, Kammler called Göring, reminding the "fat one" about some of his past indiscretions better left buried. That reminder prompted Göring to reassign Ritter to the SS working for Kammler.

"Will Ritter wear his Luftwaffe uniform during training?" Strassburg asked.

"Of course not, Major, he'll wear the proud uniform of a *Hauptmann* in the Leibstandarte SS Adolf Hitler Division."

"Any siblings?" Speer asked.

"Father, mother, older brother, and sister killed during a night raid on Hamburg. Like Horst, no one will miss him if he doesn't make it back to the Reich."

"What about the others, General?"

The crew chief, Frantz Gerhardt—older than the others but still a bear of a man—was born to wear a uniform. Göring and Gerhardt knew each other during The Great War, when Gerhardt was the chief mechanic for some of Germany's greatest pilots: Voss, Boelcke, the von Richthofens, and Bolle. After the war, Gerhardt landed a job with Dr. Hugo Eckener's Zeppelin Company, where he supervised the installation and maintaince of engines used in Zeppelins.

Strassburg reminded Kammler and Speer that Dr. Eckener was one of his father's clients and in 1936 he went with his father to America when he tried to persuade the US government to end the embargo on helium.

"And your father failed to get the embargo lifted," Kammler snidely reminded Strassburg.

Strassburg let the belittling remark pass.

Shortly after the Hindenburg disaster, May 6, 1937, at Lakehurst, New Jersey, Gerhardt lost his job with Zeppelin. The flaming demise of the giant airship killed thirty-seven people, ending the era of lighter-than-air travel. But Germany was rearming and good mechanics were in demand. Gerhardt ended up working at Blohm & Voss for Dr-Ing Richard Vogt, the chief engineer and designer of both flying boats, the BV 222 and the BV 238, and the BV 8-246 Hagelkorn.

"So Gerhardt knows the BV 238 like the back of his hand?" Speer asked.

"Absolutely," Kammler replied. "That's what got my attention."

The two first met in France in 1916. Vogt was a pilot and Gerhardt was the noncommissioned officer in charge of aircraft maintenance for Vogt's *jasta* on the Western Front. Their paths crossed again after the war. Both were employed at Lindau, the Zeppelin works on Lake Konstanz.

Kammler, looking at Gerhardt's file, said to Strassburg, "It says here that Gerhardt doesn't get along with your girlfriend, Fräulein Prien, who'll be instructing you and your crew on the ins-and-outs of the BV 238."

Strassburg said nothing.

"That could be a real problem, Hans. Is there someone else who could instruct Karl and his crew?" Speer asked.

Kammler looked at Strassburg and told Speer that wasn't *his* problem. It was Strassburg's problem as mission commander to see that the beautiful Fräulein's charms, which no doubt Strassburg had sampled, don't compromise the mission's success.

"Have I made myself clear, Major?"

"Perfectly clear, General," Strassburg replied, showing absolutely no emotion.

"I didn't know you knew the chief test pilot, Karl," Speer said, surprised resonating in his voice.

"That's because you didn't need to know, Speer, and I do," Kammler snapped, his voice elevated in volume

Strassburg, rather than backpedal at the mention of Prien's name, went on the offensive. He told Kammler if he had doubts about his ability to lead, Kammler should have Himmler ask Hitler to replace him with an SS officer. Strassburg added he was sure Hitler wouldn't mind Himmler questioning his judgment. Strassburg also argued that bumping into Prien in a hotel hallway, and spending a night with her at an inn didn't make her his girlfriend. All Kammler had to do, Strassburg said, was ask him if he liked Prien. That would have saved Kammler the trouble of sending

Olga to his room last night, hoping she and her charms would discover if Strassburg liked Fräulein Prien sufficiently for Kammler to use her to control Strassburg.

Kammler was furious. Everyone in the room had stopped talking. Strassburg looked around. Everyone was listening to the seated SS General and the standing *Fallschirmjäger* Major, with the Knight's Cross, discuss the sexual merits of two women, someone named Anna Prien and another woman named Olga.

"Now that everyone in the room knows how I feel about Fräulein Prien and the beautiful Olga, why don't you continue telling Minister Speer and myself about my crew, General?"

Dead silence, a pin dropping would have sounded like a cymbal crash. Kammler knew when he had a winning hand—and when he didn't.

This has become another embarrassment. Again it seems I've underestimated you, Major.

Forcing a smile, followed by a fake laugh, Kammler said in a very low voice, "You really do have a big pair of stones, Major. I hope you'll be able to keep them."

Henry Brock was the mechanic, the fourth member of Strassburg's crew. He was frumpy. When Kammler interviewed him, Brock was wearing a new uniform that looked as if it went through the entire siege at Stalingrad. Brock was larger and taller than Gerhardt with none of Gerhardt's nineteenth-century bearing. Initially, Kammler feared Brock wouldn't be able to wiggle into tight spaces, such as those in the wings of the BV 238, if something went wrong. But Gerhardt swore that Brock could crawl through a mouse hole if he had to and was undoubtedly the finest mechanic he had ever worked with.

"Does Brock have any other little quirks besides not keeping his uniform clean?" Strassburg asked.

"Yes and no," Kammler coyly replied. "And don't ask me to explain this. You'll see what I mean when you meet him."

"Are either Gerhardt or Brock married?" Speer asked.

"Gerhardt never married," Kammler answered. "His work is his life. He had a sister in a mental institution. Last year he stopped seeing her because she no longer recognizes him. Both his parents are dead. He may still have an uncle living somewhere in America.

"As for Brock, he and his sister grew up in an orphanage. While they seem to be close, Brock worked in the south of Germany and his sister lives up north in Hamburg. They don't see much of one another. Brock liked women, but women find him a bit—strange. Gerhardt and Brock are completely different personalities. But, while they approach their work differently, they complement each other troubleshooting an aircraft."

The plan was for Strassburg to meet the four airmen after breakfast. Before departing, Speer pulled Strassburg aside.

"It's truly been a honor working with you, Karl. All the best, I hope what you and the others do will win us the war. Heil Hitler."

"Thank you Minister. The honor was all mine."

Both knew they'd never see the other again.

Strassburg met his crew at a boathouse on the western tip of Peenemünde. After Kammler introduced Strassburg, he talked about the mission, delivered a pep talk, and then turned the session over to the Major. Strassburg was puzzled that Kammler never mentioned the bomb they'd use to destroy the dam—that it was a revolutionary new weapon, as was the delivery system, the BV 8-246 *Hagelkorn* glide bomb.

Brock, the mechanic, stepped forward before Strassburg could say a word.

Max Horst, the pilot; Wilhelm Ritter, the copilot; and Kammler instinctively stepped backwards, leaving Strassburg to deal with Brock. Smiling, they watched Brock execute his "Heil Hitler" salute, using his left hand instead of his right.

"Sir," Brock gravely stated, "I never thought I'd meet someone so famous. Would you be so kind as to write a little something on this piece of paper and sign it? I'll send it to my sister. She thinks you're really quite handsome, as I do, I mean—well—you know what I mean."

Strassburg looked towards Kammler for advice on how to handle Brock. His expression conveyed, "Who the hell is this clown? What should I do?"

Horst and Ritter choked back laughter. Kammler passed the buck to Strassburg, mouthing (but not actually saying), "He's yours! You deal with him!"

Gerhardt, the crew chief, didn't find Brock's behavior comical.

"Look, son," he said, "the Major is going to need a little time to get used to your quirky ways. Wait a day or two—maybe even a month—before you ask him again to write a note to your sister and sign it. That's, of course, if he lets you live that long.

"I'm sure if the autograph was for you," Gerhardt added, "he'd write it out for you right now. But it's for your sister, son. For all the Major knows she could be a screaming bitch—do you get my drift, son?"

Gerhardt proceeded to give the mercurial Brock something of a lecture, explaining life was different now that he was in uniform, no longer a civilian. He bluntly told Brock that he no longer could or would tolerate the "crap" he put up with when they worked together as civilians.

"You're the best damn aircraft mechanic I've ever come across in or out of the military," Gerhardt told him. "But now, just like me, you're expendable. Why?"

Brock was doing his best to stand at something resembling attention. Gerhardt paced back and forth in front of him, hands behind his back waiting for an answer.

Eventually, Brock answered Gerhardt's question with a question.

"Because I'm in uniform, Frantz?"

"Right you are, lad," the senior noncommissioned officer snapped back. "That's why everyone standing here, listening to my fucking ravings, is also expendable. We're all in uniform, boy! And why are we in uniform? Because we're in the service of our country! And that may mean giving up our lives to ensure this upcoming mission is carried out to the best of our abilities.

"If we were Japs, Russians, or Brits in uniform, the answer would be the same," Gerhardt told him. "And that answer is? Come on, son, tell me!" Gerhardt demanded, cupping a hand close to his ear, a clear signal he was listening for Brock's reply.

"That I am in the uniform of my country and this upcoming mission might call for me to give my life to achieve its success," Brock exhaled, looking straight ahead.

"Yes, son," Gerhardt replied sadly, shaking his head in agreement. "I'm sorry to say that's the answer—the only answer. We're all expendable."

What had started out as a whimsical moment had turned deadly serious.

Gerhardt turned to Strassburg.

"Henry's a good man, Major, and from now on everything should be fine. But if he fucks up, I'm sure the General, here, can find work for him on the Eastern Front, fixing tank treads during winter."

Everybody laughed, except Brock.

20.

Fog engulfed the entire island of Peenemünde as Kammler, Strassburg, and his crew boarded the launch that would take them to the BV 238, the aircraft floating somewhere in the mist, waiting to fly them to Lake Konstanz, the lake Germany shared with Switzerland and Austria on her southern border.

Once again Kammler started needling Strassburg about Prien. The noise from the launch's engines kept the others from hearing the conversation.

"I hope, your ex-girlfriend," Kammler began, emphasizing *ex*, "Fräulein Prien, still likes you enough that she doesn't crash this thing we're looking for, somewhere in this blasted fog, in a fit of revenge for you dumping her."

"I hope she doesn't as well, General," Strassburg replied, stepping into the launch. "It certainly would be a shame if Brock was found floating dead wearing a dirty SS uniform."

Brock cast off. The launch's pilot started the in-line marine engines. The launch crept slowly into the void.

Ritter, a veteran of Norway's pea-soup fog, positioned himself on the launch's bow next to Brock, his senses on full alert. Horst started to say something to Gerhardt and Ritter told him to be quiet. Then Ritter heard it. At eleven o'clock off their bow, the sound of water sloshing against metal, the giant flying boat's aluminum hull.

"Brock!" he shouted. "As soon as you see the hull to your front, look to starboard and you'll see a rope ladder hanging down from the cargo deck. When I tell you jump, jump. Once you're on the ladder I'll toss you this line. Tie the line to one of the cleats on the cargo deck's floor."

Strassburg could tell that Brock wasn't coordinated by the way he got up on the bow of the launch. The veins in his neck were starting to protrude, a clear sign the mechanic was scared to death at the thought of having to jump for the ladder. Brock knew if he missed, he'd fall into ice-cold water, maybe cramp up, and drown.

"Get down off the bow, Brock," Strassburg ordered. "I've had a lot more experience jumping off things than you have."

Ritter, in a whisper, queried Strassburg about whether he, being the mission commander, should be the one making the leap for the ladder. Strassburg took off his camouflage parka and handed it to Ritter.

"Better I get a trifle damp than we lose our mechanic. "

Ritter smiled, taking Strassburg's parka. "Nice parka, boss."

After circling the mammoth aircraft three or four times, Ritter finally spotted the ladder. The fog hadn't lifted and finding the ladder wasn't easy. Strassburg timed his jump perfectly. Landing on the lowest rung of the ladder, Strassburg called out to Ritter to toss him the line. With the line between his teeth he scampered up the swaying ladder as if he were part cat. Both bow doors were wide open. Reaching the opening he pulled himself onto the cargo deck. On hands and knees, surrounded by darkness, he began gropping the deck for one of the cleats. What he found was a shapely leg wrapped in a tight-fitting flight suit.

"Don't stop now," she whispered softly, "the farther up you go the better it gets. But that'll have to wait. For now stand and up and kiss me."

"How's it going up there? Need some help?" Kammler shouted up to Strassburg.

"It's darker than Hades in here, General. As far as needing help, I should be fine once I find the light switch."

"I think you just found mine," she moaned in hushed tones,

He gently pushed her away.

"Help me find one of those damn cleats. I need to tie off this line before someone comes up the ladder and see's what you're doing to me."

"Have it your way," she said, "you used to be fun."

With the line secured around a cleat Anna retreated to the flight deck and turned on the plane's tactical-lighting system, which gave off a dark red, low-intensity light designed to preserve night vision while being unseen by the enemy.

As Kammler prepared to jump for the ladder, Strassburg shouted a warning. "Hold on General, there's sharp edges at the leading edge of the cargo deck where the bow doors close. Before you come up the ladder I have to pad those edges or they might cut through the ladder's side ropes."

"Have you seen Fräulein Prien, Strassburg?"

"No, but she's heard us. Unless this thing houses some pretty smart rats, she's the one who turned on the plane's tactical-lighting system from the flight deck."

"Hurry up with your padding, Strassburg, it's colder down here than a well digger's ass."

With everyone safely on board the aircraft and the two facing bow doors closed, the launch headed back to the boathouse. Kammler, his outsized ego at work, felt the need to remind the crew he was in command. He ordered everyone to their stations on the flying boat or to find a comfortable seat in the lounge behind the flight deck, adding that they should relax and enjoy the flight to Lake Konstanz, where they'd spend the next six to seven months immersed in training."

"Has Major Strassburg met Fräulein Prien?" Brock asked as Strassburg entered the cockpit. Before anyone could stop him, he said, "Major Strassburg, this is Fräulein Anna Prien, our instructor and fairy godmother. She knows more about this aircraft than all of us put together. She's beautiful, too."

"That's enough, Brock," Gerhardt told him. "I'm sure the Major has good eyes. He can make his own decision about Fräulein Prien."

Strassburg laughed politely along with the others. Prien blushed slightly before managing a smile.

"Thank you for your thoughtful introduction, Brock. The Major and I know each other. We bumped into each other in a hallway at a hotel. I knocked him out. Isn't that right, Major?"

Nice going, Anna, Karl mused. *That should give Kammler something to think about.*

"As a matter of fact," Strassburg told everyone, "never before have I woken up and looked into the eyes of a more beautiful woman."

Even Kammler laughed after hearing Strassburg's comeback.

One by one Prien, as pilot, and Horst, as copilot, coaxed to life the six coughing seventeen hundred-horsepower engines in the wing nacelles of the giant flying boat. Ritter, usually the copilot, remained in the cockpit cabin, working the radio and navigating. Brock, counseled by Gerhardt, eschewed the lounge's posh seats for the jump seat on the cargo deck, on call if Prien or Horst spotted any mechanical problems. Kammler sat in the rear of the lounge. After buckling in, he started working. Gerhardt strapped himself in across the aisle from Strassburg even though there were plenty of empty seats elsewhere.

Strassburg, sitting next to a window, remarked to Gerhardt, "I wonder why they've started the engines. The fog's still thick. We won't be taking off anytime soon."

"That's where you're wrong, Major," Gerhardt replied. "Fräulein Prien has bigger balls than any man I've met. We'll be airborne as soon as she and Horst finish their preflight instrument checks."

"In this fog?"

"Yes, Major, in this fog."

He continued his monologue telling Strassburg the"long-legged bitch" was the best pilot he ever worked with. Better than Voss, Göring, or the two von Richthofens. Despite that, he still thought she should be back in Switzerland, married to some farmer, with kids sucking milk from her tits, instead of being a test pilot. Leaning closer to Strassburg than he had been, as if he was about to reveal some big secret, Gerhardt told Strassburg that the "word" was that Kammler pulled a fast one. That somehow he got this one-of-a-kind aircraft away from Göring and— Strassburg was going to win the war."

Strassburg reaction wasn't what Gerhardt expected.

"Gerhardt, you're going to have to quit sniffing those aviation fuel fumes. They're causing you to hallucinate."

"Please, sir, let me explain," Gerhardt murmured.

He told Strassburg the aircraft was supposed to have flight trials in 1945 and that few even knew it existed. But due to Generalfeldmarschall Milch's soon-to-be-made announcement that all future Reich aircraft production would be limited to fighters the BV 238 would never be finished.

When Kammler got wind of this, he made some inquires and got the aircraft since the flying boat had the capabilities he needed.

"Is all this going to make sense when you're through, Gerhardt?" Strassburg asked, seemingly baffled at the crew chief's monologue.

"Yes, Major, it damn well will," Gerhardt said. "Word's out when we get to Lake Konstanz, some *Kriegsmarine* unit is going to strip this baby down to the bone. Get rid of all this nifty-looking paneling so she can carry over forty-four thousand pounds of fuel and some big-ass bomb across the Atlantic to the States. Forty-four thousand pounds of fuel isn't enough to get us to the States and back to Germany and the way the war is going, there isn't a place going out or coming back where we can get more fuel. Since none of the four of us have families, there's no one to come back to—except maybe you. I don't know."

Gerhardt seems to know much more about this than a crew chief should Strassburg thought. *You, my 'friend,' will bear watching.*

"Something I said bothering you, Major?" Gerhardt asked noticing Strassburg seemed preoccupied.

"No, but please continue, Gerhardt."

"There's not a single bomb in the world powerful enough to take out a dam. But if we auger her into the concrete and then the bomb goes off that might cause some cracks and put the dam out of commission. Of course, we'd all end up dead. Is that the plan, Major?" Gerhardt bluntly asked.

"And what if it is, Gerhardt? You in for the ride?" Strassburg shot back. "I'm asking because after that 'we're all expendable' speech you gave Brock, back at the boathouse, I thought you'd be a man willing to die for his country. Now I'm not so sure. Maybe I should tell General Kammler to look for a replacement."

"Just testing your resolve Major," Gerhardt said, forcing a chuckle.

"And did I pass, Gerhardt?"

"Sometimes what a man wears around his neck isn't what's in his heart, Major," Gerhardt opined.

Not a single aircraft was seen in the skies during the flight to Lake Konstanz. Once the BV 238 landed, workmen would begin tearing apart all the well-appointed bathrooms, sleeping accommodations, and staterooms reflecting the art deco style of the 1930s. The aircraft was intended to be a flying symphony of chrome. Combined with panneled pastel-colored walls, multicolored zigzag carpeting, exotic woods, and beautifully etched Plexiglas panels, the flying boat was meant to impress. Plexiglas had been used instead of glass because of its shatter-resistant qualities. Soon the not-quite-finished beautifully crafted interior would be scrap. Even the galley, crew quarters, luggage, and cargo areas would be stripped and used to make parts for Luftwaffe fighters. And as soon as those fighters came off the assembly line, they'd be shot down and buried in some trash heap—forever.

Misty patches of winter fog were still clinging to the top of the water on Lake Konstanz as Prien and Horst guided the flying boat's descent to the surface. Gerhardt likened the touch down to a massive stone skipping across the water, thrown by some giant hand. During the descent, he told Strassburg about all the hazards of a water landing. The possibility of a small, unseen object floating on the surface, puncturing the hull. And worse, an ill-timed wave catching one of the wing pontoons and flipping the BV 238 onto her back, killing everyone on board.

Strassburg found Gerhardt's description of water landings extremely accurate. He hoped all the hazards Gerhardt mentioned might be avoided. All conversations ceased following the first skip; quiet settled in over the aircraft. Consequently, Strassburg overheard Prien and Horst talk through their extensive and complex landing procedure as the din of the flying boat's half-dozen engines lessened with reduced power.

Finally, the huge aircraft became one with the water, coasting to a stop. Horst feathered down power to the props, and soon they stopped spinning. While the flying boat's forward momentum stopped, it continued to move up and down with the water's chop.

"How long does this bobbing continue?" Kammler asked, addressing his question to no one in particular and looking annoyed.

"As long as we're on the water, General, there's going to be movement," Gerhardt shouted back over his shoulder.

Strassburg unbuckled his seat belt, quickly got his sea legs, and made his way to the cockpit to get a better view of where they landed. Just as he was about to enter the cockpit, Brock, appearing from nowhere, edged past him.

"Brock, I thought you were on the cargo deck."

"I was until I was summoned up here. Sorry, Major, I need to get back on the cargo deck to get the bow doors open and throw out the tow line."

Horst, Ritter, and Prien congratulated themselves on the landing, noting how rough the chop was.

"I thought we'd taxi to a pier or tie up to a buoy," Strassburg remarked. "Instead we seem to be at least a mile from land. There's nothing to tie up to."

Horst, Ritter, and Prien smiled. Ritter encouraged Strassburg to look starboard. "That's our new home, Major," which prompted laughs from everyone but Strassburg.

"What the hell is it?" Strassburg asked, confused.

"That, Major," Prien explained, "is a floating Zeppelin hangar. It was built around the turn of the century and was used well into the 1920s, when the government—before this one—wanted to turn it into a dirigible museum. The hangar used to automatically turn into the wind to accommodate landing airships. Now it's anchored to the lakebed.

"If you look at the shoreline through the mist," she continued, "you'll see an old decaying wharf. That wharf was supposed to be demolished. There were plans to build a new wharf as part of a luxury resort. Now the entire area and the hangar are off-limits supposedly because they're in such a dangerous state of disrepair."

Strassburg understood. This was all a smoke screen.

"Before I became involved in all this a week ago," Prien said, "I flew over this area many times. Never did I suspect the hangar or the wharf were part of one of the best-kept secrets of the war."

What they were looking at was part of the *Kriegsmarine* Inland Sea Research and Development Test Facility.

Kammler, somewhat recovered from the aircraft's bobbing, interrupted the friendly conversation among Horst, Ritter, Prien, and Strassburg, a conversation he caustically characterized as "Fräulein Prien's educational tour of the area." He pointed with concern to a high plume of water coming directly toward them at a tremendous speed—a boat of undetermined shape barely visible, its engines nearing redline.

"He has to be pushing forty knots," Ritter remarked casually while peering through marine binoculars at the "V" wake behind the boat.

Kammler was worried. He feared some maniac would crash into the BV 238 and sink his precious one-of-a-kind aircraft.

"So, what do we do?" he asked.

"I'm up for suggestions, General," Strassburg answered, showing absolutely no concern.

"I'm not *paying* you to ask me for advice, Major. I'm paying you to *give* me advice," Kammler barked in an edgy voice, showing obvious and mounting concern.

Strassburg reminded Kammler that the last time he got paid it didn't come from SS's coffers. And unless the boat's pilot was crazy, which Strassburg doubted, whoever was at the helm didn't want to eat a mouthful of BV 238 aluminum any more than they wanted to eat a mouthful of whatever that damn boat in front of the rooster was made of.

"So relax. Enjoy the show, General."

Kammler wasn't enjoying the show and he wasn't about to relax.

Whoever is piloting the boat is really good." Strassburg joked, "I'm glad he's on our side."

Kammler was at a loss for words.

Strassburg was certain if a collision occured it wouldn't be catastropic. The flying boat's hull was sufficiently reinforced to keep it afloat. At worst the aircraft would need a new paint job and some bodywork. Brock would be the problem if a collision took place. They'd need a new airplane mechanic because Brock's position on the bow guaranteed he'd be killed.

By now Kammler was fuming, partially because he realized Strassburg was right, that whoever was piloting the boat wouldn't want to die and if a collision did occur it would delay the mission for months—something he couldn't afford. While no one on The Committee would say it to his face, tongues would wag in hushed tones behind his back that it was his fault for what happened. There was also the likelihood that Strassburg, a Hero of the Reich, might make fun of him.

Damn you, Major, you're fast becoming a real pain in my ass. Unless you do something to discredit yourself, I'm stuck with you. I'm sure you realize this.

You're a "smart boy," Major, as Hitler told you at the Berghof. But we'll see who's the smartest, won't we?

21.

The two facing bow doors on the cargo deck below the cockpit were wide open. Brock, squatting on the open deck, resembled a seagull taking a crap. The muscles throughout the mechanic's body were tight as the skin on a drum. Filled with great trepidation, he watched as their tow showed no sign of slowing down as it speeded straight at him.

What if that crazy motherfucker can't see us through all that spray?

The noise from the tow's three supercharged diesels, humming in unison, grew increasingly loud. Brock scrambled back from the edge of the open cargo bay's doorway, realizing the chance of collision was increasing with every passing second.

He curled himself into a fetal position, pressed his body against the portside bulkhead, and waited for the impact.

Things weren't any better in the cockpit. Everyone—with the exception of Ritter, the mission copilot, and Prien—thought Strassburg might have grossly misjudged the situation. They secured themselves for a violent collision, powerless to do anything but watch and wait. Seconds before the crash, their tow, thought to weigh more than one hundred tons, veered off to port. Everyone, except Ritter, was baffled about how a one hundred and fifteen-foot–long "S" boat traveling at an estimated forty-five knots could slide into a turn so adeptly, miss them, and then stop so suddenly.

Ritter, familiar with these types of boats because of his previous assignment in Norway, said, "I've heard about these new Schnellboots, with their *Kalotte*, armored dome bridges. They aren't operational yet, but when they are, the British Vosper MTBs and the American PT boats will be no match for them or their crews."

Ritter, usually not that talkative, seemed poised to say more. He glanced at Kammler, looking for a sign of his approval. The SS General offered a slight nod and Ritter continued. He told everyone, except Brock, that what they just witnessed went way beyond the capability of British and American torpedo boats. The tow's crew wasn't showing off. It was what they practice day in and day out in all kinds of weather.

Ritter sensed the group wanted to hear more. He described in some detail the boat they had just seen in action, a prototype S-100. The deck over the forecastle was armored as well as the *Kalotte* ("skull cap"), the pilothouse. The port and starboard twenty-one-inch torpedo tubes used the same torpedoes the U-boats used. The area around the engines was better armored than previous boats. The increased fuel capacity stretched its range to seven hundred fifty nautical miles. It's speed was reported to be thirty-five plus knots. Flak cannons were located at the stern, amidships, and the bow. So much firepower was packed into such a small package; S-100s could take on ships four times their size. The red and white diagonal stripes painted on the forward deck were there so Axis fighters and dive-bombers wouldn't mistake the German boats for Allied ones during close-in skirmishes.

Kammler cut off Ritter's dissertation, pointing out the "maniac" piloting the

BV 238 flying boat towed by S-100 Schnellboot

S-100 had positioned the Schnellboot's stern to facing the flying boat's bow and seemed ready to tow them to the hangar once Brock had the tow line.

Kammler looked down the open hatch leading to the cargo deck and noticed that Brock, who was on the cargo deck, was being hailed by a young, bearded, *Kriegsmarine* Oberleutnant dressed in an old sheepskin-collared leather coat and a dirty white *Kriegsmarine* officer's cap. He tossed Brock the towline. Once the line was tied off for the tow to the hangar, the youthful officer did a theatrical bow for benefit of the people watching from the cockpit.

"A most hearty welcome," he effused, "to everyone aboard this flying sea monster, from the men, women, and children of the Inland Sea Research and Development Test Facility on beautiful Lake Konstanz. And, I might add, the only R & D facility of its kind in the world. Now if everyone up there in the crow's nest and that fellow I tossed the towline to will go back to your seats and buckle up, it'll be our pleasure to tow you, free-of-charge, to that pathetic-looking bunch of rotting boards over there." The Oberleutnant was pointing at the old Zeppelin hangar.

A slight smile crossed Strassburg's lips. *Our stay here might be the best part of the entire mission.*

Strassburg and the others found the sensation of being towed similar to that of a long train moving out of a railroad station: slow getting started, but once in motion things kept moving. Just as it seemed they were up to speed, the Schnellboot's helmsman reduced power and they started slowing down.

"Shit!" Horst exclaimed. "Sorry, Fräulein, but I just realized we're about to thread a needle."

"What's he talking about?" Kammler shouted, unbuckling his seat belt and racing to the cockpit.

"What Horst is saying. General," Prien explained. "is that our one hundred eighty foot, eleven-inch wingspan is about to try squeezing through those two open doors on the back of the Zeppelin hangar—dead ahead."

"What's happening people," Kammler screamed."First, we go skipping across the water out of control. Then some young bearded maniac, who should never have been put in command of anything, almost crashes into us, and now this. We're about to lose our wings, something *I* can't afford."

"So what would you have us do, General?" Strassburg asked facetiously,

He gave Kammler two choices. Let the tow keep dragging the flying boat through the water and chance getting their wings clipped or cut the tow and risk being spotted and attacked by some hot shot Allied fighter pilot.

"It's your call, General, but personally I think whoever had the brains to come up with this facility might also be smart enough to figure out how to squeeze ten pounds of shit into a two-pound bag."

"Don't mouth off to me, Major. We both know Hitler likes you and thinks you're a 'smart boy.' But remember, I'm the one in charge here. So what do we do now?" Kammler asked no one in particular, displeasure again apparent in his voice.

"The General and the Major might consider going back to the lounge and closing their eyes," Gerhardt suggested, "while Fräulein Prien and Hauptmann

Horst do their jobs, getting this beast through a very tight space. Let them do the worrying for the rest of us.

"And if we should lose a wing or part of the tail going through those doors, and the two of you are somewhere else when it happens, you can deny all responsibility. And being officers, you'll still get your next promotions." This quip triggered laughs and smiles even from Kammler.

These idiots have no idea why I'm mad. They probably think I'm scared. I don't give a shit about any of them. It's the aircraft I'm worried about. If that fool doing the towing makes a mistake, I'll be the one eating crow from Hitler, Himmler, and the others on The Committee, not them.

Realizing Gerhardt wasn't being insubordinate, Kammler said, "Why thank you, Gerhardt, for such sage advice. What would we do without the wisdom of *our* crew chiefs?"

Gerhardt snapped to attention, clicking his heels as Kammler passed by him on the way to the cabin in back of the cockpit

"Be sure to let us know if we lose parts, Gerhardt," Strassburg whispered as he followed Kammler.

"You do realize, Major, the General was scared shitless," Gerhardt replied, pulling Strassburg off to one side, ensuring the others couldn't hear. "He hasn't seen the crap you, Ritter, and I've seen. But he does have a sense of humor. He realized that by staying in the cockpit, while Fräulein Prien and Hauptmann Horst do their jobs, he's only adding to the tension of an already tense situation. More tension might cause them to make a mistake.

"If you don't need me, Major, I'm going to join Brock at the towline.

"By the way, I'm proud to be serving under you. This is my second Great War," Gerhardt said sarcastically, "and never before have I witnessed an officer of lower rank have the balls to address a superior officer the way you just did. Telling him he's wrong. Your father and mother have a lot to be proud of."

He saluted Strassburg in the Old Prussian way, used during The Great War, rather than with the "Heil Hitler" Nazi salute.

Does Gerhardt dislike the Nazis? Strassburg wondered. *Or more diabolically is this a ploy by Kammler to see how I'd react to someone showing signs of being anti-Nazi?*

Strassburg also wondered about the crew in general. Were they assigned to the mission because of their job skills and experience or because they are die-hard Nazis selected by Kammler for their party loyalty?

Seventy-five yards to their front, the two massive vertical slat doors at the end of the old Zeppelin hangar opened from the middle to their maximum positions. Each door was less than one hundred feet in length and rolled back-and-forth like the door on a roll-top desk.

"Wow, this is really slick!" Ritter exclaimed, mesmerized by the hangar door's opening, momentarily forgetting the mission might end before it began, if one of the plane's wingtips or tail clipped the hangar's entrance passing through.

"This could be bad, Fräulein Prien," Horst commented, his eyes racing back-

and-forth from the starboard and port wingtips. His knuckles were white, the tips of his fingers digging into the armrest on the copilot's seat.

"I'm more concerned about the tail clearing the top of the door frame," Prien told him. "The wingtips can be repaired much easier and faster than the tail can."

Strassburg, now back in the cockpit, opined, "Just be happy the General isn't here giving you both advice on how to avoid a disaster."

Strassburg was leaning forward over Anna's shoulder, his eyes darting back-and-forth from wingtip-to-wingtip. With the possibility of disaster staring him in the face, he still found time to glance down at Anna's alluring cleavage.

So close, yet so far, he thought. *How am I ever going to find a way to talk to you in private and not be spied on? I desperately need to find a way to tell you about my plan for getting you back to your parents in Switzerland.*

Out of nowhere a wisp of lingering fog blew across the cockpit windshield, blocking everyone's view of the wingtips as they cleared the hangar's entrance. Instinctively, the four of them ducked as if that might help avert disaster.

No scraping sounds were heard, leading Prien to exclaim, relief in her voice, "We're inside!"

With that she reached over and exuberantly hugged Horst who pushed her away.

"How can you be so sure we're through? The fog is still sticking to the windshield!" Horst asserted, alarm in his voice.

"Because the light is different," she reasoned. "Besides, if we had problems, we'd have heard them by now."

"You're absolutely right," Ritter cried out ecstatically, so excited he reached over from his position behind Horst and hugged her. Strassburg somewhat miffed about the hug did his best to not show it.

Then the sound of metal scraping metal was heard.

Ritter instantaneously set their minds at ease. "That's just the sound of our hull making contact with the hangar's restraining cable, slowing down our forward momentum before bringing the aircraft to a stop."

Kammler heard what Ritter said as he entered the cockpit and offered congratulations to the crew.

Those standing on the hangar's catwalks erupted in celebratory cheers.

With the BV 238 safe inside the hangar, lines were secured from the aircraft to cleats on the Zeppelin hangar's two catwalks—one on each side of a channel that ran the length of the hangar. The two doors behind the aircraft's stern began closing. Bobbing lazily on the surface of the water, the giant aircraft waited for an aluminum gangplank to be run up to her forward starboard hatch on the cargo deck. Once the gangplank was in place Kammler, Strassburg, and the crew exited the aircraft.

What they saw as they walked down the gangplank was comic book science fiction.

While the hangar's exterior appeared to be Noah's Ark—after spending thousands of years on Mount Arafat—the interior resembled a cross between the Eiffel Tower with all its nineteenth-century exposed iron beams, bolts, and rivets, and German *Bauhaus*, where form followed function, a pleasing blend of two architectural periods.

Custom demanded that everyone aboard a marine vessel—and the BV 238 was definitely a marine vessel—be piped aboard the hangar by a boson, the highest-ranking officer the first one down the gangplank. The moment Kammler stepped off the gangplank he was greeted by an elderly man, casually dressed, sporting a full head of light blond hair, a Van Dyke–style beard, and piercing blue eyes.

"Good morning, Hans, how was the flight?" the small man asked, vigorously pumping Kammler's hand.

"Interesting, Admiral. Very interesting," Kammler replied, saluting the diminutive man although he wasn't wearing a military uniform.

Strassburg was amazed. In the two years he served under Kammler, he never saw him salute anyone. Just the opposite, everyone saluted Kammler.

Prien was the last to exit the mammoth flying boat. The moment her head poked through the hatch and she stepped onto the gangplank, wolf whistles and cheers resounded throughout the hangar.

"You're right, Hans," the Admiral said, watching her stride down the gangplank. "Fräulein Prien is absolutely stunning."

When everyone was off the plane, Kammler made the introductions by name, rank, and job description before introducing the Admiral.

"This is Admiral Manfred Kohler," Kammler told Strassburg and his crew. "He'll be your host until you leave on the mission. He'll see to it the BV 238 is refitted for the mission and your training, education, and language skills are adequate for your survival until you're repatriated. I'm sure you have questions about this base and what is done here. All that can wait until you're settled in."

The Admiral informed Horst, Ritter, Gerhardt, and Brock they'd be billeted in a château on the mainland. Arrangements were made for Fräulein Prien to live with a family on one of the base's many farms. Strassburg's accommodations were in the Zeppelin hangar. While they were at the facility, they'd receive civilian clothes. Their military uniforms would be placed in storage and returned to them when they returned to Germany after the war.

Kammler cautioned them to be pleasant to everyone they met, to say nothing about the mission to anyone, and if anyone asked why they were here to tell them it was for special training.

"If you're questioned further," he sternly advised, "report that to my office and I'll handle the matter. Any questions? Seeing no hands, "Then I'll see you back here at 3 p.m. for the orientation."

Privately, Kammler told Strassburg and Kohler to start the orientation without him, if he hadn't returned by 3:15 p.m.

"In case something comes up, Hans, where can I reach you?" Kohler asked.

"I'm having lunch with Dr-Ing Vogt at Friedrichshafen around noon," Kammler told him. "I'll need one of your Schnellboots to get me there. When I return

I'll have plans on how to rig Vogt's BV 8-246 *Hagelkorn* glide bomb in the BV 238 and how to release it. I'm not expecting any problems since Vogt designed both the glide bomb and the flying boat. While I'm gone, please show the Major your wonderful facility."

***

Strassburg had been busy sizing up Kohler while introductions were made and everyone was gathering up their gear for the trip to the mainland. Kohler appeared to have spent most of his life at sea. For some reason, Strassburg thought they'd previously met. Kohler wasn't a big man, but Strassburg immediately sensed the aura of leadership—qualities that cause others to follow, regardless of rank, station in life, or age. Strassburg judged him to be a person not easily impressed. But for some reason, in Strassburg's case, all it took was a handshake. Kohler was convinced that here was a young man capable of holding his own with the best of them. He saw in Strassburg a man much older than his years, an unfortunate by-product of leading men in combat, something Kohler was all too familiar with. He knew that men—good and bad—were capable of rising at least once in their lives to a moment of extreme heroism when bravery and courage were required. He also knew these acts were seldom, if ever, repeated. But what Kohler saw in Strassburg was a man with at least three such acts of bravery to his credit. Consequently, when the two were alone, he told Strassburg that it was "truly an honor and a privilege" to meet him. Strassburg was deeply moved; he was speechless.

"I didn't mean to embarrass you, Karl," Kohler said after witnessing Strassburg's genuine modesty. "I hope you don't mind me calling you Karl when it's just the two of us talking. I would be honored if you'd join me for dinner tonight."

"It would be a privilege, sir," Strassburg replied, "but does your wife know you've invited me? I don't want to intrude."

Sadness swept across the Admiral's face. "My wife died two years ago, Karl. But my cook, Raul, will be happy I'm bringing a guest home tonight for dinner. Raul's a Spaniard, and the volume of most of his splendid dishes could feed a navy. I'd love your company tonight. With Kammler tied up at Friedrichshafen with Dr-Ing Vogt, we can talk freely."

"Excuse me, sir, but the General said he'd meet us back here at three," Strassburg reminded the Admiral.

"Yes, so he did," Kohler conceded. "He also said if he wasn't back at 3:15, we should start the briefing without him. I can say with some certainty we won't be seeing Kammler until probably tomorrow morning. And when we do see him, he won't be smiling."

A mysterious smile crossed the Admiral's deep-lined face.

Strassburg, his curiosity piqued, asked Kohler how he met Kammler, a man so very different than the Admiral.

"This, Karl," Kohler gestured with his arms, "The Inland Sea Research and Development Test Facility."

***

The origins of the facility stretched back to 1919 with the Treaty of Versailles. Under treaty terms, Germany was forbidden to construct or acquire any type of underwater warship for her navy. In order to sidestep that provision and preserve Germany's U-boat expertise, a network of civilian companies was set up to build U-boats for foreign navies. Great Britain was Germany's biggest competition. But who would want a British boat if they could get a German boat, considering how German U-boats controlled the seas during The Great War?

Under the cover of manufacturing U-boats for foreign navies, Germany began building U-boats and doing sea trials using *Kriegsmarine* personnel before turning the boats over to foreign buyers. By using different German crews to do the sea trials Germany began rebuilding her skilled U-boat crews. But after a while the countries buying the U-boats wanted their own sailors to perform the sea trials.

Kohler characterized the U-boats built for foreign customers as inferior. The reason for this was that most of their foreign clients decided what features they wanted on their boats and those features did nothing to increase the boat's performance or survivability.

Everything changed when the Nazis came to power. Hitler decided to immediately rebuild Germany's U-boat fleet. Dönitz knew Kohler from The Great War and asked him to come up with a way to design and test U-boat designs in secrecy. Hitler wasn't ready to openly break the Treaty of Versailles. Hitler demanded that *Kriegsmarine* personnel design the U-boats, rather than having German companies design, engineer, and construct the boats, while only *Kriegsmarine* personnel carried out the sea trials. Now U-boat manufacturers and independent entrepreneurs, like Professor Walter, would build what Dönitz and his staff designed.

Strassburg instinctively felt he could trust the Admiral so he rolled the dice and took a huge gamble.

"Then you know about the project Walter is working on and Dönitz doesn't know about it?" Strassburg asked.

Kohler smiled. "You took a big chance asking me that, Karl and yes, I know what Walter is working on because Kammler asked me about the project's feasibility. And, no, Dönitz doesn't know because he has no need to know. Brilliant independents like Professor Walter do some of the U-boat designing and those designs come through here for my evaluation. As you can imagine, once these designs are approved, they demand the utmost secrecy during development. Initially, Dönitz wanted this facility to be at the mouth of a major river, a security nightmare. I convinced him to let me build it at one of our inland lakes, away from the prying eyes of the Russians, British, and French. What better place for secrecy? In addition to the main facility's remoteness and appearence, an old rotting rusting-away Zeppelin hangar and a tumbledown wharf the area was blessed with small farms and resort towns—no industrial sites other than Friedrichshafen, a perfect place for a major naval R & D center.

"If something needs testing, that can't be done in the hangar there's a fifteen-mile peninsula on our side of the lake at the northwest end that blocks anyone on the Swiss side from seeing what we're doing."

Kohler paused, could he trust Strassburg? He, too, decided to take a chance.

"About the dam Karl, Dr-Ing Vogt's *Hagelkorn* glide bomb isn't an option. For now that's all I can tell you."

Strassburg didn't know what to say. It was obvious Kohler wasn't about to share why the glide bomb wouldn't work. Strassburg changed the subject. Again he asked Kohler how it was that the R & D center was instrumental in his meeting Kammler.

"We're back to that, are we?" Kohler said, sounding somewhat miffed, remembering how they met. "It began with the Allied bombing of German cities and industrial centers. The Nazis realized they'd have to move everything underground to protect their assets until Göring's Luftwaffe regained air supremacy. Something we all knew wouldn't happen. A power struggle began between Himmler and Speer over whether the SS or the Ministry of Armament would manage construction of those underground cities. Himmler won, he tapped Kammler to head the project."

"Nordhausen and the underground city in the Jonastal region of Thuringia?" Strassburg asked.

"You're well informed, Karl," Kohler acknowledged, "and while Kammler is one of our best and brightest engineers, he had no experience designing and building complexes that large."

"And you did, because you built this facility," Strassburg said, "and because of that, Himmler told Kammler to talk to you about how he should design and construct Nordhausen and the city in Thuringia."

Kohler sported a mischievous smile.

"Yes, Karl, that's how I met Kammler."

Just then a whistle tooted on the lake outside the hangar.

22.

"What the hell was that?" Strassburg asked. "Sounds like the horn on an ocean liner."

"So you heard it?" Kohler asked impishly, as if anyone could not have heard the blast. Grabbing Strassburg by the arm, he directed him to a window and pointed. "That's some of our security."

Strassburg couldn't believe what he saw.

"Sir, you've got to be kidding!" Strassburg exclaimed. "That old lake steamer—that's you're security?"

"Part of it, but don't let her looks fool you. She's modeled after one of those surface raiders we used against the British at the outbreak of the war. You know, disguised merchant ships armed to the teeth. In order to justify her existence, we use her to ferry Swiss and Germans back-and-forth between our two countries, so no one will suspect her real purpose."

Strassburg was very aware that border security between Germany and Switzerland was tight. His parents, now living in Switzerland, could not visit him in Germany and he could not visit them in Switzerland. He wondered, who could travel between the two countries?

Kohler told him that before he could answer that question Strassburg needed a history lesson. Then Strassburg would appreciate how everything works—why some people could cross the border and others couldn't.

Historically, the area around the lake was known as Swabia—long before there was a Germany, Austria, or Switzerland. For thousands of year's people had lived around the lake. Many of the current residents could trace their lineage back to Roman times.

One of the qualifications for serving as a border guard in any of the three countries was your family must have lived around the lake for at least three hundred years. Consequently, all the border guards knew each other. They also knew the border-area residents. Because of the war what a person did for a living determined if they were permitted to cross borders. If a border guard in one neighboring country didn't know a person—and his opposite number also didn't know that same person—that individual couldn't go from country-to-country unless they had the proper papers. Even if the guards knew an individual—but that person was in the military or had anything to do with the military or war production—that individual was barred from crossing the border. Farmers, doctors, dentists, domestics, and trades people could cross back-and-forth among the three countries as long as they refrained from publicly voicing opinions about the war.

Kohler's wife's family was Swiss. Her family had lived on the Swiss side of the lake for five hundred years. She happened to be visiting them when she died. But because Kohler was a high-ranking officer in the German military the consensus among the Swabian officials was not to let him cross the border into Switzerland for her burial.

Four S-100 Schnellboots, five modified Seehund midget U-boats, and one Walter XXII prototype U-boat, which patrolled the lake in random patterns, provided security for the R&D center in addition to the steamer.

The Zeppelin hangar, the main feature of the facility, was steeped in rich history. The floating megalith had once housed the finest airships of their day. They provided a civilized and luxurious form of transportation unmatched by any type of winged aircraft. Consequently, Kohler was committed to preserving as much of the original hangar as he could without compromising the facility's R&D mission. The hangar's exterior retained vestiges of the past because it served a purpose. Occasionally Allied camera planes would perform flyovers looking for signs of a German and Austrian military presence. Something that was big, rusting, and falling apart wasn't likely to house anything but rats.

The hangar was twelve-stories tall and slightly more than nine hundred feet from bow to stern. Its beam was two hundred thirty-three feet. The once open space where Zeppelins had "lived" was now a tidy array of offices, shops, conference rooms, laboratories, catwalks, overhead cranes, electrical and hydraulic lines, storerooms, elevator banks, stairs, and balconies.

Kohler remarked that the first time Kammler saw the hangar he said it reminded him of a jail. Kohler asked him whether the prison camps he was building were as nice, and if not, be quiet and learn something. Kammler apologized and listened.

Three large atriums had thoughtfully been placed in the roof of the hangar. Each one provided natural light and a feeling of openness for the workers inside. From the air the atriums appeared to be nothing more than rotted away portions of roof reinforcing the notion, among the locals, that the hangar was in such a bad a state of disrepair and neglect that at any moment it might collapse. Except for the seemingly endless number of government safety inspectors, who kept checking for something and who weren't inspectors but members of the R&D's staff, no one ever ventured close to what once had been the lake's main tourist attraction. The fear was that any moment the structure might collapse and suck anyone close to it, under water to their death.

Everything in the hangar ran on electrical power generated by five enoromus generators housed in a soundproof room built into the hangar's foundation, thirty feet below the lake's surface. The generators were powered by diesel fuel stored in tanks next to the generators. The fuel got to the tanks by running through pipes along the lake's bottom from a pumping station located in the old wharf, four miles from the western end of Friedrichshafen.

The hangar's foundation had three decks. The first deck was divided into storerooms for spare parts and seldom-used equipment. The second housed the five generators and diesel. The third had underwater docking stations for the Seehund midget U-boats and the Walter XXII prototype U-boat.

The support part of the complex was on the mainland. It was a complete village surrounded by farms that supplied all the food the facility's staff required. The farms were so productive that half or more of what they produced was sold in local markets. The village and farms were centuries old.

When Kohler got Dönitz's permission to build the center he offered everyone who lived there more money than their farms, homes, stores, and shops were worth. Some stayed, giving legitimacy to the facility, but most moved out. Slowly, Kohler and his staff moved in, no one the wiser.

Besides the hangar, wharf, and farms the facility contained a school, chapel, small clinic, general store, police and fire station. The only thing added was a huge underground garage under the gas station. Its main use was storing captured Allied vehicles for gray missions and research. The Admiral told Strassburg to not be surprised if he saw an Allied tank freshly painted Wehrmacht gray sitting out under a tree being worked on or washed when the weather got better.

Strassburg thought it was strange that Allied vehicles, at times, were parked out in the open. Word might leak out to the Allies, he thought. But Kohler explained, what they found out was that many people believed they were looking at new Wehrmacht prototypes waiting to be tested.

At 3 p.m., Strassburg's crew was back at the hangar for the orientation, tour of the hangar, and Q&A session. Kammler was absent.

While the tour was going on, Strassburg pulled Kohler aside so he could ask him a question that was worrying him about the scope and importance of the Inland Sea Research and Development Test Facility.

"What if I–or any member of the crew was captured and we purposely or accidentally revealed the facility's location and the work done here? Germany would lose a great asset. We both know the Allies would bomb this place into dust if they knew it existed."

Kohler, barely able to control his rage, said, "So, what you're about to ask me, Karl, is who's the imbecile who decided to risk everything we're doing here by telling the six of you about this place in connection with a mission destined to fail. Correct?"

"Yes"

"The imbecile's your boss, Karl, SS General Hans Kammler. Kammler's power and influence go way beyond being a General in the SS. The man's so well connected and has so much dirt on so many people, most of *us* fear if anything happened to Hitler, Kammler could possibly gain control of the Reich."

"*Us*, Admiral? So you're in on some conspiracy?"

"This isn't the place Karl—later. The irony is Kammler might even be able to turn things around, subjecting Europe to Nazi domination for the next fifty years. Right now, Hitler is a blessing to the Allies. Hitler and his birdbrain decisions are costing us the war—a war we never should have started."

Strassburg point-blank asked Kohler why he believed the dam mission was doomed. He laconically told Strassburg he'd understand why when Kammler returned tomorrow to the hangar.

Kohler then addressed Strassburg's question about how Kammler came to use the Inland Sea Research and Development Test Facility for this nefarious project.

"He got permission to use this facility by going directly to Hitler. Convincing Hitler that doing the training for the dam mission and the BV 238's conversion here was worth the risk."

"Didn't you object?"

"Whom could I object to? Dönitz? If I did I'd have to tell him about the bomb and the mission. Hitler? He's the one who told Kammler to 'get the job done' any way he could. So I lied and told Dönitz that I overheard two SS Generals bragging he might soon be working for Himmler. Dönitz demanded that Hitler see him immediately. When he did, he asked Hitler if there was any truth to the rumor.

Hitler told Dönitz that things would soon start being done at this facility that were none of his business or the business of the *Kriegsmarine*. Hitler is desperate and this new super bomb is his pride and joy. As for how I know about the bomb, we'll talk more tonight when were alone."

Strassburg's confidence and trust in Kohler were growing as he listened to the man speak so intelligently and forthrightly about so many subjects—and people. So he frankly asked Kohler if one of his crew was SS, spying on him on Kammler's orders.

"I honestly don't know, Karl, if Kammler put a sleeper in your crew. I wouldn't put it past him. We've been talking back here in hushed tones way too long," Kohler cautioned Strassburg. "Start mingling with the others. As I told you before, we'll talk more tonight."

Everything kept getting more complicated. Strassburg's back was killing him. His head ached. For all he knew, Kammler had the Admiral in his back pocket and ordered him to find out if Strassburg could be trusted to lead the dam mission.

During the Q&A session Strassburg purposely didn't sit near Prien. Previously, during the orientation and the tour, they occasionally made polite small talk, which seemed natural. Strassburg hoped that if one of his crew were a spy, his coolness toward Prien would give the mole nothing to report. Only Ritter, the copilot, was showing any interest in Prien. This made sense: Ritter and Prien were about the same age and single, whereas Gerhardt, the crew chief, was some thirty-plus years older than Prien and despised her, thinking she should be married and tending to babies. Horst, the mission pilot, was a dozen years older than Prien and still brooding over the deaths of his wife and children. Clearly, he wasn't ready to get involved with a woman. That left Brock, the mechanic, who, while appearing uninhibited, likely wouldn't make a play for Prien once he saw Ritter, an officer, showing interest in her.

Strassburg somehow had to tell Prien to encourage Ritter's advances. This might take Kammler off the scent of any relationship between Strassburg and Prien.

If Kammler ever suspected the truth about their relationship, he'd hold Anna hostage. Strassburg wasn't sure what to do if that ugly scenario transpired. Things were becoming even more complicated with Strassburg living at the Zeppelin hangar and Prien living at a farm on the mainland. Communication was difficult.

There it was—the framed *Pour le Mérite*, or Blue Max, Imperial Germany's Great War medal, for valor—situated under an oil painting of the U-boat Kohler commanded during the Great War. Strassburg spotted it immediately as he entered the combination library, study, and parlor at Kohler's quarters in the hangar.

The room, which served so many purposes, was well organized, the result of Kohler's long service in cramped quarters aboard U-boats. The walls were paneled in walnut. The floors, constructed out of oak planking off the decks of wooden ships, served as frames for beautiful Oriental rugs of nomadic and urban designs. The room sharply contrasted with the skeletal, iron beam and girder open look, characteristic of the rest of the hangar. The furniture was from Germany's imperial period, the 1880s through the end of The Great War. It was comfortable and masculine without being ponderous.

"You keep looking at my *Pour le Mérite*, Karl," Kohler commented, standing aside, watching Strassburg's eyes dart back-and-forth between the painting of the U-boat on the stormy sea and the Blue Max below it.

"When you've lived as long as I have," Kohler reminisced, "you accumulate a lot of remembrances. See anyone you know here in these pictures?"

Strassburg immediately started looking at an array of framed photographs scattered about the room. He sensed he was about to discover something he preferred to forget. A chill ran through his body.

Finally, he saw it—the picture. Strassburg bit deep into his upper lip.

"I knew you looked familiar," he said in a hushed tone. "I just couldn't remember where I saw you—because I never did. You're Reinhard Kohler's father."

"Yes, I am or should I say *was*," Kohler replied, his eyes becoming moist. "Can you tell me about Crete, Karl?" Kohler asked in a plaintive voice. "When we received notification of Reinhard's death, all it said was 'Sorry for your loss. Your son was a splendid officer. He died a hero. Please accept his Knight's Cross, postmortem.'"

"Where's your son's Cross, Admiral?" Strassburg asked, thinking it strange it wasn't in a frame next to the Admiral's *Pour le Mérite*.

"It's buried with my wife, Karl," Kohler mournfully replied. "She died two months after we were notified that Reinhard was killed in action. She went to sleep one night and never woke up. I think she died of a broken heart."

All of this reminded Strassburg about how *his* mother reacted to the deaths of his two sisters.

For a while quiet filled the room. Then they both started talking at the same time. Again silence.

Strassburg sucked in a lung full of air. "I was the last person to see Reinhard alive. He died in my arms, as did twenty-two others at the base of Hill 107 on May 21, 1941, near the Maleme Airfield on Crete."

"Then you knew him, Karl?"

"No, sir, I knew *of* him," Strassburg told him, hoping to clarify the matter, "but I didn't *know* him. You probably knew that Reinhard was a mortar platoon leader. I was a pathfinder. The two jobs are different. We only met at parties and briefings. Word was your son was one hell of a good officer. We spoke once about the war and that was it."

"If I may ask, Karl, what did you talk about?"

"A lot of us were starting to have moral concerns about how the war was being pursued. How Germany might have started something she shouldn't have."

"Do you still feel that same way?" Kohler asked.

Strassburg hesitated. Kohler was asking a loaded question. "Why are you asking me this, Admiral?" Strassburg replied, serving up his own question.

Kohler's reply was candid, honest, and blunt. "To find out if I can trust you. Why else would I ask such a question? Please, take your time before answering. Your life—and the life of Fräulein Prien—depends on what you say."

Strassburg felt another chill run through his body. *Is this a threat? Or does Kohler, a high-ranking German naval officer, have anti-Nazi sentiments, like I do?*

Strassburg was at a top-secret naval facility in the middle of a lake. There was no chance—absolutely no chance—of escape. So if he guessed wrong about Kohler, it wouldn't matter. He'd be dead and so would Prien. However, if Kohler despised the Nazis and Kammler, like Strassburg did, there might be some way for him and Prien to get out of this alive. At the very least, Prien might survive. Kohler had spoken disparagingly about Kammler, so Strassburg took a chance—a very big chance. He spoke in a tone that left absolutely no doubt about his intentions.

"What you're really asking me is if I'd bomb that dam in the States. The answer is no, even if it means I'll be shot as a traitor and Anna will be killed because she loves me."

Kohler once again became teary-eyed. He hugged Strassburg as a father hugs a son.

"I lost a son," he said with melancholy in his voice, "but I feel I've just gained another. I was praying you'd say something like you did. If you hadn't, I don't know if we could ever have figured out a way to stop this foolishness."

Startled, Strassburg asked, "Who's we, Admiral? You mentioned *us* during the Q&A session this afternoon when you referred to 'us' fearing if something happened to Hitler, Kammler could end up running the Reich."

Kohler thought about what Strassburg asked. He hesitated. Then he spoke.

"I can't tell you that, Karl. If you knew the answer and Kammler found out about what I'm proposing you and I do to stop this madness much grief and pain could come to five members of a cell I'm a member of. And that's one of many cells throughout Germany that are trying to put an end to this insanity."

Kohler conceded to Strassburg that even he didn't know who all the "we's" were except for the five people who populated Kohler's very compartmentalized underground cell.

Strassburg was curious about how Kohler knew about his feelings for Anna. After all, the couple had met only twice—once at the Platterhof, and that was an accident, and once at the inn at Werder.

"I know about you and Anna," Kohler confessed, "because 'we' have 'eyes and ears' just like Kammler has—just not as many. When I saw how the two of you were going out of your way to avoid each other, I figured you either didn't like each other or you didn't want Kammler or any of your crew to know your true feelings for one another. And by that love-smitten gleam in your eyes, when I mentioned Fräulein Prien, it seems I guessed correctly."

Anticipating Strassburg's concern for Anna's safety, Kohler told him, "Don't worry, Karl, *we'll* see to it that Anna gets back safely to her parents at their home in Interlaken before you and the others leave for the States."

"Before I leave?" Strassburg asked. "How the hell—excuse me, sir—are you going to pull that off?"

Kohler smiled. "Before I tell you that, Karl, I need to talk to Fräulein Prien about her athleticism."

"Her athleticism?" Strassburg asked in a perplexed voice. "What's that got to do with getting her back to Switzerland?"

"A lot, Karl, a whole lot."

This time it was Strassburg during the hugging.

"Thank you, Admiral, thank you so very much," he gushed.

"My pleasure, son."

Strassburg recalled the Admiral cryptically had alluded to some major problem with the Hagelkorn, Blohm & Voss's glide bomb, which was pivotal to destroying Boulder Dam.

"Ah, yes, the *Hagelkorn*," Kohler said, shaking his head and laughing. "Kammler's grand solution for getting his wonder bomb to the dam. The solution he never checked out personally and at this very moment is trying to find a way to make it work. If he doesn't, and he won't, he's faced with telling our glorious Führer the bomb attack is a one-way suicide mission. Either that, or another target has to be selected."

Strassburg could clearly see that Kohler was enjoying the fact that Kammler had egg on his face. He admitted he was savoring every moment and in the same breath labeled Kammler an "obnoxious ass." Kohler speculated that Kammler was, right now, making frantic phone calls, trying to find another way to deliver what he called "that cursed bomb" to the dam.

Strassburg was a trifle miffed that Kohler still refused to tell him what the overwhelming problem was with the glide bomb.

Kohler's response showed exactly how shrewd he was.

"Because, Karl," he began, "if I told you what the problem is, and when Kammler tells you there's a delivery-system problem, you wouldn't sound genuinely shocked. And you must sound genuinely shocked, especially when he tells you *you're* the one who's going to have to solve the problem."

What a clever fox you are! Strassburg thought.

"So you think it'll end up being a suicide mission?" Strassburg asked.

"No," Kohler replied, smiling, "because you'll see to it that it isn't."

Strassburg laughed and asked Kohler if he had similar concerns about the Wall Street bomb.

"Karl," Kohler said, looking over the top of his glasses, "we both know that won't happen, don't we?"

How the hell does he know that? Strassburg wondered.

Kohler's chef, Raul, announced dinner, and Kohler led the way to the table.

"We don't dare delay, Karl. Raul is a refugee from the Spanish Civil War. He is as temperamental out of the kitchen as he is excellent in the kitchen. My late wife left countless family recipes and notes, which Raul follows faithfully. Although once in a while he can't resist inserting a few Castilian touches of his own."

Raul overheard the Admiral's comments, prompting him to roll his eyes in a gesture, in effect, saying, "The things I put up with as an artist to please this man."

Strassburg immediately recognized the bond of affection the two men shared—how much they enjoyed playing their little game of the patron not appreciating the artist's culinary creations.

The meal was an excellent blend of Swabian cuisine accented with touches of the Castilian. The beef in the *Zwiebelbraten* was from one of the facility's mainland farms. It was served with a light onion sauce of Raul's design atop a plate of spaetzle, crinkly flower noodles made from milled wheat, also from one of the facility's farms. The soup was a *Maultaschen*, a spinach-filled dumpling served in a light beef broth. Accompanying the meal was a local wine, a favorite of the Admiral and Raul. It was fruity and robust, complementing the main course. Dessert was a rich Black Forest cherry gâteau, another favorite of the patron and the artist.

After supper, Strassburg and Kohler pushed themselves slowly away from the table, thanked Raul for his delightful cuisine, and returned to the comfort of the oxblood–colored leather, overstuffed chairs in the library part of Kohler's living room.

"Cognac or scotch, Karl?"

"Scotch would be grand, sir," he replied, shifting in his chair because of back pain.

"Single malt neat?" Kohler asked.

"That would be wonderful, sir."

Kohler held up a bottle of Laphroaig from the famed Scottish distillery on the Isle of Islay.

"It's peaty and smoky," Kohler said, describing the liquor. "The Scots left it behind when they fled Dunkirk. But by what's going on in North Africa and Eastern Europe, they'll most likely be taking it back to Scotland in a couple of years. At least I hope so. And be sure to have some of these delicious cheeses Raul put out to fatten us up. Your old boss, Göring, loves the stuff."

"What's the matter, Karl?" Kohler asked, noticing Strassburg was squirming in his chair, as well as his detached demeanor.

"It's my back, and that—the picture on the wall of the U-boat you commanded during The Great War."

"You're wondering," Kohler replied, "what kind of a man would willingly allow himself to be sealed up in an iron coffin and spend his life underwater?"

"Yes, that's right, sir."

"Well, the same kind who's stupid enough to jump out of a perfectly good aircraft like you and my son did," Kohler joked.

They laughed. Then they toasted the men they knew—men who never returned from their missions.

Kohler pointed to the picture of his U-boat breaking through the nighttime waves on the North Atlantic's choppy surface. He told Strassburg that he could never lead men into battle on dry land—to see them die. Something like that would haunt him for the rest of his life. Kohler explained that in a U-boat every one either lived or died when the depth charges came. Because of that, he knew he'd never have to write one of those dreadful letters, telling a parent, a spouse, or loved one that their son or husband had died under his command.

"I admire men like you, Karl, and my son, who lead men, knowing sooner or later you'd have to write one of those horrible letters."

Strassburg sat there quietly. Eventually, he asked Kohler, "Who signed the letter, notifying you of your son's death?"

"Some Major with the letters KS," Kohler coldly replied. "No signature, just the initials. The damn letter read like a battlefield after-action report, not a condolence letter."

Kohler choked back tears.

"That's because it *was* an after-action report," Strassburg explained. "I was the only one left in any condition to write anything. Someone obviously took my report, copied it, and sent it to the families of those who died. I'm guessing they could only read the capital letters of my name, KS, and used those initials to identify the person writing the letter."

"Oh my god!" Kohler exclaimed, head down, eyes looking nowhere.

Raul entered the library.

"Please excuse me, Admiral," the chef apologized. "I forgot to refill your humidor. Would either of you gentlemen care for a cigar with your drinks and cheese?"

"We'd love one, Raul," Kohler told him, recovered from what Strassburg told him.

Looking at Strassburg, he added, "I think the Major and I need to discuss a certain young lady and what he should tell her—using you, Raul, as the messenger."

23.

K ammler looked terrible, stepping off the deck of the Schnellboot onto the star-board catwalk inside the hangar. Strassburg never saw him look this way be-fore. It was 9:30 a.m.

"What's the matter, General?" he asked, feigning genuine surprise. "You look absolutely dreadful."

"Spare me your concern, Major. *You've* got trouble," Kammler barked.

Not according to Admiral Kohler, General. It's you who has the trouble, not me.

"Your dam mission is now a suicide mission," Kammler brusquely an-nounced.

"I don't understand!" Strassburg said, forcing concern into his voice. "Is this some bad joke?" he asked. "There's a problem with the *Hagelkorn*?"

Kammler shook his head. Strassburg reminded him that back in Speer's of-fice he assured them—personally—that by using the *Hagelkorn* to deliver the bomb, Strassburg and his crew wouldn't be committing suicide.

"Keep your voice down, Major," Kammler asked. "I know what I told you, Speer, The Committee, and our beloved Führer. I don't give a shit what you, Speer, or the others think. But I *do* care about what Hitler thinks. He'll be a problem if you and your crew are blown to bits delivering that damn bomb. So shut up and help me solve this problem."

Kammler then made it personal. He told Strassburg the problem had to be solved if for no other reason than to spare his mother and father in their new home across the lake the news that their last child was—dead.

"And spare you, General," Strassburg bristled, "the embarrassment of hav-ing to tell Hitler you screwed up."

"That's ridiculous, Major, absolutely ridiculous!" Kammler said in a voice so loud two seamen checking the mine racks on the Schnellboot's stern turned to see who was yelling.

"Keep your voice down, General, this isn't the place to discuss this problem. Smile. I'll laugh. Make it look like what you said was a joke. Let's get out of here and find a place where we can talk—in private."

The pair nondescriptly walked to a quiet and dark corner of the hangar to continue their highly charged discussion. There, Strassburg asked Kammler who besides himself and Vogt knew about the problem.

"As far as I know, only Vogt and now you."

"Good. For now don't tell anyone else," Strassburg told him.

"Don't you want to know what *the problem* is?" Kammler asked.

The answer for Strassburg was a matter of common sense, as well as his pre-vious conversation with Kohler. Vogt designed both the BV 238 and the *Hagelkorn*. Kammler had just told him that beside himself, Vogt was the only person aware of the problem. Strassburg reasoned that since the BV 238 could carry a fifty thousand-pound payload when stripped of its finery, the problem had to be the *Hagelkorn*.

Strassburg did some quick figuring. The *Hagelkorn* weighed about sixteen hundred pounds. It stood to reason there was no way a sixteen hundred-pound glide bomb could carry a nine thousand-pound bomb, let alone be dropped from twenty thousand feet and be expected to hit a target fifty miles away.

"You got the glide ratio to the target, as well as the weight of the payload the *Hagelkorn* could carry, wrong," Strassburg asserted. "How does a doctor of engineering make such a big mistake?"

Kammler ignored the barb and said, "Instead of carrying nine-thousand pounds, as I was told, the payload is only nine hundred and fifty pounds."

"Ouch!"

"Don't be a smart-ass, Major," Kammler roared. Remember, this could become a suicide mission if *you* don't come up with a solution—and fast. Any suggestions would be deeply appreciated."

Strassburg's sharp and insightful mind already was probing for alternatives. He asked Kammler if Dr-Ing Vogt thought the BV 238, if placed on autopilot, might deliver the bomb fifty miles out from the dam once the trajectory was established, allowing the crew to bail out to safety.

Kammler had asked Vogt about that very same possibility, never mentioning the dam. Vogt told him too many things could go wrong during a fifty-mile journey on autopilot, and someone was needed—actually two people were needed—to constantly check the autopilot to ensure it was performing as set.

Besides, the BV 238 had to remain intact for use as a backup for the Wall Street mission if the V-2 failed to take out the US financial hub. During his monologue, Kammler let slip the backup plan was code-named "Howard," an ingenious ruse devised to get the huge flying boat through US air defenses.

So, "Howard," whatever it is, will allow us to get the BV 238 into US air space without getting shot down—I wonder. And thank you General for telling me you don't trust me. Saying someone has to stay with me, if the plan calls for flying the aircraft into the dam. So there's at least one member of the crew watching me to make sure I do as I'm told—are there others?

No matter what plan they came up with to get the bomb to the dam, Strassburg told Kammler they'd still need the BV 238 to carry it. So they'd still need to gut the plane's interior and get the fuel bladders, and extras, in case of leaks. They'd also need to have Kohler install a new ventilation system in the hangar to handle the exhaust from the BV 238's almost continually running six engines. Strassburg intended to run the engines until they failed to determine what spare parts to stock at the various refueling and maintenance spots along the route to the dam. He told Kammler to tell Prien to set up a flight simulator, resembling a BV 238 cockpit at Friedrichshafen, and start training Horst and Ritter on takeoffs and landings in all types of weather. He also told Kammler to make sure that Gerhardt and Brock immersed themselves in the workings of the BV 238 and that the entire crew should hone their English-language skills, especially colloquial English, as spoken in the American Southwest. They also should become knowledgeable about contemporary American culture—films, sports, politicians, important places, and landmarks.

"Yes, *Mein* Führer," Kammler sarcastically said after listening to Strassburg's extensive to-do list. "Your wishes are my command. And what will you be doing while I'm doing your bidding?"

"Getting the keys to one of the Admiral's cars on the mainland. I want to check out an idea that might might keep us all alive."

"Mind if I come with you?" Kammler asked.

"Of course not, General, I'll get the keys from the Admiral and twiddle my thumbs at the dock, while you tell Prien, the crew, and the Admiral what *I* need then to do."

And I thought you worked for me, Kammler laughed as Strassburg walked off toward Kohler's office.

"I saw you talking to Kammler as he stepped off the Schnellboot," Kohler remarked, a slight smirk forming at the corners of his mouth. "Kammler never looks happy. It's those lifeless fish eyes of his. But today he really looks miserable."

Strassburg told the Admiral he'd been right about the *Hagelkorn* and whoever gave Kammler the information about the weight it could carry would soon be playing winter sports on the Eastern Front.

"So, what are you planning to do, Karl?"

"Redesign the mission and make Kammler think it will work. If I don't Kammler will pick the target. He'll convince Hitler and the others to let him pick someone else to lead the mission. That 'someone else' most likely will be SS and you know how the SS likes nothing better than to kill thousands of people."

"And Germany will still loose the war."

"Of course. We both know the Wall Street mission won't work," Strassburg reminded Kohler, "and I'm the only one who can stop the second bomb from being used."

Strassburg switched gears.

"Remember telling me about the support facility on the mainland? While Kammler was telling me about the problem I had an idea that might work, but I have to take some measurements. That BV 238 manual on your desk, would it happen to say how wide the inside cargo area is?"

Kohler picked up the thick manual and started flipping pages back-and-forth, looking for the dimensions in question.

"Sorry, Karl," Kohler finally concluded, "but there's no mention here of what you're asking. It has the outside hull dimensions, not the interior. I'm guessing that the inside width of the hull, where the cargo area is, might be around eight to nine feet."

"How about the height of the two cargo doors in the nose?" Strassburg asked while jotting down notes.

"Probably seven feet," Kohler guessed. "If you want I can contact Dr-Ing Vogt at Blohm & Voss and get the exact numbers."

"For now, Admiral, what you told me is fine. I'll need transportation to the mainland and one of your cars at the wharf. Please call the garage, tell whoever's in charge I'll be coming by."

Kohler telephoned a dispatcher to ready one of his Schnellboots for the trip to the mainland, where a car would be waiting for Strassburg.

Even in February, driving through the countryside along the lake was pleasant and relaxing. As yet, the war hadn't touched the region.

If only Anna could be here with me, Strassburg thought, everything would be perfect— except for the damn war.

The garage was just as Kohler described it: one pump for gas, another for diesel, two bays, and a small office. The place appeared in need of paint and repair. An American Harley-Davidson motorcycle, painted in Panzer gray, leaned against a leafless tree.

Strassburg pulled up in front of one of the bays. A tall bearded man in his early thirties came out to greet him.

"You Strassburg?" he asked.

"Yes, and you're Leutnant Kempner?" Strassburg said, smiling.

"Yes, but please no mention of rank. I'm just a poor garage owner, and as you can see by the peeling paint, I'm trying to eke out a living in wartime. So how can I help you?"

Strassburg asked if Kempner had any captured US Army vehicles. Kempner pointed to the Harley. Strassburg admired the motorcycle and told Kempner he was interested in trucks.

"They're all underground." Kempner told him, motioning Strassburg to follow him.

The elevator bounced to a stop. Kempner pulled up the strap on the top door, which automatically opened both the top and bottom doors.

"Here we are. Karl's your first name, correct?"

"Yes, and yours?"

"Otto. And here we have most of our enemies' vehicles."

Strassburg gasped.

"Good grief!" It looks like you have at least one of every type of vehicle they have."

"Probably. What kind of truck are you looking for?"

"An American deuce-n-a-half."

"Over here,"Kempner told Strassburg, pointing to one that was battle scarred.

"How much weight can it carry and what's the width and height?

"As is," Kempner said in a matter-of-fact tone, "it can't carry anything. A Panzerfaust took out the rear axle somewhere in North Africa."

"Any way of rebuilding it," Strassburg asked, "so it can transport nine thousand pounds?"

"Shit! That's a lot of weight, Karl. This thing's only designed to carry two point five tons. When do you need it?" Kempner asked, concern mounting in his voice.

151

"Two months from now. Sometime in May would be great."

Kempner placed an arm around Strassburg's shoulder as if he had known him all of his life.

"Most people want things tomorrow, Karl. The beginning of May you'll have your truck rebuilt so it can carry five tons. I assume you don't want anyone suspecting what's in the bed, especially something that weighs five tons, right?"

"Correct. What's the width and length of the bed, Otto?"

"Looking at it, my guess is—probably six feet wide, seven feet deep."

"How about from the ground to the top of the cab?" Strassburg inquired.

"Maybe a little over nine feet."

"Ouch, the height's a problem," Strassburg told him.

"How high do you want it?"

"How about six and a half feet?"

"No problem," Kempner replied. "We'll do a little chop and channeling with the windshield, seats, etc. They'll go up and down. When they're up, no one will know they're collapsible."

"Thanks, Otto," Strassburg said. "Is it possible to get a Jeep and two Harleys, along with the truck?"

"How about a slightly used Russian T-34 just in from the Eastern Front?" Kempner joked. "We're having a special on tanks this week!"

24.

When Strassburg returned to the hangar, he called a meeting with Kammler and Kohler. He outlined his plan to both men, beginning with the BV 238 landing on Lake Mead, the lake behind the dam, taxiing up to a landing, and offloading Kempner's vehicles. When the convoy was on the road, and over the midpoint on the dam, they'ed fake an accident. The truck with the bomb in the back would "accidently" slip off the pavement and into the lake in back of the dam. Pressure from the water would activate a timer connected to the bomb's detonator. Before the bomb cooked off everyone would be safe in Mexico, staying there until the war ended.

"Smart!" Kohler exclaimed.

"Its absolutely brilliant," Kammler exclaimed. "So how long have you known the *Hagelkorn* wouldn't work, Major?" his voice trembled with anger.

Strassburg was livid. "What you should be asking General, is why *you* didn't know the *Hagelkorn* wouldn't work before *you* met Vogt yesterday. *You* were the one who told Minister Speer—in his office—there was no need for him to validate the information about the *Hagelkorn you* received from one of *your* SS buddies— inaccurate information that said the *Hagelkorn* would work.

"Now that *I've* come up with a workable plan to deliver the bomb," Strassburg thundered, "saving *you* the embarrassment of having to tell Hitler *you* screwed the pooch by not checking details *yourself*, you're asking *me* how long *I've* known *you* screwed up. How long should I have known?"

Kammler realized that once again, Strassburg had bested him.

"Since I told you this morning on the catwalk that it wouldn't work," Kammler sheepishly answered. "That is the answer you wanted, right?"

Kammler's tone and words belied his actual thoughts.

Slick, Major, very, very slick! Once again you've put me in an untenable position, embarrassing me this time in front of someone who's important and powerful. All this because that imbecile, Speer, asked me if he should check into the Hagelkorn's ability to deliver the bomb to the dam and I told him I had everything under control. Bah— what an ass I was. Damn you, Strassburg, you're a crafty son-of-a bitch, a worthy opponent. This is more fun than I've had in years!

Once Kammler simmered down, Kohler asked Strassburg to tell them how he came up with his plan. Strassburg glimpsed at Kammler as if asking permission to speak. Kammler responded by waving his hand nonchalantly, indicating approval.

A vengeful and caustic thought passed through Kammler's malignant mind. *Yes, Major, by all means tell us how you came up with the solution and with such speed. We're all holding our breath to hear how you saved my ass!*

Strassburg recounted his dinner the previous night with Kohler, where he learned about the garage on the mainland, the captured Allied vehicles, and how later that night he kept thinking about "Howard" and the *Hagelkorn* might not be the ideal delivery vehicle to take out Wall Street if that became the mission.

"And realizing we had the world's largest flying boat," Kammler interrupted, an acid tone to his voice, "you naturally thought about requisitioning a truck from the Admiral's garage, putting the bomb on the back, and driving it off the dam or to Wall Street, correct?"

"As a matter of fact, General, that's exactly what I thought."

Kohler confirmed the fact that sometime during last night's dinner conversation with Strassburg he mentioned the gas station on the mainland and the garage under the station filled with captured Allied vehicles. He also said Strassburg had come to his office this morning after learning from Kammler the glide bomb wouldn't work. He recounted their conversation about the size of the flying boat's cargo bay—that Strassburg requested a car and asked him to call the officer-in-charge at the garage to determine if any vehicles there were from the US military.

Once again Kammler found something to question. "The bomb weighs more than nine thousand pounds, Major. No American army truck rated to carry that much weight would ever fit into the BV 238's cargo bay."

Strassburg conceded Kammler's point.

"You're absolutely right General. One of their five-ton trucks won't fit in the aircraft's cargo bay. But one of their two-and-a-half-ton trucks, reinforced by Lieutenant Kempner's crew, will. And since Houtermans hasn't assembled the bomb, we'll have him disguise it as an electric generator and place it in the truck's bed."

Kammler slowly shook his head up-and-down massaging his chin with his fingers.

"Yes, that could work," he reluctantly admitted, but still skeptical, he said, "You mentioned taxiing the plane to some boat landing on the lake. Where would that be, Major? And why wouldn't it be crawling with American vacationers? There can't be that many landings, so finding one that's seldom used could be a problem."

Strassburg reminded Kammler how back in Speer's office the Minister showed him a map of the lake behind the dam, noting there were not just a few but numerous landings scattered all around the lake's shoreline.

"Okay, so there are numerous landings. My point is Major the lake's a recreational paradise in the middle of a desert. It'll be the end of summer when you land there. All those landings will be choked with hundreds of recreational power boats," Kammler shot back, his trademark smirk on his pockmarked face.

Both Strassburg and Kohler laughed.

"It's wartime there as it is here, Hans!"

Kohler shook his head and looked at Strassburg, "Explain it to the General, Major."

"Sir, there's gas rationing there as there is here so the likelihood of recreational powerboats being on the lake is slim to none.

"Also," Strassburg added, "as you pointed out it'll be the end of August when we arrive and the area around the lake is desert. If you were on the water that time of year, it would seem like you're in a sauna. Who in their right mind would waste their precious gas coupons to power a boat for recreational purposes knowing they'd be drenched in sweat?"

Kammler continued his pointed questioning, probing how Strassburg planned to get the bomb onto the dam and escape to Mexico.

Strassburg patiently explained his five-man team—two in the truck, two riding motorcycles, and one driving a Jeep—would be dressed in US Army uniforms, masquerading as part of an engineering unit transporting a generator to Los Angeles, California.

"Yes, yes, I assumed as much," Kammler snapped.

Strassburg, unruffled, continued, "I've told you there's a road over the dam. When we're at the midpoint, we'll blowout a tire. Naturally we'll have to stop to change the tire. During the tire changing the truck will 'accidentally' slip into gear, roll off the jack, and crash through the guardrail into the lake.

"Naturally," Strassburg deadpanned, "I'll apologize profusely for what happened to whoever's responsible for the dam's security. I'll tell him I'll report everything to my commanding officer, and the five of us will drive away. Just before we get to the US border with Mexico, we'll dump the vehicles, change from our US military uniforms into civilian clothes, cross the border, and—"

"Great, Major," Kammler interrupted, clapping. "I also like *our* plan for another reason. It works if we need to implement 'Howard.'"

"What the hell is 'Howard'?" Kohler interrupted.

"'Howard' takes place if we fail to take out Wall Street with the V-2," Kammler explained. "If that happens, the Major and his crew will abort the dam mission. They'll fly to one of the lakes in Upstate New York and drive the bomb to Wall Street. Hitler will be a happy man," Kammler boasted, "when I tell him about *my* new plan. Bravo, bravo!"

Strassburg abruptly changed the subject. He pointedly asked if Kammler had secured the new Swiss milling machines Dr. Cranz wanted.

"They should be arriving any day, Major" Kammler confidently said. "I've sent one of our best negotiators to persuade the Swiss it's in their best interest to sell those machines to us *tout de suite.*"

25.

D r. Peter Yost—powerfully built, handsome, his dark hair sprinkled with flecks of gray—was staring into the gray mist rising off Lake Zurich, situated outside his office window on the *Uto-Quay*. Yost glanced at his Rolex, surprised it wasn't even eleven o'clock. So far, it had been a busy morning.

Yost was enjoying the final puffs of a voluptuous eight-inch *Montecruz Individuale*, the cigar she gave him before abruptly departing. Yost watched, along with his secretary, as the woman hobbled through the snow, having just lost one of her stiletto heels. Leaning on the phony priest for support while he removed his bogus clergyman's collar, the two tried walking in lockstep without much luck. They finally disappeared into the mist coming off the lake.

What an evil lot these Nazis are, Yost thought. *How fortunate the world will be when they're gone!*

His private thoughts had to wait. Right now, Yost's attention was fixed on a copy of the *Constance Missal*, a liturgical book thought to be the earliest volume printed in Europe. Yost was concerned that it be properly cared for since he would be responsible for it until its rightful owner claimed it. With all the last-minute commotion taking place the counterfeit priest had forgotten to take the tome with him.

Yost knew there were only three known copies of the *Missal*: one in the Morgan Library and Museum in Manhattan; one in Zurich; and the volume given to him by the small, balding, and bespectacled man pretending to be a priest.

"What a twosome," Yost commented to his secretary. "The very attractive Fräulein Muller from the German Free Trade Delegation, brings this bogus priest holding the *Missal* with her so she can get what she wants: an audience with me."

"What did she want Dr. Yost?"

"Fourteen of our latest milling machines. She knew I'd never see her so she brings along "Dirty Collar" with the *Missal*, knowing I'd grant him the audience. Then when her charms don't work the two of them bolted out of here, as if some Russian T-34 tank was about to go "where the sun don't shine," forgetting to take the *Missal* with them. Damn these people!"

Muller and the "priest" arrived at Yost's office together. If it hadn't been for the man's dirty priest's collar, Yost would have been fooled into believing he was a clergyman. In other circumstances, Yost thought, the man might be an aging pimp and Muller his means of support. Shaking the man's clammy hand was like holding a dead fish.

Dirty Collar wasn't one for small talk. He got right to the point as Yost unwrapped the precious *Missal*.

"If you would, Dr. Yost," Dirty Collar said, "please tell me how much it will cost and how long it will take for you to duplicate the outside and a few of the inside pages."

"What pages would you like duplicated, Father?" Yost asked.

"It doesn't matter," Dirty Collar said, annoyed at Yost's question, "any few pages will do. Just so when we open the thing there's something to look at."

Yost buzzed his secretary on the intercom.

"Heidi," he politely requested, "if you'd be so kind, ask Jon to join us in my office. I need him to authenticate something and to give me an estimate on the time and cost it will take to duplicate a cover and some pages."

Yost placed his hand over the receiver's mouthpiece.

"This usually takes forty-five minutes to an hour," he told his visitors. "Can you wait?"

"Actually, Dr. Yost," Muller cut in, "the *Missal* is only one of the reasons that we're here. Forty-five minutes should give us plenty of time to conduct *our* other business."

Addressing Dirty Collar, she said, "Wait outside, Henry. Sorry, Father Henry, Dr. Yost and I need to discuss some Reich business."

"Father" Henry complied.

"And, Henry, take the *Missal* with you," she ordered. "When Dr. Yost's technician shows up, give it to him. That way he won't disturb us while we're discussing more important matters. Understand?"

"Perfectly, Fräulein."

Muller got down to business once Dirty Collar left the room.

"I'm here on behalf of the German government to negotiate a deal for your most current milling machines. I need fourteen. There seems to be some reluctance on the part of your government to sell us those machines—the ones capable of much higher tolerances than the ones we bought from you in 1941."

So that's it, Yost thought. *This is all about the milling machines. The Missal was the bait to see me.*

Muller laid her cards on the table. She conceded that six months ago, purchasing the milling machines wouldn't have presented a problem. That's when Germany was winning the war. Now, things were different. Von Paulus's Sixth Army was surrendering at Stalingrad. The Americans and British were bombing Germany day and night. Rommel's brilliant victories in North Africa had come to an end. The *Ubootwaffe's* happy hunting days in the North Atlantic seemed to be over. However the fact remained that Switzerland still needed German coal to heat its homes and run its factories as well as German food to fill its people's bellies.

"All true," Yost admitted, "but just as we need you for certain things you also need us."

"Oh, why is that Dr. Yost?"

"Because of our neutrality, Fräulein Muller."

Muller brushed off the remark fully knowing it was true.

"So why don't you get up from behind that cluttered desk of yours and go sit with me in one of those comfy chairs over there. We'll kick off our shoes, put our feet up on the ottoman, and I'll show you why Germany is still going win this war despite what has happened."

"What a grand idea, Fräulein Muller. Please, lead the way. I'm always open to seeing things differently. But as far as those milling machines go, I'm not the person you should talk to."

Muller dismissed Yost's comment as false modesty.

"First let me show you some things that might cause you to see things our way."

She sat down in a chair directly across from Yost and opened her briefcase. Pulling out a sheaf of official-looking papers, she began explaining what seemed to be a series of military reversals were actually well planned ploys to divide and conquer the Allies. During her presentation she kept crossing and uncrossing her long legs. The more she shifted her legs the higher her skirt crept up her legs. Now and then her skirt creeped up passed the tops of her hose, exposing just a hint of her pale-white Rubenesque thighs.

Then she reached for more papers. In the process she appeared to lose her balance. Her skirt went higher. Her legs spread apart revealing more than just her thighs. Muller recovered, faking modesty. Instead of pulling out more documents Muller took two cigars from her briefcase: a *Montecruz Individuale* for Yost and a small *Hoyo de Monterey Colorado* for herself.

She offered the *Montecruz* to Yost causing her to bend forward, exposing the deep cleavage between her generous breasts.

"Please, lick," she alluringly told him. "It will give you more pleasure."

Bending even lower she attempted to light his cigar. As fate would have it the one button holding her blouse shut opened. Coincidently, a mere fraction of a second later one of her bra straps slid off a shoulder. What was a girl to do? Feigning surprise and embarrassment, she slowly—with great theater—began fondling her naughty appendage back into its cup. After Fräulein Muller got everything tucked away, she stood up and pulled down her skirt, assured Yost would see something he liked. Instead he began licking the *Montecruz Individuale* she gave him, all the while remaining silent as a clam. Never before had anyone remained passive during one of her "presentations."

Standing there, the small *Hoyo de Monterey Colorado* dangling from her lips, she coyly muttered, "I'm so embarrassed. Please, forgive me. So far I've been doing all the talking. You must be bored. Permit me to show you something that won't bore you."

With that she pulled her skirt up around her waist, wiggled out of her panties, and kicked them behind her. The show was far from over. Next, she turned around, bent down, picked up her panties, turned back around facing Yost, and placed them in the breast pocket of his jacket. "There, that's more like it," she said, adjusting the panties as if they were a handkerchief.

Yost still didn't move; he never uttered a word. She was running out of options. She undid the garters from the tops of her stockings and with her legs spread wide moved towards Yost. Anticipating what was coming Yost stood up, sauntered over to his desk, pressed down one of the buttoms on the intercom, and spoke to his secretary.

"Please, come in here, Heidi," he said in a matter-of-fact tone. "It seems Fräulein Muller is having some clothing issues. She needs your help."

Muller was shocked. This just didn't happen. She had two options—both bad. If she opted to reattach her garters, her skirt would remain up while Yost's secretary and god knows who else entered the room viewing all of her parts below the waist. Or option two: she could lower her skirt and leave her hose around her ankles and look very foolish walking out of Yost's office.

Muller remained frozen in place, considering her options when the door opened. Yost cavalierly tossed her the panties.

"February is a cold month, Fräulein. The wind coming off the lake can be brutal. We wouldn't want those fantastic assets of yours to get a bad case of frostbite would we? Your choice of course."

Muller's face was scarlet. She pulled down her skirt, stuffing her panties in her coat pocket, hobbling as fast as she could out of Yost's office. Outside in the snow one of her heels caught in the top of one of her hose, causing her to lose her balance, along with her shoe. Dirty Collar, following closely in her wake, bumped into her, causing the two to eat a mouthful of snow.

Heidi, Yost's secretary, watching the show along with Yost, commented, "Such a pity! In all the excitement Father Henry forgot the *Missal*."

26.

Switzerland is a small country, made up of twenty-six states, called cantons. Among the oldest of the cantons is Appenzell, a land of unsurpassed beauty with rolling hills, green meadows, and the snowcapped Alps.

When most outsiders talk about the canton of Appenzell, they tend to mean the region of Appenzell. The region and canton often are confused. Appenzellers don't see themselves as Appenzellers—you're either a Vorderlander from Heiden, a Mitterlander from Teufen, or a Hinterlander from Herisau.

Yost's people were Mitterlanders, where the cow is king and the inhabitants have lived off their cheese production from time immemorial. Their economy, as well as their manners and customs, all revolved around the dairy cow. While other regions in Switzerland evolved into dairy farming co-ops, the Mitterlanders considered themselves their own lords and masters, solely responsible for all facets of cheese making and marketing. Yost's family had farmed in Appenzell from before Hannibal crossed the Alps. During the thirties, before the war, Peter, the second son, ran an extremely profitable export business, selling some of France's finest soft-ripened cheeses to an exclusive clientele of restaurants and hotels along the East Coast of the United States.

The second of three brothers, he knew he would never run the family farm. Under Swiss law the firstborn son is next in line upon the father's death.

Of all his father's sons, Peter was the one with the most drive, intelligence, and understanding of change. Yost's father was a man of vision. Realizing Mitterlander dairy farmers were facing change, triggered by advances in technology and marketing, the elder Yost sent Peter to the United States for his education; he attended the University of Illinois in Urbana-Champaign, where he earned a bachelor's degree in progressive and scientific agriculture. At the Harvard Business School in Boston, Massachusetts, he obtained an MBA. After graduation, he went up-and-down the East Coast of the United States with the sole purpose of taking orders from high-end hotels and restaurants for the finest cheeses Europe had to offer.

<hr />

What Yost proposed intrigued many. Few thought he could do it. Others had tried and failed. The most sought-after cheeses were the soft-ripened, highly perishable, unpasteurized French, like Brie and Camembert, or the washed-rind cheeses, like *Pont-l'Évêque*, not the harder Swiss ones, like Emmentaler.

US law stated that unpasteurized foreign cheeses like raw-milk Brie and Camembert must be aged at least sixty days before their export to the States and eaten within six to eight weeks after their arrival. So the problem was time. How could time be trimmed to get his cheeses from the small independent French dairy farmers to the mouths of US consumers in order to comply with US law?

Many complex steps were involved in transporting the cheese from farm to market: first the cheese had to be made, then it had to be washed and wrapped for shipping; French officials needed to check it for quality before shipping it to the US; once the cheese arrived in the United States, customs and food inspectors had to check it before importers could send it to distributers; at distribution centers it was subjected to local health inspections before being transported to restaurants and hotels; and then it waited at those restaurants and hotels until one of their patrons ordered it.

Yost solved the problem of time by having his cheeses chaperoned. He hired men to travel with large consignments of cheese, starting at the farms in France and ending up at the American restaurants and hotels that ordered it. The men he chose as his cheese chaperones were second and third sons of Swiss families—men who were personable, single, well educated, loved to travel, multilingual, and willing to learn the import–export business.

The easy part for Yost was lining up the French farms needed to supply the cheeses. The more difficult task was finding four- and five-star restaurants in the States willing to sign up as clients. Peter's enticement was a free cheese primer and menu for any restaurant or hotel willing to carry his high-quality products. Yost's cheese menus were high-end marketing pieces, rivaling the finest wine lists. They included histories of the various farms where his extraordinary cheeses originated. They were generously illustrated with beautiful maps and photos of the farms and the surrounding countryside. They became sought-after guides to the finest French and Swiss cheeses, leather-bound, printed on the finest papers, banknote quality four-color engravings, and beautiful four color and black-and-white photographs. Restaurant patrons often asked waiters if they could purchase one of Yost's cheese menus for gifts or for their libraries. The deal was always the same: if a restaurateur or hotelier agreed to purchase Yost's line of fine cheeses, they received the classy and tasteful menu free-of-charge.

For fifteen years, Yost's company was the sole supplier of the finest European cheeses to upscale hotels and restaurants from Boston to Miami. Clients were added from around the world as Yost's import–export business flourished.

The Swiss Bureau of Engraving held his print shop in such high regard, word was, if something went wrong at the Bureau, give it to the "Mitterlander" and *he* or one of his "cows" would fix it.

Yost's success came crashing to a halt when Germany brought France to her knees in less than six weeks in the summer of 1940. No more high-quality European soft cheese would reach fine American restaurants. His thriving business vanished in a month. But Yost, a crafty soul, wasn't devastated by this turn of events. He simply replaced one commodity—cheese—with another.

That new commodity came knocking at his door, courtesy of a former cheese supplier, a wealthy French dairy farmer who happened to be a Jew. Prior to the Nazi invasion of France—seeing the dark war clouds on the horizon—the farmer sold his business for what he could get for it. With the money he made from the sale and his life savings he and his family fled to Brussels. In Brussels, he purchased uncut blue-white diamonds, one- to three-carat, high-quality stones.

When German Panzers and Stukas attacked France, the farmer and his family bolted Brussels and went to Zurich, arriving on Yost's doorstep. The farmer was desperate. He wondered whether Yost, with all his connections and international business experience, could spirit him and his family to the States, where they could start a new life.

And so the legend of "the Magician" was born.

Yost began living two lives: his legitimate life as a successful international businessman, and his secret life as something of a twentieth-century *Scarlet Pimpernel*.

The Swiss were caught in a financial pincer. The Allies restricted Swiss imports–exports, claiming the Axis was using the Swiss as surrogates. The Axis squeezed Swiss exports, charging they were aiding the Allies. Consequently, the besieged Swiss had to obtain both Allies and Axis approval for anything entering or leaving the country. Yost cleverly took advantage of these circumstances.

With his in-depth knowledge and experience in international commerce and his intimate knowledge of the key players, he was able to grease the skids for the Allies and the Axis when they needed to conduct business beyond their borders. These transactions ran so smoothly that neither side looked into the details about how Yost got things done. But they did have suspicions.

His secret life, his clandestine business, was aided by his legal expediting business. Using his trusted contacts and savvy (amassed running his highly successful cheese import–export business), Yost started to scurry refugees out of countries the Nazis overran. Somehow he managed to remain one step ahead of the dreaded SS. But in order for his exploits to continue, there could be no traceable connection to the Swiss government. If the Nazis established a link, they would punish the Swiss by cutting back on gas, oil, coal, and other goods the Swiss needed to import in order to survive.

Yost had major hurdles to overcome. The biggest was finding new identities, false identities for refugees—identities that could never be unmasked by either the Nazis or officials in the escapees' new homelands. Oddly enough, the Nazis provided Yost with a solution when they brutally destroyed entire towns and in the process obliterated countless birth and other records.

Beginning in 1941, Yost tapped into the International Red Cross to pinpoint towns and small cities razed by the Nazis—places where everything was so completely destroyed that it was impossible to prove or disprove if a person or a family had resided there. Once Yost had that information, he used it as raw material for crafting a client's new identity provided the person could speak or learn the language where his papers claimed he or she was from. Yost cleverly used his high-quality printing operation—the presses used to print his slick cheese menus—to produce these new identities, family histories, personal papers, seals, and forge signatures.

But there was a problem. He no longer needed the printing part of the business because he no longer printed cheese menus. So he had to find a legitimate need to justify its existence. A friend of Yost's, a German lawyer living in Switzerland, came up with the perfect cover. Every church, synagogue or mosque in nations where the war raged had a Bible, Torah or Koran, considered by its congregation as priceless. Some, like the *Constance Missal*, were invaluable.

Yost offered a new service: preserve original Bibles, Torahs, Korans and other treasured religious documents in a safe and secure Swiss vault, and in their place create a high-quality reproduction for parishioners to use until the war ended. These reproductions were of such high quality that only scholars might discern the difference between an original and a Yost fake. However, these reproductions were costly. Only cathedrals, synagogues, mosques and churches with large—and perhaps wealthy—congregations could afford the high-caliber counterfeits.

Most commissions only covered the spine, front, and back covers, along with two or three facing pages. The pages were there so when the book was opened it appeared the reproduction was real. This subterfuge dramatically trimmed reproduction costs.

Yost's operation reproduced priceless Gutenberg Bibles and even some handwritten manuscripts dating to the sixth century A.D.

Word quickly spread about Yost's reproduction business and its attention to detail. Soon it became the only acceptable source in Europe and the United Kingdom for storing and reproducing religious works of art. But all that craftsmanship was also employed to manufacture government-quality seals, birth certificates, exit and entry visas, ration booklets, and other vital documents needed to spirit refugees to freedom from the Nazis.

The ex-cheese man had become "the Expeditor," "the Precious Document Protector," and "the Magician," who made people "disappear."

It was 1 p.m. when Yost's secretary buzzed him on the intercom, announcing the arrival of his old friend, the lawyer.

27.

Between April and May 1943, one hundred and nine Nazi U-boats were lost in the Atlantic due to Allied advances in anti-submarine warfare. The Allies, during that same time span, lost only five hundred and fifty thousand tons of shipping. This netted out to one U-boat lost for every Allied ship sunk—a ratio Germany couldn't sustain.

The vaunted Afrika Korps ceased to exist on May 12, 1943. Consequently, the entire North African coast now was in Allied hands.

On the evening of May 16, the British bombed and destroyed four hydroelectric dams on the Ruhr River. Coming in at an altitude of just sixty feet, the Lancaster bombers skipped five-ton bombs across the water behind the dams at Mohne, Eder, Sorpe, and Ennepe, crippling one of Germany's biggest industrial complexes.

The war was turning against the Axis on all fronts. With more defeats on the horizon, The Committee knew if the uranium bombs failed to destroy America's Financial District on Wall Street and the Hoover Dam in the Southwest, the "Thousand-Year Reich" would be another failed attempt at empire.

The refitting work on the BV 238 was finished on May 12. Flight trials on Lake Konstanz began the next day.

In the meantime, Raul, the Admiral's chef, kept passing Prien messages from Kohler and a somewhat reluctant Strassburg, encouraging her to keep visibly expressing her friendship with Ritter, the mission copilot. The ploy was designed by the Admiral to convince Kammler and the crew that Strassburg and Prien had ended their wartime fling.

For Strassburg, the gambit seemed to work a little too well, but that seemed fine with Prien. She thought she'd have some fun making Strassburg just a tad jealous. After all, they weren't even engaged.

While the BV 238 was put through its paces, other flying boats also were tested on Lake Konstanz. That was Kohler's idea. He wanted things to look normal to any prying eyes on the Swiss side of the lake.

The four US Army vehicles Strassburg selected for the mission were ready on May 23. The truck tapped to carry the bomb was loaded with six tons of metal to simulate the bomb's weight. This successfully tested its reinforced chassis to determine if it would support the bomb's weight.

The next day the vehicles were driven on-and-off the flying boat, which was afloat in the hangar, some twenty times to determine whether there were loading or unloading problems. There weren't.

Gerhardt (the crew chief) and Brock (the mechanic) suggested adding more tie-downs on the cargo deck, where the truck would be lodged. Three days later, with the suggested tie-downs welded to the deck, everyone kept their fingers crossed while Prien, Horst (the pilot), and Ritter (the copilot) got the monstrous flying boat with all the mission vehicles and a nine thousand-pound bomb stand-in airborne. Kammler, Kohler, and Strassburg watched the exercise from the deck of one of the Schnellboots. Prien successfully flew three touch-and-goes before turning the controls over to Horst and then Ritter. Both mission pilots completed their maneuvers without any problems.

Kohler radioed Gerhardt shortly after the flying boat landed.

"Do any of the welds around the tie-downs have cracks?" he asked.

"No problems with the welds," Gerhardt reported back.

Brock got so excited after the last touch-and-go, he slapped Prien on her ass. Brock was so embarrassed, he stayed in the cockpit and kept apologizing to Prien until Gerhardt couldn't take it any longer and told him to get back on the cargo deck.

Fuel bladders and transfer equipment arrived at the Zeppelin hangar on June 3. The following day the bladders along with the transfer equipment were installed behind the vehicles on the BV 238's cargo deck. Spare bladders were stowed in the extreme rear of the aircraft—insurance in case any of the bladders sprang irreparable leaks. The entire crew, including Strassburg, practiced refueling the bladders, as they would at the various repair and maintenance stopovers on the journey to the dam.

On the same day the bladders and transfer equipment arrived at the hangar, similar equipment arrived at the U-boat pens at Bordeaux on the French coast, a massive submarine base topped by thousands of tons of concrete and steel. The bladders were immediately installed in the tankers. Aviation fuel was pumped into the bladders; spare parts and everything needed to support the mission were loaded aboard the tankers the next day. When everything was stowed and accounted for, hatches were spun shut and the journey to the resupply points began. Once they were safely at sea, the tankers would surface to receive any last-minute instructions.

As previously agreed both tankers carried two sets of bladders and transfer equipment. One set filled with fuel would remain on the tankers. The empty set would be taken ashore at the various refueling sites. Here fuel from bladders on the tankers would be pumped into the ones onshore to refuel the BV 238 when it landed. After transferring fuel to the shore bladders, the tankers would steam to their next resupply point. On their return journey to Bordeaux, the tankers would pick up the empty bladders, technicians, and unused parts they had previously dropped off on their outbound cruise, leaving no sign of anyone or thing at the four refueling sites.

On the morning of June 6, Kammler received reconnaissance photos of the four-resupply points. Each site proved suitable for the mission.

Strassburg's four-member crew had sufficiently honed their English-language skills and knowledge of American trivia to successfully pass as GIs whose parents had immigrated to the States when they were young and had learned American English as a second language.

In the meantime, Strassburg went through rudimentary pilot training with Prien as his instructor. Kammler saw to it the two were never alone. Strassburg sharpened his flying skills to the point he could take off or land the BV 238 in the event Horst or Ritter was severely injured or killed.

The bomb arrived at the Zeppelin hangar at the end of June. Houtermans reconfigured it to fit inside a generator housing supplied by Kohler—the detonator kept separate.

<hr>

July 4 was the start of history's largest tank battle: the Battle of Kursk. Twenty-seven divisions of the German Ninth Army, in conjunction with Army Group South, attacked the Soviet-held Kursk salient in Operation Zitadelle. The battle ended on July 17—a disaster of epic proportions for Germany—guaranteeing she would lose the war if she failed to get America out of the global conflict and concentrate all her resources on the war with the USSR.

<hr>

Kammler, Kohler, and Strassburg had lunch together on July 19. After the meal, Kammler made an announcement Strassburg, his crew, and the Admiral anticipated.

"Himmler called me before lunch," Kammler said. "He told me Wall Street would be destroyed on August 18. However, if word of the mission's success hasn't reached you by August 20, you're instructed to abort the dam mission and proceed with Howard."

Strassburg, always curious, asked Kammler why the alternative mission was called "Howard."

Kammler, smiling, asked Strassburg if he knew of the American millionaire, Howard Hughes.

"The man's fascinating," Kammler explained. "He inherited a million-dollar company from his father and could have coasted through life. Instead, he became a famous aviator, setting transcontinental speed records from New York City to Los Angeles. In 1938, with a crew of four, he flew around the world in a little under four days. Now, he's a major player in the US aircraft industry."

Kohler knew this but was baffled. He wondered what Howard Hughes and his aviation accomplishments had to do with Strassburg's mission.

"Hughes has a contract with the US government to build the world's largest flying boat," Kammler told him. "He's building it out of plywood, which is interesting.

"Anyway," Kammler continued, "when I found out about this—and knowing the dam mission would be diverted to Wall Street if the rocket attack failed—I figured we needed a ruse to allow the Major and his crew to get to New York. And what better way to do that than to claim the BV 238 is Hughes's seagoing monster." Kammler laughed, in effect, congratulating himself on his brilliance.

Kohler asked Kammler if he knew for sure Hughes's airplane could fly.

"Who cares if it can or can't?" Kammler replied. "If the Major is challenged by some hotshot fighter pilot on his way across country to Wall Street, he simply radios the fighter, identifying himself as Howard Hughes, and tells the pilot he's test-flying a prototype of his new flying boat. No fighter pilot in his right mind is going to shoot down Howard Hughes, one of the richest and most powerful businessmen in America and a Hollywood filmmaker."

"Are you sure that some fighter pilot wouldn't shoot down the BV 238 even if he thought Hughes was the pilot?" Kohler asked Kammler.

"No, but I hope for the Major's sake—and the sake of his crew—I am," Kammler answered, laughing.

28.

The four men standing on the open-grilled catwalk, leaning on the rusty rail in front of them, stared down at the creature they all helped create. The catwalk was nearly touching the dark underside of the thousand-ton concrete roof covering the monstrous cavern below them. They were at the submarine pen on the island of Helgoland. One end was open, empting toward the North Sea. None of the men seemed to notice the pungent smell of salt air mixed with diesel fumes. The diesel aroma came from generators supplying auxiliary power to the strange-looking creature floating in the brackish water below them.

"What an ugly-looking beast," Kammler remarked. "I didn't think when the two were clamped together they'd look like this."

Cranz, the retired V-2 rocket scientist, stood next to Kammler, chuckling.

"What did you expect, Hans? You're looking at the first of its kind," Cranz remarked, pride punctuating his every word. "Give this idea fifty years to evolve, and it'll be a thing of beauty—sleek and deadly. This is only the beginning. But enough of my ramblings I assume everything is working as it should?" Cranz asked the third man, the Captain of the U-tug/barge combination.

The man Kammler chose to command the Wall Street mission was intelligent—an engineer and an officer in the SS—but he wasn't one of Dönitz's seasoned U-boat commanders. He'd never been in combat. His command experience was limited to supervising engineering projects. However, he had worked on the tug/barge combination as first assistant to Cranz and Walter.

"Yes, Doctor, everything is working just as we thought," the Captain replied. "Before you arrived, the General and I toured the barge and the tug."

Speer, the fourth man on the catwalk, asked about the crew.

The Captain explained there were three crews: one for the U-tug, one for the barge, and a team of underwater technicians who would set up the barge in the wreckage of the 1926 freighter off America's East Coast.

"They're all SS, Minister," the Captain noted. "They're all loyal to the Führer."

Wonderful! Speer thought. *That, by itself, should guarantee the mission's success.*

Speer asked whether any of the crew had combat experience on U-boats, a query that obviously annoyed both the Captain and Kammler.

"No, Speer," Kammler answered, sounding peeved, "no one in the crew has experienced combat of any kind. But they built and tested everything you're looking at. They also did all the sea trials. They know the ins-and-outs of every pipe and valve on the tug, barge, bomb, and rocket. Besides, none of the Captain's crew will be exposed to combat either above or below the waves. Once the rocket leaves the barge, the five technicians, who launched the rocket, will leave the barge and head south to the coasts of South Carolina or Georgia. Then they'll make their way to Mexico. Satisfied?"

"No, Hans," Speer asserted. "But as usual, I suppose it'll have to do."

Kammler ignored Speer's barb. He turned and faced the Captain. The two exchanged "Heil Hitler" salutes. The Captain then climbed down the catwalk's ladder to the tug's deck and disappeared down a hatch into the beast's interior.

Auxiliary power to the tug and barge was cut. Hatches were closed and locked. Then, as if by magic, water started waking out from behind the tug's stern. At first there was no movement. Then slowly the beast pushed itself out of its pen, into the low rays of the afternoon sun, reflecting off the water's calm surface.

Cranz, who was facing Kammler and Speer, said in an emotional and hubris-laden voice, "Gentlemen, we've just witnessed the birth of a new weapon system, one destined to change how war is fought. I just hope it will be enough to win us *this* war."

While Cranz slowly made his way down the ladder to the concrete pier below, Speer asked Kammler, "And how is Strassburg doing, Hans?"

"Brilliant, as usual," Kammler replied. "He's also, as usual, one big pain in my ass. Thanks for reminding me."

At that moment Speer noticed that Kammler didn't have his ever-present briefcase. When Speer mentioned this, Kammler showed no concern. This perplexed the Minister of Armament. "I know how you can be so anal over the pettiest, most insignificant things," Speer said, "and not absolutely livid over having misplaced your briefcase."

"Sorry to disappoint you," Kammler replied, his words cloaked in indifference.

Speer shook his head. He followed Cranz down the ladder, leaving Kammler alone to stare out at the last vestiges of the tug's wake as it disappeared beneath the sun-reflected water.

You ended up being such an ugly beast, didn't you? On your return to Helgoland the detonator in my briefcase will put an end to your ugliness. That way if this little venture lays a goose egg there won't be any loose ends.

29.

On August 11, Kammler gathered Strassburg, Kohler, and the mission's crew in one of the hangar's conference rooms for a brief meeting.

"You're departing on August 16," he bluntly announced.

Their departure was timed for the morning between when the British flew back to their bases from night raids on Axis targets and the Americans left their bases for daylight air raids.

From Lake Konstanz to Clipperton Island, the BV 238 would fly under Portuguese markings. Portugal was a war-time neutral and since the aircraft showed no armament and her lines were not that of a bomber, there would be no reason for any combatant to attack the flying boat. At least this was Kammler's theory.

The mission's cover story, should friend or foe make radio contact with the crew, was cholera had broken out in Angola, Portugal's African colony. The BV 238, a Portuguese aircraft with which none of the combatants were familiar, was flying out of Switzerland, bound for Angola, with drugs, doctors, and nurses to combat the disease. Kammler noted that Strassburg spoke Portuguese, which added plausibility to the cover story.

The crew was silent. Kammler could tell everyone thought the cover story thin.

Kohler was worried about what would happen in the event some German, Swiss, or Italian fighter challenged the BV 238 and wouldn't back off. Kammler assured the Admiral and everyone in the room that once it was known the aircraft was on a mercy flight, there wouldn't be trouble.

However," he added, "per Hitler's directive, I've had all Axis frequencies on your radios blocked, so you won't be able to communicate with any Axis aircraft."

"What!" Ritter shouted. "That's the stupidest thing I've ever heard. Why?"

Strassburg was thinking the same thing. He also was surprised that Ritter, normally quiet, was so vocal. Previously, the only time Ritter seemed talkative was with Anna.

Kammler was peeved.

"Because, Ritter," Kammler asserted, "Hitler is afraid that if somehow the Allies find out what we're planning, they might tell you to abort the mission over one of our frequencies. Now, I know that's a stretch," Kammler conceded, "and everyone on The Committee has told Hitler that, but he's still insisting, so that's the way it is."

Kammler wasn't shy about showing his frustration. He tried to smooth things over by pointing out that once the aircraft was flying over the Sahara, the crew wouldn't have to worry about fighters attacking them until they crossed into US airspace.

Horst, the pilot, asked Kammler if they would have all the current Allied, Axis, and neutral codes, radio frequencies, and call signs before leaving on the mission.

Kammler acknowledged this was an important issue, and before they departed on August 16, Strassburg would be given the frequencies needed to dial in and monitor all radio traffic. He stressed they'd be able to communicate with the Allies and neutrals, but not the Axis.

"I don't have the codes now," Kammler admitted, "because the Allies change them at one minute after twelve on the sixteenth of every month. Our intelligence—in this case, the Abwehr—won't have them until 3:30 a.m."

Brock, the mechanic, raised his hand. He wanted to know where the Portuguese markings would be stripped off the aircraft and what would replace them.

"You'll change the markings at Clipperton Island, Brock," Kammler instructed. "I'll give the Major the replacement markings, along with a diagram of where they go, before you leave."

With no more questions, Kammler announced that he and the Admiral were hosting a picnic in the crew's honor on August 13. Everyone who worked on the project at the facility, including families, was invited. He cautioned the crew to say nothing about the mission at the picnic.

"Where's the picnic, and what's the time, General?" Brock blurted out, causing everyone to smile, roll their eyes, and shake their heads.

Brock's enthusiasm for the picnic triggered a laughing spree.

"How about the park on top of the cliff next to the old wharf complex?" Kammler suggested. "Let's say 2:30 p.m., if that fits in your schedule, Brock."

Kammler was barely able to keep a straight face.

"Great, General," Brock gushed. "I'll be there!"

30.

The picnickers all wore civilian clothes. Arriving in a mixture of prewar trucks, sedans, and other vehicles on loan from the base's garage. Prien and Ritter arrived in a sporty 1936 two-seat roadster, top down. She was driving and had to park the car near the edge of the cliff since all the other spaces were taken.

"Who's that?" Strassburg asked Kohler.

"That's one of Kammler's secretaries. At least that's how he's introducing her to everyone," the Admiral explained, a tinge of sarcasm in his voice.

"She's gorgeous. What's her name?" Strassburg asked.

"I'm not sure she has a name, Karl. Kammler just keeps introducing her, as 'This is my secretary,'" Kohler quipped, a twinkle in his eye.

Upon spotting Strassburg, she sauntered over, pulled him to her breasts, and kissed him on the cheek as if she had known him for years. She continued holding him close, signaling something more than just a friendly greeting.

"Hans has told me so much about you, Major," she raved. "I'm so happy to meet a true Hero of the Reich. He said you're the only one who ever made him back down. Is that true?"

Strassburg was becoming more and more uneasy. Embarrassed by her closeness and uncomfortable where the conversation seemed headed.

"Are you the one who brought back those stockings from Paris, the ones I gave Fräulein Prien over there?" Strassburg asked, fumbling for something to say.

"As a matter of fact, I am. Hans told me that hasn't turned out too well," she gloated. "Unfortunately, things don't always work out the way we wish, do they? But then there's always the next one," she added, her hand moving from around his waist to where it shouldn't.

Oops! This is not good, Strassburg mused.

Strassburg forced a smile and pulled away, hoping his move wouldn't arouse suspicions he still harbored feelings for Prien.

"And about the General backing off," he said, picking up on her comment, "I'm sure no Major ever made the General back off."

"Nice comeback, Major," she said. "Yes, I see why Hans likes you. You're as Hans said, 'a very worthy opponent.' Presently, no one else seems capable of filling that need. While this has been fun," she said, a slight hint of malice in her voice, "I think we both know this stimulating repartee isn't likely to lead to us spending a night under the sheets. Be sure to let Hans know when you need more stockings.

"Isn't that your ex over there?" she asked, letting go of his arm.

"Look at her. Wow! Those long shapely legs I bet she's good in bed," she spitefully speculated.

And with that, Kammler's secretary abandoned Strassburg and ambled toward Prien, who was speaking to Kohler.

What the hell was that all about? Strassburg wondered.

"You'd better leave, my dear," Kohler said to Prien in a soft but authoritative voice. "It seems the General's secretary is heading this way. You know what to do," he cryptically added. "Good luck. I doubt we'll ever see one other again,"

Kohler kissed Prien on her cheek. She hugged him.

"Thank you so very, very much, Admiral, for all you've done for us," Anna dolefully said. "Good-bye."

And with that she turned and walked away, joining the other women watching the men play soccer.

Raul, the Admiral's chef, who'd spent hours preparing the picnic's cuisine, cornered Strassburg.

"Oh, there you are, Major," he casually said. "I've been looking all over for you. I need some men to help me carry the rest of the food down by the wharf and bring it up here. The Admiral told me to find you and ask if you wouldn't mind getting a few men to help me."

"Of course, Raul, I'd be happy to," Strassburg told him, hoping their conversation sounded unrehearsed.

Strassburg and the others met Raul at the wharf. Just as they began bringing the food to the picnic area, screams erupted from the park above them.

"Shit!" one of the men exclaimed. "What the hell's going on up there?"

Another speculated perhaps someone spotted an Allied fighter coming off the lake and sounded the alarm. Most doubted that was the reason behind all the screams since no one heard the all-too-familiar roar of an aircraft's engine coming in low, close to the ground.

"One thing's for sure, we're not going to find out what's happening up there by staying here," Strassburg yelled before dropping the load he was carrying and running up the steep hill to the park.

Mothers were running around, trying to gather up their children. Men were congregating at the cliff's edge.

"What's going on?" Strassburg shouted. Gerhardt grabbed his arm and pulled him aside.

"It's Fräulein Prien, Major," the crew chief replied. "Ritter, who was with her watching the men play football, said she went back to their car for something and while she was getting it, somehow, she must have released the emergency brake. The car rolled off the cliff with her inside."

"What! She was inside the car? Has anybody seen her in the water?"

"We're not sure, Major. In all the confusion, if anyone knows, it'd be Ritter. But he's so upset. The Admiral couldn't get anything out of him that makes any sense. Seems he really liked her."

Kammler joined Gerhardt and Strassburg.

"The Admiral's on the radio, calling the hangar," he reported. "He'll have boats here in a few minutes."

"But has anybody seen her?" Strassburg shouted, fear in his voice.

"Like I said, Major, we don't know," Gerhardt answered.

Hastily, Strassburg started unbuttoning his shirt.

"Forget it, Major," Gerhardt told him, "the water's far too deep and too cold

173

for anybody without a wet suit and diving gear to go in looking for her."

"So all we do is wait?" Strassburg lamented.

"That's all we can do, Karl," Kohler told him, having just put down the radio, and joined the trio of Kammler, Strassburg, and Gerhardt at the edge of the cliff. All four were staring into the black water below.

Seconds later a blast from the old lake steamer's ocean-liner horn sounded her arrival. Far in the distance, two Schnellboots were seen roaring out of the hangar, their signature rooster tail wakes high in the sky behind them. A third Schnellboot was coming hell-bent for leather from the broken-down wharf to the spot where the car plunged into the water.

"How deep is it?" Strassburg asked, forgetting Gerhardt's assessment in the heat of the moment.

"It hasn't changed, Karl," the Admiral told him, placing his arm around Strassburg's shoulder. "It's still too deep for free divers to go down to the bottom and way too cold to go into the water without wet suits. The divers on the Schnellboot will have their suits on in a moment. Be patient, Karl, be patient."

"So we wait, Major, and hope for the best," Gerhardt said, hope absent from his voice.

◂▬◼▶

And wait they did, into the night and through the morning of the following day. At noon, Kohler and Kammler met with Strassburg, his crew behind him. The Admiral and the General looked grim.

"Sorry, Karl," the Admiral mournfully began, "her body hasn't been found and might never be recovered. It's pointless to continue the search. The General will see to it her parents in Switzerland are notified of her death a few weeks after the bombs go off in the States."

Kammler, all the while, was carefully watching and assessing the crew's reaction to Prien's death. His shrewd and devious mind determined that Ritter, the copilot, was the hardest hit, with Brock, the mechanic, a close second. Strassburg, who should have been the most devastated, seemed a distant third. Kammler found this strange, disturbing, and puzzling.

"I'm surprised," Kammler said to Strassburg. "I thought you'd be taking Prien's death the hardest."

"We had a great night at the Platterhof," Strassburg admitted, "but that night at the inn on the Havel turned everything sour. Ritter was the one who really liked her, but after a while he'll get over her. You always do. War lets you do that."

◂▬◼▶

Kohler pulled Strassburg aside during the 4 p.m. smoke break. Outside the hangar the wind blew briskly so no one could eavesdrop on their covert conversation. Kohler reported to Strassburg that Raul had replaced the wet suit, fins, and Draeger Anna used during her escape earlier that day, when no one was around. Everything was cleaned and some parts were replaced. All the equipment she used was back where it belonged. If Kammler sent someone snooping around everything would appear normal.

174

The Draeger was one of Germany's greatest advances in underwater technology during World War II. It allowed the user to breathe underwater without having bubbles come to the surface, disclosing the user's location. It was perfect for clandestine operations. Strassburg learned about the device from Kohler when the two discussed ways to spirit Anna safely to Switzerland to be with her parents.

"How about the clothes she wore at the picnic?" Strassburg asked.

"Raul's burning them as we speak," Kohler replied. "Don't worry, Karl, everything is working just as we planned. Before you get to the dam, Anna will be safe with her parents at their lodge outside of Interlaken."

"And you're sure all the gear she used appears not to have been used in months?" Karl asked, still worrying about Kammler discovering the truth.

"Yes, Karl, everything is as it should be," Kohler assured him.

"I hope so," Strassburg nervously added. "Kammler's a cagey bastard and in case he starts sniffing around we don't want him to find anything suggesting that Anna didn't drown in the lake. What about the border crossing?"

"What border crossing?" Kohler mused. "Remember what I told you the first night when we had supper together—that long before there was a Switzerland, Germany, or Austria, there was Swabia? Anna will cross into Switzerland where the guards on both sides are locals. Her papers show she's a Swiss domestic who's no longer needed to do house cleaning chores in Germany. He hair will be cut short, she won't be wearing make up, her hands are rough from doing aircraft maintainance, and with that outdated nineteen twenties's dress, my wife's old gardening oxfords, and not wearing stockings she'll look to be what her papers say she is."

"A domestic going back to Switzerland."

"Exactly, Karl, and if for some reason the first crossing doesn't look right, she'll move to the next, just as Raul told her to do. She'll appear to be twenty years older than she is—she'll be fine, Karl."

"I know," Strassburg acknowledged, "but I can't stop worrying."

"You have to, Karl. So much depends on you stopping this foolishness that if you don't—"

"I know, Admiral, you're right."

Kohler encouraged Strassburg to get his mind off Anna and turn his attention to how he was going to stop the mission from succeeding and how he was going to handle the crew so they'd never suspect what he was doing.

What Strassburg regretted most was not having been able to brief Anna in person, a chore carried out by Raul.

"After the night we had at the inn," Strassburg lamented, "we never got a chance to talk to each other privately and—"

Strassburg never finished the "and" part.

"The way the war is going, Karl," Kohler contended, "it can't go on much longer, and when it ends you'll go to Switzerland and she'll be waiting for you. Now go back inside before someone gets suspicious."

Part III

31.

At dawn on August 16, Strassburg and his four-man crew strapped themselves into their seats aboard the BV 238 after saying their good-byes to Kohler and Kammler. The crew was silent while the two huge hangar doors slowly opened. A Schnellboot, the same one that greeted them on their arrival, towed the aircraft out of the hangar and into the haze on the lake's surface.

Once free of the tow, Horst and a somber Ritter coughed the plane's six engines to life. The aircraft taxied west into intermittent patches of haze. Its speed and noise increased as its six three-bladed props bit deeper and deeper into the air, the result of Ritter pushing the engines' power setting to their maximun limits. Skipping over the water with the grace of a dolphin, all engines at maximum RPM, the hull and outrigger pontoons at the end of the wings finally broke free of the water's surface.

Everyone cheered as Horst banked the big aircraft south, up into the skies over Austria, and down into Italy's lush Po Valley. Their route was designed to avoid Swiss airspace but give the impression the flight originated in Switzerland. Their departure was perfectly timed to avoid flights of British and American bombers and their fighter escorts.

The flight was routine until they passed Brindisi in eastern Italy near the Strait of Otranto, where the Adriatic meets the Ionian Sea. They were still over land when they encountered a lone German fighter, a Focke-Wulf 190A-5. The FW pilot tried raising them on radio but couldn't because of Hitler's decree. The pilot fired a few 20-mm rounds across the BV 238's nose in an effort to "encourage" them to communicate.

"What the hell do we do now, Major?" Horst yelled over his shoulder at Strassburg, who was sitting at the navigator's station, tending to the radio.

"He probably wants us to land, and we can't," Strassburg told him in a calm voice.

"We sure can't raise him, Max. Hitler—in his infinite wisdom—had the General block every fucking Axis frequency on our radios," Ritter reminded Horst, who was perspiring.

"Calm down, Max, calm down!" Strassburg advised the pilot. "There's always a way out if you don't panic."

Strassburg, long accustomed to surviving combat situations, considered the options.

Let the Focke-Wulf force us down. We land on soil and our flotation hull gets smashed. That's the end of it. Only it won't be the end of it because we're still in Axis territory and Kammler might be able to recover the bomb.

Or we land and the bomb's outer casing cracks and the entire area becomes radioactive for a hundred years.

Or we put out a distress call over Allied channels, fighters show up, they shoot down the Focke-Wulf, and we continue to the dam—if we can.

"Mayday! Mayday!" Strassburg said in Portuguese, speaking into the radio's microphone.

Then in English, with a Portuguese accent, he said, "We're a Portuguese mercy flight en route to Angola. We've got drugs, doctors, and nurses on board to deal with a recent cholera outbreak. A German fighter is attacking us. Mayday! Mayday! We're a little south of Brindisi."

Horst was becoming more and more agitated. He started screaming at Strassburg for sending the Mayday message, prompting the Allies to send aloft fighters to shoot down the Focke-Wulf.

Enough was enough. Strassburg shot back, "The mission comes first, Horst, shut up."

Strassburg needed desperately to buy time, hoping Allied fighters would arrive before the Focke-Wulf shot them down.

"Horst," he ordered the pilot, "give Ritter the controls. Ritter, when that Focke-Wulf makes his next pass, fly right at him. Maybe when he sees this monster coming straight at him, he'll think we're crazy and back off."

"And what if he doesn't?" Horst screamed while handing the controls to Ritter.

"Then we're fucked!" Ritter told him, no evidence of panic in his voice.

Twice Ritter was able to pull off his collision maneuver, causing the Focke-Wulf's pilot to pull up before the two aircraft became a fiery mess.

Strassburg and Ritter knew they'd never get a third chance to play chicken with the Focke-Wulf. The pilot was climbing and banking in a tight turn. In less than a minute the fighter would be on their tail.

Strassburg, expecting the worst, told Horst to do something useful. "Tell Gerhardt and Brock to put on their chutes and prepare to bail out."

Before Horst could utter a word, Gerhardt, followed by Brock, rushed into the cockpit. They were breathless. The FW, they reported, was no longer attacking them. It had exploded.

"Look there, Major," Brock said, squeezing his way passed Gerhardt, "two American P-47s."

"Yes, son," Gerhardt lamented. "They shot down the Focke-Wulf. They came at him out of the sun. The poor bastard never knew what hit him."

A few seconds later, one of the American P-47 pilots radioed, saying, "Good luck with the cholera mercy flight. Out."

Strassburg radioed back a "Thank you."

He told Ritter and Horst to switch seats and go back to their prescribed altitude.

Ritter felt the entire bloody incident was avoidable. He argued if Kammler had ignored Hitler's orders and left the radios alone, the Focke-Wulf's pilot would still be alive.

Horst told Ritter to be quiet. They were there to take orders not question them, he said. Strassburg said nothing, thinking Horst was an asshole and a trouble-maker. All five were happy to be alive, but their survival had come at a high cost. The Focke-Wulf pilot was only doing his duty. Ritter was right: the episode should never have happened.

The balance of their journey toward the delta of the Rio Muni was uneventful but breathtaking. Looking down from eighteen thousand feet, the earth below seemed like a painting.

The azure-blue waters of the Mediterranean, peppered with tiny specks of rolling whitecaps, abruptly changed into subtle shades of the ocher along the North African shoreline. Continuously swirling sand formed dunes as high as small mountains in the Sahara. Farther south the sand slowly mixed with spots of green until everything, as far as the eye could see, was shades of brilliant green, forming Central Africa's massive jungle canopy. Finally, an ever-widening ribbon of thin blue snaked its way east toward the South Atlantic, an hour of sunlight left to illuminate the delta of the Rio Muni.

"There it is!" Strassburg pointed. "Keep a sharp lookout. Our refueling site is in one of those small inlets about a mile-and-a-half from the ocean."

Horst was impressed with the whiteness of the sand as well as the palm trees and tropical vegetation, which would help conceal the huge aircraft while the ants below serviced and refueled the flying boat.

"Hard port!" Ritter called out, pointing.

Barely able to make it out, Horst said, "Got it. Thanks."

That tanker Captain couldn't have picked a better spot to drop off fuel and supplies. Horst's landing was his smoothest since their training began on Lake Konstanz. The refueling and maintenance crew watched the landing and commented on how the big flying boat landed with all the grace of an eagle. After Strassburg's crew introduced themselves to the refueling and maintenance team, they got down to work, with Gerhardt and Brock supervising. Strassburg, along with the two pilots, rested on plush beds in the cabin behind the cockpit. The cabin was designed for the comfort of Reich officials traveling on business but Strassburg got little rest. He worried and wondered whether Anna was safe with her parents in Switzerland.

Four hours later they were again airborne. The BV 238 flew almost due west over the moonlit waters of the South Atlantic, heading to their second refueling and maintenance site on the southern channel of the estuary of the Sao Francisco River near the coastal town of Penedo, Brazil.

Flying over what seemed to be endless water in the Mediterranean during daylight had been exceedingly boring. Now, flying over three times that amount of water at night was even worse—boring beyond words. The boredom was broken when Strassburg feed hourly course corrections to Ritter, who was now the pilot. Ritter would then place the corrections in the autopilot.

Gerhardt, concerned that Ritter, the only member of the crew with experience flying over large expanses of water, might fall asleep supplied him with copious amounts of strong black coffee. Occasionally, Ritter asked Gerhardt to wake up Strassburg and have him shoot a star fix, part of their celestial-navigation procedure to ensure they remained on course.

Horst took over the controls at daybreak. Brock relieved Gerhardt at the same time. A few minutes past noon, local time, Strassburg, perched in the copilot's seat, spotted the two channels in the delta of the Sao Francisco. While he couldn't see it, Strassburg knew tanker A was waiting, silently underwater, off the coast of the southern delta, to sanitize the area once they were back in the air on their journey across South America to San Ambrosio Island in the Pacific off the coast of Chile.

32.

"Damn," Horst spoke out in a somewhat disgruntled voice as he looked down off to port at the southern channel of the delta, "that sure doesn't look like what we left behind in Africa, does it?"

The Rio Muni's delta had been beautiful and tranquil and the Sao Francisco's delta was mostly flat with patches of ungainly palms, beach grass, and scrub vegetation—all mixed together in a tangled mess. The river's main channel was to the north, where the sand dunes were more stable, making it more navigable, more accessible, and more populated. More population meant more prying eyes, and since some of those eyes might be British, Kammler insisted locating the second refueling site somewhere in the delta's southern channel. He didn't want to run the risk of having some local report to the Allies that the world's largest flying boat was dropping in for "a spot of tea." By choosing the southern channel, where the dunes constantly shifted, the tanker and the aircraft could only go upstream or downstream during the height of the incoming tide. Long before the flying boat arrived, tanker A had gone upstream and located a spot that met the navigational needs of both the tanker and the flying boat—providing the sands held their positions.

The unloading of fuel, parts, and service personnel couldn't have gone better or been better timed. No sooner had everything been offloaded than the tanker's lookout announced the incoming tide. Hearing that news, the Captain ordered the boat's engineer to start and reverse engines, driving the tanker back out to sea beneath the waters of the Atlantic. Submerged, the tanker would silently wait for her sister tanker to arrive.

Horst, still basking in the praises he received for his magnificent landing at the Rio Muni's delta, said to Ritter, "Why don't you take this one and show us how it's done?"

Ritter, quiet by nature, took over the controls without fanfare. Eyeing a three-hundred yard spot in the channel without bends, he called out to the others, "Buckle up, this is going to be fun." With that he dropped the nose of the aircraft toward the channel, as if it were a Bf109 fighter about to engage a British Spitfire.

"What the hell are you doing?" Horst yelled, fumbling with the toggle on his harness, attempting to close it.

"Seeing if she performs as well as those BV 222s I flew in Norway," Ritter deadpanned, a slight smile on his lips

Maybe I won't have to scuttle the dam mission after all, Strassburg thought as he grabbed hold of the radio console for support. *If Ritter doesn't pull this off, the mission may end here.*

Obviously, something was going on between Horst and Ritter. Strassburg wasn't sure what it was until Horst barked, "Pull up now, you fool. That's an order! I'm in charge here."

"I thought the Major was," Ritter replied, no hint of stress in his voice. "And since he hasn't told me to pull up, shut the fuck up! Sit back. Relax. Enjoy the moment—what it feels like flying combat. You're too used to flying those nice controlled, completely thought-out test-flight maneuvers. This is what it all comes down to."

It was doubtful Horst heard a word Ritter said. The man was too scared. What happened next was breathtaking. The huge aircraft seemed to somehow pop out of the sky and the next moment it was floating in the channel. Everything happened so smoothly, so fast, that no one besides Ritter was sure what took place. Instead of auguring in, as Horst had prophesized, the huge beast landed in the middle of the channel with all the grace of a ballerina coming off *en pointe*. With the engines shut down, water rocking the hull side to side Gerhardt felt as if he was a baby being rocked in his cradle by his mother. Gerhardt made his way from the cargo deck to the cockpit.

"How the hell did you do that?" he asked, laughing. "I've been through a lot. I've never experienced anything like that. Fantastic, Ritter! Utterly fantastic."

Ritter smiled. "If you liked the landing," he quipped, "you're really going to love the takeoff. You either finesse these things, as Max did back at Rio Muni, or cut the bullshit, have some fun, and—well—have everyone crap in their pants."

"That doesn't answer Gerhardt's question," Horst piped in. "How in hell did you do it?"

"The same way I got that Focke-Wulf pilot to back off when I went head-to-head with him over Italy," Ritter explained.

Horst remained bewildered. What Ritter told him didn't make sense.

"What Ritter is telling you, Max," Strassburg patiently explained, "is that in combat you do things based on what *feels* right at the time."

"You mean like taking risks you don't have to. Like what Ritter just did," Horst asserted.

"Ritter wasn't taking risks," Strassburg explained. "He did something he knew he could do based on experience. Just like when he took on the Focke-Wulf pilot. He knew when the pilot first saw the airplane ten times the size of his fighter coming straight at him, he'd die if he didn't back off—"

"And he did," Gerhardt said, finishing the sentence. Gerhardt, a veteran of two wars, understood Strassburg's assessment of Ritter's actions. Horst, one of B&V's best test pilots but lacking combat experience, did not. Strassburg knew it was pointless to continue the discussion.

With the arrival of their tow Brock tossed out the line. The flying boat appeared to be under a cammo net after being towed into overhanging vegetation. Surprisingly, the officer-in-charge of maintenance turned out to be an old friend of Ritter's—not SS, like most of the crew on the tanker. The two served together in Norway. After swapping lies about their previous exploits in Norway, Ritter, who liked eating fish, asked his friend how the fishing was around the area. The maintenance officer scratched his head, telling Ritter that for the last three or four days fish were rarely seen in the channel near the refueling and maintenance site. He was puzzled by the scarcity of fish since they were plentiful previously. Mosquitos were sparse, too, and no one had seen any flesh-eating piranhas.

While Brock supervised work on the flying boat, Strassburg, Gerhardt, and the pilots caught up on sleep. Ritter awoke after an hour, found his friend, the OIC, and the two continued reminiscing about their "Norwegian vacation." Ritter was in the process of offering his friend a cigarette, when he spotted a log, more than thirty feet long, covered with what appeared to be spots of green algae, floating against the current, drifting toward the gangplank leading up to the open doors on the BV 238's bow.

"What the hell is that?" Ritter asked, pointing to the log.

"I'm not sure," the OIC confessed. "I'll get one of my men to push it out of the way before it hits your aircraft.

"Fritz," the OIC ordered, "get over here and push. Shit! What is that thing?"

In an instant the log came out of the water and started slithering up the gangplank.

"Oh, my god, it's a giant anaconda," Ritter shouted, eyes nearly coming out of their sockets

"What?" the OIC asked, gasping for breath.

"I saw its baby brother at the Berlin Zoo before the war," Ritter replied.

"So, what the hell do we do?" the OIC shouted loud enough to wake the dead.

"You tell me!" the copilot replied.

The maintenance crew was lightly armed with P-38 pistols and MP40 sub-machine pistols, none of them good shots. Both men knew, the chances of a 9-mm round stopping something the size of the anaconda was slim to none. The OIC thought that shooting the beast with the weapons at hand would only "piss him off." But since no one seemed to have a better idea, "what the hell."

Strassburg, who typically slept with one eye open, shot out of bed, hearing the all-too-familiar rattle of 9-mm rounds being pumped out the business end of a Schmeisser MP40. Spotting Horst's US Government 1911 lying next to the snoring pilot, Strassburg grabbed it, jacked a round into the chamber, flipped up the safety with his thumb, and went to investigate the reason for the Schmeisser's hissy fit.

At first, Strassburg couldn't believe it. The giant snake, crawling up the airplane's gangplank, swiveling his head back-and-forth, appeared to be performing a maintenance check. Ritter, the OIC, and a seaman, as well as members of the tanker crew, were frantically trying to unjam the Schmeisser.

"Put that fucking thing down!" Strassburg screamed. "You're going to kill yourselves. You've already shot holes in the plane's hull, and you haven't even touched whatever it is that's considering crawling up my pant leg."

Strassburg dropped the safety on the 1911 and proceeded to clean the magazine of its seven .45-caliber rounds in ten seconds. At first, the critter thrashed around like he'd been hit with a million volts of electricity. Then, just as fast it stopped.

"Fucking A! Nice shooting, Major," one of the tanker's seamen exclaimed, shocked at how fast events had unfolded. "The thing's dead, right?"

"Sure looks that way, doesn't it?" Strassburg remarked.

"Remember you saying how, up until three days ago, the fishing here had been fantastic?" Ritter reminded the maintenance officer.

"Yeah."

"Well, maybe that thing we thought was a log was the reason the fishing, here, turned sour," Ritter joked. Brock came running to see what all the commotion was about.

"That's a hell of a lot of fresh meat lying there on the gangplank, Major," Brock commented. "Think it's edible?"

"Probably," Strassburg answered, trying to keep a straight face. "And I bet it tastes like chicken."

"Really!" Brock exclaimed.

"No Brock, that's a joke. An old joke," Ritter explained.

Gerhardt, like Strassburg, was a light sleeper. He watched the entire scene play out, taking notice that all seven rounds Strassburg fired went into the snake's head while it swiveled from side to side.

Major, you are one hell of a shot.

Horst, slow to awaken, thought he heard explosions in his sleep.

"What's going on?" he asked Gerhardt. "Someone blasting away a sandbar blocking our way out of this resort?"

"Go back to sleep, Max. Show's over," Gerhardt told the pilot.

33.

The third leg of the journey was timed so they'd land at San Ambrosio Island during daylight. That meant flying west over the Andes at night. Their landing in the waters around the island wouldn't be in gently rolling surf, as it had been at Rio Muni. They were headed for a turbulent splashdown in the Pacific six hundred and fifty miles off the coast of Chile, aiming for a small piece of rock surrounded by pounding surf and high vertical walls, a wart on the face of the Pacific that time had forgotten.

Back in Speer's office, when the three were planning the mission, Kammler decided they should fly a south–southwest course, a route that veered away from the United States. A more direct route would have taken them to the Archipiélago de Colón, off the Ecuadorian coast, nearer to the States and closer to the Panama Canal. Mission secrecy was paramount and getting anywhere near the canal would invite trouble. The only land that met the mission's need for secrecy and could serve, as the third refueling site was San Ambrosio Island. To get there meant navigating peaks higher than nineteen thousand feet at night, a challenge even in daylight.

⬦▰▰▷

As they flew west the flat land below abruptly became hilly, a prelude to the Andes. Horst remarked to Strassburg, "Guess everyone's up tonight." Strassburg ignored Horst's remark. The light from the sun became dimmer, the light from the stars becoming brighter.

Strassburg laid out the schedule. Horst would fly the first six hours of the leg. Strassburg would be at the controls for the next six hours, followed by Ritter, who would land the BV 238 in the Pacific off the coast of San Ambrosio. Brock would keep Horst awake, and Gerhardt's job would be to keep Strassburg awake. Brock would be on duty when Ritter took over from Strassburg. Horst protested, saying Strassburg's crew schedule was crazy. He argued they needed everyone looking out for the Cordillera of the Andes and the massive Sierra de Ramón mountain range peaks during the crossing. Horst labeled Strassburg's plan "madness."

"It would be, Max, if I wasn't such a damn good pilot. But since I am, just relax as you always do whenever there's a crisis." Strassburg's comment caused everyone to laugh—everyone except Horst.

"Sorry, Major," Horst apologized, "I meant no disrespect."

Strassburg told Horst that under most circumstances he'd be right— but not tonight. Strassburg didn't intend to fly *over* the mountains. His plan was to fly *between* them. Strassburg pointed out that he was the only qualified navigator aboard the BV 238 and had plotted the flying boat's course between the peaks. Furthermore, they'd be flying at under thirteen thousand feet so there wouldn't be any "tight squeezes." Consequently, he'd pilot the plane though the "easy stuff."

Strassburg went on to explain that Ritter would be doing the "hard" flying, landing in "god knows what" conditions in the waters surrounding San Ambrosio. And if Ritter should have a problem landing at San Ambrosio, Horst would be there to save his ass. "Won't you Max?" Strassburg quipped. Once again everyone

187

laughed except Horst.

It happened around midnight. They were crossing Chile's Sierra de Ramón mountain chain. Gerhardt was telling Strassburg an amusing story about one of Göring's exploits during The Great War, when the BV 238 hit a small downdraft followed immediately by a strong updraft.

"What the hell was that?" Strassburg shouted, startled by a loud cracking sound apparently coming from the cargo bay.

Silence prevailed. Gerhardt rushed down the ladder to see what caused the sound. He reappeared minutes later white-faced, telling Strassburg they had a problem—a big problem. One of the tie-downs holding the truck in place on the diamond plate broke its weld. The one thing they needed and didn't have was equipment to weld steel to aluminum. All they could do was pray the other welds held and the remaining tie-downs were strong enough to keep the truck in place until they got to San Ambrosio.

"So from here on," Gerhardt urged, "easy on the air pockets, Okay?" He hoped to inject a little humor into a humorless situation.

At first, Strassburg remained silent. Then he replied, "I think we both know that getting to the island is the least of our problems. Landing without the truck coming loose while we skip "lightly" over the waves, like some three hundred-pound prima ballerina spinning on one toe—that will be the problem."

34.

"Brock, wake up the Major and Gerhardt," Horst ordered the mechanic. "We're at San Ambrosio and it doesn't look good."

"Look good?" Brock mumbled as he exited the cockpit. "It looks like shit, sir."

No one knew what to expect when they got to the island. But no one expected the island's five hundred-foot vertical basaltic rock walls to be encased in pea soup–thick fog—a fog with *Siren*-like arms, stretching more than a half mile into the Pacific—waiting to grab some unsuspecting mariner and dash him against the island's cliffs. While they could see the top on the island, it was impossible to determine where land met water. The scene was theatrically eerie, verging on the bizarre.

One hundred thousand years ago, San Ambrosio was a volcano. Now there was no visable sign that the island had been a volcano. San Ambrosio was approximately forty-five hundred yards long and nine hundred yards wide; its top a colorful mixture of multi-colored plants, barren rock and small ravines. Various types and sizes of broad-leaf trees, shrubs, ferns, and herbs dotted the landscape, encouraged to grow by the warm and moist climate. The top seemed to be held in place by cliffs that fell directly into the sea. The island had no beaches and few inlets. In one of those inlets the crew from the tanker constructed a small floating dock for servicing and refueling the aircraft when it arrived.

Ritter took his place in the pilot's seat. Strassburg's plan was to have Ritter keep circling until someone spotted the dock through the fog. Once they knew where the dock was, Ritter could land as close to it as possible, which meant spending less time bobbing around in the Pacific, waiting for the tow to find them. The less bobbing, the less chance of having another tie-down break its weld and the truck with the bomb coming loose and possibly sending the BV 238 to the bottom of the Pacific.

The fog wasn't lifting. But their concerns about finding the dock melted away as soon as they saw a red star shell, followed by two more, shoot up through the fog and explode in the sky to their eleven o'clock. The maintenance crew obviously had heard the plane's engines and shot the flares, indicating the area where they wanted the flying boat to land.

"Thank goodness they want us to land on the leeward side," Horst remarked. "There's way less chop on that side."

Ritter was at his best. The flying boat became one with the chop with hardly a skip.

"So, what happens now, Major?" Ritter asked.

"Taxi just a little into the fog and cut the engines," Strassburg replied.

Brock seemed petrified that Strassburg wanted the big aircraft to taxi into the unknown. "How far in is in, Major?" he asked.

"As far in, Brock, as Ritter wants to take her."

"Then what?" Gerhardt asked.

"We twiddle our thumbs and wait for instructions."

Instructions came in the form of a periscope wake.

Brock, in his usual position when they needed a tow, was perched on the forward edge of the cargo deck, bow doors open, waiting to throw a line to whoever showed up to tow them. At first, he couldn't tell what it was, but when he did he had a conniption fit.

"It's the fucking tanker," Brock yelled. The bastard's coming right at us. They're not slowing down."

The crew chief was standing directly behind Brock, his hands on the mechanic's shoulders.

"Steady, son, steady," Gerhardt told Brock in a voice filled with confidence. "Stay where you are, I'm sure those fish men don't want to bump into us any more than we want to bump into them. They're just waiting to see if we crap in our pants before they reverse their engines—smile, Brock—start waving at that one-eyed Cyclops son-of-a-bitch. You'll see, son, everything will be fine."

Gerhardt's words of encouragement were followed almost instantaneously by more of the periscope rising out of the water, a sure sign the underwater boat was surfacing.

"Forget what I just said, Brock. Now might be as good a time as any to say a few prayers."

U-tankers were immense, much larger than the BV 238. The massive flying boat with her engines off couldn't move. Collision was imminent. If the two collided, both would sink to the bottom of the Pacific. The question was how soon.

While the crew of the BV 238 would most likely survive because they were above the waves, the tanker's crew—being below the waves with the mass of the aircraft bearing down on top of them—would not. The periscope continued to rise.

"What the fuck?" Up in the cockpit, looking down at the periscope rising out of the water, Strassburg began to laugh. "The damn thing's a Biber."

A Biber was a midget U-boat, dubbed a "beaver," displacing six and three-quarter tons with a crew of one—not the monstrous IXD U-tankers Brock thought it was.

"I bet the sadistic bastard who's driving that piece of shit," Gerhardt barked to Brock, "is the same asshole who was driving that damn Schnellboot. The one who towed us to the hangar the day we landed on the lake back in February."

"What do you think, Brock?"

Brock didn't answer; he fainted sunny-side up.

Back at Bordeaux, when he was told about the mission and the problems

190

associated with using San Ambrosio Island as a re-supply point, the tanker's captain realized he'd need one vehicle capable of doing two things. Get everything off the tanker, needed to service the aircraft to the small floating dock his men would need to build and tow the flying boat to the the same dock once it landed in the waters off San Ambrosio. The captain told Kammler his problem. Kammler knowing about the little U-boat and what it could do secured one for the mission.

Gerhardt slapped Brock back to consciousness. After which Brock tossed a towline to the Biber's pilot. Brock then hollered to the pilot, asking how long they'd have to wait to start the tow because of the fog.

"Can't wait!" the pilot yelled back.

"Then how the hell do you know where you're going in this fog?" Brock shouted.

"Can't tell you that," the seaman answered jokingly. "If the Allies found out we'd lose the war."

Brock looked at Gerhardt and asked him if what the seaman told him was true. The crew chief looked skyward, hands clasped, as if praying. "Why me?" Gerhardt plaintively asked no one. "Why the hell did it have to be me?"

It was winter on the island, three hundred miles below the Tropic of Capricorn. Winter storms appeared and vanished at a moment's notice. The officer-in-charge told Strassburg he didn't want to rush him but the sooner they refueled the aircraft and fixed the broken tie-down, the sooner the BV 238 would be airborne and that would make him very happy. According to the OIC the sea would often go from being smooth as glass to whitecaps six-feet tall in barely a half hour.

The problem re-mounting the steel tie-down to the aluminum cargo deck was the maintenance crew not having the equipment needed to weld steel to aluminum. The best they could do was to weld the steel tie-down to a steel plate, drill holes through the plate and the deck, and bolt the two together.

Gerhardt balked, telling the OIC that the bolts might pull through the aluminum decking.

"You're absolutely right, Gerhardt," the OIC replied. "The steel bolts could pull through the aluminim decking. But it's the best we can do with what we have. If you can think of a better solution, let's hear it."

Gerhardt remained silent.

"So we bolt a steel plate, with the tie-down welded to it to the deck and Horst here finds us a nice puffy cloud to ride on," Strassberg told him.

"Don't bet on it, Major," Gerhardt sarcastically replied. "If we encounter rough weather, let Ritter do the flying, he's got big stones."

Strassburg thanked Gerhardt for his "sage" advice and told him he'd keep it in mind.

Horst looked angry but didn't say a word.

It seemed to Strassburg that Gerhardt, through looks, had signaled Horst to remain silent.

Strassburg wondered if Gerhardt was Horst's "real" boss.

Gerhardt and Brock returned to the dock to supervise the refueling and maintenance. Ritter joined Strassburg, Horst, and the OIC. Strassburg asked the OIC where he and his men were staying.

"On top of the volcano," the OIC joked. "Don't worry, the thing's been dormant for more than a hundred thousand years and since your plane won't be ready for four hours, let's climb to the top. I guarantee the view looking out over the Pacific will be worth all your huffing and puffing. The fog will be gone by the time we get to the top."

Horst asked him what the top looked liked.

"Like what the world must have looked like a million years ago, when the dinosaurs ruled the earth."

The dinosaur reference triggered Horst's memory of the crew's encounter with the giant anaconda. He asked the OIC if he or any members of his crew had encountered any strange creatures on the island.

"No," the OIC told him. "We left all those back in Germany, so they can keep screwing up things, making sure we lose the war."

35.

Strassburg and the two pilots figured it might take sixteen to eighteen hours to fly the four thousand miles over the Pacific from San Ambrosio to Clipperton Island, assuming they'd be able to maintain a constant air speed of two hundred and fifty air knots per hour, even if they encountered headwinds.

They'd depart at 3 a.m. the next day, so their landing at Clipperton would be shrouded in darkness. Strassburg and his team reckoned it would take four to six hours to refuel and perform maintenance at Clipperton before getting airborne at noon on August 19. The distance from Clipperton to the dam was eighteen hundred miles to the north and east. Strassburg's goal was to land in the waters of Lake Mead between 7 a.m. and 8 a.m. on August 20.

Back at the hangar on Lake Konstanz, Kammler gave Strassburg a 1930 US Army Corps of Engineers topographic map of the shoreline around Lake Mead. The map showed all the recreational boat sites, where a flying boat the size of a BV 238 could land and unload vehicles. Strassburg selected three potential sites, deciding to pick the actual site after viewing the trio of sites from the air.

Strassburg and Kohler knew the Wall Street mission would never happen. The rocket with the bomb would never leave the barge. That meant "Howard"—a disaster waiting to happen—would be implemented. Back at the hangar, the two devised a plan to foil Howard. Instead of *flying* the bomb to Wall Street, as Kammler proposed, Strassburg and his crew would land on Lake Mead and Strassburg would tell his crew they'd be *driving* the bomb cross-country to Wall Street. Along the way Strassburg would engineer a breakdown, someplace where the only inhabitants for miles around were rattlesnakes. Their only option would be to leave the bomb where it was. Strassburg would pretend arming it, giving everyone time to escape the blast—a blast that would never take place. When everyone had gone their separate ways, Strassburg would telephone the authorities; tell them about the bomb, where it was located, and after the war, he'd meet Anna in Switzerland and they'd marry—that was the plan.

Strassburg was restless, his sleep fitful. He couldn't doze more than a half an hour at a stretch. He kept thinking about whether Anna was safe with her parents in Interlaken.

Gerhardt awakened the crew at 2:30 a.m. After the four washed down some coffee, Horst and Ritter went to the cockpit, where they did engine run-ups, checking their instruments and gauges for discrepancies. Strassburg studied his maps. When everything was running and working smoothly, they waved their good-byes to the maintenance crew.

"You look tired, Major. Everything Okay?" Gerhardt asked.

Strassburg was tired. He told Gerhardt he'd been thinking about that tie-down, which he hadn't been doing. He asked Gerhardt if he thought it would hold.

"We won't know the answer to that one unless it breaks, will we?" the crew chief replied caustically.

Strassburg let Gerhardt's sarcasm pass, chalking it up to fatigue after a night with little or no sleep.

At 3 a.m. on August 19, the BV 238 headed for a point on the globe of 10 degrees 17 minutes north, 109 degrees 13 minutes west, the longitude and latitude of Clipperton Island off Mexico's Pacific coast. The six-square-mile coral atoll was named after the early eighteenth-century English pirate, John Clipperton, who discovered it in 1722. The average height of the island was six feet above sea level. It had 6.89 miles of coastline. A stagnant freshwater lagoon dominated the atoll's center. The only drinkable water came courtesy of May–October rains.

Strassburg carefully reviewed photographs of Clipperton given to him by Kammler. He noticed the atoll was covered with various palm trees and other vegetation, some of which tanker B's Captain would use to camouflage the fuel bladders and aircraft spare parts unloaded off the tanker prior to the BV 238's arrival. The island's sixty-nine-foot-tall extinct volcano would serve as an observation tower, as would the old French lighthouse. The volcano also was a prime location for one of the two Rheinmetall MG C/38 cannons the maintenance crew would use to defend themselves, if attacked by the US Navy. The barracks, abandoned in 1940 after the fall of France, remained in somewhat stable condition and would house the maintenance crew.

Strassburg told Horst to let Ritter fly the aircraft. Strassburg wanted to show Horst aerial photos of the atoll. "Look here at all of these anchorages inside the reef. If a storm comes up, we should be fine."

The pilot agreed. The problem wouldn't be finding a suitable anchorage. The problem at Clipperton would be getting over the coral to one of those anchorages and back out into the Pacific without ripping out of the bottom of the flotation hull or one of the outrigger pontoons. Horst was also edgy about the US Navy paying them a visit when they were moored inside the atoll's reef. Shrugging his shoulders Strassburg told him there was no way to tell when or if the US Navy would stop by for a visit. Kammler told Strassburg that in the late 1930s Roosevelt visited the atoll and wanted to make it a US possession, a move that might have been connected to some top-secret project. Kammler wasn't sure. Now, with the war going on, US warships occasionally cruised by the atoll, checking its condition.

"They ever come ashore and look around?" Horst asked.

"The Japs don't think so, according to Speer," Strassburg said. "From what they could tell, looking through a periscope, the Americans limit their reconnaissance of the atoll to viewing it from outside the reef using binoculars."

"That's most likely because their ships draw too much water to get over the coral," Horst reasoned.

Strassburg agreed. He also observed the US Navy surely wouldn't hesitate to send a landing party to the island if they thought something was afoot.

"So we cross our fingers and—"

Horst broke off the conversation as the flying boat suddenly gyrated, rising seven or eight feet before pancaking, then dropping twelve feet, and knocking both men to the floor. Ritter pulled back on the yoke and increased power. The aircraft climbed.

"Sorry," he told the two as they pulled themselves up off the cockpit's floor. "There may be more of this shit at this altitude. I'll try climbing above it."

Suddenly Brock poked his head through the hatch leading up from the cargo deck.

"Major, we just popped another tie-down."

"Is Gerhardt Okay?" Strassburg asked. "Is it the one we repaired?"

Brock was near panic. Horst appeared frightened by the news.

"Gerhardt's Okay, Major," Brock reported. "He's keeping an eye on the situation. He told me to come up here and tell you what's going on. The tie-down, fixed by the maintenance crew at San Ambrosio, is holding, but it's loosening up a little."

Looking at Ritter, Brock smiled a weak smile. "Gerhardt told me to tell you to knock off the fancy flying."

"Go back and tell Gerhardt to talk to the autopilot. That's when the hiccup occurred," Ritter told Brock.

Horst was flying the aircraft when the sun started slipping over the horizon. Ritter spotted the tiny atoll at one o'clock off in the distance. Horst turned the stick over to Ritter, who was skilled at night water landings.

"Get both your asses up here now!" Strassburg yelled down the open hatch to Gerhardt and Brock on the cargo deck. "Then go back in the cabin and buckle up in one of those posh seats. Stay there until Ritter lands this thing and we're dead in the water. If that truck comes loose during the landing," Strassburg warned, "most likely it'll puncture the hull and we'll sink like a rock. If you're up here in the cabin, you'll have a better chance of surviving."

Gerhardt was obstinate.

"Survive only to be shot because I failed to deliver the bomb," he shouted. "No thank you, Major. I'd rather stay down here and go down with the fucking aircraft. Brock can do what he wants. I'm staying."

Fear was in the crew chief's voice.

"Suit yourself, Gerhardt," Strassburg shouted back.

Brock wisely climbed the ladder to the cockpit, went to the cabin behind cockpit, and buckled in.

Strassburg, perplexed by Gerhardt's strange outburst, let it pass. His focus shifted to what was about to take place—the treacherous water landing just seconds away. If either the truck broke loose from its tie-downs or some coral below the surface ripped out the bottom of the aircraft's hull, the result would be the same. The flying boat would fill with water and sink to the bottom of the Pacific. Of the two options, the truck breaking loose would give the crew more time to escape. Either way, the bomb would be lost forever.

Strassburg, the two pilots, and Brock were strapped into their seats. Everyone's fate was in Ritter's hands. Their survival rested in his flying skill and luck. For a fleeting moment Strassburg's thoughts drifted away from the perils of the upcoming landing. He thoughts turned to Anna. He wished he could have traded places with Ritter and escorted Anna to the "farewell" picnic before they departed on the mission. He resented not having the chance to plan their future. But thanks to Admiral Kohler, Anna was safe, out of Germany. Strassburg remembered Kohler saying that the only chance the two of them had of coming out of this mess and ending up together after the war was if they stayed away from each other.

Pray for us, Anna, and pray that the Admiral and Raul make it out of Germany.

Strassburg was jarred back to reality by the sound of cheering. Then Gerhardt give him an enthusiastic slap on the back.

"We're down, Major," the crew chief gleefully remarked. "We made it! Everything in the cargo bay—despite the weakened tie-downs—is secure."

Strassburg was stunned to see Gerhardt standing in back of him.

"I'm surprised you changed your mind, Gerhardt," Strassburg ribbed. "I thought you'd still be camped out on the cargo deck, prepared to go down with the ship like all good Captains."

Gerhardt's face was flushed. Then he smiled. His explanation as to why he had abandoned the cargo bay, "thin beer."

"It's simple really," he began. "I figured if all of you survived, and I didn't, then you'd be stuck trying to handle Brock. And we couldn't have that, could we?"

Strassburg forced a smile, nodding agreement, pretending to accept Gerhardt's weak attempt at a humorous, anecdotal explanation of his actions. Beneath the humor and the forced smile, Gerhardt knew he'd made a big mistake when he told Strassburg, "If *I* fail to deliver the bomb."

Fuck you, Major! Was the only thought continuously looping through Gerhardt's mind.

The long and onerous journey, spanning continents and oceans, as well as the inherent danger of the mission, was fraying the crew's nerves. Could this be what triggered Gerhardt's sudden outburst on the cargo deck? Or was it something else? Strassburg wondered.

Nice going, Gerhardt, Strassburg thought, *but that still doesn't clear up the "I" thing, does it? Thank goodness we've only got eighteen hundred more miles of this craziness before we get to Lake Mead.*

Horst and Ritter were too busy searching for breaks in the coral and their tow to notice Strassburg was deep in thought. Strassburg was thinking about the crew. *Ritter was an experienced combat veteran, unflappable under pressure. Horst and Brock hadn't seen combat—at least that's what Kammler told me. In times of crises they exhibited fear and unpredictability.*

And then there's Gerhardt, the "rock"—at least I thought he was. Despite his being away from combat for twenty-five years, he seemed to have rock-solid nerves,

196

until moments ago when he had his little tantrum about staying on the cargo deck. And what was the meaning of his "I blew the mission" comment?

Unless, of course, I'm just "window dressing" to satisfy Hitler, and Gerhardt is the real mission commander.

Strassburg recalled the incident at the hanger. *That mission briefing just before the picnic when Kammler called Gerhardt by his first name, Frantz. Kammler never calls any subordinate by their first name. He always addresses them by rank.*

"So who is Gerhardt? For that matter, who are any of the others?"

36.

The team from the tanker assigned to tow them through a break in the reef had done their homework.

"These guys are damn good, Major," Gerhardt announced, watching the tow maneuver the BV 238 to the dock. "Not once did I hear our hull scrape over coral, although I saw it in the water beneath us."

After making landfall, the OIC introduced himself and his maintenance crew to Strassburg and the others. Handshakes and introductions were brief; refueling, repairing the tie-downs, and general maintenance were the priorities. Horst and Ritter, tired by stress, located two unoccupied, low-strung hammocks and proceeded to lie down. Refreshed by the balmy night winds off the Pacific the two had little trouble falling asleep. Gerhardt and Brock got right to work. They supervised the tanker's maintenance crew on tasks needed to get the aircraft ready for its final leg of the journey.

Strassburg, unable to sleep, struck up a conversation with the maintenance crew's OIC. Strassburg wondered if any American warships were spotted nosing around the atoll. In fact, they had. The incident occurred about a week before the seaplane arrived. A US Navy destroyer appeared at dusk out of the west, steaming east. The tanker crew grew tense with the arrival of their unwelcomed guests. Outside the reef seamen aboard the tanker quickly rigged her for crash dive so all the tanker Captain had to do was give the order. The American "tin can" started to make a slow wide three hundred sixty-degree "recon" of the atoll. The tanker slipped quietly under the water to *schnorchel* depth, the Captain making sure to keep the atoll between the tanker and the destroyer. Finally, after some nail-biting moments the destroyer steamed east. But at any moment more American warships could appear on the horizon.

"If we see more US warships," the officer-in-charge told Strassburg, "I don't care what that SS General said and neither does our SS Captain. We're all getting back on the tanker on the double. You and your crew are welcome to join us or try to make it through the opening in the reef and go wherever you're going."

"So you don't have any idea what this is all about?" Strassburg asked, amazed that Kammler wouldn't have told the tanker's SS Captain about the mission.

"Look, Major," the plainspoken OIC said, "we were in the *Ubootwaffe* until that big SS muck-a-d-muck General somehow got us away from Dönitz's command and assigned us to the SS. Our present Captain is SS, but like most Germans he's a 'mushroom.'"

"'Mushroom'? I don't understand."

"You know," the officer-in-charge, explained, "we're all kept in the dark about everything. First, we were told our tanker and another one were to be refitted as minelayers. Then the SS gets involved and we're refitted to carry aviation fuel in bladders, airplane parts, and two maintenance crews to remote spots all over the fucking globe. We're told to wait for that big-ass flying boat of yours to show up, top it off, make any repairs required, getting you on your way ASAP. And once you're back in the clouds, get the hell out of here, leaving no trace we were ever near these godforsaken shit holes. Then go back to Bordeaux. Trust me, Major, we have no idea what's going on."

The officer-in-charge sounded peeved about all the secrecy. Strassburg tried not to sound judgmental but asked him if he had a problem with the situation.

"You bet your ass I do. We all do. We're the ones holding our dicks, pissing into the wind, losing boats and crews, while those pukes in Berlin keep making their dumb decisions causing us to keep losing the war."

"Your point is?" Strassburg probed.

"As a courtesy," the OIC asserted, "it might be nice if those screwups in Berlin told us why we're taking such big risks."

"If you knew that," Strassburg said, "you'd shit in your pants. Besides, why would it be different in this war than it has been in other wars?"

"I'm not following you, Major?"

"Throughout history have the ones doing the fighting ever really known why they were fighting?

The officer-in-charge had to think about that.

"You do it," Strassburg reminded him, "because someone above you tells you to do it and so on up the ladder. And usually the person at the top hasn't a clue how to end it."

"That's grim."

"Sorry that's just the way it is. By the way, any wireless news about what's happening in Europe and the rest of the world?"

Strassburg was hoping to find out if there was news about Wall Street.

"Sicily fell to the Allies on the seventeenth," the OIC reported. "Other than that, same old shit. We just keep losing more ground to the Russians, British, and the Americans."

Fueled and serviced, the BV 238 was ready for takeoff.

"Well, Major," the officer-in-charge, said, "it's been grand. Good luck. I hope you, your crew, and that floating monstrosity we fueled and serviced win us the war. God knows we tried and couldn't. But for a while, before the Yanks came in, it looked like we might do just that."

Brock ran up to Strassburg and the OIC toting paint, stencils, and two large decals of a fierce-looking duck-like Disney character, dressed in a flying helmet and goggles. The duck needed to be placed on each side of the aircraft under the cockpit. The stencils contained an experimental 'N' number, NX37601 for the tail and various size Hughes Aircraft Company logos to be stenciled on the wings and fuselage, once the Portuguese markings were removed.

Strassburg gave Brock the nod to hand everything to the OIC.

"Oh my god!" the OIC exclaimed, surprise written across his face. "Those fools in Berlin really have gone off the deep end. That crazy Austrian with that ridiculous mustache is coughing up fur balls."

The entire maintenance crew, along with Strassburg, Ritter, and Brock, laughed. Strassburg noticed Horst and Gerhardt remained stoic.

"You really want my men to put these on your aircraft?" the OIC asked.

"That's the idea. We intend to win the war by making the Americans laugh themselves to death," Strassburg wisecracked.

Once the BV 238 cleared the coral reef and their tow headed back toward the atoll, Strassburg and the others waved good-bye. Horst had the stick. Ritter started the engines. Once the engines were warmed up, he pushed the six throttles up to full rev, adjusted ailerons, and flaps for takeoff. Within minutes the aircraft was airborne. Minutes before crossing into Baja, California, death came a-knocking.

37.

The flight was uneventful until Horst began battling a series of violent updrafts and downdrafts. The aircraft shook as if it were having an epileptic fit. After three savage bounces Strassburg and the two pilots heard a bloodcurdling scream coming from the cargo bay. Strassburg ripped off his headphones and rushed to the ladder leading down to the cargo deck. Gerhardt, coming up the ladder, blocked his way.

"What's the matter?" Strassburg barked.

"It's Brock," Gerhardt reported. "The tie-downs holding the Jeep in front of the deuce-and-a-half ripped out. The Jeep rolled backwards. Brock was between the two vehicles. He's dead."

"Out of my way," Strassburg yelled, pushing Gerhardt aside before doing a fireman slide down the ladder.

Brock—eyes open, expressionless, blood streaming from his mouth—was indeed dead. He was held upright against the deuce-and-a-half by the Jeep. Strassburg quickly ascended the ladder to the cockpit, confirming Brock's death to the two pilots.

"What do we do about the Jeep?" Horst asked.

"Gerhardt, Ritter, and I will tie the Jeep's rear bumper to the truck's front bumper," Strassburg answered. "I'm hoping that'll keep it from moving. We all better pray that more tie-downs don't break loose of their welds."

Horst, concerned about the position of Brock's body asked Strassburg what he intended to do about the corpse. Strassburg told him it had to stay where it was, fearing that any attempt to move it would trigger more problems.

"That's the best you can come up with?" screamed Horst, appearing hysterical.

"What's done with Brock's body is my concern. Not yours!" Strassburg barked at the pilot. "Your concern is flying this airplane. Make sure we don't hit any more rough air pockets. Understood?"

Horst was mute. Strassburg started to return to the cargo deck.

"Follow me!" he ordered Gerhardt and Ritter.

Once the trio was on the cargo deck, Strassburg ordered Gerhardt to get a line. The three of them lashed the Jeep to the truck. Once they landed on Lake Mead they'd say a few prayers before dumping Brock's body into the lake.

"Lake Mead?" Gerhardt asked sounding surprised. "I figured we'd be heading cross-country and land on one of those lakes in their state of New York. We've heard nothing about the rocket with the uranium bomb taking out Wall Street."

How the hell does he know it's a uranium bomb? Strassburg thought.

"Last-minute change of plans, Gerhardt," Strassburg curtly replied. "We're still taking out the dam. Wall Street's someone else's problem."

They fiddled with lines for twenty minutes, tying both the Jeep and the truck to the cargo deck's starboard and port aluminum bulkhead. Strassburg hoped the lines would take some of the stress off the deck tie-downs by transferring it to the sides of the aircraft.

"Think it'll hold if Horst keeps bouncing us around?" Strassburg asked Gerhardt.

"Your guess is as good as mine," the crew chief replied. "I still don't understand why these tie-downs keep breaking their welds."

"We can discuss the welds after we win the war," Strassburg derisively said. "Go back to the cockpit. I'll be up in a few minutes. I want to see if there's any more cracks in the remaining welds or if any of the nuts are working loose from the bolts."

"That's my job" Gerhardt fumed.

"No, Gerhardt," Strassburg pointed out, losing patience. "Your job is to do what I tell you to do. Get back up the ladder with Ritter. *Now!*"

After checking the welds and the bolts and not discovering any additional problems, Strassburg returned to the cockpit. Gerhardt was absent from the flight deck.

"Where's Gerhardt?" Strassburg asked.

"Turn around, Major!" Gerhardt ordered. "We need to talk."

"Be with you in a second," Strassburg replied over his shoulder, continuing his navigation discussion with a very nervous Horst.

"Now might be best, Major," Gerhardt barked. "We won't be going to Lake Mead."

Strassburg turned around slowly. Gerhardt's 1911 was pointing directly at Strassburg's chest, hammer back, safety down.

"By the way, the name's not Gerhardt, Major. It's Oberst Gerhardt Gent of the SS Adolf Hitler Leibstandarte Division."

"At least Kammler got the Gerhardt part right," Strassburg quipped.

Gent ignored Strassburg's feeble attempt at humor.

"And the man you're so diligently talking to about course corrections," Gent said, "is Major Horst Göring, no relation to the *Reichsmarschall*. And our queer copilot, sitting next to Major Göring, is who he says he is. Quite a lot to think about at one time, isn't it, Major? Just tell me where you hid the detonator for the bomb, and I'll shoot you in the head and not the gut."

"Before we decide where you're going to shoot me, Gerhardt—sorry, I mean Gent—tell me why Kammler didn't replace me with you before we took off from Lake Konstanz."

"Three reasons, Major," Gent, confided, "Hitler likes you. You're a Hero of the Reich. And General Kammler, other than not liking you, couldn't fabricate a reason to replace you with me that Hitler and the others would buy. Believe me, he tried."

"What about Ritter? Why was he picked for our merry band?" Strassburg asked, stalling for time.

"Because the 'fat one' Göring, the *Reichsmarschall*, doesn't like Ritter—"

"And?"

"And whoever Göring doesn't like, Himmler automatically does like. Also

Ritter, like you, is a Hero of the Reich. But not nearly the hero you are, or should I say *was*. He's also the best combat flying-boat pilot in the Luftwaffe. He has no family, so there'll be no one asking troublesome questions about what happened to him after I kill him."

"What about you, Oberst, and Major Göring, here? Did you both do what Kammler said you did?" Strassburg asked, stringing out the conversation as long as possible.

"I served in the Great War," Gent said, "as General Kammler told you. Major Göring is one of the best test pilots B&V ever had. Ten times better than that blonde bitch you were screwing—just not as pretty. And I'd be happy to tell her that, if she was still alive."

A split second later, the click of a hammer being cocked resonated through the cabin and the cockpit.

"The bitch is behind you, Gent, and she's not happy," a voice asserted from the shadows behind Gent. "In fact, she's pissed and she's holding a gun that's pointed at your head. Surprise! Surprise!" Prien said in an assured, confident voice.

38.

"How in hell" were the only words Gent (aka Gerhardt) managed to blurt out as he turned to face the voice from the shadows, a voice he thought was dead, a voice he despised—the voice of a woman he thought should be pumping out babies and wearing an apron in the kitchen instead of test-flying world-class airplanes.

The reason for not finishing the sentence was a *click* followed by a *swish*. Gent never heard the *splat* like the others did, an unusual-looking knife sticking out of his left ear. Gent died instantly.

With everything happening so fast, no one noticed Göring (aka Horst) pulling out his Government 1911 and crash it down on the back of Strassburg's head. Unconscious, Strassburg crumpled to the cockpit's floor. As Strassburg collapsed, Horst fired two shots. His first shot missed. His second hit Prien in her left shoulder, missing bone and arteries. That was the bad news. The good news was that after Horst's second round hit her, she managed to place two rounds into Horst's heart, blowing out all four ventricles. After that, she collapsed to the cabin's deck, as if she were a rag doll.

Ritter, the only one left standing, was the one who threw the strange-looking knife into Gent's ear. After checking out the plane's autopilot, making sure it was working properly, Ritter went over to Prien's limp body to see how badly she was wounded. He determined the bullet that struck her was a full-metal jacket (FMJ) designed to penetrate and break bones, not cause lead poisoning. Prien was lucky the round that hit her had just gone through soft tissue and exited her back.

Ritter poured a packet of antibacterial sulfonamide, a sulfa drug, into the wound's entrance and exit holes. He bandaged Prien's shoulder, leaving her where she was until he attended to Strassburg. When Prien regained consciousness, her shoulder would hurt like hell. Young and strong, her recovery would be fast, allowing her to travel in a week or less. Strassburg's condition was far different and could be complicated. Head wounds often were fatal. Ritter, unsure what to do, picked up Strassburg and carried him to one of the chairs in the cabin he converted into a bed.

He propped him up with pillows, elevated his head, loosened his clothing, and removed his boots. Then Ritter belted Strassburg onto his bed so he'd remain upright. Now, the copilot-turned-medic turned his attention to Prien. He placed her unconscious body on the chair/bed across the aisle from Strassburg and belted her as he did with Strassburg. After doing this, Ritter returned to the cockpit to check the instruments and gauges to ensure they hadn't been damaged by the gunfire. Everything was operating normally. He then tended to Gerhardt and Horst.

After retrieving his knife from Gerhardt's ear, he wiped it off on Gerhardt's shirt, folded it, and stuck it back up his sleeve. He pushed the two lifeless bodies down the hatch leading to the cargo deck. Life was starting to look a whole lot better to Ritter as he looked at Gerhardt and Horst lying facedown on the deck below.

Ritter was surprised how easy it was to enter into US airspace. He crossed his fingers, hoping to ensure their good luck would continue. He knew if Strassburg failed to regain consciousness and give him the current US codes and challenges, no matter what was plastered on the side of the aircraft, US fighters would shoot down the seaplane.

He flew cautiously over endless miles of desolate landscape barely fifty feet off the deck, evading US radar sweeps. Finally, there it was, Lake Mead their final destination. Ritter found the area surrounding the lake extremely bizarre and un-nerving. He was used to flying out of beautiful Norwegian fjords, unlike the fjords Mead was a massive man-made freshwater lake nestled between three hundred-foot cliffs of sandstone surrounded by desert bereft of vegetation.

Failing to spot any people, Ritter made his landing approach. No people around meant no one would report the presence of a huge and strange-looking air-craft to local authorities. Ritter ruminated about the upcoming landing. *With any luck the Jeep won't come loose and the only way to find that out is to land this big son-of-a-bitch now.* Ritter made one of his smoothest landings. *Such a shame*, he thought, no one but himself to see his first touchdown in the United States. Now what? He mused. *I know what the plan is, but without Strassburg giving me instruc-tions, I can't do anything but dump the bodies of those two SS assholes, along with poor Brock, into the lake and wait for Strassburg to regain consciousness—maybe.*

Ritter noted on Strassburg's map where they were on the lake. He set the sea anchor and opened the doors, windows, and hatches to cool the plane's interior. He returned to the pilot's seat, put his feet up on the instrument console, and snoozed.

Prien was the first to regain consciousness.

"What happened?" she moaned.

"You were shot," Ritter bluntly said. "Then you killed the bastard who shot you."

"Horst?" she asked, still somewhat foggy.

"Close enough," he answered. "You're going to need this. It's morphine to control the pain. I've already given you one shot. Just remember, I can't give you more of this stuff until six hours from now. If I did, you might become addicted."

The pain was intense, but Prien still managed a smile. That was before she looked across the aisle and saw Strassburg, unconscious, strapped to the bed.

"How bad is he, Will?" she asked, not sure she wanted to know.

"I have no idea," he truthfully replied. "I'm a pilot, not a doctor."

"Then all we can do is wait?" she asked, biting her lip.

"I'm afraid so, Anna, but while we're waiting, mind telling me where you hid?"

"Behind all those back-up fuel bladders along with my gear and some food. I must smell like a goat." She laughed. "But speaking of bladders, could you help me up and walk with me to the head? I'm not sure I can make it by myself."

She looked back at Strassburg. "He'll be Okay while we're gone, won't he?"

39.

Sometime during the night Strassburg groaned, his first sign of life.

"Will, wake up!" Prien whispered, her voice filled with excitement. "I think Karl's regaining consciousness."

It took Strassburg an hour to explain everything to Ritter and Anna once he awoke and the cobwebs cleared from his brain.

"This is all great, Major," Ritter remarked. "But—"

Strassburg interrupted. "From now on, Will, drop the 'Major.' Call me Karl. And I'll call you Wilhelm."

"Do us both a favor," Ritter joked, "call me Will."

"Then, Will, it is," Strassburg said, smiling.

"The thing is, Karl, we've been anchored here for hours. It's nighttime and dark. I'd like to start the engines, find the landing spot you picked out, unload what we need, and once that's done take this floating palace to the center of the lake and sink her, along with the truck and the bomb before the prairie dogs and rattlesnakes spread the word there's two Germans, a Swiss, and one big-ass flying boat in their swimming pool."

"You're right on all counts but one, Will," Strassburg told him. "The truck with the bomb comes off the plane along with us. We'll put everything in an old abandoned mine near the landing location I've marked on one of my maps. Until I figure out what to do with the bomb, it stays in the mine."

"You're still the boss, Karl," a wide grin forming on his handsome face.

Just before sunup, everything they needed, including the bomb, was unloaded and stashed in the mine. Once that was done, Ritter ran up the engines one last time. After positioning the airplane in the center of the lake, the bodies of Brock, Gerhardt, and Horst—along with what they didn't need still inside the aircraft—he opened the seacocks. Twenty minutes later, everything rested three hundred feet underwater.

Strassburg did some fishing, caught some, and brought back driftwood for a fire, while Ritter disposed of the flying boat. After breakfast the conversation became serious. Will asked Karl for one of the Harleys.

"Three's a crowd and both of you seem Okay," Ritter remarked, sadness in his voice.

Strassburg encouraged Ritter to stay. Ritter insisted it was time to leave, to disappear. He reminded the two that before Anna started chumming around with him, Kammler suspected his sexual preference was contrary to Nazi doctrine. But because of Anna's visible interest in him, he avoided the fate Nazis reserved for Jews, gypsies, and homosexuals.

"Did Kohler—" she started to ask.

"Admiral Kohler knew," Ritter said, "and, just like Dönitz, didn't care. The only thing either one of them cared about was performance."

"Kohler knew?" Strassburg asked, sounding surprised "Why didn't he tell me? All the time I thought you were trying to move in on Anna."

"I was, Karl," Ritter laughed. "for our protection. Kohler thought if he told you about me, you wouldn't appear jealous. Everything had to look like the two of you no longer cared for each another."

"Jealous! I was never jealous," Strassburg said, grinning while Prien and Ritter smiled at each other.

Strassburg asked about the knife Ritter used to take out Gerhardt, noting he caught only a glimpse of it before being knocked unconscious.

"The switchblade? I picked it up in Italy while I was training Italian pilots how to support their torpedo boats in the Mediterranean."

Prien wondered about Ritter's escape plan.

"It's better for all of us if you don't know," he explained. "Once I leave, you won't hear from me again. I hope you don't mind, Karl, but I took the papers, money, gas rationing, and food stamps Kammler gave Brock, and with what Kammler gave me, I'll be fine. The one thing I'll tell you is this: I won't be going back to Europe. All my family there is dead."

"What do you think you'll end up doing, Will?" Prien asked. "You're such a fantastic pilot."

"Find a company that builds rockets, become one of their test pilots, and walk on the moon."

Strassburg laughed. "You do realize no one is building those types of rockets, don't you?"

"They will, and I'll be there when they do. Within thirty years men and women will be in space. I just hope we'll do it for exploration and not subjugation."

Strassburg told Ritter he was welcome to anything Brock had but cautioned him about using the bogus passports Kammler handed out to the crew. Strassburg feared they might be traceable. Ritter already was on top of that situation. He showed Strassburg his collection of passports: four American, six British, five Norwegian, and four Canadian.

"Where the hell did you get those?" Strassburg asked, astonished at the number of passports.

"Don't worry, Karl, I didn't kill anyone to get them. I traded women's silk stockings."

"Will, sweetie," Anna asked, trying to appear coy, "you wouldn't happen to have some extras, would you?"

"Passports or stockings?" he asked her, his infectious smile spreading across his unshaven face.

Immediately after breakfast, while the sun was still low in the east, the three hugged as if they had known each other for a lifetime.

Ritter got on the Harley and took off for parts unknown. Anna was crying.

"Think we'll see him again?" she asked, waving good-bye with her uninjured arm as long as she could see the dust trail behind his Harley.

"I doubt it, Anna," Karl replied. "I don't see either of us going to the moon anytime soon."

Anna thought it over. "I'll bet you that in thirty years we'll see pictures of Will or someone like him standing on the moon."

Strassburg was feeling better. The drugs Ritter had given him, taken from the crew's medical kit, were working wonders. In fact, Strassburg was feeling a bit frisky. He asked Anna if she was wearing underwear.

"Karl!" she said, feigning shock. "You know I'm not. The stuff I had on was filthy. Will washed it for me in the lake before breakfast. It's out there on a rock, waiting for the sun to bake it dry."

"Feel good enough for a back rub?" he asked.

"Oh, so that's what we're calling it now?" she quipped, reaching down inside the waistband of his pants with the hand of her good arm as he pulled up her skirt around her waist.

40.

Anna and Karl played house in the mine for three days. It's cool interior allowed them to escape the sun's blistering heat. Karl fished in the lake during the cool hours before dawn and after dusk. At night, under light from the stars, the two took short walks along the beach when Anna felt like walking. Her shoulder was giving her less pain every day. Life was wonderful. Both wished it could continue. Both were realists and knew it wouldn't. They needed to return to civilization, get their lives in order, contact their parents, and let them know they were Okay. They also knew they had to be careful. Kammler might have agents on the lookout for Karl and the other members of the crew now that neither target had been destroyed. Anna suggested they cross the US-Mexico border, as was the original plan for Karl and his crew and head to Mexico City.

"It's a huge city, sweetie. We could easily disappear in one of its many neighborhoods. I could go to the Swiss embassy and ask for asylum. I'm sure they'd grant it to both of us."

Knowing Kammler, Karl thought he probably had people stationed at all or some of the border crossings, watching to see if any of the crew showed up. But Anna was right Mexico was their only option. Recalling a discussion he had with Kohler about where to cross and avoid detection, Karl recommended they enter Mexico at El Paso on the US side and go into Ciudad Juárez on the Mexican side. The reason for choosing El Paso was the large number of farm workers that daily crossed back-and-forth between the two countries. Karl reminded Anna of the risk they'd be taking. Lines of worry crossed her beautiful face.

"Is that why you're growing a mustache?" she asked.

"Yes, and you should change your appearance too," Karl said in a serious voice.

"What? Grow a mustache?" she asked jokingly. "I thought about it but decided not to! Instead, you're going to cut my hair as I told Raul I would do but didn't. And don't look so scared. I'll tell you how to do it. I can see you as a poor man's Clark Gable and myself as a tall, fantastically beautiful, Jean Harlow," she mused. They both laughed.

Their laughter was short-lived, as Anna's mood changed and her tone became somber. "What about the bomb, Karl?"

Karl conceded he didn't have the foggiest idea about what to do with the bomb on the deuce-and-a-half in the back of the mine. He couldn't call the Americans because he didn't know whom to call. Even if he had known they'd either laugh, thinking he and Anna were nuts, or shoot them when they saw what they brought them, from as Karl put it, his "ex-employers. And once the Americans had the bomb, some high-up government official might convince Roosevelt to drop it on Germany just out of spite.

"What about the Wall Street bomb?" Anna asked. "Whenever I asked about it you seemed so sure it would fail."

"Yes, because Kammler was unwilling to go beyond the SS for assistance, fearing someone might grab some of his power." Back in Speer's office, Karl explained, "when we were trying to figure out how to get the bomb to Wall Street, since the Reich didn't have a plane that could cross the Atlantic, we developed the plan I told you about. Everything seemed doable except the observation part from the air."

"Observation part? I don't understand," Anna said, wrinkling her brow, bewildered.

Karl explained the ploy about using a shipwreck one hundred fifty miles off the coast to disguise the barge housing the rocket and Speer getting hold of a 1937 US Coastal Survey chart of the area showing hundreds of shipwrecks. One of the shipwrecks, a small Canadian coastal freighter sunk in 1926 by the US Coast Guard for illegally running whiskey into the States, was deemed the perfect spot to anchor the barge and not have it observed from the air.

Anna listened intensely as Karl proceeded to tell her why the plan would never work. In 1939, a hurricane dubbed the "Long Island Express" ripped through the New England area, creating a new shoreline. In addition to altering the shoreline, it shifted the sand and silt on the sea floor. That shifting of sand and silt, in combination with normal currents, was enough to change the stability of the floor around the 1926 shipwreck. Naturally, none of those changes appeared on Speer's map, published in 1937, two years before the storm. While Dönitz's *Ubootwaffe* had updated charts, Strassburg never mentioned to Kammler or Speer the need for an updated chart. No one besides Strassburg and Kohler realized the problem with the out-of-date chart.

"So the Wall Street mission failed," Anna said, "because of shifting sand, silt, and changing currents?"

Karl smiled. He told her there was more to it; something called the proxigean spring tide. The highest and strongest tide on the US East Coast occurred once every eighteen months when the moon was the closest it gets to the Earth and is aligned with the sun. He went on to tell her that one of those tides was happening now. It was powerful enough to shift the barge with the rocket inside off its plumb, so nothing would work. And since there was no news of Wall Street being destroyed, everything in combination was what doomed the mission. If Kammler had sought Dönitz's advice, as to what was the best time to launch the rocket, the plan might have worked.

"Ironic, isn't it?" he said. "The term 'spring tide' comes from our German word *springen*, meaning 'rise up.' It was probably the tide that prevented the rocket from just doing that—rising up."

Anna expressed worry as to the fate of the now failed and useless rocket inside the barge.

"Yes, the fate of the rocket and the barge," Karl pondered, "but what about the tug that got it there? You realize Kammler could never allow the tug to make it back to Helgoland," he opined. "I know how Kammler operates, how he thinks. Kammler doesn't like loose ends. If the tug made it back to Helgoland and one of the crew should talk about what they did, that's a loose end. The same with those two U-tankers, once they've picked up the four maintainance crews, after they've cleaned up the resupply sights, somehow Kammler will see to it they don't make it back to port."

"How?"

"On the way back to Helgoland, there'll be an explosion somewhere on the tug, sending her to the bottom of the Atlantic—the same with the U-tankers. I don't know how Kammler will accomplish it, but he will. As for the barge—with the rocket and the bomb inside it—it'll eventually fall over and be carried off by the tides."

"Where?" she asked.

Karl thought about that. "Someday, if the barge remains watertight, it'll float up to the surface, and when that happens someone might find it and open it. Maybe by then," he ruminated, "the world will be smart enough to deal with such evil."

Anna thought for a moment about what Karl said, finding it chilling. If the barge did make it to the surface, then there'd be proof the Nazis tried to attack the United States. Proof of the diabolical plot devised by Kammler, Speer, Walter, Houtermans, Cranz, and all the others.

"Do you really think," Anna asked, "that someday people will live in peace?"

"No," Karl asserted, "but wouldn't that be nice?"

41.

Before departing, Karl and Anna sealed everything they didn't need deep in the abandoned mine. They made sure the truck with the bomb was well hidden, insurance against the horrible weapon being found accidentally. Karl repainted the Jeep using paint from the flying boat's paint locker, making it appear to be US army surplus. They filled the Jeep with supplies needed to get them to Flagstaff, Arizona, and headed east along the south rim of the Grand Canyon, the mighty Colorado River flowing below.

Late that afternoon, when the sun was low in the western sky, they arrived at a particularly beautiful spot overlooking the canyon. The light was soft and the purple shadows were long. Anna and Karl took a deep breath, marveling at the splendor of their surroundings.

"The war seems so far away in this beautiful place," Anna remarked.

"And god seems so close," Karl replied as they watched a pair of eagles ride thermals over the canyon's north rim.

It was something about the way the brisk wind blew Anna's hair across her face that caused Karl to look into her eyes. "This seems as good a place as any," he said. "Will you marry me?"

"I thought you'd never ask," she said, teary-eyed, reaching up with the hand on her good arm and pulling his head to her lips.

After a romantic engagement dinner, spooned from cans of *Wehrmacht* field rations while fighting off the occasional scorpion, they returned to the Jeep and drove south into the night, camping at the outskirts of Flagstaff. The next morning they covered the one hundred and thirty-five miles from Flagstaff to Phoenix well before noon. Lunch was at a roadside diner. Just beyond the diner was a two–gas pump filling station. Karl filled the Jeep's gas tank, paying for the fuel with ration stamps and cash, and headed to Tucson. The Americans they met along the way were friendly, courteous, and helpful. Some even offered aspirin to Anna to ease the pain of her "broken" collarbone.

"So far, so good," Karl said, laughing. "No one has even asked me about the New York Yankees or the Brooklyn Dodgers."

The afternoon sun was a scorcher when they arrived in Tucson. Anna asked Karl how people could live in such heat day after day, year after year, her eyes squinting in the bright sunlight, perspiration wetting her brow as well as the front and back of her dress. Anna wasn't wearing a brassiere. Karl smiled, hoping the sun wouldn't find a cloud to hide behind.

"They simply adapt to it, Anna," Karl answered. "When O'Gorsky returned to Germany, he said the same thing about the North African desert. They wondered how people could live in *that* heat."

On the fringe of Tucson they spotted a well-kept motor lodge and decided they'd spend the night there. The manager's wife was something of a character.

"How can I help you folks?" she began.

Seeing Anna's arm in a sling, she remarked, "If you folks were from around these parts, I'd think he'd done it to you, dearie," she said, nodding in Karl's direction. "Men around here sometimes tend to treat their women rough. Anyways, how can I help you?"

"We'd like a room for the night, please," Anna replied.

"Please!" the manager's quirky wife said. "Don't hear many 'pleases' around here. You folks got any luggage?"

"Sorry," Karl said, sounding forgetful. "I'll go out and get it."

After Karl departed the front desk, the woman shook her head, bent toward Anna, and whispered, woman-to-woman, "Men are like tits on a boar hog, ain't they, dearie?"

Bewildered and startled, Anna asked, "I'm not sure I know what you mean."

"Useless, dearie, useless. That's what they are, just plain useless."

Karl returned, toting their luggage. They signed the register and paid for a room for one night. Anna picked up the room key, while Karl carried their luggage.

After closing the door behind them, Karl plopped down on the bed to relax. Anna took off her shoes and dress and studied herself in the full-length closet mirror.

"I know it's hot out," she said to Karl, "but we really need to eat. And I need to get some unmentionables." She pirouetted in front of the mirror.

"What! My ex-country's canned food isn't good enough for you?" he joked. "Besides, you only need *one* pair of underwear."

Anna took the bait.

"First off, buster," she teased, "*you* wear underwear, *I* wear unmentionables. And if you'd quit ripping off my unmentionables, I wouldn't have to buy more. Besides, I need a garter belt for those stockings Will gave me before he left."

"Okay. Can't argue with that," he said, stroking his pencil-thin mustache like a villain in some American Western movie.

Anna found what she wanted at a woman's clothing store. Karl carried her packages, sampling what life would be like when they were married. While they were out on the town, they picked up a bus schedule. Destination: El Paso, Texas. When they got back to the motor lodge, the manager's chatty wife served them a late lunch of toasted cheese sandwiches and ice-cold Coca-Cola.

Dog-tired from the heat and craving medication for her shoulder, Anna went back to the comfort of their cool, one-foot-thick, adobe-walled room. Anna examined her purchases while Karl drove the Jeep to a deserted side street, removed the license plates, wiped the vehicle clean of telltale fingerprints, and rejoined Anna back in their room.

"Feel like sex?" he asked, seeing her spread out on top of the sheets, wearing only her new panties.

"Kind of tired, sweetie, how 'bout you?"

"Same."

It was as if they'd been married a lifetime.

They missed supper, sleeping straight through the night. When they awoke the first rays of the morning sun had started trickling through tiny spaces between the closed slats of their room's window blinds. After showering, dressing, and packing, they checked out of the motor lodge and walked to a nearby truck-stop diner for breakfast.

The only other people in the diner were the cook and two customers sitting at the far end of the counter. One of the customers, a middle-aged trucker built like a tree stump, was shoveling sunny-side up eggs into his mouth with a fork in his left hand and pieces of chicken-fried steak with a fork in his right. The other was a small man, wearing a white suit and a Panama hat, who seemed overly engrossed in a two-week-old Mexico City newspaper while nursing a cup of coffee.

Both men looked up when Karl and Anna entered the diner. The trucker kept eyeing Anna as he continually pushed forkfuls of chicken grease and eggs into his mouth. The other man kept giving Karl and Anna quick glances before burying his face in his aging newspaper. Karl was nervous, cautious, and careful. He sensed the man in the white suit was out of place. Not wanting Anna to look at the man, he tried distracting her with small talk. "Of the two dresses you bought yesterday," Karl said, eyeing the edge of the dress, which was just a bit above her knee, "I think I like this one the best."

"Why thank you for noticing," she replied, looking up from the menu and smiling. "Maybe I won't have to train you that much after all to compliment me. It's a second," she continued. "But I don't think anyone can tell the difference, do you?"

"Who made it?" he asked, trying to sound interested.

"It's a Claire McCardell," she explained. "I love the pale rose-color jersey material. The design is simple, made for comfort, an adjustable waistline, Magyar sleeves, and deep pockets. How 'bout these low-heeled, open-toed wedges and these silk stockings Will gave me? Do you like them, too?" she asked, pulling the hem of her dress up beyond where it had been and then pushing it back down.

"What's the problem, sweetie? Since when are you interested in what I'm wearing?" she asked, looking at the menu.

"I'll tell you later."

After breakfast, Karl and Anna headed to the bus stop. Karl told Anna his concerns about the man in the white suit, saying no one in their right mind would wear a suit in such heat and no one would keep reading, over and over, the front page of a two-week-old newspaper, the date printed in big type under its masthead.

Just as the doors on the bus to El Paso were closing, the man in the white suit boarded.

42.

Their US–Mexican border crossing from El Paso to Ciudad Juárez was smooth. Border agents in both countries briefly glanced at their passports before stamping the documents and waving the couple through checkpoints. Once they passed through Mexican customs, they made their way to the Ferrocarril Mexicano, the railroad station. There they pushed their way through crowds of people to get into the station. Inside, it was worse—pandemonium—people running around, others standing and trying to talk and be heard, huge lines everywhere. The longest line was the one where people were waiting to buy tickets to the Federal District, Mexico City, the crush of people winding around the building's interior perimeter.

"Oh my goodness," Anna commented, "I never expected this."

Karl reminded her that this mass of people was the very reason they chose to cross at El Paso–Ciudad Juárez. With throngs of migrant farmworkers constantly crossing back-and-forth across the border, chances were slim that an SS agent would spot them, especially with their disguises—or so he hoped.

"We seem to be the only Europeans here," Anna said in a worried voice, "and that bothers me. What about you?"

"Absolutely," Karl replied, scanning the crowd to their front for anyone who looked to be Northern European or German.

"We also seem to be the only ones concerned the train might be delayed. This sure isn't like the trains in Switzerland and Germany," Anna remarked, thinking Karl was directly behind her.

"No, it isn't, Senorita Prien," the Mexican soldier behind her agreed. "You'll find Mexico is very different from the countries you and Major Strassburg are from."

<hr/>

"Karl" was the only sound Anna managed to utter before the huge white-gloved hand belonging to the soldier behind her clamped her mouth shut, holding her tightly to his chest with his other hand.

She turned to Karl for help. What she saw were three large men standing next to him. Two of them were in uniform, holding Karl in a vice-like grip. The third, the one wearing street clothes, was behind Karl discretely pressing what she thought was a gun to his spine. Suddenly a fourth man appeared, the man in the white suit from the diner.

"They have us, Anna," Karl said in a tone filled with defeat. "Don't struggle. It might open your wound."

The little man in the white suit—the man they saw in the diner—said matter-of-factly, "Okay, now that we're all friends, my large associates here are going to release the two of you. You have two choices. One, you can be on your way to who knows where and risk having Kammler's friends hunt you down. Or two, you can come with us to the ticket window, purchase two very expensive tickets to the Federal District, and be safe.

"It's up to you, of course," he added. "But if you should choose the second option, let me welcome you to Mexico on behalf of a group of people who hate the

215

Nazis as much as the two of you do—and have suffered at their hands just like you.

"I'll be brief," he continued, "because people are starting to stare at us. By contacting you the way we did, in this crowd, if anyone was watching they'd never suspect who we are. They'd think we were *Federales*."

"Clever, very clever," Karl laconically said, remaining unsure whether the man in the white suit and his companions were some of Kammler's thugs or anti-Nazi "friends." Karl took the man up on his offer, hoping he wasn't making a fatal mistake.

"Please," Karl said, "lead the way to the ticket window."

Instantly, the man in the white suit started screaming.

"Welcome to Mexico, Senor Gable and Senorita Lombard."

Everyone in the immediate area stopped to see what the commotion was all about.

"Are you crazy?" Karl said in hushed tones. "Everyone is *really* starting to stare at us now."

Karl and Anna literally froze in their tracks as "White Suit" started hugging and kissing Karl.

With one arm locked in Anna's good arm and his other arm around Karl's waist, the little man escorted his new friends to the railroad's first-class ticket window, where no one was waiting in line. The agent on duty was sleeping, bored by the lack of business. The two men, dressed like soldiers, flanked Karl, Anna, and White Suit. The other two, the one dressed in plain clothes holding the pistol and the third soldier, stood behind them.

"Wake up, you lazy ass!" White Suit yelled at the dozing ticket agent. "Senor Gable, here, wants to purchase two rides on our luxurious *Americana del Sur* car to the Federal District."

The agent shot-up, it was as if someone had just stuck a red-hot poker up his ass. No one ever purchased even one ticket, let alone two, to ride on the car because of the hefty cost. The only reason the Mexican government offered such luxurious accommodations was to show its neighbor to the north it had come a long way since Pancho Villa flipped his middle finger at his neighbors to the north at the turn of the twentieth century.

"That will be one hundred ninety Norte de American dollars, senor," the ticket agent told Karl. The agent's eyes grew bigger each time Karl peeled off another Hamilton and Jackson.

"Thank you, and welcome to Mexico," the agent shrieked as Anna and Karl were hustled to their luxury accommodations on rails.

"Wave! Start smiling! Walk like you're film stars," White Suit ordered, walking as fast as he could to keep up with his new Hollywood friends. "These people are poor. Most likely they have never before seen anyone famous. They'll talk about this day for as long as they live."

Karl helped Anna board the train. The three men dressed like soldiers handed their luggage to Karl. When Karl, Anna, and their mysterious protector were safely on board, the three soldiers, along with the man with the gun tucked under his shirt, melted into the crowd.

"Keep waving and smiling," White Suit insisted. "The train will leave any moment now."

"I thought it wasn't scheduled to leave for twenty minutes," Anna said as she continued to smile and wave at the crowd.

"Ah, but that was before Senor Gable, here, bought those very expensive tickets."

43.

"Please, please, sit down, my friends," White Suit told them, gesturing with his hand to a much sat-on garnet-colored crushed velvet sofa. The ornate railroad car and its plush furnishings looked like they came from the era of money baron J. Pierpont Morgan.

"Drinks?" the mysterious man asked

"Forget the drinks," Karl told him rather briskly. "Who the hell are you?"

"Ah yes, please forgive me for not introducing myself. My name is Roberto Sarducci. I'll be your conductor and chef during your trip to the Federal District. You have already met my brother, Raul, have you not? Admiral Kohler's chef."

"What!" Anna and Karl exclaimed, looking briefly at each other, then back to their rescuer.

"I didn't mean to alarm you back in the station, my friends," Sarducci said, "but we had to get you out of there quickly. Actually, your disguises are quite good. If I hadn't seen you both at the diner, I might have missed you at the train station."

Karl was skeptical. He wondered about the entire Gable–Lombard hoopla thing. Sarducci picked up on this.

"If there were SS at the station," Sarducci explained, "the last thing they'd be expecting from you was to show yourselves in such a bizarre way. And you, Karl, do look a little like Gable when he was young. "Ahhh, but you were the problem, my dear," Sarducci said, addressing Anna. "You don't look a bit like Carole Lombard. You're much taller, way more beautiful, and, of course, Lombard's been dead for more than a year."

"If that drink's still available, I'll have it now," Karl told Sarducci, sounding exhausted.

"Make that two," Anna added.

As Karl and Anna settled in for their journey, they learned about the Sarducci brothers and their past. Raul and Roberto fought against the Fascists in Spain during the civil war. They fled their homeland with only the clothes on their backs. Raul went to Germany, posing as a Fascist, hoping to continue the fight in the belly of the beast. Because of his background as a restaurateur, and through connections in the German underground, he met Admiral Kohler who wanted Hitler and the Nazi's out of Germany as much, if not more than the Allies did.

"What do you think will happen to your brother and the Admiral now that Kammler and the others realize both targets haven't been destroyed and never will be?" Anna asked, worried about Raul and Kohler's futures.

"Absolutely nothing," Sarducci said. "The day after Karl and the others left for the States, my brother and the Admiral were in Switzerland. From Switzerland they'll go to Palestine."

"Why Palestine?" Anna asked.

"The Admiral's late wife was Jewish. She has family there."

"Do you think we'll ever see them again, Roberto?" she asked.

Sarducci flat-out told them that would never happen due to the inherent danger for all concerned.

"Unfortunately," Sarducci lamented, "when the war ends, there will still be Nazis floating about out there—probably forever. However, if things work out the way the Admiral hopes, and those hopes are shared by a group of Ashkenazi Jews, the one place there won't be any Nazis will be Palestine."

Anna wanted to ask more questions about the Admiral and Raul. Sensing that, Sarducci cut her off, apologizing but bluntly saying that he couldn't tell them anything more about the Admiral's plans because of security considerations. Sarducci did confide that he and his brother are part of the anti-Nazi underground and that Admiral Kohler helped him get away to Mexico, where he helps to relocate refugees fleeing war-torn Europe.

Sarducci, deep in thought, looked down at his folded hands. He told Karl and Anna that his family was originally from Venice, where they were silversmiths, practicing Jews, and depending who was the Doges (ruler of Venice) were either persecuted or not. When the Spanish started bringing silver back from the New World, during reign of King Charles II, they moved to Spain and became silversmiths to the Spanish nobility. The family converted to Catholicism to avoid persecution like they experienced in Venice. Some family members, seduced by Spain's vast variety of cuisines, ventured into the culinary arts, like Roberto's brother, Raul.

Roberto and his wife owned and operated two small jewelry stores, one off the Zocalo Capitalino in the Federal District and one in Taxco, where he had his workshop. He confessed there wasn't much business because of the war, but he and his family, a good Mexican woman and their beautiful young daughter managed to get by. "Things could be a lot worse. But enough about myself, and my family, I have, as you say, my marching orders concerning the two of you."

Karl and Anna exchanged glances, worried a shoe was about to fall.

"I see by the look on your faces that you are worried by what I just said. Don't be," Sarducci reassured them. "I'm here to get Karl to the States as a naturalized citizen and Anna, here, back to her parents in Switzerland."

Karl and Anna said nothing. The looks of disappointment on their faces said it all. Sarducci then proceeded to address his agenda.

"About the bomb, Karl. I hope it's not on the bottom of Lake Mead inside that wonderful aircraft, because if it is, that would definitely be a shame, as well as a problem."

"The bomb?" Karl asked.

"Yes, the bomb, Karl," Sarducci replied, realizing trust might still be a problem. "But before you say anything, read this." And with that, Sarducci handed Karl a sealed envelope.

"Oh my goodness!" Karl exclaimed as he read the letter before handing it to Anna.

"Karl!" she exclaimed. "It's from your father. He knows the Admiral and Dr. Yost."

"That's the part I didn't understand. Who's Yost?" Karl asked, his mind swimming with questions.

219

"Before the war, he—" Anna started to say before Sarducci interrupted her.

"Please, Senorita Prien, I'll explain how Dr. Yost fits in later." Sarducci confided he showed the pair the letter in order to gain their complete trust so they'd tell him where the bomb was located. Karl still remained leery, cautious. He was fretting about just how widespread knowledge was about the bomb. Sarducci told him that fewer than eight people, outside the Nazis, knew about the weapon and that Karl's father, Dr. Yost, and Admiral Kohler planned to keep it that way. Once again, Sarducci pressed Strassburg concerning the bomb's whereabouts. Karl still remained wary.

"Before I tell you that," Karl asserted, "you have to promise me that it will never be used against Germany."

"You have our promise, Karl," Sarducci solemnly said. "The bomb will never be used against Germany. So, where is it?"

"It's still on the truck," Karl reported.

"And where's the truck?" Sarducci asked.

"In an old abandoned mine on the south shore of Lake Mead. If you have a map of the lake, I'll point out the mine's location."

"Good," Sarducci said, nodding his head in approval. "This will make things a lot easier."

"What things?" Karl and Anna asked in unison.

"It's better you don't know," Sarducci said. "But I can tell you this: the bomb won't be given to the Americans until after the war in Europe is over."

Sarducci recognized his new friends were tired, especially Anna. He thought it might be best for them to go into the railroad car's bedroom and rest. In the meantime, he'd prepare dinner, and during the meal he promised to answer all their questions.

After what he considered was a reasonable amount of time for Karl and Anna to rest, perhaps sleep, Sarducci gently knocked on their bedroom door, announcing dinner will be served at their convenience.

Karl was dressed in extremely comfortable Egyptian cotton lounging pajamas. Anna's apparel was something closer to an evening gown, white silk with spaghetti straps, low cut in the front and back, with a slit on the side revealing a healthy portion of leg. Anna looked stunning. In love with her gown, Anna opted to wear it to dinner, a decision that clearly delighted Karl and Roberto. She also found her shoulder had sufficiently healed to allow removal of the dressings and the sling, a painful decision but one that revealed two of her best assets.

"Ta-da!" she exclaimed, twirling around, careful not to extend her left arm too far out as she made her grand entrance from the bedroom.

"What do you think?" she asked.

Karl had left their bedroom earlier to talk to Roberto about news of the war. As Anna announced her entrance, Karl turned, winked at Roberto, and said, "I thought you said dessert was being served *after* the main course!"

Sarducci, faithful to the Latin-lover stereotype, replied, "No, my friend, what you're looking at is far sweeter than any dessert."

Conversation at the table quickly became serious. It began with Roberto prompting Anna to talk about Dr. Yost, something she had tried to do before her "siesta," as Roberto put it.

"Before the war," she explained, "Dr. Yost dealt in fine cheeses. My parents' lodge at Interlaken was one of his customers. He is still one of my parents' closest friends. It seemed to me at the time there was no one he didn't know—and nothing he couldn't get—from anywhere."

"That's still the case," Sarducci said, smiling. "Only now because of the war, he also provides another service. He relocates people—like you, Karl—by providing them with new biographies and documents, allowing them to become citizens in new lands. And because of how he does it, no one ever has to look over their shoulder for fear they'll be jailed or deported." Having said that, Sarducci reached into the breast pocket of his jacket and retrieved two envelopes: one for Karl and one for Anna. He proceeded to tell the two about living in Mexico. "It seems I keep giving you envelopes to open, but before you open these, let me explain something. Karl will live in Mexico until he get's US State Department approval to immigrate to the US where eventually he'll become a naturalized citizen. Anna, you will return to Switzerland. This envelope is yours, Anna. And this one is for you, Karl. They contain papers, passports, and bank accounts—everything you'll need to live in Mexico. Certain documents will be updated when the time comes for you to leave. But for now, what is inside these envelopes is all you'll need."

Anna looked at Karl. Her facial expression said it all: she was very displeased.

Sarducci, recognizing her reaction, counseled patience. "Before either of you say anything, you might want to look inside your envelopes."

"Why?" Anna asked, her eyes becoming teary. "We won't be together here or when the war is over, so what does it matter?"

Sarducci was playing a game: first, the bad news and then the good news. "Yes," he replied to Anna, looking as sad as he could. "I'm afraid you'll have to go back to Switzerland and live with your parents. Unless, that is, you allow my other brother, the one who's a Catholic priest, Father Donatello Sarducci, to marry you to Senior Gable here, when the two of you get to Mexico City.

"You see, Anna," Sarducci continued, his brown eyes sparkling, a smile forming impish dimples, "the Admiral, along with your mother and father, felt betrayed when they discovered you weren't on your way to their home in Interlaken. Figuring you'd stowed away on the BV 238, they sent a message to Dr. Yost, telling him what they thought you did. Very naughty! Yes, very naughty, indeed. "This really gets complicated, so please bear with me," Sarducci admonished. "Yost told your parents what Admiral Kohler told him. The Admiral then got back to Yost, telling him to get word to Manning Dorff, in the States, who—"

"Hold on, Roberto," Karl interrupted. "Did you say Manning Dorff?"

"Ah, so you remember Senor Dorff."

"How could I not remember Dorff?" Karl replied. "He's the American attorney my father used in 1936 to negotiate a helium-export deal with the Americans. Dr. Hugo Eckener, the manager of Luftschiffbau Zeppelin, my father's client, wanted to use helium to lift his Zeppelins rather than hydrogen. Helium being inert was the ideal gas, and America was the only source. Since the Americans didn't like Hitler, my father needed an American law firm with political connections to negotiate the deal. So, he used Dorff."

"And you went with your father to the States," Sarducci recalled, "as a reward for doing so well on your entrance exams at the Kaiser Wilhelm Institute for Chemistry. See, I know a lot about you."

For years Karl was baffled by his father's relationship with Dorff. In public, the two went to great lengths, appearing they never met before. Yet, when others were absent, they acted like they'd been friends forever. Years ago, Karl had queried his father about his relationship with Dorff. The elder Strassburg simply replied that someday his son would understand.

"After the war," Sarducci said, "I'm sure your father and Dorff will tell you all about their relationship. But for now, let me continue. Many conversations flowed among Dr. Yost, Admiral Kohler, Manning Dorff, Karl's and your father, Anna, and myself about the two of you. The upshot was that your parents, Anna, wanted to slap your wrists for stowing away, as you did, on the BV 238 and not coming home to Interlaken." Sarducci was doing his best to stifle a laugh.

"So this has all been a big joke," she said, sounding slightly peeved. "You were in on this, too, weren't you?" she said, looking at Karl.

"Look," he said, "you damaged my reputation as a tough guy when you clocked me while I wasn't looking in the hallway at the Platterhof. Then, to make matters worse, you stole my virginity."

"Are you looking now?" she asked. "Then try ducking this, buster!" she shouted, throwing the contents of her salad at him. Anna laughed hysterically as some of the salad stayed on Karl's nose.

"So I take it you don't have a problem marrying Karl?" Sarducci asked, a twinkle in his eye.

"As he said,"she sighed, "I stole his virginity. So if marrying him is what it takes to have him forgive me, then what's a girl to do? Yes, I'll marry him!"

"What I don't understand," Karl said, genuinely baffled, "is how Admiral Kohler and Dr. Yost sent messages back-and-forth without Kammler knowing."

"For a physicist," Anna quipped, "you're really not that bright, are you, Karl? Yost put the messages somewhere with the cheese he sent to Raul."

"Bravo, Anna, bravo," Sarducci said while clapping. "Those marvelous cheeses the Admiral frequently served contained coded information in the artwork on the labels. Since no one but Raul touched the cheeses, and only the Admiral could decode the messages, there was no way Kammler knew what was going on under his nose."

"Okay, I'll admit it," Strassburg conceded, "I didn't see that one coming. But how did the Admiral get messages back to Dr. Yost?"

"In the orders for more cheese," Anna answered.

"Was Dr. Yost," Strassburg asked, "the one who kept the Nazis from getting those milling machines Dr. Cranz wanted?"

"Yes," Sarducci laconically replied.

The pieces of puzzle were beginning to fit together quite nicely in Karl's hyperactive mind.

"And you knew," Karl surmised, "if we managed to land on Lake Mead and got away from the crew, we'd head straight for the border and the Swiss Embassy in Mexico City, seeking asylum, correct?"

"Correct, or as we call it in Mexico, the Federal District. And with El Paso the nearest and biggest border crossing from Lake Mead," Sarducci continued, "I was quite sure that was where you'd cross into Mexico. As you both found out, hundreds of people cross the border there every day. And since crossing in the midst of a large crowd would be the best way to avoid detection—well — "

"You also figured," Strassburg, pointed out, "we'd want to get rid of the Jeep as soon as possible, because in the event we were stopped by the police my credentials may not have checked out."

"Correct again, Karl," Roberto acknowledged.

Strassburg was on a roll.

"And since Tucson is a fairly big city, I could ditch the Jeep on one of those seldom used side streets because we wouldn't need it if we caught the bus to El Paso. And that's exactly what we did and that's why you were sitting at the counter at the only diner near the bus stop."

"Well done, Karl, well done indeed." Sarducci was pleased. "I realized it was a gamble going to Tucson like I did because you might have taken a different route to the border. But being so shorthanded, I had no other choice than to take a chance the two of you would be at the diner near the bus station, which is what you did."

Anna felt she was being left out of Karl and Roberto's Agatha Christie/Hercule Poirot–type wrap-up conversation.

"I hate to get between this love fest you two seem to be having, but maybe the next time you decide to wait at a diner for someone to show up, Roberto, you might splurge and purchase that day's newspaper. That two-week-old newspaper and wearing a suit in a place where no one ever wears a suit made you stick out like a sore thumb."

Sarducci conceded his mistake, admitting he realized it when Karl kept pretending not to look at him.

◄━▇█▊►

It was nearly midnight when the train pulled into the Mexico City railroad station. They inconspicuously left the luxurious railroad car and Sarducci flagged down a beat-up 1931 Chevrolet sedan that he claimed was a taxi. The driver took them to a hotel near Sarducci's jewelry store. He instructed the two to be at his place

223

of business at nine thirty the next morning.

The next day, after they finished their continental breakfast at the hotel, Karl and Anna window-shopped while they waited for Sarducci to open his jewelry store. Their conversation was masked in Polish to avoid any possibility of some SS agent spotting Karl even though he had a mustache. Karl learned Polish when his family lived in Warsaw. Anna learned Polish as a university student in Bern.

Eventually, Sarducci and his brother, Father Donatello, arrived at the jewelry store.

"You're both Catholic?" the priest asked.

"Yes, Father, we are." They both replied at the same time.

"You both want to get married?"

"Yes, we do, Father," again in unison.

"Do either of you want confession?"

"In my case, Father, it might take a day or two," Karl joked to the priest.

"What about you, my child?" the priest asked Anna.

"I'm with him, Father," she replied.

Father Donatello, realizing it would be time wasted to press the issue, asked, "So where are the rings?"

Karl and Anna looked at each other bewildered. "We don't have rings, Father," Karl told the priest.

Father Donatello looked down. He shook his head side-to-side. He pursed his lips. "My children, you're getting married in a jewelry store. Look around!" he said with a broad sweep of his hand. "Please, take your time! I'm sure you'll find something you like. Besides, my brother could use the business."

After a few minutes of walking around the store, carefully combing through Roberto Sarducci's inventory of rings, peering into the various jewelry cases, Anna picked out two rings: one for her and one for Karl.

Father Donatello brought Karl and Anna together. He kissed his stole, slipped it on, and the service began.

Karl and Anna were married two months when they received a package from Manning Dorff, the Washington, DC, attorney and friend of Karl's father. It contained their new European identities, courtesy of Dr. Yost.

Yost's papers described them as Polish. Prior to the war, the papers said they lived in a village near the German border, where on September 1, 1939, the German Fourth Army crossed the border into Poland. Every person, building, horse, barn, cow, fence, pig, and chicken, in the village was destroyed. No buildings were left standing. The entire area resembled a farmer's freshly plowed field. The destruction was so complete, so vast, that all church records, including archives of births and deaths and land holdings going back centuries were lost.

Yost's bogus papers showed the couple anticipating war, selling their business and farm months before the conflict broke out, and moving to Antwerp, Belgium. One steamer trunk contained their clothes, gold earned from the sale of their

Polish business holdings, and—most important—"copies" of pertinent church records about their family were all they managed to bring with them.

The couple kept meticulous records of everything they bought and did, including the uncut diamonds they purchased in Antwerp and how they managed to keep one step ahead of the Gestapo until they secured passage to Mexico. Their life together was documented by a detailed paper trail.

In December 1943 Karl and Anna went to the US Embassy in Mexico City and filled out immigration papers. The clerk told them not to get their hopes up. But that was before they showed him their letter of credit from Credit Suisse and their letter of sponsorship from the DC law firm of Schmidt, Guthrie and Dorff approved by Edward Reilly Stettinius, Jr. U.S.Undersecretary of State. Two weeks later they were told they were welcome to come to "the land of the free and the home of the brave."

Once they were in the States, Karl and Anna looked for a place to set up their import business—selling wholesale, high-end handcrafted silver masterpieces, made in Mexico to large, upscale department and jewelry stores, on the East and West coasts.

Deciding they didn't like either coast, they opted for a life in the Midwest. Chicago, the city with the world's second largest Polish population, the first, being Warsaw, seemed a natural choice. They explored many of the city's neighborhoods looking for a place to settle down. The "crowded" nature of city life prompted them to opt for the suburbs, where trees, bushes, and open space were more prevalent.

The small, quaint Village of Golf—population one hundred and ten, counting people, cats, dogs, horses, cows, and chickens—located eighteen miles north of Chicago was the ideal location. The couple purchased a house on a two-acre parcel of land. The house had been a stable the previous owner converted into a cozy four-bedroom home with a large library. Karl turned the library into his office. Less than a fifth of a mile west of their home was a post office and a train station, providing easy access for communication and travel—two things needed to service their clients.

1944 was a good year for the Polish couple—unlike most of the world.

Epilogue

Germany surrendered on May 7, 1945, but Japan fought on.

Early in the morning of May 11, four days after Germany surrendered, Dr. Mark Weber, one of the senior members of the Manhattan Project at Los Alamos, New Mexico, looked out the window in his cabin on "Bathtub Row." Weber was in charge of bomb upgrades and replacement parts for *Little Boy*, the name of the uranium bomb America would use to destroy Hiroshima. Blocking his driveway was a US Army two-and-a-half-ton truck. Curious as to why the truck was parked there, Weber put on his robe, slippers, and after doing his usual morning below-the-belt scratch went outside to inspect the truck.

Under the tarp, on the bed of the truck was a large electric generator with a note attached to it. The note said the generator wasn't a generator.

Weber wasn't sure how long he stood there, looking at the bomb disguised as a generator. All he remembered was a wave of nausea passing through his body. He returned to the Weber-family cabin, dressed for work, and kissed his wife and two children good-bye. He told his wife she could use the car since he'd drive the mysterious truck, parked in the driveway, to work.

Weber worked at Site "Y," the Quonset hut where his team, under the hands-on supervision of his boss, Dr. J. Robert Oppenheimer (aka "Oppie"), the head of the Manhattan Project, was upgrading *Little Boy*. When his wife asked why the truck was blocking their driveway, all Weber said was "Don't ask!"

Weber's habit was to arrive at Site "Y" early in the morning to get a head start on the day's work before his colleagues arrived. He lifted the bomb, disguised in its electric-generator housing, off the US Army truck using the crane arm of a tank-recovery vehicle. He buried "the present" under the continually growing mountain of "obsolete" parts that really weren't obsolete. Weber and his team, under Oppenheimer's supervision, were ordered to make *Little Boy* better, more powerful, than its original design. Weber and others knew this was a mistake—the discarded parts should never have been discarded and replaced with the "upgraded" parts. These continued requests to make the bomb more powerful came from politicians who knew nothing about nuclear physics. They thought that by changing a few widgets and gadgets here and there that the physicists could squeeze a few more ounces of death and destruction out of *Little Boy*. The meddling politicians wanted to nail the lid firmly shut on Japan's coffin, guaranteeing her immediate surrender. Their motivation: The politicians desperately wanted to avoid a bloody US invasion of the Japanese home islands, likely to add another estimated million-plus American casualties to the already bloody tally.

Weber figured that until he found the right moment to tell "Oppie" about the Nazi bomb, it would be safe under the discarded bomb parts.

⊷▆▌▐▶

On July 16, 1945, the United States exploded what the world acknowledged as mankind's first nuclear bomb. It happened above the white sands at Alamogordo, New Mexico. Code-named "Trinity," and nicknamed "Gadget," it was a plutonium

226

bomb. At the time the bomb was built, the United States had just enough fissile material to make three bombs. Since the plutonium design was more questionable than the uranium design, it was decided to build two plutonium bombs and test one to see if it worked. It did.

⊷▮◖◗

Early on the morning of July 10, before the others arrived at Site "Y," Weber made a startling discovery. Actually, it was more of a problem than a discovery. Either way, if it wasn't corrected—and corrected fast—it would cost the United States another million-plus of her sons and daughters.

The plan had been that on July 14, *Little Boy*, the uranium bomb whose design had not been tested, was to be shipped to the San Francisco Naval Yard at Hunters Point, California, and from there taken by ship to Tinian, a Pacific Ocean island in the Marianas. At Tinian, *Little Boy* would be placed on board a B-29 Superfortress and dropped on Hiroshima. Now, none of that would happen because *Little Boy* was a dud.

As is, *Little Boy* would be lucky to produce a "fizzle," an explosion slightly more powerful than a conventional ten thousand-pound blockbuster bomb—not exactly what the politicians in Washington, DC, had been hoping for (certainly not worth the billions of American taxpayer dollars spent to produce it).

The reason the bomb was a dud was the continued tinkering, fine-tuning, and "upgrading" of parts to make it perform like its plutonium brother. It was the old adage, "If it ain't broke, don't fix it." The design was supposed to be a "sure thing" and it would have been if it hadn't been for the upgrading.

If anyone beside Weber had discovered the problem, who knows what might have happened? Weber was a cool head, not easily rattled. He figured that since only a handful of people knew what the bomb looked like—because up to this stage it hadn't been fully assembled—why not just substitute the Nazi bomb for *Little Boy*, ship it out on the fourteenth as planned, and hope the Nazi's hadn't designed a dud.

The only person Weber told about the switch was his boss. Oppenheimer went along with the swap after he examined *Little Boy*, confirming it was a dud and that the Nazi bomb would work. Both men knew that no one in DC —or the rest of the country for that matter—would give a rip if the bomb dropped on Japan was American or German. All they wanted was a bomb that would force Japan to surrender. They wanted the war to end so that no more American lives and treasure would be spent in the bloody conflict. So what, if a hundred thousand more Japs died to get that coveted surrender.

Weber's Nazi gift became: *The Bomb That Never Was.*

⊷▮◖◗

A little after sunrise on September 11, 2001, two fishermen in a small boat, off the coast of New Jersey, spotted a long cylindrical object, more than one hundred and thirty feet long. It was floating in the shipping lanes leading to the port of New York. They thought it might be a small freighter that overturned during a storm and become a danger to shipping traffic. One of the fishermen called the US Coast Guard. They also called a local radio station in Belford, New Jersey, to report their

227

discovery, thinking they had found something newsworthy.

Because of the horrendous events that took place on September 11, the station's manager forgot about the sighting until several weeks later. When he called the tipster for more information all he got was a recording saying the number had been disconnected. Curious as to what the object might have been, the station manager called the US Coast Guard only to be told that no one on the morning of September 11 ever called the Coast Guard about an object floating in the shipping lanes leading to the port of New York.

On July 19, 2005, a television news network reported on its website that the model of the atomic bomb—the one dropped on Hiroshima and displayed in the Ray Bradbury Science Museum at Los Alamos, New Mexico—had been removed and replaced with a new model. The museum said the switch was done for "security reasons." When the museum's director was asked what aspect of the old model was classified, the only thing he said was that the new model was more historically accurate.

The Beginning

Characters

Real People

Adolf Hitler: Der Führer, the Nazi "Top Banana.'"

General der Waffen SS Dr-Ing Hans Kammler: Nazi engineer in charge of building underground cities: V-1 cruise missile and V-2 rocket operations, Rheinbote, HDP, and other projects; a leading Nazi, almost invisible to history, a real "bad ass."

The Committee: a term concocted by J. R. Shaw, the author, as a catchall moniker, referring to Hitler's cronies:

> **Albert Speer:** architect who became Nazi Minister of Armament.

> **Herman Göring:** Nazi *Reichsmarschall*, Commander-in-Chief of the Luftwaffe, the German Air Force.

> **Martin Bormann:** Hitler's go-to guy, Nazi Party Secretary.

> **Dr. William Ohnesorge:** Nazi Minister of Post.

> **Dr. Joseph Goebbels:** Nazi Minister for Propaganda.

> **Heinrich Himmler:** chicken farmer who became head of the much-feared SS, or Schutzstaffel, an elite Nazi party quasi-military force that served as Hitler's bodyguard and as a special police force; among other things, the SS operated the infamous Nazi concentration camps.

Dr-Ing Fritz Houtermans: brilliant German engineer and physicist.

Dr. Werner Heisenberg: German physicist, 1932 Nobel Prize winner, in charge of Germany's nuclear bomb project; Heisenberg wasn't a Nazi.

Professor Hellmuth Walter: German engineer, inventor of revolutionary U-boats and a closed-cycle hydrogen-peroxide propulsion system known as the Walter Drive.

Grossadmiral Karl Dönitz: Head of the *Ubootwaffe* (Germany's submarine fleet) from 1936 to 1945.

Dr-Ing Richard Vogt: Head of Blohm & Voss's project bureau, designer of the BV 222 and BV 238 flying boats; B&V is a German engineering company that built aircraft and ships for Germany during World War II.

Baron Manfred von Ardenne: Nazi scientific entrepreneur who had an extensive laboratory complex at Lichterfelde-Ost.

Fritz von Halban and Lew Kowarski: research assistants to Frederic Joliot-Curie, who, with the aid of the French underground, Nazi resistance, smuggled uranium ore out of France to North Africa.

Sir Claude John Eyre Auchinleck: British Commander-in-Chief Middle East; a British General who was seriously outclassed by Field Marshal Erwin Rommel, Germany's famed "Desert Fox."

A Word about Historic Personalities and Their Families

Whether history judged them good or evil, the real people used in the plot of this book had, and may still have, living family and relatives. These people are in no way responsible for the actions and policies of their famous or infamous relatives.

Fictional People

Major Karl Strassburg: *Fallschirmjäger*, German paratrooper, recipient of the Knight's Cross with Oak Leaves and Swords.

Anna Prien: lead test pilot for Blohm & Voss (B&V).

Arnold Strassburg: Karl Strassburg's father.

Admiral Manfred Kohler: head of the Inland Sea Research and Development Test Facility (There was never an Island Sea Research and Development Test Facility)

Manning Dorff: Washington, DC, lawyer, friend of Arnold Strassburg.

Dr. Peter Yost: the Magician.

Dr. Gerhard Cranz: retired V-2 rocket scientist at Peenemünde.

Hauptmann Rolf Muller: *Fallschirmjäger* friend of Karl Strassburg.

Oberleutnant Fritz O'Gorsky: *Fallschirmjäger* friend of Karl Strassburg.

Raul Sarducci: Admiral Kohler's chef.

Roberto Sarducci: silversmith, Mexico City.

Father Donatello Sarducci: Roman Catholic priest, Mexico City.

Max Horst: BV 238 pilot.

Wilhelm Ritter: BV 238 copilot.

Frantz Gerhardt: BV 238 crew chief.

Henry Brock: BV 238 mechanic.

Dr. Mark Weber: physicist at the Los Alamos nuclear research laboratory in New Mexico.

A Word about Fictional People

Its fiction, folks! If you think you've read about one or more of the fictional personalities who populate *The Bomb that Never Was*, it's either a coincidence or the author having some fun.

Places and Things

Friedrichshafen: a town on Lake Konstanz where there used to be a floating Zeppelin hangar like the one mentioned in *The Bomb That Never Was*.

Lake Konstanz: a lake in southern Germany, bordering Switzerland and Austria; Europe's third largest lake.

Swabian Sea: another name for Lake Konstanz.

St. Gallen, Switzerland: town in Switzerland near Lake Konstanz.

Interlaken, Switzerland: a Swiss town located in the canton of Bern.

Lichterfelde-Ost: a Berlin suburb.

Obersalzberg complex: located in the Bavarian Alps until the Allies trashed it at the end of World War II.

Hotel Platterhof: the luxury hotel in the Obersalzberg complex.

Berghof: Hitler's villa below the Obersalzberg complex.

Helgoland, Germany: a five hundred twenty-acre North Sea Island where German U-boats were based.

231

Rio Muni: a river on Africa's west coast that empties into the South Atlantic Ocean.

Sao Francisco: an eighteen hundred-mile-long Brazilian river that empties into the South Atlantic Ocean.

San Ambrosio Island: an island off Chile's South Pacific Ocean coast.

Clipperton Island: a three and a half square mile island off the Pacific Ocean coast of Mexico.

Los Alamos, New Mexico: location of the US nuclear research laboratory, an important Manhattan Project facility in the race to build the American atomic bomb.

Lake Mead: lake behind Boulder Dam; it is one hundred twelve miles long when full of water; it has hundreds of miles of shoreline; it is five hundred thirty two-feet deep; it covers two hundred and forty-seven square miles.

Peenemünde: a German island in the Baltic Sea, where the V-1 "buzz bombs" (something like a cruise missile) and V-2 rockets (ballistic missiles used to bomb London and other places) were developed, built, and tested.

Abwehr: Nazi military intelligence.

Operation Sea Lion: the code name for the Nazi invasion of England that never occurred.

88: the common reference to the 88-mm flak gun used on tanks, anti-aircraft flak cannons, and anti-tank guns, one of the most versatile weapons of World War II.

Tiger I: heavy German tank, its main gun was the famed 88.

Steinhoff Plan: a plan to launch V-2 rockets vertically from floating containers off the English coast in the English Channel.

Kuhwerder: an island in the Baltic Sea.

RLM: Reich Air Ministry during World War II.

BV 8-246 Hagelkorn (Hailstone): a German glide bomb that never made it off the drawing board.

BV 222: a large six-engine flying boat; its first flight was in 1940; thirteen of these aircraft were built.

BV 238: a mammoth flying boat, the largest aircraft constructed by the Axis powers in World War II; it was powered by six massive seventeen hundred and fifty-horsepower Daimler Benz DB 603C engines; it could fly an estimated four thousand five hundred miles without refueling, attain speeds of two hundred forty-eight miles per hour at an altitude of nineteen thousand six hundred and eighty-five feet, and carry a forty four thousand-pound payload; just one of these aircraft was built and flown.

Operation Merkur: code name for the Nazi airborne invasion of Crete.

WP: white phosphorous.

Blitzkrieg: Nazi "Lighting War."

RAF: Royal Air Force (Great Britain).

Hauptmann: a German military rank, equivalent of a US Army Captain.

Oberleutnant: a German military rank, equivalent of a US Army Lieutenant.

Leibstandarte SS Adolf Hitler Division: Hitler's bodyguards.

Kriegsmarine: the German Navy.

MAS: Italian Schnellboot, or "fast boat."

Bathtub Row: formerly part of a private boy's school, purchased by the US government to house senior members of the Manhattan Project at Los Alamos, New Mexico.

1942 Wannsee Conference: a meeting held by SS Chief Heinrich Himmler in a stately mansion, previously owned by a wealthy Jewish family, where members of the Nazi government planned the "Final Solution" (i.e., the extermination of Europe's Jews).

Knight's Cross with Oak Leaves and Swords: during World War II, Germany presented one hundred fifty-nine Knight's Cross with Oak Leaves and Swords to her heroes; during the same war, the United States presented four hundred sixty-four Medals of Honor to its greatest heroes.

1926 shipwreck in the waters off the US East Coast: could be, there are hundreds of wrecks in the area.

Walter Drive: a revolutionary propulsion system, developed by Professor Hellmuth Walter during World War II.

U-barge and U-tug: one of the better *ideas* the author came up with while writing *The Bomb That Never Was*.

Schnellboot: Nazi torpedo boat.

V-2 rocket: more than three thousand were launched against the Allies during World War II; this revolutionary weapon was a direct ancestor of the intercontinental ballistic missile (ICBM).

Underground cities in the Jonastal region of Thuringia and Nordhausen: cities SS General Hans Kammler was building using slave labor.

"Spruce Goose": the huge flying boat designed to fly hundreds of troops and equipment over the Atlantic Ocean; it was the brainchild of famed aviator, moviemaker, and business tycoon Howard Hughes; it flew just once.

Appreciation

Again, thank you for buying the book. I hope you've enjoyed reading it as much as I've enjoyed writing it. If you want to find out what happened to everyone after the war look for, *The Pieces*.

The Author

J. R. Shaw is a pseudonym. I'm a person who likes privacy. I like being a shadow, but I hope you—my readers—will bring *The Bomb That Never Was* into the light. Any discrepancies in spelling, dates, names, nomenclature, grammar, punctuation, and other things are because I either wanted it that way or made a mistake.

Portrait Photography by
Larry Simon (larry@larrysimon.net)

Excerpt from the Next Book: *The Pieces*

The day before the wedding, Arnold Strassburg took his son aside and told him an amazing story. It involved his mother. Karl was his parent's only surviving child and one day he would acquire his mother's burden. If he and his wife, Anna, had children upon Karl's death their first-born would inherit the "family burden"—and so on until the line ended. Karl was increasingly suspicious he wasn't going to like what his father was about to tell him. Suspicious that it had something to do with the war.

Karl's father counseled patience. No questions until Karl had heard the entire story. Karl always saw his father as unflappable, a man not prone to exaggeration. So he knew that whatever it was that was weighing so heavily on his father's mind, it would have an enormous impact on his life and Anna's.

"Before the Reich fell," the elder Strassburg began, "your mother received a package from Willie."

Willie was a cousin by marriage to Karl's mother. More formally, he was Dr. William Ohnesorge, the Third Reich's Minister of Post. Karl interrupted his father, asking if Willie survived the war. His father was unsure, but suspected he had. "Willie's a survivor, Karl. If I were to venture a guess, I think in all likelihood he cut a sweet deal with the Soviets and as we speak is living the good life in some dacha along the Black Sea."

Curious as to what was inside the package Ohnesorge sent his mother Karl asked, "What was inside that has you so edgy?"

Arnold told his son the package contained two things: a letter and a piece broken off an ancient tablet.

"And—" Karl probed.

"The broken piece is sapphire, Karl," Arnold confided to his son. He described it as being as big as his hand. Arnold Strassburg had big hands.

"That's impossible," Karl asserted. "No one has ever found even one piece of a sapphire that big. And, you're telling me that the piece was off of something even bigger. Who told you it was a sapphire?"

Karl's father sidestepped his question, saying he'd get to that later. He pleaded for Karl's indulgence.

In his letter Ohnesorge apologized for what he and the Nazis did during the war. He pleaded she say nothing to anyone about the piece he sent to her. Ohnesorge ended the letter, saying that if Hitler somehow survived the war she should do whatever was necessary to make sure Hitler never got his hands on it. Never explaining why this was important. Karl's father characterized Ohnesorge's letter as the ravings of a lunatic, something Ohnesorge definitely was not. The tone and contents of the letter were troubling; something Arnold couldn't ignore.

The troubling letter and the piece kept nagging at Arnold. The incident demanded closure and that couldn't happen until he knew more about it—everything. He decided to seek the counsel of a friend in Zurich—the same person who constructed Karl and Anna's Polish identities, allowing them to live in the States, Dr Peter Yost. Arnold contacted Yost and brought the piece to Zurich. Yost grew dark and troubled when he read the letter and saw the piece. Arnold somehow got the impression that Yost had previously seen the piece. Yost took the letter and the piece and agreed to show them to folks he thought might be able to shed some light on the matter.

Months passed. Then two months before Karl and Anna came to Switzerland for their Swiss wedding, Yost telephoned Arnold saying that some senior Swiss government officials wanted Arnold and his wife to come to Zurich to discuss the letter and the piece. The day after the Yost-Strassburg conversation, two men dressed in dark suits knocked on the Strassburg's door at their home in St Gallen, Switzerland. They told Arnold they were from the central government in Bern. They asked him to call Yost.

Yost told Arnold that the two men were there to escort Arnold and his wife to Zurich, where all would be explained. Arnold asked Yost if he alone could come because of his wife's delicate health. Arnold's wife had never recovered from the deaths of their two daughters in Germany before the war. Yost agreed that Arnold could come alone.

In Zurich, Arnold and Yost met with two of the seven Ministers who ran the Swiss Republic. They told Arnold the story of the pieces.

Karl was dumbstruck when he heard the story. *Could this really be happening?*

Look for *The Pieces* in 2016

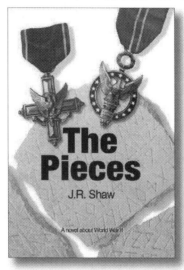

Printed in the United States
By Bookmasters